The De

MJ White is the pseudonym of bestselling author Miranda Dickinson, author of twelve books, including six Sunday Times bestsellers. Her books have been translated into ten languages, selling over a million copies worldwide. A long time lover of crime fiction, the Cora Lael Mysteries is her debut crime series. She is a singer-songwriter, host of weekly Facebook Live show, Fab Night In Chatty Thing.

Also by MJ White

A Cora Lael Mystery

MJ WHITE

THE
DEADLY
ECHOES

hera

First published in the United Kingdom in 2024 by

Hera Books
Unit 9 (Canelo), 5th Floor
Cargo Works, 1–2 Hatfields
London SE1 9PG
United Kingdom

A CIP catalogue record for this book is available from the British Library.

Print ISBN 978 1 80436 709 4
Ebook ISBN 978 1 80436 708 7

This book is a work of fiction. Names, characters, businesses, organizations, places and events are either the product of the author's imagination or are used fictitiously. Any resemblance to actual persons, living or dead, events or locales is entirely coincidental.

Look for more great books at www.herabooks.com

Printed and bound in Great Britain by Clays Ltd, Elcograf S.p.A.

I

For Katy & William

Thank you for being Cora's biggest cheerleaders.

This one's for you!

x

"For now they kill me with a living death"

King Richard III, William Shakespeare

PROLOGUE

My darling,

I'm sorry.

I wanted there to be another way, but this is all I have.

If you're reading this, I'm gone. Please don't look for me. I know you won't understand. I know I'm breaking your heart. Life is just too hard and there are too many problems I can't solve. I'm not up to the task like you thought I was.

All I ask is that you forgive me for not being enough.

You have been the perfect partner, the person I most wanted to do life with. You have given me our beautiful children and the home we love. None of this is a reflection on you. You couldn't make this better: the problem is mine.

Live your life. Stun the world with your beauty and resilience. Be the parent for our kids that I failed to be. Find someone who deserves you like I never did.

I love you. You will be my last thought as I go.

Don't look for me. It's already done.

x

ONE

LANEHAN

He was ranting when she found him.

Soaked in blood from his close-cropped red curls to his once-white trainers. Flailing his arms around as if being attacked by a swarm of assailants. Eyes horror-wide and wild.

'It's my fault,' he repeated, over and over, bloodied hands gripping PC Steph Lanehan's sleeve, frantic fingernails digging red stains deep into the fabric. 'I did this!'

Horrified bystanders crowded the street around him, some already with phones aloft. She had to get him out of view – and fast.

'Take a breath, sir. You're safe now,' she assured him, the steady tone the result of years of studied practice, masking her rising panic.

'I did this! It's all my fault!' The man's voice was a childlike wail, rising in volume as he clung onto Lanehan's arm. They couldn't handle this alone: already the situation was beyond their capabilities.

But then, there was no way they could have prepared for a situation like this. Who would have expected to deal with a blood-drenched man bursting out from a boarded-up building in a small village centre in broad daylight?

Lanehan glanced to her left, seeking assistance. PC Rilla Davis was radioing it in, her voice hushed and urgent. But it was too late to prevent a spectacle. The bloodied man had made sure of that.

Evernam wasn't the largest village in the area, but thanks to the livestock market at its northern edge, it attracted enough business to maintain two main streets filled with local shops. The village centre provided the heart of the village, home to around four thousand people, if you included the farms and hamlets on the peripheries. Januarius Street was the older of Evernam's two shopping streets, with several of the Victorian buildings currently under renovation. The building from which the man had emerged had once been a grocer's shop, amongst other things, and rumour had it that it would be converted to living accommodation when its renovations were complete.

The man in Lanehan's care kept staring back at it, his voice catching as if terrified that monsters were about to emerge from its darkened doorway.

Lanehan was confident she'd seen it all, but the job could throw you a sick surprise, even after many years of service. When they'd been called out to a disturbance in Evernam's village centre, she'd expected a drunk or kids acting up. The usual trouble they'd encounter as officers of a rural police force, more of an annoyance than a potential crime.

Not *this*.

'Can you tell me your name, sir?' she pressed on, relieved when Davis arrived on the other side of their charge. Holding an arm each, they began to steer the hysterical man towards a small alleyway that passed from the street to a quieter space behind the run of shop units.

He sagged between them, a sticky, babbling, dead weight. Gritting her teeth, Lanehan shouldered his bulk. Old injuries and battle wounds from her years on the beat protested, but she pushed the pain aside, as she always did.

'CID and SOCOs are on their way,' Davis hissed, the effort required of her to keep the man standing evident as she spoke. 'Tell us your name, sweetheart.'

Lanehan resisted a grim smile. Things had to be serious if Davis was calling someone *sweetheart*.

'Mark… Mark Lingham.'

'Okay, Mark, can you tell us what happened?'

They had reached a gravelled area at the back of the shops, where a dark blue van and a few cars were parked, and a row of overflowing industrial wheelie bins stood sentry. Heaven only knew when they were last emptied. With a joint heft, Lanehan and Davis propped the man against the nearest bin. In the warm September sun, the stench of blood and baked fetid rubbish sacks made it hard to breathe.

Lingham's stained face crumpled, his head shaking like a kid refusing to speak.

'Are you hurt, Mark?' Lanehan asked.

Another shake of the head. There certainly didn't appear to be any visible wounds, now that Lingham was still and Lanehan could better inspect him. But if the blood wasn't his, whose was it?

'We need to know what happened so we can help you, sweetheart.'

The man wailed this time, a pained, elongated 'No-o-o-o…'

'Mark, listen to me, okay? You're in a bit of a state, love. Can you tell us how it happened?'

'*I* made it happen. I did this. It's all my fault…'

'Right, so what did you do?' Davis kept her expression steady, but Lanehan clocked the eye-roll.

'I made it happen.'

'You've said that, but how? Did you get into a fight?'

'No.'

'Did someone hurt you?'

He was staring at his hands now as if the bloodstains had just appeared there. '*So* much *blood*…'

'Where has the blood come from?' Lanehan pressed.

'I can't…' Lingham's face crumpled again, pain etched into every line.

'We need to get you checked by the paramedics. They're on their way. Then we can get you cleaned up. But I need to

4

know what happened, Mark, so we can best help you. Do you understand?'

Tears burgeoned in his eyes, escaping in red-stained streams coursing down his face as he slumped to the floor. 'You can't help me. I can't help *them*...'

'You don't have to help the paramedics, sweetheart,' Davis soothed, crouching down beside him. 'That's not how it works, is it?'

'Help them to a nice box of chocs when it's all over, maybe,' Lanehan added, the brief break in tension welcome. Contingencies raced through her mind. Who was Mark Lingham? Why had he been in the boarded-up shop unit? How had he got into this state? And, most importantly, whose blood was he drenched in? 'How long?' she hissed to Davis.

'Thirty minutes, they reckon,' her colleague replied under her breath.

'Too bloody long. And the ambulance?'

'First responder's on his way. Ambulance unit's about twenty minutes behind.'

'Right.' Lanehan placed her hand on Mark Lingham's own, where it rested on his knee. His skin was cold and sticky to the touch. Her stomach churned in response, but she blocked the sensation. There was quite enough bodily fluid present here as it was – nobody would thank her for adding her partially digested bacon sandwich to the mix. 'Mark, where did this happen to you?'

He refused to answer.

'Okay. Could you take us there?'

The man observed her for a moment, his cheeks bearing white streaks between the blood where tears had cut through. 'I can't help them,' he repeated, causing Davis' shoulders to tense again. 'And neither can you.'

Confused, Lanehan pressed on. 'Help who?'

'It's not possible... It's too late...'

'Let PC Davis and me be the judges of that. Who can't we help, Mark?'

Lingham's blood-rimmed stare returned, rounding on Lanehan. 'The others.'

TWO

MINSHULL

'Holy *shit*.'

Detective Sergeant Rob Minshull blinked in the gloom of the derelict space, as if the sight before him might vanish from view.

'Told you it was bad, Sarge,' Lanehan muttered, her expression grim.

Bad didn't begin to cover it.

'This is how you found them?' he asked.

'Yes, Sarge. We touched nothing. Had to wrestle the guy out to stop him trashing the scene, though. We walked in here and he went for the bodies. Just *went* for them, like he wanted to attack them. Rilla and me had to grab him fast.' Nervous fingers played with the radio attached to her vest. 'Not sure whose blood he's wearing, but I'd say we can narrow it down to four possibilities.'

Minshull wasn't certain he'd ever heard anyone refer to four mutilated corpses as *possibilities* before. 'That's one word for them.' Checking his blue shoe-covers were in place, he gingerly stepped around the periphery of the unlit unit, careful not to disturb anything.

What the hell had happened here?

In the centre of the dusty concrete floor, four bodies lay. They were arranged in a circle, their feet at the centre and their blood-soaked bodies stretching away. That would have been remarkable enough, but what made the scene unique in

Minshull's experience – and chillingly freakish to witness – was the presence of the objects. Five items for each victim. All appeared to have been deliberately placed, identical distances apart. Completing the circle was another group of belongings without a body at their centre. Is this where the bloodied man should have lain?

The belongings themselves appeared to be randomly chosen: an old cricket ball, a child's toy car, a roll of silver electrical tape, a folded jacket. But the placing of them piqued Minshull's interest. There was something careful, studied even, about the way they had been arranged. But what was the significance?

'What do we know about him?' he asked, facts being paramount now to keep his mind in focus. It would be too easy to let the scene distract him, and he really didn't want that to happen. The stench of blood, excrement and death was overwhelming here: the sooner he could establish the initial details and vacate the premises for the soon-to-arrive SOCO team to get to work, the better. Minshull was certain he wouldn't forget this scene easily.

'His name's Mark Lingham. He's local, owns a business in town. We're working on the rest.'

'So we're assuming the deceased are known to him?'

'Maybe,' Lanehan shrugged. 'Until we can get some sense out of him, that's all we have. I guess we know they all met him at least once. Poor sods.'

'Pathologist's on the way, Sarge,' DC Dave Wheeler said, arriving beside Minshull and Lanehan. 'Bloody hell.'

'Literally.'

Wheeler shot him a wry look. 'Nice.'

'Who's the Duty Pathologist?'

'Dr Amara.'

Minshull shared a fleeting grin with his colleague. At least that was something. If anyone could decode this bizarre crime scene, it was Dr Rachael Amara. Unflappable, fiercely intelligent and self-confessed strange, she was their best hope.

8

Minshull and Wheeler made a slow circumnavigation of the space together, pausing to inspect details from a safe distance.

'Throats slashed,' Wheeler noted, his voice reverentially low. 'That explains the volume of blood.'

'So we're looking for a knife.'

'That'd be my guess.'

Minshull peered at the tallest of the four bodies. 'It's a hell of a lot of blood, though, even for four bodies.'

'Maybe there was a struggle?'

'Possibly.'

'And Lingham said it was his fault?'

'According to Steph and Rilla,' Minshull confirmed, the bloodied confession in the street an incongruous detail that seemed at odds with everything else. 'But I'm not sure how he'd have managed it. These victims are all tall, well-built adult males. I saw Mark Lingham being examined by the paramedics – he's small, wiry. I guess he could be fast…'

'Fast enough to slit four throats without anyone stopping him?' Wheeler asked, mirroring Minshull's thoughts.

'Exactly. Why didn't they fight back? Even one of them could have easily overpowered the guy.'

'Drugged?'

'Possible, I suppose.' Minshull stopped walking, allowing himself a moment to take in the whole scene. Why didn't it feel right? And what was the significance of the objects placed around each body with apparent care? 'We need to get these seen by Dr Amara and bagged up as soon as possible. And we need to inform the Guv.'

'I don't envy either of us that task.'

Minshull returned Wheeler's grimace. It was imperative DI Joel Anderson should be informed. The problem was that their superior had been battling dragons of his own for weeks now.

The team was a detective down, thanks to a major case that had caused DC Les Evans to fall victim to a savage attack from which he was still recovering at home. It could be months before he was back on the team. In the meantime, Anderson's superior was refusing to provide cover. And, like the proverbial law of sod, Evans' absence had coincided with South Suffolk's criminal fraternity apparently calling open season on crime. Everyone on the team was doing the work of two people, and the strain was already showing. A quadruple murder in a quiet rural town was the last thing anyone needed.

Anderson was not going to be happy.

'And Cora?' Wheeler's question was careful.

Minshull understood his colleague's concern. The presence of belongings, especially so prominent in the placing of the bodies, suggested that police consultant Dr Cora Lael should see them in situ. Her ability to sense emotional echoes from objects could provide invaluable insight into what happened here and the mind and identity of those responsible.

But this was the worst murder scene Minshull had encountered in his career. Maintaining his composure was taking all his strength of mind. Asking a civilian to witness it first-hand — even one as important to South Suffolk CID as Cora — was out of the question.

'I can't ask her to do this.' The statement carried more truth out loud than he'd intended. 'At least not until the bodies are out.'

'And even then?' Wheeler glanced around the space, at the ugly scars of blood spatter on every wall and surface of the unit. It was horrific enough without the victims in place.

Minshull shook his head. 'I'll ask the Guv, but I reckon Cora seeing the items bagged and away from this place is better.'

'She might hear something in here.'

'I can't ask her to see this, Dave.'

Wheeler gave a slow shrug. 'Your shout.'

'I'll call the Guv,' Minshull said. 'Can you make sure nobody else comes in here until the SOCOs arrive?'

'Consider it done,' Wheeler replied, a little pale. 'Might just stand sentry by the door, though, if you don't mind.'

The putrid stink was enough to turn anyone's stomach, even the famously cast-iron innards of Dave Wheeler. Minshull couldn't blame him for preferring fresh air. 'Be my guest. I'll be back as soon as I've made the call.'

'Right-o.' Wheeler blessed him with a grim smile. 'And they say nothing exciting ever happens on a Monday morning, eh?'

Minshull allowed his smile to remain until he reached the threshold of the unit.

Outside was a tangled mess of official business and local shock. Police tape flapped in the strengthening breeze, banks of dark clouds gathering overhead, mirroring the mood of those on the street. A storm was imminent, its oppressive air already claiming the space. His uniformed colleagues were doing their best to secure the scene, fielding fevered questions from bystanders who had been drawn by the commotion. Knowing Suffolk village communities as he did, Minshull was certain the news would have travelled the length of the Evernam grapevine by now. Probably out to the surrounding villages, too.

Lanehan and Davis were standing at the edge of the cordon, talking to the newly arrived SOCO team, who were unloading their van. Both remained stony-faced, but Minshull could tell they were shaken. Who wouldn't be?

Spotting the chief SOCO, Minshull raised a hand and headed over.

'Afternoon, Brian.'

Brian Hinds raised a characteristically wry eyebrow. 'We must stop meeting like this, DS Minshull. People will talk.'

'Let them.' The hackneyed joke was as welcome as the officer who made it. Minshull was acutely aware that in Brian Hinds' occupation, as in his own, humour was an indispensable tool of the trade.

Hinds chuckled. 'Brave as ever.'

'Always.' Minshull let the warmth of the joke last as long as he could before the necessity of the situation extinguished it. 'It's a nasty one in there.'

'So I heard. Four victims?'

'The surviving fifth claims he did it. Paramedics are checking him now. Once they're done, he'll be taken back to the station. It's not like anything I've seen before. I'll be interested to hear your thoughts.'

The chief SOCO nodded. 'Who's been in the building?'

'Two PCs who were first on the scene, the suspect, DC Wheeler and me. We've done our best to keep disruption to a minimum.'

'Good. Anything else we should be aware of?'

'Any sign of a murder weapon. Our man's not making much sense at the moment, and it's not on his person, but I don't think it can be far away if what he says is true.'

'If?'

'Early doors,' Minshull replied. 'Could be straightforward, but it doesn't feel like it's going to be.'

'One of those, eh?' Members of the SOCO team arrived beside Hinds, offering smiles to Minshull. Hinds nodded. 'We'll keep a lookout.'

'Appreciate it. Dr Amara's on her way, so I'll get Uniform to send her in as soon as she arrives.'

'And that's when the fun will begin,' Hinds grinned, heading into the building.

Minshull walked to the edge of the cordon, mobile phone in hand, the strengthening breeze providing respite after the stench of the crime scene. It didn't remove the smell from his clothes, though. It never did. Until he could get home and change, Minshull knew he would carry the odour of sudden, calamitous death around like a bad omen.

Anderson answered after a single ring. 'How bad?'

'Four fatalities. One surviving male who claims it was his fault.'

'And was it?'

Minshull watched two uniformed colleagues coaxing a group of onlookers away. 'Not sure, Guv.'

'Right. Fun and games, then. So, what are we looking at?'

'Not a straightforward murder. I don't know what it is. You should be getting some initial photos soon. You'll see what I mean then.'

'Hang on, email just in from Dave... What the *hell*? What are those things around the bodies?'

'Belongings, I assume. Until the SOCOs have catalogued everything, I won't be able to inspect them. But there are five objects around each body, and a fifth set without a body at the centre.'

'Significance?'

'Until I can get a closer look, it's impossible to say.' He filled his lungs with fresh air. 'But Cora might.'

'You want her there?'

'No. No, I don't think we can ask her to do it on site. Back at the station, when everything's bagged.'

The *click-click-click* of Anderson's tongue against his teeth sounded down the line. Minshull could almost hear his superior's brain whirring. 'I think you're right. But you should give her the heads-up soon, make sure she's ready to come in when we need her.'

'Will do, Guv.'

Minshull smiled as he ended the call. How times had changed... Only a few months ago, DI Joel Anderson would have resisted any involvement of Dr Cora Lael, her remarkable ability to sense sounds and voices from objects being at odds with standard police procedure. But recent cases had shown Minshull's superior the error of his ways.

Minshull liked the change.

More uniformed officers had arrived now, strengthening the police cordon around the immediate area. As he'd suspected, word had travelled fast; the crowd had grown significantly since he and Wheeler had entered the crime scene.

It wouldn't be long before someone's smartphone video of the unfolding events in Evernam would make it to the press.

Minshull wanted to hope they'd be granted enough time to deal with the initial business of investigation before the media laid siege to the village, but experience had taught him to expect the worst.

A multiple murder and an apparent public confession were too much to keep under wraps.

Taking one last blessed lungful of fresh air, Minshull turned on his heel and headed back into hell.

THREE

ANDERSON

Detective Inspector Joel Anderson pinched the soft skin above the bridge of his nose and willed his headache away. Opposite him, the stony face of his superior, Detective Chief Inspector Sue Taylor, remained unmoved.

It was fast becoming one of *those* days.

But then, it had pretty much been one of *those weeks* for the last month since he'd lost a detective to an enforced leave of uncertain duration. In a team already stretched and chronically underfunded, the staff shortage was a blow Anderson wasn't certain they could withstand. He never thought he'd miss DC Les Evans, but the last few weeks had been a revelation.

'Ma'am, with respect, we have three active investigations already. The news from Evernam suggests a major murder inquiry: multiple victims, a potential killer at large. My team simply can't cope without extra help…'

'If your team can't cope, Joel, maybe we should replace them.'

It was salt rubbed into an already gaping wound: a line crossed. Anderson discarded all his remaining scraps of politeness as he glowered at his superior. '*My team* are phenomenal. They've withstood more injustice and demands than any other team in this constabulary. How we haven't lost them to another force is a miracle.'

'Then they'll be more than capable of handling this.'

'*Ma'am…*'

'No.' DCI Taylor slapped her desk, the crack-shot of the sound temporarily silencing Anderson. 'This discussion is over.' She stood and pointed to the door. As if that would be enough to send Anderson scurrying from the room like a first-year probationer. How little she knew him...

Despite fury firing every sinew, Anderson didn't rise from his seat. 'The press will be all over the case,' he returned, the coolness of his tone thinly masking white-hot threat.

His superior's eyes narrowed.

Anderson pressed on. 'We have form, after all. Abducted child. Murdered schoolteacher. Missing man back from the dead to wreak revenge. They've had quite the run of scandalous headlines lately, courtesy of South Suffolk Police. You think they're going to ignore a quadruple murder in a peaceful village with a killer on the run? Reckon that'll fall in our favour?'

She was paler now: he'd won.

And yet the victory was as bitter as his words. A DCI's first motive shouldn't be image protection. DCI Taylor knew it, too: it had long been the unspoken shadow in their interactions over the years.

'I'll have to speak to my superiors.' The noticeable dip in volume was enough. 'The decision is out of my hands.'

Now Anderson stood, slowly, eyes trained on her. 'Appreciate that, Ma'am. Now, I need to get back to my team.'

It was only when he reached the end of the third-floor corridor that Anderson set his frustration free, slamming his hand against the scuffed wooden double doors to the stairwell. They flew open, one door thudding against the wall beyond. A shadow of a dent where contact was made revealed this was not its first assisted journey into the ageing plaster.

How *bloody* dare she?

The CID office felt like a sanctuary after the battle-stale air of Taylor's office. DC Drew Ellis offered him a weary smile as Anderson passed his desk; DC Kate Bennett giving a nod while pinning a selection of gruesome photos to the noticeboard beside Minshull's vacant desk.

'Guv.'

'How's it looking, Kate?'

Bennett stared at the board. '*Bloody*, Guv. It's looking bloody.'

'Aye, it's that all right.' He turned to Ellis. 'Any more from Rob and Dave?'

'SOCOs had just arrived when I spoke to Dave half an hour ago,' Ellis replied. 'And Dr Amara's on her way.'

'Good.' Anderson allowed the remaining stress of his meeting to leave his body with a hefty sigh. 'At least we have a team there.'

'Good meeting, Guv?' Bennett's wry smile was a bright spot in an extremely dark day.

'I've no idea. But I made our case – *again*. What happens next is anyone's guess.'

'Les would have a sweepstake already in play.' Ellis' remark summoned a sudden melancholic pause as Anderson and Bennett agreed.

'No doubt. But I'd defy even DC Evans to pick a winner in this one.'

'You know we're here for the lot, Guv.'

Anderson met the earnest expression of the team's youngest detective. The shock of the murder in his home village must be still sinking in – but Anderson feared further revelations might test Ellis, especially if it transpired that he knew the people involved. 'You shouldn't have to be, Drew. But thanks. For now, we soldier on and pray that Dr Amara and the SOCOs can find something to give us a bloody advantage. Heaven knows we need one.'

He saw a look pass between Ellis and Bennett.

'What?'

'Control sent over a report, ten minutes ago. A woman called 999 after finding a suspected suicide note from her husband. Uniform were already on their way there when…' Bennett kept her eyes on Ellis.

What weren't they telling him?

'When what?'

Apology flooded Bennett's expression. 'When her husband ran out of a derelict building covered in blood, claiming responsibility for four murders.'

Anderson stared at his colleagues. 'Our bloodied man left a suicide note?'

Ellis and Bennett nodded.

The dull ache across Anderson's brow became a full-company advance. 'Where is he?'

'Paramedics gave him the all clear. He's been arrested and they're bringing him here now. Should be around half an hour.'

Behind its wall of pain, Anderson's mind battled contingencies and theories into place. Was the suicide note a cover story? Or had the blood-covered man expected to kill himself after murdering the others?

'Right. Someone needs to go and visit her. Kate, can you do that? Find out who we have already at the house and liaise with them.'

'Guv.'

'Thanks. Drew, if Rob isn't back by the time our suspect is ready for interview, I'll need you to jump in with me, okay?'

'No problem, Guv.'

'Okay, good. For now, this case takes priority. Shelve everything else for the rest of the day.' Let Sue Taylor take her sweet time with the high-ups discussing Evans' temporary replacement. At least with her occupied, Anderson's team could get on with the job at hand. 'I'll call Rob and Dave to update them. Let me know as soon as our man's in. And can someone stick the kettle on? I think we're going to need it.'

Ellis gave a small salute. 'Already on it, Guv.'

Anderson strode into his office and closed the door. With Wheeler unable to perform his usual beverage-making duties he at least had a cat in hell's chance of getting a decent coffee from Ellis. On a day of few positives, that was a noteworthy win.

FOUR

MINSHULL

'A suicide note?'

'Apparently. Kate's on her way over to see Mrs Lingham now. When we know more, I'll update you.'

'Okay. Thanks Guv.' Ending the call, Minshull glanced across the police cordon, the new information competing with events unfolding inside the building. Had Mark Lingham intended to murder the men in there and then end his own life? Or had he intended to flee the scene, the suicide note left to prevent anyone from following him?

If that was the case, what happened to cause his shocking emergence onto Januarius Street and his apparent confession of guilt? Had the reality of killing four men derailed his plan?

The ends of the threads lay stubbornly untied.

'Madam, *please*! Calm down!'

Dave Wheeler's raised voice caused Minshull to turn back. So rare was it for his colleague and friend to shout that it summoned Minshull across immediately.

A woman had slipped past the tape and was loudly confronting Wheeler, her indignant retorts intended for all to hear.

'I demand to be let in!'

'That's not possible, madam. It's a crime scene. You can't go in there.'

What was she doing?

Minshull jogged across, Wheeler's relief tangible as he arrived at the DC's side.

'Everything okay here?'

'Sarge, can you explain to this lady that she's not permitted here?'

Minshull felt the force of the woman's stare as it swung to him. 'This is a restricted area, madam. I must ask you to step back behind the cordon...'

'You don't understand, officer. I need to be in there.'

'With respect, you don't. Now please move away from the entrance.'

'But I'm a councillor for Evernam...'

'And I'm a detective sergeant in charge of this investigation. Please move away.'

'I *have* to go in there...'

What was her problem? Minshull couldn't believe the audacity of her request or the height of her self-entitlement.

Regrouping, Wheeler held up his hands, ever the oil on troubled waters. 'I hear what you're saying, madam, but there's a crime scene in that building. Our teams are working as hard as they can, but I'm afraid it takes time...'

'And *I'm* saying that, as this community's local representative, I have every right to know what's happening in there.'

This was ridiculous. Dealing with the belligerent woman was only delaying them from working. They couldn't afford to waste time here. Without another thought, Minshull stepped in, tired now of this woman's refusal to listen to reason. 'What's happening in there is a major murder investigation, madam. People have lost their lives.'

He caught Wheeler's look in his peripheral vision, but the sudden silencing of the councillor justified the means. He let the statement sink in for a moment, then pressed on. 'If you leave your details with DC Wheeler here, I'll make sure you are the first to be informed when we know what we're dealing with.'

Staring blankly, she nodded and slowly wandered away.

'Bloody hell, Minsh, laid it on a bit thick there, didn't you?' Wheeler said as they walked back to the entrance of the building. 'What happened to softly-softly?'

'You'd battled with her for long enough, Dave. She wasn't ever going to listen to niceties. The shock did the trick, didn't it?'

'Yeah, but announcing it as a multiple murder before Dr Amara has examined the scene?'

Minshull sighed. 'Mate, there are four men in there with their throats cut. It's academic.'

'All the same...'

'It's done, okay?'

Minshull bristled as he walked past Wheeler. The last thing he needed was a lecture from his colleague. What was the matter with everyone today? Was he ever going to be allowed to do his job?

It didn't help that they were all exhausted, that the team had been at breaking point for weeks. Anderson was a bad-tempered grizzly prowling the CID office, ready to snarl at anything in his path. Minshull still hadn't dealt with the fallout of their previous case that had robbed them of a detective. Dealing with a multiple murder investigation might shatter the team once and for all. Minshull couldn't allow that to happen...

'Sarge?'

The PC guarding the entrance to the building raised his hand. Minshull and Wheeler approached.

'What's happening, Steve?'

'Dr Amara wants a word.'

'Okay, thanks.'

Shaking off his frustration, Minshull ducked into the building.

Dr Amara was standing by the empty circle of belongings when Minshull entered. She offered a smile, incongruously bright against the darkness around her.

'Bit of a strange one we have here, eh?'

'What do you think?' Minshull asked.

'Aside from the objects around the deceased and the odd arrangement of bodies, the method of dispatch appears straightforward. The injuries are more or less identical, the fatal cuts were clearly made quickly – viciously, I would say – and all at the same angle, which suggests to me a right-handed attack.'

Minshull nodded. 'The surviving man apparently left a suicide note.'

'Oh?'

'His wife reported it not long before he was found outside. Could this have been a suicide pact gone wrong?'

The pathologist considered this for a moment, her black kohl-rimmed eyes sweeping across the scene. 'I suppose it's possible. I need to inspect the wounds more closely when I get these gentlemen back to my lab, but my initial sense is that one person made these injuries. In haste. Perhaps our survivor planned to take his own life after taking theirs, but reconsidered at the eleventh hour?'

'Maybe.' The theory was sound but seemed a bad fit for the scene before them. Minshull changed tack. 'Any idea what the body placements and objects signify?'

'Not a Scooby.' She met his surprise at her chosen term with a sheepish grin. 'Apologies. My four-year-old niece's favourite *phrase du jour*. Scooby Doo – clue? I'm afraid I've become a firm fan of it.'

'Ma'am?' One of the SOCOs beckoned from the furthest, darkest corner of the space. Dr Amara and Minshull hurried over. Illuminated by a halo of light from the officer's torch, a large carving knife lay, its blade and handle smeared thickly with blood.

'It was under the tarpaulin here,' the officer informed them. 'I just caught the glint of metal when I was inspecting this corner.'

'Excellent spot,' Dr Amara congratulated her. She raised her eyebrows at Minshull. 'Looks like we have our potential murder weapon, Detective Sergeant.'

'Brilliant work,' he replied, gratified by the crinkled-eye smile of the SOCO above her mask.

'What've we got, Sarge?' Wheeler arrived at his side. 'Bloody hell...'

'Indeed. Get this recorded and bagged, and we'll notify Forensics. This needs to be fast-tracked and checked against Mark Lingham and the four victims.'

'*And* the victims?' Wheeler stared back. 'Are you suggesting one of the deceased killed the others?'

Minshull pinched the bridge of his nose. 'I'm not suggesting anything. But as we have precious few theories to follow right now, we can't rule anything out.'

'Wise,' Dr Amara agreed. 'It's a strange one, that's for sure.'

FIVE

BENNETT

DC Kate Bennett killed the engine of the CID pool car and waited a moment in the resulting silence, her hands resting on the steering wheel, staring at the converted barn ahead.

It was a location straight out of a countryside interiors magazine. Manicured grounds, flowers in pots and planters standing sentry along the wide, sweeping, York-stone gravelled drive, a verdant paddock to the left of the house where two white horses grazed serenely. *A Perfect Suffolk Country Retreat*, the headline would read.

Except that the woman within its architecturally aesthetic walls currently believed her husband had taken his own life.

Bennett took a breath that induced aches from every muscle in reply. She was beyond exhausted – all the team were. The past four weeks had been the busiest and most frustrating she could remember. The thought of summoning more energy to deal with this case made her heart sink.

It didn't help that her home life was as chaotic as life in CID. Her soon-to-be ex-husband – when the divorce came through – had sold their marital home without her consent and was now threatening to withhold any payments if Bennett pursued her claim against him. Not content with betraying her and setting up a home and a family with another woman, Russ Bennett now seemed intent on stealing her financial rights, too. She would fight – and her solicitor assured her she would win – but the process was brutal. She felt hollowed out, battered on every side, and each day required a gargantuan effort to leave her rented house instead of curling back up in bed and willing the whole damn mess away.

At least she had good news for the frantic woman in this perfect house. Good news that her husband had been found alive. That he had been found drenched in the blood of four dead men – claiming responsibility for their murders – would be a harder message to deliver.

Best to get it over with.

Bracing herself, she left the car and rang the doorbell.

The large oak door opened immediately, revealing a uniformed officer.

'Good to see you, DC Bennett.'

'Hey Janey.' Bennett held up her warrant card as a matter of protocol, smiling at the Family Liaison Officer assigned to Isabel Lingham. 'How's it going?'

PC Janey March grimaced. 'It'll be better now you have news. Is he okay?'

'Not sure *okay* is the term I'd choose, but he's alive.'

'Has he been arrested?'

Bennett nodded. 'It's an odd one. What's your impression of the wife?'

PC March pulled the door closed a little, lowering her voice. 'She's in a heck of a state. Go easy on her, yeah? I've only just managed to calm her down.'

'Will do. Was she on her own when she found the note?'

March nodded. 'She'd just returned from the school run. They'd had breakfast together before taking the kids, and then she found it when she got back. She thought he'd gone out to Evernam Woods to do it – I sent Liam Bullivant and Andie Simmons out there to check while I stayed here with her.'

'Are they still out there?' Bennett asked.

'As far as I know. Should I call them back?'

Bennett considered this. 'Might as well. Ask Control for the okay from DS Minshull, but I don't see why they'd need to continue the search seeing as he's been found.'

'No problem. Let me take you in and I'll get on it.'

Bennett was ushered into a wide, oak-floored hall, then followed PC March to an open-plan living area that stretched the width of the building. Though the day beyond its windows was dulled by the building storm, the space was light-filled and airy. A well-appointed kitchen occupied one end, a generous seating area the other. The space was tidy apart from one corner where a mound of children's toys had been hastily piled beneath a clothes horse drier filled with red and white school polo shirts, pairs of black trousers and sentry rows of white socks.

An ashen-faced woman sitting on an armchair by the window sprang to her feet as Bennett and March entered. She was dressed in a long linen tunic and white cropped leggings, a large silver charm in the shape of a wave hanging from a long turquoise beaded necklace around her neck. Her blonde corkscrew curls were pulled into a high ponytail. She stared at Bennett with desperate, dark-shadowed eyes.

'Isabel,' March said, her voice gentle, as if she was addressing a child, 'this is DC Kate Bennett. She has some news for you.'

'Have you found him?' Isabel Lingham demanded.

'It's probably better if you sit down,' March soothed. 'Shall I pop the kettle on?'

'No. I – I've had enough tea… *Thank you*.' The thanks seemed a conciliatory gesture to smooth the sharp edges of her reply. 'Just tell me where Mark is.'

Bennett noted the wringing hands, the restlessness of the body. The air around the woman seemed pained, completely at odds with the comfortable surroundings. It felt unfair to be the bringer of news that would irrevocably change the lives of everyone connected to Mark Lingham, even if the first part of her message would allay fears of his demise.

'Mrs Lingham, let's sit down,' Bennett said, her tone enough to cause Mark Lingham's wife to comply. 'I know you've gone over this with my colleague, but I just need to ask a couple of questions, and then I can tell you where we are.'

Isabel Lingham stared back, her fingers turning and twisting together.

'Did you see your husband this morning?'

'At breakfast.'

'And how did he seem?'

'Fine. Laughing and joking with the kids, talking about seeing the guys at rugby practice tonight, work – the usual stuff.'

'He didn't appear overly anxious, or on edge?'

'He was chatty,' Isabel Lingham conceded. 'But no more than usual. Mark does everything at a hundred miles a second, but that's just him.'

Bennett made careful notes. 'So, where did you find the letter?'

'It was…' A sob rose in Mrs Lingham's throat. She battled it away. 'Sorry. It was in the kitchen. By the kettle.'

'And has Mark ever done anything like this before? Or talked about it?'

'No.' Her hands became very still, fingers stretching out on her lap. 'He's never threatened to end his life before. He's had his demons, as most people have. But he's settled and successful and happy with us. Mark's a kind and generous man. He's gentle. He couldn't hurt himself… Please, find him. Bring him home. I'm going out of my mind here.'

It was time to tell her. Bennett nodded at March, who slipped out of the room. Sitting on the sofa nearest Isabel Lingham, Bennett steadied herself. Adrenaline had begun to fill the space where exhaustion had been, and it was enough to sharpen her focus.

'We've found him. Alive,' she began, because to start with anything else felt cruel. 'He's being checked by paramedics.' Bennett withheld the rest for now, plotting a careful course around the information she was here to deliver.

The effect was instantaneous: Isabel Lingham crumpling in a relieved rush of breath, her head dropping to her hands.

Bennett waited respectfully. You couldn't rush someone when delivering this kind of information. The hours of fear and worry had clearly taken their toll on Mark Lingham's wife: she deserved time to process the news.

Seeing a box of tissues on a low oak coffee table beside the sofa, Bennett reached for it, resting the box on the arm of Isabel's chair.

After a while, Isabel raised her head, smudges of black mascara imprinted on her palms where she'd held them to her eyes. She grabbed a handful of tissues, wiping her face quickly.

'Where is he? Is he okay? Can I see him?'

'My colleagues are with him now and are likely to be for some time.' Bennett paused, willing the correct words to follow. 'Mrs Lingham, your husband was found very distressed and making some concerning claims.'

Isabel's brow furrowed. 'Claims? About what?'

'He was discovered leaving an empty retail unit in Januarius Street, Evernam, where my colleagues discovered the bodies of four men. Mark's clothes, face and hands were covered with blood. He was insisting that he was responsible.'

How were you supposed to make this kind of message palatable? Even as she spoke, Bennett winced at her words. Lingham's wife stared hollowly back – and when she didn't reply, Bennett felt compelled to continue.

'My colleagues in the ambulance service have confirmed that the blood on Mr Lingham's clothing and skin is not his own. He hasn't sustained any injuries and appears to be physically well. But he's very distressed, as you can imagine.'

'I need to see him.' The statement was barely more than a whisper.

'I understand that, Mrs Lingham. But we need to talk to your husband about what he's said.'

'But I – I had breakfast with him this morning. My children sat down to eat with him, and everything was fine. Are you telling me that, in the time it took me to run the kids to school, he wrote a suicide note, went into the village and murdered four people?'

It sounded preposterous, but given what they knew, it was possible. 'Mark told my colleagues it was his fault the men were dead.'

Isabel Lingham blinked back, fire igniting in her eyes. 'Which men? Who are they? How does Mark know them? How do you even know they're connected?'

'We're working on identifying them now.'

'So bring him home while you're doing that. Let me take care of him. Until you know who the victims are, how can you possibly link them to my husband?'

A dull ache appeared and assumed stubborn residence at the centre of Bennett's brow. 'Mrs Lingham, we have four dead men in a building your husband was seen emerging from, bloodied and claiming responsibility. We need to ascertain exactly what his involvement was.'

'Has Mark been arrested?'

'He's helping us with our enquiries...'

'Don't give me that! *Has* he been arrested?'

'I believe so.'

'This is a joke!' The change in Lingham's wife was startling. She fixed Bennett with a thunderous stare, spitting fury with her words. 'I'm calling my solicitor immediately. Mark is clearly distressed, and you're making him say things when he doesn't know what's going on. Where is he being held?'

'He'll be taken to Police HQ in Ipswich...'

'Right. I'm going there...'

'Mrs Lingham, I must request you stay here for the time being.'

'Not on your life! You think I'm going to stay at home while you throw murder charges at my husband?'

PC March, summoned by the sound of raised voices, hurried into the room, placing herself between Bennett and Isabel Lingham. 'Okay, okay, we need to calm down.'

'She's accusing Mark of murder!'

'No, Isabel, she's telling you what Mark's said.' March extended a hand towards her. 'We have to investigate his claim and why he made it. And the best place to do that is at the station. Mark has volunteered to accompany our colleagues there. He will have the option of a legal representative before any questions are asked. Now, if you want to call your solicitor, you can. But you have to stay here so we can do what we need to.'

The PC's soothing words snatched some of the fire from Isabel Lingham, although she refused to sit. Bennett sensed her cue to leave and stood.

'I'll keep PC March updated, and as soon as you can see Mark, we'll make it happen,' she replied gently, ignoring the woman's furious scowl.

'I'll stay here with you for as long you need me,' March assured Isabel, before turning to Bennett. 'Thank you, DC Bennett.'

Bennett held her composure until she was out of the house and back in the pool car. Only when she was behind the wheel did she slump in her seat, the effort of the interview finally taking its toll. The call of her bed was strong, the caffeine she'd imbibed today not nearly enough to combat the exhaustion.

Resigned to the long day stretching ahead of her, Bennett started the engine and steered the car out of the Linghams' drive and onto the main road towards Ipswich.

SIX

MINSHULL

'Mark Lingham?' DC Drew Ellis stared at Minshull.

'Yes. Do you know him?'

Ellis shifted uneasily. 'Everyone does. He's on the cricket team, and he's a regular at the pub.'

'How well do you know him?'

'He's just someone I see around. One of the lads, only he's the oldest.'

As soon as the call had come in from Evernam, Ellis had noticeably kept his head down. Having moved there over a year ago and being a member of the local rugby and cricket teams, it was inevitable that this conversation would happen. Minshull had seen his DC anticipating the questions he now faced.

'I'm sorry to ask,' Minshull added, lowering his voice despite them being alone in the CID office. 'But as you live in the village…'

Ellis shrugged. 'It's okay. It's just… the thought of who the deceased might be, you know? I haven't known victims in the job before.'

'It's tough when it happens.' Minshull clamped a hand on his shoulder, hoping it offered some comfort. 'And it's likely to be people you've seen in Evernam even if you don't know them well. I'll do what I can to keep you away from the worst of it, but…'

'I appreciate that, Sarge. I know we'll all have to pitch in.'

'Good man. For now, see if you can find out who owns the unit on Januarius Street. If we can establish that, we can look for connections with Lingham. Someone had to have granted access to him and the others.'

'Sarge.'

Minshull watched the DC slope back to his desk. Poor sod. It was never easy when a personal connection to a case emerged. Once they had positive IDs on the victims, the pressure would only mount on Ellis. Minshull wished he could reassign him far away from the investigation, but with manpower and resources as tight as they were, it was impossible.

Wanting to do something, he moved to the tiny kitchen at the corner of the CID office, filling the kettle and fetching mugs from the sink drainer. Any action was better than inaction.

The steadily boiling water acted as a foil to his thoughts. How had the five men gained access to the building? Had someone let them in? Had Lingham arranged for a key? The back door was bolted from the outside, so the only means of access would have been the Januarius Street entrance. There were no signs of forced entry, so a key must have been used. But why were the victims there? And who had invited them?

The man Minshull had seen being attended to by paramedics shortly before his arrest was of slight build, around five feet seven inches in height. By Minshull's reckoning, the shortest of the victims was over six feet tall; all of them well built. How had Lingham overpowered four men considerably taller and heavier than himself? And how had he dragged them into the bizarre arrangement on the concrete floor?

How long had the murder taken to commit? Minshull glared at the swirling steam from the kettle's spout as if it was respons-ible for his circling train of thought. He'd know more when Bennett returned from Lingham's home, but already time was against him. How long before word got out beyond Evernam? How long before the media caught the scent?

'Lingham in yet?' DI Anderson barked, arriving in the CID office like the silent assassin his team secretly acknowledged he was.

Minshull dropped the teaspoon he'd been fidgeting with, its clatter causing Ellis' head to rise from his desk nearest the kitchen. 'Just arrived, Guv. But his wife's requested the family solicitor be present, so we're waiting on his arrival.'

'Anyone we know?'

'Um...' Minshull pulled a ripped envelope from his back pocket and consulted the name he'd hastily scrawled on it. 'Jasper Carmichael?'

Anderson stared pointedly at the note. 'Run out of paper, have you?'

'No, Guv. I couldn't find my notebook when Kate called.'

His superior's eyes narrowed. 'Judging by the disaster of your desk, Rob, I'm not surprised. Carry on down that road and you'll be giving Les Evans a run for his money in the Messiest Desk stakes.'

'I've been busy...'

Anderson's sigh was lost in the kettle's steam. 'It was a joke, son. Lame as it was.'

'Ah. Sorry.'

His superior received Minshull's apology with a wry smile and a heavy hand patting his shoulder. 'Don't sweat it. Make me a decent coffee and we'll forget it ever happened, eh?'

'Ooh, Sarge, if you're making...' Ellis grinned, his mug held aloft.

'One for our young DC too,' Anderson winked. 'Good work, DS Minshull.'

Cursing himself for falling into the trap, Minshull groaned and reached for Ellis' mug.

–

An hour later, Kate Bennett returned, just as the call came up from the custody suite that Mark Lingham and his legal brief were ready for interview. Bennett looked ready to drop, but then so did everyone else. She batted away Minshull's concern when he asked her if she needed a break.

'Like any of us have time for that. Cheers, though.'

'How did it go with Isabel Lingham?'

'Hard to say.' Bennett rubbed the back of her neck. 'I'm not likely to be invited back without a warrant, though.'

'*That* good?'

'Let's just say I was glad Janey March was there.'

'I suppose telling someone their partner is alive but now a chief suspect in a quadruple murder investigation isn't the best launch point for a friendship,' Minshull grinned.

'Oh, don't. I'm hoping I don't have another of those conversations for a long time.'

Minshull felt a kick of guilt, even though the situation was unavoidable. 'Sorry for sending you out solo.'

Bennett gave a slow shrug. 'It is what it is, Sarge. I know it wasn't your choice.'

'All the same, I know it sucks.'

'Thanks.'

'What impression did you get from Mrs Lingham about her husband?'

'She insisted he wasn't capable of harming anyone, although clearly he'd considered harming himself, according to the note he left.'

'Did she have any concerns about him prior to this?'

'She mentioned something about demons...' Bennett opened her notebook and scanned a page. 'Um, here – *He's had his demons, as most people have*. But she was adamant he couldn't have hurt the people in the unit.'

Having finally located his own notebook, Minshull added the point to his notes. Staring at what they knew so far didn't exactly fill him with confidence. There was little to go on and frustratingly large gaps in what they had collected so far. 'So he says it's his fault but his wife thinks him incapable of murder. Why do I feel like we're missing something?'

'It's a weird one for sure. Any news on the victims' ID, Sarge?'

'Nope. I'm hoping something comes back soon. Check with Control would you? See if they've had any worried calls from family or friends. Two of the victims were wearing wedding rings so there must be wives or husbands somewhere. And they're all of working age, so maybe employers concerned about their whereabouts?'

'Evernam's a tight knit community. You'd think someone would have noticed they were missing.'

'You would, Kate. But you and I know it's never as straight-forward as that.'

'Ah Kate. Glad you're back.' Anderson emerged from his office, his smile fading when he glanced at Ellis. 'A word in my office, Rob?'

'Guv.'

Minshull saw dread fall across Ellis' face like a veil. Heart sinking, he followed Anderson into his office.

'Close the door, would you? Best to keep this between us for the time being.'

Minshull complied, closing the concern of his colleagues from view. 'News, Guv?'

'Brian Hinds just called. We have driving licences for three of the four victims. I need you and the team to find out what you can about them, contact next of kin and so on.'

'Who do we have?' Minshull asked, the news simultaneously welcome and grave.

Anderson consulted the sheet of paper in his hand. 'Krish Bhattachama, thirty-nine. Jack Markham, forty-two. And Otto Wragg, forty-one. No name for our fourth victim yet, but Brian's going through the notebook found next to the body, so it's possible he'll find something there.'

Minshull noted down the names and ages. On paper the relative youth of the deceased was starkly evident. 'How old is Mark Lingham?'

'Forty-nine. His fiftieth birthday is next Tuesday.'

'Might that be significant?' Minshull mused.

'What, the dire prospect of turning fifty pushed him to become a multiple murderer?' Anderson scoffed. 'I know getting older can be a challenge, Rob, but most blokes just buy a leather jacket or start cycling in neon Lycra at weekends.'

'I didn't mean...' Minshull backpedalled, realising his mistake.

'No, no, it's a point worth considering. Us fifty-odd year-olds need to be watched closely for signs of late-onset psycho-pathy. Perhaps I should warn Ros to hide the sharp knives in case the urge to slash my friends' throats suddenly arrives...'

'*Guv...*'

Laughing, Anderson held up his hands. 'Fine, I'll stop. But grant me a bit of levity in the middle of this crap, eh?'

It was Minshull's turn to relent. Jokes had been the only saving grace of the CID team in recent weeks. Now more than ever it was important to keep morale afloat. 'Sorry, Guv. Reckon I left my sense of humour at home this morning.'

'Quite surprised to find I brought mine, to be honest,' Anderson replied wryly. 'Perhaps my wife packed it for me with the sandwiches I'm not going to eat later.'

'Italian deli again, is it?'

'Too bloody right. Between battling with Sue Taylor and having four corpses drop unexpectedly on us I've more than earned my illicit lunch.' He grinned. 'And if you and the others want coffee and buns bringing back you'll pretend you didn't hear that.'

'Guv.'

The moment of lightness was what he needed, but all too soon it ebbed away. Minshull felt the sinking of his spirits as he considered the list of victim names he'd written on his notes.

'We'll have to tell Drew. Chances are he knows them or has seen them in the village.'

'True. Poor kid. This is going to hit him hard.'

'I think that's dawning on him already,' Minshull replied. 'I've asked him to locate the owner of the unit as a first priority.'

Anderson nodded. 'Wise. Best keep him occupied with that for now. I'll ask Kate to start looking for next of kin for our known victims. When we've spoken with Lingham we'll brief Drew with everything we know. I think that's kinder.'

'Agreed. Are you accompanying me for interview, Guv?'

'I will, aye. But we'll hold back on revealing the names we know to Lingham and his brief for now. See if Lingham volunteers them.' He hefted a sigh that spoke of too much pressure and far too little sleep. 'Right then, Rob, shall we?'

SEVEN

ANDERSON

The man waiting for them in Interview Room 3 didn't look like a murderer. But then, few of the murderers Anderson had encountered during his police career ever had. This was the first suspected murderer of four concurrent victims he'd interviewed, however, so all bets were off. In this job, you couldn't ever think you'd seen it all. There was always something nasty waiting to bite you on the arse if you did.

Mark Lingham cowered beside his legal representative, uncomfortable and exposed in a regulation grey sweatshirt and tracksuit bottoms. His clothes were already bagged up and on their way to forensics, the sight stomach-churningly gruesome, according to PCs Lanehan and Davis.

'Drenched in blood,' Steph Lanehan had informed Anderson, calling from the scene. 'Never seen anything like it, Guv. Like someone had tipped buckets of it over him.'

Lingham was clean now, but the way he rubbed his fingers over the skin of his clean palms suggested he could still see the blood.

Out, damned spot! Out, I say!

Anderson had learned that in school. Act 5, Scene 1 of Shakespeare's *Macbeth*: Lady Macbeth driven mad by the memory of murder, frantically washing imagined blood from her hands. Was Mark Lingham experiencing the same thing?

His solicitor eyed Anderson and Minshull accusingly as they made their introductions. *One of those*, Anderson surmised.

Some lawyers would make master poker players, their faces unreadable. Not Jasper Carmichael, it would appear. Minshull had informed Anderson that the solicitor was the family's representative – he hazarded a guess that the man had never had to deal with a multiple murder charge for his regular client. Could he be out of his depth, too? Perhaps this show of mistrust was designed to mask his lack of experience. Go on the offensive from the outset. Blag it until the coppers believe you...

'If you have everything you need, we'll make a start,' Minshull offered.

Jasper Carmichael nodded. Mark Lingham kept his eyes fixed on his hands.

Anderson started the recording. 'Interview conducted 11:40 a.m., Monday 9th September. Detective Inspector Joel Anderson and Detective Sergeant Rob Minshull present.'

'Mr Lingham, could you state your name and age for the recording, please?'

Lingham's voice cracked on his first attempt to speak. When he managed it, the tone was thick and laboured. 'Mark Lingham, forty-nine.'

'Thank you. Can you tell us, in your own words, what happened this morning at 62 Januarius Street, Evernam?'

There was a pause. The solicitor opened his file, pen poised. He made no attempt to encourage Lingham or make any kind of eye contact.

Anderson and Minshull waited.

Lingham's fingers continued to rub his palms. Then, as Anderson was about to speak, Lingham lifted his head.

'They're dead. All of them. I couldn't stay in there.'

'Who is dead?' Minshull asked.

'*All* of them.'

'Mr Lingham – *Mark* – can you tell me their names, please?'

Lingham shook his head, the muscles in his jaw working. Carmichael glanced at his client but said nothing. Was he giving Lingham time to formulate his reply?

When the silence began to stretch too long, Minshull intervened. 'Okay, let's go back to this morning, then. Can you tell me what you did prior to going to Evernam?'

'Normal stuff. Got up, made breakfast, then Issy took the kids to school...' His voice drifted away, his stare glassy.

'How many kids do you have?' It was a clever move from Minshull, Anderson observed. Make conversation. Keep Lingham talking.

'Three. Kyra, Fin and Seb.'

'Good kids?'

Lingham blinked. 'The best.'

'And your wife came home after running them to school?'

'Yeah. She works from home, so...'

'And what do you do for work?'

Lingham mumbled something.

'Louder for the recording, please.'

'I run a lettings agency. With a partner.'

Minshull made notes. 'And who is your business partner?'

'Is that important?' Carmichael interjected.

Minshull's expression bore no hint of irritation. 'It helps us build a picture, that's all.'

The solicitor glanced at Minshull and returned to his notes. Lingham fell silent.

'Mr Lingham?' Minshull prompted. 'Who is your business partner?'

'Gavin Quartermain.'

'How long have you run the agency?'

Lingham gave a long sigh, eyes fixed on his hands. 'About fifteen years.'

'And how's business?'

The stare sharpened a little. 'Can't complain.'

Minshull offered a slight smile. 'So, were you expected at work this morning?'

A pause.

Anderson kept his eyes trained on Lingham.

40

'No.'

'But it's your business,' Minshull prompted. 'Don't you have to be in the office?'

'Not today.'

'How come?'

'Gav didn't want me there.'

'Why not?'

Another hefted sigh crossed the interview desk. 'Because he was meeting an investor. I just... get in the way.'

What did that mean? Lingham's tone had changed: whether this was the reality of his situation sinking in or something else, Anderson couldn't tell. Minshull betrayed none of his own opinion but left a significant pause while he wrote down what Lingham had said. Longer than was necessary to record the suspect's reply, but long enough to make him sweat.

The effect was immediate: the hand-rubbing began again in earnest, a frown shading Lingham's features as he stared down.

'And did Mr Quartermain call you at all, prior to the investor meeting?'

Lingham shook his head.

'For the recording?'

'*No.*' The word was sharp-edged, irritated. The kind of reply a sulky teen would launch at an overbearing teacher.

Anderson glanced at his DS, proud of his work. Now they were getting somewhere...

Minshull let Lingham's reply hang in the air far longer than was comfortable. Then he looked up from his notes. 'So you weren't expected in the office. Why did you go into Evernam this morning?'

'I had to see...' Lingham's lips suddenly snapped shut, cutting off the answer he was about to give. Regrouping, he stated, 'I – I had some stuff to do.'

'Did you go there to meet your friends?'

'No.'

'How did you travel into the village?'

41

A slow blink. 'In my van.'

Anderson watched Minshull's steady note-taking. 'Make and model?'

'Ford Transit.'

'Colour and year?'

'Uh... navy blue, 2022 model.'

'Numberplate?'

Lingham gave it. His solicitor didn't flinch. Anderson found himself watching Carmichael rather than Lingham, wondering what Lingham might have disclosed to him. For now, the solicitor's expression gave little away.

'Okay. So, you drove to Evernam in your van and parked it, where?'

'Behind the unit.'

'The unit in Januarius Street?'

Lingham nodded.

'Do you own the unit?'

'No.'

'Do you let it out for a client?'

'No.' Lingham was staring at his palms again.

'Do you know who owns the unit?'

'No.'

'Do you have a key for the unit?'

'What? No... I just park behind it. Lots of people do.'

'And were there any other vehicles parked nearby?'

'I don't... I didn't notice.'

Minshull's pen worked another line on his notepad. 'So you went into the unit?'

'Yes.'

'How?'

'Sorry?'

'Did you go in through the front door or the rear?'

'I didn't... I don't remember, I'm sorry.' Lingham glanced at Carmichael. His solicitor gave a slow nod. What did that mean?

42

'Did someone let you in?' Minshull pressed on. 'One of the friends you were meeting, perhaps?'

'No.'

'Was the door already unlocked?'

'I didn't know they... It wasn't what I expected.'

Minshull kept his gaze steady, but Anderson saw the grip tighten on his pen. 'What did you expect? Had you agreed to meet there? Was it one of the errands you had to run?'

'I... Maybe.'

Minshull relented, pulling back as Anderson had seen many times. Push for answers and then retreat, in the hope that the person opposite you at the interview desk would be compelled to fill the sudden silence.

But Mark Lingham simply returned to his hand-rubbing, his gaze pointedly averted from the DS.

'Mr Lingham, did you leave a note for your wife this morning?'

'I don't see how that's relevant.' Carmichael stated, his uncharacteristic intervention causing both Anderson and Minshull to look at him. Anderson suppressed a grin. Was the solicitor on a coin meter? Did he lapse into silence until you paid him?

'It's relevant, Mr Carmichael, because Mrs Isabel Lingham called 999 to report a suicide note from her husband this morning, around twenty minutes before he emerged, bloodied, from the unoccupied unit at 62 Januarius Street.'

Silence.

Minshull folded his hands and waited for a reply. When none came, Anderson accepted the baton.

'Mr Lingham, did you intend to take your own life?'

'I... I just needed some space.'

'Have you talked to your wife about this in the past?'

Lingham's fingers increased their motion. 'She knows.'

'Is that why you chose the empty retail unit?' Anderson asked as gently as he could. Surprise registered beside him as

43

Minshull's eyebrow rose a little. Anderson ignored it. 'Did you intend to harm yourself there?'

'It was supposed to be... I didn't think they'd...'

'Didn't think who?'

'The others. It wasn't meant to be like this. It's all my fault.'

'Who are the others, Mr Lingham?'

'You can't help them. No one can.'

'I'm aware they are past help.' Anderson kept his tone steady, stare heavy on Lingham, who visibly winced when he looked up. 'But we can help their families and friends who are left. And the men who died deserve justice. We can't do either of those things unless we know who they are. So, I'm asking you again: who are *the others*?'

Lingham held Anderson's stare for a heartbeat, then released the names on a long sigh, as if they were attached to his breath like ribbons on an invisible kite string. 'Otto... Denz... Krish... Tim...'

Anderson and Minshull stiffened. The missing name.

'Tim?' Anderson repeated, a battle to keep the sudden adrenaline from his voice.

'Stapleforth.' Lingham stared back at his hands.

Minshull made steady notes, only looking up when he'd added the last name. 'And who is Denz?'

It took Lingham a while to register. 'Jack Markham. Everyone calls him Denzil, have done since he was a kid.'

'How long have you known them?'

'Grew up with them. In the village. I was a little older, but they started hanging around with me when we joined the rugby club and then the cricket team.'

'Were you meeting them at the unit?'

'I didn't know what they were planning... They shouldn't even have been there.'

He was meandering again, eyes glazing. Jasper Carmichael looked at his client, concern worrying his brow.

44

'Were they trying to stop you hurting yourself, Mark?' Minshull asked, as gently as he could.

Lingham's hands went to his temples, his answer a long, agonised wail. 'They were there because of *me*. It's *my* fault... And now they're *dead*...'

—

Outside in the corridor, Minshull slumped against the wall. Anderson punched his hands on his hips and stared towards the double doors that led to the cells.

'What the hell are we supposed to make of that?'

'Search me, Guv. Were they trying to stop him and he lashed out? Or were they there to help him and it went wrong?'

'Help him?' Anderson asked. 'Help him do what?'

'The bodies, the belongings around each one, the fifth space without a body at the centre... That doesn't tally with Lingham being suicidal. Or panicking and lashing out with the knife. Why arrange the bodies like that and all the belongings around them?'

'Unless they were part of it, too.'

'How? A pact?'

'Ludicrous as it sounds.'

It was preposterous to even consider it, but with so little else to go on and the already bizarre nature of the crime scene, it was a theory they couldn't afford to rule out.

'Did they want to be found like that? Is there a significance in the layout?'

'If there is, I've yet to discover it.'

'Maybe we'll have more of a clue when we've spoken to next of kin.' Minshull shook his head. 'So, what's the plan now?'

Anderson groaned. 'Let Lingham talk to his solicitor again. Maybe Carmichael can advise him to tell us more.' The solicitor had requested an urgent meeting with his client, and for once, Anderson was glad of the hiatus. Maybe it would give them time to work out what the hell the truth was.

'But Lingham said he did it.'

'No, he said it was *his fault*. Two very different things. For now, we keep an open mind. Maybe Lingham lashed out. Maybe they were all meant to die today. Or maybe they were there against their will, and someone else did the job...'

'You think that's possible?'

Anderson wished he knew. 'Right now, anything's possible. First and foremost, we need to add Tim Stapleforth to the list of suspected victims. Let's head back. We need to break the news to Drew. And then... we need to find their families.'

EIGHT

ELLIS

DC Drew Ellis pushed his chair back from his desk and rubbed his eyes. Today had begun as a nightmare and was rapidly descending into hell. Worse than the body blow of the Evernam news was the impending horror of learning the full details. He kept catching DC Bennett's not-so-subtle glances in his direction. The thought of what she might not be telling him twisted his guts.

Of course he knew Mark Lingham. He was a stalwart of the cricket team, a constant presence at the bar of The Shire Horse pub at the centre of the village. At one point, Ellis had been part of Lingham's friendship group, until Mark found a new clique and moved to the other side of the pub. Were any of this new inner circle now lying in their own blood at 62 Januarius Street?

'I've got the owner's details,' he said, turning to Bennett. 'Email just came in. He's a non-dom, living in the Caribbean. His secretary's going to send us the details of the current agency letting it and also the last building company to do any work on it. But she reckons it's been unoccupied for at least eighteen months.'

'Do you remember what it was before?' Bennett asked. Ellis noted the way she subtly shifted her monitor to obscure the screen from view. What was she working on?

'No. It's been empty for as long as I've lived there. I'm hoping the letting agent can give me a history of recent tenants. How are you getting on?' He gave her monitor a pointed look.

She paled a little. 'Oh. You know. Background stuff.'

Bennett looked dead on her feet. They all did, of course, but Ellis knew about everything his colleague was dealing with away from work. Since she'd opened up about her impending divorce and the mess that her git of an ex had left her with, Ellis had been more aware of how incredible Kate Bennett really was to have kept going.

She was impressive, full stop.

Not that he'd tell her that.

For now, it mattered that she'd let him in. That glimpse into the world she masked so skilfully at work was a privilege Ellis didn't want to take for granted.

'Four bodies,' he stated, more out of a need to be part of things than to discover who the murdered men were. 'It's grim.'

'It is. Can't be easy for you, being in your neck of the woods.'

'Honestly? It's the worst.' The smile Ellis offered wouldn't convince anyone. 'How are you holding up?'

For a moment he expected Bennett to brush off his concern in the brusque way she usually did. But instead, she rubbed her eyes and stared back. 'Let's just say it's not my favourite day at work.'

'Going to see Lingham's missus can't have been fun.'

'It wasn't.'

'Next shout on this job we should do together.'

Bennett sent him a wry smile from her desk. 'We don't have the manpower, Drew. I'll manage fine on my own, thanks.'

'I wasn't talking about *you* not coping. I need backup for me.'

'Oh, poor baby.'

'Cheers.' The spark of fun between them was exactly what Ellis needed. Glad of the distraction, he decided to push his luck. 'We should grab a drink tonight after work. If this shift ever ends.'

Bennett made no attempt to hide her surprise. 'Pint of cola calling your name, is it?'

'One time! That was one time! And we were on a stakeout, *and* I was driving…'

'Yeah, well, nice idea, but I have a hot date with flatpack furniture tonight.'

'I could help with that.'

Bennett scoffed. 'What do you know about flatpack furniture?'

'More than you think I do.' He pulled a face. 'Or maybe not. But think of the comedy value of watching me try.'

'Tempting, that.' Bennett grinned. 'Anyway, St Just is out of your way now. You'll probably just want to go home… Oh, Drew, I didn't mean…'

Ellis blanched, the thought turning his stomach. 'Home to *Evernam*? No, funnily enough, I'm not in a hurry to get back to the scene of a quadruple murder, where half the residents know I'm a copper, and the victims may well be blokes I know. I've even considered camping out at my folks' place till this blows over.'

'I'm so sorry. I didn't think.'

'Don't sweat it. But think about the flatpack, yeah? The offer's there.'

Bennett's laugh betrayed her relief at the subject change. 'I'll bear it in mind.'

The CID office door opened slowly, heralding the return of an ashen-faced DC Dave Wheeler. 'Wotcha, kids. What's the latest?'

'Wading through background searches,' Bennett replied grimly.

It was all Wheeler could do to raise his eyebrows. He looked ready to drop.

'Brian Hinds sent the names over, then?'

Ellis stared back. 'They've been ID'd?'

'Yeah, sorry, kid.' Wheeler flopped down on his chair, chucking the pool car keys on his desk. 'Three so far, waiting on a fourth. I expect Minsh will fill you in, soon as he can.'

Ellis turned to Bennett. 'You know already?'

She couldn't even look at him. How long had everyone known, while he'd been sat there, dreading the news?

'Thanks for nothing!'

'I'm sorry...'

'Who are they?' He was on his feet, fury searing through him.

'I can't say yet...'

'Can't, Kate? Or won't?'

'Drew – *Drew*, boy – Minsh told us to wait until we know more. This is going to be a bastard for you when it all comes to light. But their families need to know first. That's what Kate's doing.'

'And what am I supposed to do?'

'Do what we all do when faced with a pile of crap in this place,' Wheeler replied, risking a gentle smile. 'Stick the kettle on.'

Still shaking, Ellis did as he was told. As he set about the task, the conversation recommenced behind him, kept at a respectful volume but audible over the kitchen noise.

'How's it looking?' Bennett asked.

'In Evernam?' Wheeler shook his head. 'Shock, like you'd expect. I imagine the whole village knows now.'

'Are the press there yet?'

'No, thank goodness. Won't be long, mind. Those bastards turn up faster than bloody wasps at a picnic the moment there's a whiff of trouble.'

'At least they aren't there now,' Bennett offered. 'Let's hope they stay away until we've got the bodies out.'

'Amen to that.' Wheeler stretched his arms above his head, wincing at the pull. 'Tell you what, though, there was one woman who just wouldn't leave us alone. Not a journo, either. *Councillor*, she said she was.'

'Did she give you her name?'

'*Ohh*, now she did, but… What was it? Eve? Yvette? No – Yvonne someone or other?'

Ellis paused mid-pour, the freshly boiled kettle hovering over the mugs. 'Yvonne Stapleforth?'

Wheeler clicked his fingers. 'Yeah, that sounds about right, Drew. Frantic about getting in the unit, she was. Which was ironic, seeing as those of us who *had* been in it were all desperate to get out.'

'Stapleforth?'

The three DCs turned towards the door to discover Minshull and Anderson standing on the threshold. Minshull's hand was still on the door handle, as if the name had frozen his body mid-movement.

'Yes, Sarge.'

'Councillor Yvonne Stapleforth?'

Ellis nodded, Minshull's apparent shock setting alarm bells chiming. 'She lives in Evernam. I used to play rugby with her son, till he moved to the cricket team.'

Anderson's frown cast his eyes into deep shadow. 'What's his name?'

Ellis was suddenly aware of tension filling the room. When he glanced at the point where his hand met the kettle's handle, he saw that his knuckles had grown white. 'Tim.'

Anderson cursed loudly. Minshull stared at Ellis, his expression one of shock and compassion.

'How well do you know him?'

'Pretty well. He's a decent bloke. Older than me but solid, you know? One of the lads…' Fear began to grip his insides. The way Minshull and Anderson were looking at him, a sense of foreboding prickled his skin. 'Why?'

Minshull gave a slow, weary nod. 'Then we have all four names. I'm sorry, Drew. I think you should sit down…'

NINE

MINSHULL

Watching the slow, anguished collapse of his colleague was something Minshull never wanted to repeat. It had been inevitable, of course, from the moment the murders were uncovered in Evernam. Drew's involvement with the close-knit village community made it almost impossible that he wouldn't know the four dead men, even in passing.

He knew all of them, of course. Better than Minshull had anticipated.

'I was in the pub with them all on Saturday night,' Ellis said, emotion choking his words. 'They were at another table, but they were part of the banter. I can't believe they won't be there again.'

'Do you have any idea who might wish them harm?' Anderson asked, crouched beside Ellis' desk.

'No. They'd upset people by being cliquey lately, but that was just because people thought they were being idiots. Not a reason for anyone to want them dead.'

'We need to find their next of kin,' Minshull said, flanking the other side of the DC's desk. 'I hate to ask, but can you…?'

'I can, Minsh… *Sarge*,' Ellis corrected himself.

Minshull waved away the slip. 'I can try to reassign this if it's too much?'

Grim determination flashed in the young DC's red-rimmed eyes. 'I want to. I just need to do… *something*.'

'Thanks, mate.'

'Good work, son,' Anderson soothed, rising to his feet. 'Right. Someone needs to visit Councillor Stapleforth.'

'I'll go,' Wheeler offered. 'I spoke to her more than anyone.'

'No,' Minshull replied, the gut-kick of the insistent councillor's identity still stinging. 'It should be me.'

'Don't go alone,' Anderson warned. 'As it's a death notification, you need a seconder. I'll ask Tim Brinton for a PC to attend with you.'

That was something, at least. If he hadn't allowed his annoyance to dismiss the councillor's concerns at the unit, he might have discovered something that could progress the case so much further on than where they were. And while he would never have let her witness the carnage of the crime scene, the cruel fact that her son was likely in the unit while she argued outside it stuck like a knife in his gut.

'Before you do, a quick word?' Anderson was already striding out into the corridor beyond the CID office.

Minshull followed. 'Guv?'

Anderson watched the office door swing shut. 'We need Cora.'

'I know. I just couldn't ask her to go to the scene...'

'Understood. But we need to brief her now. Have her on standby for when the objects and murder weapon are released. Maybe even have her visit the unit when SOCOs are done?'

'I'll call her on my way back.'

'Do that,' Anderson replied. 'Whoever arranged those belongings around the bodies intended them to signify something. And they may have left more attached to them than DNA.'

Anderson's acknowledgement of Dr Cora Lael's ability to hear audible voices from discarded objects – the 'audible fingerprints', as the CID team had learned to refer to them – revealed how far he had come. Time was when the DI had doubted Cora's skills, observing them as a threat to the case rather than an advantage to the investigation.

How times had changed.

Minshull thought of it as he headed down to the uniformed division to meet the PC that Sergeant Tim Brinton was arranging to accompany him. Cora was now a vital part of the team; he'd missed her input in the investigation thus far. It was time to rectify that.

He missed her, full stop.

Their last investigation had revealed cracks in his trust of her ability – a fact he regretted more than he could express. While he was doing his best to repair the damage, the fissure still remained. He should have trusted her completely. Because what she had heard was true.

'Audible fingerprints' was the explanation that made sense to everyone on the team. Physical fingerprints on objects found at a crime scene could hold important clues to the identity of those responsible: in the same way, their thoughts and voices could leave an imprint the moment they touched something. Cora was able to hear these audible traces and had developed her ability to lean into the sounds around the voices, building a three-dimensional soundscape of where the object had been handled and the sounds that had been present a sense of location, even suggesting how much air was around each sound, indicating the height of a room, or the size of a space.

What might she hear from the objects placed so deliberately around the four dead men and the empty space where a fifth body should have been?

Minshull had already decided to visit Cora this afternoon, rather than call. The news demanded a personal delivery, handled as carefully as possible. Cora might have already seen far more than a civilian should in the cases she had assisted South Suffolk CID with, but she needed to be prepared for the horror of this.

But first, he had a personal wrong to put right...

–

Half an hour later, he was on the road to Evernam. Sergeant Lucy Blake sat stoically in the passenger seat as Minshull drove. She'd been at the station for as long as Minshull had been in CID and was already one of South Suffolk Police's most respected officers. Even though the seriousness of the news he carried demanded two officers be present, he was glad not to be doing this alone. At least with Blake with him, he had a hope of the councillor allowing them into her home. Given his attitude to her in the village, he wouldn't blame her for refusing him entry.

They reached the cordon in Evernam and asked after the councillor but were informed by one of the uniformed officers that a concerned friend had persuaded Mrs Stapleforth to go home. Thankfully, the PC had taken a note of her address before the councillor left.

The route to the new address led them about a mile out of Evernam to a large white house set back from the road, accessed via a long, uneven gravel track. By its size and proportions, Minshull guessed it had once been a farmhouse, surrounded by fields now long since portioned off and sold. It was the way of many such farms in the area, property and land becoming far more profitable than crops and livestock.

The ageing pool car creaked and groaned as it bumped along the track, Minshull wrestling it around the largest potholes as best he could. It was a relief to reach the flat circle of gravel in front of the house, although his reason for being there quickly overshadowed all else.

'Ready?' he asked Blake.

'As anyone can be,' she grimaced back.

The frantic barking of several dogs answered Minshull's pressing of the doorbell, followed by scuffles as the animals were herded away from the hall. As their barks faded, the wide oak door opened.

'*You.*' Yvonne Stapleforth's expression grew thunderous the moment she recognised the detective on her doorstep. 'What the hell do you want?'

'Councillor Stapleforth, I'm—'

'I know exactly who you are, DS Minshull. Come to reprimand me in my own home, have you?'

Minshull kept his tone low and respectful, bearing the verbal blows as penance. 'There's been a development in our investigation that I need to make you aware of. This is Sergeant Lucy Blake. May we come in?'

Yvonne Stapleforth eyed Blake and folded her arms. 'No, you may not! Whatever it is, say it here and then get off my property.'

'I really think we should discuss this inside...'

The councillor stood her ground. 'Oh, you do? And I suppose there's a really good reason why you think harassing me on my doorstep and barging into my house is warranted?'

Minshull took a long, steady breath. He didn't want to deliver the news here, but if she gave him no option, he would. Beside him, Blake shifted a little.

'The development concerns you.'

'Me? How?' Her frown deepened. 'If you're here to yell at me for earlier, I'll call my solicitor...'

'It concerns your son.'

The effect was immediate; the fight and fury sucked out of Yvonne Stapleforth. She reached for the door handle to steady herself, an expensive-looking square cut diamond ring catching the light as she did. Fear flooded her eyes as she stared back.

'Michael?'

'No, ma'am. Tim.'

The name knocked the wind from her completely. 'You should come in,' she said, her tone oddly flat after the fight's passing.

Sharing a look with Blake, Minshull followed the councillor inside. Parquet flooring gleamed beneath their feet, reflecting the light of chandeliers hung from high ceilings. Each room was framed by elegantly moulded plaster coving, with decorative ceiling roses. It resembled the kind of country hotels Minshull's mother loved to visit, dragging his architecturally unimpressed father along. Antique furniture edged the sitting room that Councillor Stapleforth led them into, offset by two large pale grey sofas that bookended a richly detailed Persian rug. A marble fireplace between them displayed a lavish arrangement of fresh flowers where the fire would usually be.

It was comfortable, classically elegant – and faceless, Minshull thought. A well-appointed façade, but what might it conceal?

He and Blake sat on one sofa while Yvonne Stapleforth sank onto the other.

'What's happened?' she asked, a fearful shadow of her former formidable self.

'We found several bodies in the empty shop unit on Januarius Street this morning. I am afraid we have reason to believe your son may be one of them.'

She made no reply.

Minshull pressed on. 'We're awaiting the report of our scene-of-crime officers and the duty pathologist currently working at the unit, but some information has come to light that places Tim at the scene.'

'What information? Who said that?'

'He was named by an individual we're currently questioning in relation to the investigation.'

'Who?'

'I'm afraid I can't say at this moment.'

'Then how do you know for sure?'

Minshull hesitated. Without formal identification, they didn't. But it was vital they advise families of the discovery as soon as possible. 'When was the last time you heard from Tim, Mrs Stapleforth?'

'Two days ago. But he can't be in Evernam because he's working away in Manchester all this week. He called me from his hotel.'

'When did he call you?'

'Yesterday afternoon.'

'Are you sure?'

'Of course I'm… He said that's where he was…' Her face crumpled.

'Is there anyone who can come to be with you?' Minshull asked, a lump unexpectedly appearing in his own throat. 'Can I call anyone for you?'

'My husband… He's down at the lodges.'

'The lodges?'

'We have some holiday lodges near Evernam Woods. Alec is getting them ready for our late summer guests.' She picked up her phone from the arm of the sofa, her fingers shaking as she moved them across the screen. 'I'll call him.'

Blake made steady notes while Minshull sat and waited, wishing he was better at delivering news like this. Wheeler could do it with such warmth and compassion; Minshull's words sounded cold and formal by comparison. He didn't mean it to come out like that, it just did.

This time, at least, he could blame exhaustion for his tone, rather than awkwardness. Even if he knew the latter was more in play than the former ever would be.

Why had Yvonne Stapleforth been so insistent earlier that she needed access to the unit? *Frantic*, Wheeler had described it – and Minshull had felt that, too. Had she suspected her son might be inside? And why was her first question regarding her other son, Michael? Minshull gathered these questions in line, waiting for an appropriate time to ask them.

'My husband's on his way.'

'Thank you. We'll stay with you until he arrives.'

The councillor nodded, the fire gone from her.

'Can I ask, why were you in Januarius Street this morning? Why did you want to go into the unit?'

The councillor's gaze drifted to the storm clouds beyond the sitting room's large picture windows. 'It's my local patch. I was concerned.'

'Forgive me, Mrs Stapleforth, you were more than concerned.'

'Yes.' She closed her eyes. 'I heard something terrible had happened in there. I thought... I thought my son was involved.' A sob stole her breath.

'Michael?'

She nodded.

'Can I ask why that was?'

'It was my first thought.' Tears escaped from her perfectly made-up eyes as she shook her head. 'Michael is my eldest. I've feared hearing the worst news for that boy from the day he was born. Dreamed it. Battled the certainty that one day it would happen...'

'And you thought Michael was inside the shop unit?'

'I was terrified it was true. I had to see for myself...'

'I hope you understand why I couldn't let you in there this morning.'

She observed Minshull and Blake over the tissue she pressed to her face. 'I didn't appreciate your manner. But now I know people died there... You have to understand, DS Minshull, as a mother I was blinded by the need to keep my son safe. *Both* my sons,' she added quickly. Why was that?

'I'm sorry I didn't ask why you were there,' Minshull offered. 'We were dealing with the recent discovery, and tensions were high, as I'm sure you'll appreciate.'

She waved it away with her tissue. 'Of course.'

'Councillor Stapleforth – Yvonne – this is likely to be one of the most significant cases South Suffolk CID has handled. You should prepare yourself for that. We're doing everything we can to identify the victims and apprehend the person or persons responsible, but we're dealing with an unprecedented situation. We're going to make mistakes in the course of things – *I'm* going to make mistakes. For that, I apologise.'

'I appreciate your honesty, DS Minshull,' she conceded, her chin lifting in defiance once more. 'But Tim isn't one of the victims in that place. Whoever named him is mistaken.'

There was nothing more Minshull could do until the SOCO team could move the bodies so that formal identifications would be possible. His only hope was that more identifying information might be found on the fourth body. While he understood Yvonne Stapleforth's refusal to believe the fourth man was her son, if Tim Stapleforth was one of the dead men, it was better his mother knew as soon as possible. Minshull couldn't imagine what waiting for news like that must feel like.

With a quiet Sergeant Blake by his side, he waited for Alec Stapleforth's arrival in near silence in the house. When the tall bear of a man finally entered, Minshull shared the same news he'd delivered to Yvonne. Like his wife, Alec had dismissed the notion immediately.

'He's in Manchester. He told us he was.'

'Did he say where he was staying? The name of the hotel, perhaps?'

'He didn't need to. But he said he was there and that's enough for us. It can't be him.'

Along with this denial, Minshull witnessed the same badly concealed relief that Michael Stapleforth hadn't been the reason for a police visit. It was impossible to miss.

'Do you know where Michael is?' he asked, careful to keep his question neutral.

'He's travelling,' Yvonne Stapleforth blurted, but her husband's hand gently resting on her shoulder stilled her words.

'We haven't heard from him for a couple of weeks,' Alec admitted. 'We didn't exactly part on good terms the last time he came home.'

'Oh?'

Alec Stapleforth's expression hardened. Minshull sensed the frustration of many years setting the father's features like stone. 'It was about money. It always is.'

'Alec, please...'

60

'No, Yvonne, it's important here.' He turned back to Minshull. 'I don't know where Michael is, DS Minshull. My best guess is that he's holed up somewhere with those so-called friends of his, drunk or stoned. But he *isn't* in that building. And neither is Tim.'

Something about Alec Stapleforth's assertion itched at Minshull. How could he be so certain that neither of his sons were in the Januarius Street location when it was clear the Stapleforths didn't know exactly where either of their sons were? Minshull made a note to check police records for any mention of Michael Stapleforth. If his parents' obvious fear was anything to go by, plenty could be waiting to be found on file.

Dropping Sergeant Blake back at Police HQ in Ipswich, Minshull reversed his car back out of the car park and headed for the waterfront side of the town, to a huddle of three unremarkable brick buildings on the edge of a trading estate.

Parking as close as he could to the middle building, he killed the engine and made a call.

'This is a surprise, DS Minshull,' Dr Cora Lael's bright greeting was edged with weariness. Minshull empathised with that feeling.

'Can I grab you for a quick chat? I'm in the car park.'

'Oh. We're snowed under here, Rob. I'm working double cases, and I haven't had space to think.'

'Just five minutes? It's about a new investigation.'

There was a pause, Minshull willing her to relent.

'Fine,' she replied at last. 'But you're buying coffee.'

Relief flooded Minshull's aching frame. 'Absolutely.'

TEN

CORA

Rob Minshull ordered coffee from the small mobile catering van by the council offices like he was surrendering his worldly goods to an arresting officer. Cora said nothing as she waited, wondering what lay in store for her in the case Minshull had come to share.

Since officially joining the South Suffolk CID team as a special consultant, Cora was becoming used to the summons from Police HQ in Ipswich. Every new case brought with it an opportunity to further explore her ability, to push the boundaries of the emotional echoes – or audible fingerprints as she'd come to term them – she could sense from objects she was asked to inspect. Even though she was tired already from the relentless workload in her day job as an Educational Psychologist for South Suffolk Education Authority, the prospect of assisting Minshull and the team excited her.

But today the darkness she'd caught in Rob Minshull's tone tempered the thrill. It had been unmistakable when he'd called her from the car park, although she couldn't exactly define it. A warning. An edge. A sense of foreboding.

The granite-grey clouds that remained stubbornly over Ipswich all morning were now painted by rays of bright sunshine, a stark contrast of soothing light and threatening shadow. As Cora and Minshull moved to a bench near raised flowerbeds separating the car park from the approach to the buildings, the split personality of the sky gave a dramatic backdrop.

'I can't stay long,' she said the moment they sat.

'Neither can I.' Minshull risked a smile. 'Sorry to pull you away from work – I wish it was just a social call.' He took a breath, the gravity of what he was about to share heavy in his inhale. 'We have a murder investigation. Multiple bodies, I'm afraid. The crime scene was discovered this morning, in Evernam.'

'Evernam? I thought the most controversial thing that happened in Evernam was the annual livestock fair.' Seeing her smile not mirrored, Cora relented. 'How did they die?'

'Their throats were cut. We found a knife at the scene that we're treating as a suspected murder weapon.'

An involuntary shiver traversed Cora's spine. 'What do you need from me?'

'The victims were found in a bizarre arrangement. Five objects placed at deliberate intervals around each body.'

'Belongings?'

Minshull blew steam from his cup. 'We're assuming so, except there's no obvious link between them. We'll know more when we have ID, but for now, it's a puzzle.'

'And you want me to listen to them.'

Minshull nodded. 'The objects are being taken to Forensics for testing, but I can arrange for you to inspect them once they're cleared.'

'Okay. When is that likely to be?'

'I wish I could tell you. They're being fast-tracked, but you know how resources are.'

'Tell me about it. How's everyone doing – without Les?'

Minshull took a sip of coffee, wincing at the heat. 'We're all trying to stay positive, but the workload is insane. Unless we're granted temp cover for him, I don't know how we'll cope.'

'Have the bodies been identified yet?'

'Unofficially. SOCOs found driving licences for three of the victims, and the fourth was named by a man we arrested at the scene. But until we get formal identifications on the bodies, we can't know for certain.'

'You've arrested someone?'

'At the scene, yes. He was wandering around on the street outside, drenched in blood and very distressed. Insisted it was his fault that the four other men died.'

'Wow.'

Minshull grimaced. 'I know. What's odd is that there was a fifth collection of objects, placed identically to the others, but with a space at their centre where a fifth body might have been.'

Cora observed him carefully. 'Do you think the man you arrested should have been the fifth victim?'

'I don't know. Maybe? If that was the case, why claim the murders were his fault?'

'Could be shock. Or guilt that he survived while the others didn't?'

Minshull considered this. 'Would you be able to tell? From, you know, the audible fingerprints on the knife and the objects around the bodies?'

It was a careful question, a gesture Cora both appreciated and hated in equal measure. With all they had gone through on previous cases – and their personal friendship outside of work – such caution should no longer be necessary. But Minshull's belief in Cora's ability had stumbled during the last investigation, a mistake he was doing his best to make amends for.

'It's possible. It depends whether the perpetrator was wearing gloves or not. But I should be able to sense heightened emotion, anger, fear. Circumstantial, of course, but it could help you and the team piece together what happened.'

'Okay. Thanks.'

Cora watched him cradle his paper coffee cup. 'How bad was it?'

Minshull's body belied the answer before he spoke. It was impossible to miss. She saw it in the tension in his shoulders, and the stoic expression he maintained. Did he realise how much of his body language betrayed his true reaction? Cora suspected not.

'Horrific,' Minshull admitted. 'The worst I've seen. I should warn you, the crime scene photos you'll see in the office will be distressing.'

'I understand.' Cora willed conviction into her reply, but in truth, her nerves had been building since Minshull had mentioned the multiple murders – and the presence of a knife and blood. Four dead men, all presumably killed with stab or slash wounds: it was a prospect that scared her. She'd witnessed many horrors since her first case with the police. Was she ready to face this?

'Are you sure? Because this won't be like anything we've asked you to work on before.'

'I am,' Cora replied, her intention set. 'I'm part of the team, right?'

'Right.'

They shared weary smiles.

'I'll call you as soon as we're ready,' Minshull said, making to stand. 'I have to get back, but thanks.'

'You're welcome.' Cora stood, too. 'Keep me updated?'

'Sure.' He was already backing away, the call of the myriad of concerns summoning him from this place. 'We'll speak soon.'

Cora watched Minshull's car pull out of view, then turned and walked slowly back inside.

Dr Tris Noakes looked up from the stack of papers covering his desk when Cora knocked on the door of his office. 'How was the good detective?'

'Not so good.' Cora sat on the chair opposite his. 'There's a new case they're bringing me into.'

'Do you need to go? I can have a look at shifting some work around here if you do.'

'Not yet. Forensics need to release the objects first. Might be a couple of days.'

Tris put down his pen. 'You're nervous about this one.'

Was it that obvious? Cora loved many things about her boss, not least that he was a self-confessed fan of her ability and a fervent cheerleader for her own efforts to explore it further. But the way Tris could read her was unnervingly accurate. She shifted a little in the chair.

'I'm still getting my head around it.'

'It's a bad one?'

'Sounds like it could be. Strange, too.'

'Define strange.'

Cora laughed despite herself. 'The objects they want me to assess were placed around four bodies. Rob thinks they might be specific belongings for each of the deceased, but until the police have formal IDs, he can't be certain. What's odd is that they were arranged in very deliberate patterns. Identical spacing, identical number...'

'A code?'

Cora considered this. 'Possibly. I won't know until I can inspect them.'

'So, why are you nervous?'

Circumspection was of little use where Tris Noakes was concerned. 'Because there are multiple deaths involved. Because it suggests a level of premeditation I haven't encountered before.' She took a breath; the ache of her bones suddenly pronounced. 'And because the items found at the scene include a knife.'

'Ah.'

'I haven't encountered a suspected murder weapon before. And the fact it was used as recently as this morning...' She shivered again. 'What if I hear more than the person using it? In the periphery sounds?'

'Do you think you might?'

'I don't know. It's possible. Rob was shaken by what he'd seen at the crime scene – really unnerved by it. I haven't seen him respond like that before. I might *hear* the act that he saw the aftermath of. And I don't know if I'm ready.'

'I don't know that anyone would be ready for that.' Tris offered a sympathetic smile. 'The only thing you can do is try not to build preconceptions beforehand. See it as objectively as you can: as a new area your ability can shed light on.'

He was right, of course. Cora could and would approach it as she had every other task assigned to her by South Suffolk Police. She just hoped her nerves wouldn't hinder her.

Now all she could do was wait.

ELEVEN

WHEELER

It had been a hell of a day already, with no sign of the building catalogue of horrors abating any time soon. DC Dave Wheeler was glad to be back at his desk, his much-maligned Norwich City mug of coffee beside him and the familiar hum of the CID office soothing his ears. Even if today it was muted, it was home. He'd weathered countless storms from his desk in this office: this one might be longer and heavier, but it too would pass.

Right now, this was the only certainty keeping him going.

He glanced at the half-open door to DI Joel Anderson's office. His superior and close friend was bearing the brunt of everything as usual. No change there, except Wheeler worried for him. Every kick and knock in recent years had hit a little deeper with Joel, and now, with a detective down in his team and the caseload mountainous, the damage was starting to show.

He listened for any sounds of Anderson on the phone, but all was quiet save for the distant thrumming of angry fingers on a keyboard that probably needed counselling, given the amount of fury it faced daily from the detective inspector.

Slipping away from his desk, Wheeler headed over and gave the door a gentle knock.

'Yes?' Anderson's frown softened the moment he looked up. 'Ah, Dave, it's you.'

'Fancy another coffee?' Wheeler asked.

Anderson held up a mug. 'Still got one, thanks. Come in, eh?'

Closing the door behind him, Wheeler entered the office and took a seat at Anderson's desk. 'How goes it?'

'Shitshow, as ever.' Anderson's wry smile was a balm to his words. 'How are you holding up?'

'Oh, you know.' Wheeler hoped his shrug was a sufficient reply.

It wasn't, of course. 'Listen, if you need a break…'

'I'm good.'

'But that crime scene was a bastard, right?'

Wheeler deflated a little. 'Worst I've seen for years.'

'I'd say it gets easier, but we both know that's bollocks. Anything more from the SOCOs yet?'

'Still waiting. Should get an update soon.'

Anderson nodded. 'I know they'll be doing all they can. Bet it's the worst Brian's seen for a while.'

'Worst of his career, he reckons.' Wheeler took the opportunity of being away from his colleagues to press his friend. 'So what did Sue Taylor say?'

The instant grimace on Anderson's face bore testament to many years of fruitless battling with their superior. 'Wouldn't budge on a temp DC. I half-wondered whether to get Steph Lanehan seconded to us seeing as we had her before with the Hannah Perry case. I was hoping precedence would be in our favour. But by the sounds of it, Steph has enough to deal with.'

'Tim Brinton can't spare her?'

Anderson shook his head. 'She apprehended Lingham, along with Rilla Davis, so she's too important to the ground operation. Brinton wants to keep her there for the foreseeable. Which I understand, but it doesn't help our staffing issue.'

'Probably for the best, Guv, given what Steph's had to deal with this morning.' Wheeler remembered the state of his colleague when he'd arrived on the scene and shuddered. 'Proper shaken, she was. Steph's seen most things, but that bloke was something else.'

'She'll deal with it, I'm sure.'

'Oh, she will. But still, I worry for her sometimes.'

Anderson acknowledged this. Wheeler knew he understood. You looked out for your colleagues, no matter what. Despite the jokes and supposed rivalries across the divisions, when it came down to it, you were one family. That was how it always had been – and how it should remain.

'How was Lingham when you interviewed him?' Wheeler asked, secretly glad that he hadn't had to be part of the suspect's interrogation.

'Changeable.'

'Lying?'

'Who knows? His solicitor's one of the keen ones. I reckon he'll have him *no comment*-ing in the next round.'

'Do you think he did it?'

'According to Minsh, he was the only one who could have done it. Door to the back of the unit locked with no key, only one entrance onto the street that was busy with Monday morning shoppers. It's unlikely that anybody could have dashed out before Lingham emerged and not have been seen.'

'But not impossible?'

Anderson chuckled. 'Nothing ever is, is it? Lingham's van was parked at the back of the unit, but he insists it's a local parking spot. There are other vehicles there, which backs him up.'

'Are we taking the van in?'

'Aye.' Anderson rubbed his temples. 'Whenever that's likely to happen. Our forensics bods are busy assisting with a bad house fire over the border in Norwich, apparently. Whole family died.'

Wheeler winced. 'Norfolk's resources low again, then?'

'As ever. It's only a matter of time before they merge the services, and then we'll be in for endless fun.' Anderson glanced at a list on the notepad beside his poor, beleaguered keyboard, his shoulders stiffening. Wheeler knew what was coming. He'd long learned the signs with his friend. 'I had word from Control that they'd received a call from relatives of Otto Wragg…'

70

Of course. Everyone else would have calls like these today; Wheeler wouldn't be an exception.

'I can't do it alone, Guv. Not if it's a death notice.'

'I know. I've asked Tim Brinton to release someone from uniform to accompany you. They're on their way up now.' Apology folded into the creases on his brow. 'Sorry, mate.'

'No worries,' Wheeler replied brightly, though his tone fooled nobody in Anderson's office. 'Just grab a load of those *maritozzi* buns if you're going to Tutti's, yeah? I could use something to look forward to.'

Twenty minutes later, Wheeler was driving a pool car towards the village he'd been only too happy to leave earlier, the comforting presence of PC Margi Hickman in the passenger seat.

'Fancy a mint, Dave?' Margi asked, producing a packet of extra strong mints from her pocket.

'Don't mind if I do, Marg,' Wheeler accepted, the ordinariness of the exchange soothing. Hickman had been at the station forever, and nobody was quite sure how close retirement might be for her. But it was good to be with someone who knew the job inside out. Especially for this one. 'Thanks for coming on this shout.'

'Uniform to the rescue of you soft CID-ers, eh?' the PC laughed, her gentle jibe no more than a good-hearted nudge. 'Happy to help, DC Wheeler. Now if you need me to butt in at any point, just give me the nod. Otherwise, I'll stay the strong, silent type.'

'Type I like best,' Wheeler grinned, his smile feeling alien. 'We'll play it by ear, okay?'

-

The Wragg family occupied a large farm about half a mile outside Evernam. According to Control, it had been Otto's mother-in-law who had placed the call, as her daughter had become concerned when her husband failed to arrive to collect his children. The couple were estranged, although some contact remained. They currently shared the school run and other parental duties, their three young children staying alternate weekends with their father in a cottage on the edge of the family land.

Otto Wragg's wife and her mother were waiting in the open doorway of the farmhouse when Wheeler arrived, the older woman's expression grave beside her daughter's tear-stained concern. A tall man stood between them, his eyes trained on the CID car as Wheeler parked. Wheeler's heart sank when Otto Wragg's wife stepped forward, revealing the unmistakable bump of an advanced pregnancy.

He remembered watching his own wife, Sana, like a hawk during her two pregnancies. She'd brushed off his concern, as she always did, but Wheeler had patrolled their home for danger like a prowling cat. He'd been determined to protect Sana from any adverse news. How would Otto Wragg's clearly distraught wife take the news he was bringing? Who would protect her as he'd vowed to protect Sana?

'Is there news?' the older woman demanded the moment Wheeler and Hickman left the car.

Wheeler walked over as quickly as he could, not wanting to shout his reply across the wide paved driveway. 'Good afternoon. I'm Detective Constable Dave Wheeler from South Suffolk CID, and this is my colleague, PC Margi Hickman. Can we—?'

'It's bad,' Wragg's wife wailed, clamping a hand to her mouth too late to catch her words. 'Two coppers always means bad news.'

'Shh, now,' her mother snapped, turning back to the officers. 'I'm Sheila Kersey. This is my daughter, Susannah, and Otto's brother, Aldo. Please come in.'

Wheeler and Hickman followed the family into the farmhouse, its low beamed ceilings clearly a challenge for Otto Wragg's brother. He hid his frustration badly, the smile he wore tightening with each wooden beam and low doorway navigated. Wheeler wondered if Aldo Wragg lived here: he couldn't imagine the constant irritation avoiding concussion around the house would bring.

They entered an open-plan kitchen and living area that traversed the back of the house. Aldo leaned against the kitchen island with visible relief, while Sheila and Susannah shared a sofa near the large bifold garden doors. Evidence of a young family littered the room – a scattering of crayons on a stack of paper across the coffee table, floppy cuddly toys strewn over the floor and across the back of the sofa, and a sole striped sock dangling listlessly over the arm of the chair in which Wheeler sat. It warmed his heart and chilled him at once. Familiarity in the face of oncoming pain.

Hickman settled on the chair next to Wheeler, her brief smile in his direction a signal of her readiness to support him. He gave a slight nod and turned to face the family.

'Thank you for seeing us. I'm afraid I have some news that will be difficult to hear.'

Wragg's wife crumpled into her mother, who faced Wheeler like flint.

'This morning, a discovery was made in an empty shop unit on Januarius Street in Evernam. There are four bodies. We have reason to believe that Otto might be one of them.'

The news punched the air from the room, Susannah Wragg's wail filling the space as her mother and brother-in-law stared numbly back.

'How do you... What makes you think Otto is there?' Sheila managed, a tremor in her question at odds with her highly controlled demeanour.

'His driving licence was found at the scene. My colleagues are still investigating, so we'll know more when we can move the deceased. But it's important that you know it's a possibility.'

'When will we be able to see him?' Aldo asked.

'Not for a while yet, sir. The scene has been secured, and our duty pathologist is present, but there's much to do while everything remains in situ.'

Wheeler opened his notebook slowly, careful not to let his hands betray any of the stress he felt. At times like these the needs of loved ones of the deceased were paramount: nobody wanted to see a police officer struggling to deal with their emotions. It was part of the job: professional coolness in the face of unimaginable horror. That didn't make the masking of your own feelings any easier to accomplish, mind, but you did it because the families deserved respect.

'Can you tell me how Otto has been lately? Has he mentioned any problems, any issues that might have been causing him concern?'

'Nothing,' Sheila rushed. Wheeler caught the flash of a stare she sent across the room towards Aldo and the rush of air from the tall man in response.

'Anyone he'd had problems with? Disagreements?'

'Otto gets on with everyone,' Sheila returned – quick, again, Wheeler noted. 'That's part of the problem.'

'*Mum…*' Susannah Wragg's sudden interruption appeared to take her mother by surprise.

'What? It's not a secret.'

'It's private…'

'Anything you can tell us will be in complete confidence, Mrs Wragg,' Hickman soothed. 'It helps us build a picture…'

'He's estranged from my daughter because he was spending far too much time *getting on* with a young woman in the village,' Sheila declared, ignoring the protests that immediately followed from Susannah and Aldo. 'It's important they know.'

'It isn't why he didn't show up to get the kids,' Susannah bit back, her anger tripping over her sobs. 'That woman means nothing to my family!'

'That woman is the reason my grandchildren have a part-time father!'

74

'Okay, if we can all take a moment?' Wheeler interjected. A full-on brawl wouldn't bring him any closer to establishing the circumstances surrounding Otto Wragg's disappearance. The calmness of his tone stole the thunder from the room, Susannah and Aldo retreating to stung silence while Sheila glowered back. 'It's important we get as much information as possible to help us work out what may or may not have happened. I sincerely wish I didn't have to bring this to your door, but it's vital we gather as much information as we can, as soon as possible. We're treating the deaths as suspicious, which means there's a person or persons at large who should be brought to justice. The sooner we can do that, the sooner you can start to deal with this horrible situation.'

'How about I make everyone a cup of tea?' Hickman suggested. It was met by muted ascent, enough to diffuse the tension. As the PC made her way to the kettle, Wheeler moved to less divisive ground.

'What does Otto do for work?' he asked.

'He's a developer,' Aldo replied. 'Before that, he owned a building company.'

'What kind of development?'

'Apartments, flats mainly. In here and in Spain.'

'And how long has he been doing that?'

'About eighteen months. He started with the outbuildings on a friend's farm, turning them into holiday lets. Then he won the contract to develop a warehouse on the outskirts of Ipswich into an apartment complex. The work came in from there.'

'Does he work alone?'

Aldo shook his head. 'He has a small team. And a silent partner who helps with investment. Then he lets out the properties with a lettings agency his friend owns.'

Wheeler made notes. 'Do you know the names of the partner and the friend?'

'Tim Stapleforth is the investor. And Mark Lingham is the friend. Of Lingham-Quartermain? You'll see their boards up all over this area.'

Stapleforth. The frantic councillor's name. And Lingham, the suspect currently in custody. So they were connected. Wheeler pushed the elation at discovering a link far down within him. But as this could be a major step forward, and with everything at stake and his colleagues under intense pressure, he allowed himself a small swell of pride that he now carried information that could prove vital to the investigation.

Keeping his voice steady, Wheeler pressed on. 'How's Otto's business been lately?'

'Good.'

'He hasn't mentioned any problems with his team? Or Mr Stapleforth? Or the lettings people?'

'No.' Aldo let out a sigh. 'But there were the threats...'

'They don't need to know that,' Sheila Kersey snapped, causing Wheeler to look up from his notes.

'They already know,' Aldo fired back.

'Know what, sir?'

'Otto mentioned some threats he'd received at his office. Hand-delivered, typed, no indication of who'd sent them. I told him to report them to you guys, and he did.'

Wheeler frowned. 'When was this?'

Hickman slipped between them, delivering tea. Wheeler knew she was listening: the smallest glance as she handed him a mug confirmation that she was ready to act if he needed her.

'A few weeks ago.'

'And Otto reported these threats to us?'

'Yes.'

'Okay.' Wheeler nodded at Hickman, who made her way out of the room. 'Did he have any idea who might have sent them?'

'It could have been anyone.' Wragg's brother glared into his tea. 'People round here hate developers, despite being only too happy to palm off their land to the highest bidder when it suits them.'

'So, it could have been someone objecting to a recent development?'

'Who knows? There are enough nutters in the area who are desperate to make a point.'

'Campaigners?'

'*Idiots*. People with nothing better to do.'

Wheeler made a note, playing for time. Out in the hall of the farmhouse, Hickman would be checking with Control for Otto Wragg's report of the threatening letters. He wanted to give her sufficient time. 'Mrs Wragg, how did Otto seem to you in recent days?'

Susannah stared back. 'Difficult.'

'More than usual?' It was a risk, but Wheeler saw the flicker of recognition in the young woman's expression.

'No,' she replied, a sad smile briefly brushing her lips. 'As bloody-minded as usual. Still insisting he'd done nothing wrong.'

'And with your kids?'

'His usual self. They love him, and he dotes on them. He's a good dad.' Her hand grazed her belly as she said this, quickly returning to her side.

'Is that why you contacted us today?'

Her gaze dropped immediately to the tissue in her hands. 'He may be a lying git to me, but he's always there for the kids. Never misses a day when he's having them. He's spent ages getting the cottage ready for them to stay. He was excited about picking them up.'

'How old are your children?'

'Four, two and eleven months.' Susannah Wragg took a deep, shaky breath.

'Where are they now?'

'My husband's taken them out,' Sheila said. 'We didn't want them here when you visited. They've seen enough...'

'Good idea.' Wheeler looked up as Hickman returned, a single shake of her head, the signal he was waiting for. He turned to Aldo Wragg, who was now seated on a stool at the end of the kitchen island. 'Mr Wragg, how certain are you that Otto reported the threats to us?'

'He said he did.'

'And you believed him?'

'Of course.'

Wheeler nodded. 'My colleague has just checked with the station. No such report was made.'

'What? But he said...'

'He *says* a lot of things.'

'Not helpful, Sheila.'

'Do you know why he would say he'd contacted us when he didn't?'

Aldo stood, narrowly missing a beam. 'That makes no sense. He assured me he'd sorted it.'

'And by *sorted it*, did you take that to mean he'd reported the messages to the police?'

'He said he did.' He glared at the kitchen worktop. 'I don't know why he'd lie.'

'Because it suited him.'

'Sheila, please...'

'No, Aldo, it needs to be said. All of this started when *that woman* got involved.' Sheila glared back. 'You want a name, officer? *Mattie Kemp.*'

'Mum!'

'Mattie Kemp got her claws into Otto, and all hell broke loose. Ten months ago. Plenty of time for him to make...'

'Sheila, enough!' Aldo glared at Sheila, the tension crackling between them.

'We'll take it into account,' Wheeler interjected, the tension around him becoming worrying. The last thing anyone needed was an all-out war. 'Do you think Ms Kemp could be responsible for the threatening letters?'

'I wouldn't be surprised...'

'Mum, *shut up!*'

Everyone turned to look at Susannah Wragg.

Tear-stained and red-faced, she kept one hand on her belly as she faced the warring factions of her family. 'I don't think Mattie would have threatened him. She had him already.' Pain was etched into her words as she spoke. Wheeler felt for her. 'He said there was a deal he'd been banking on that had turned sour. He wouldn't go into details, but it was causing him concern.'

'When did he mention this, Mrs Wragg?'

'Last week. He said he hadn't slept trying to work it out.'

Wheeler made a note, keen to wrap things up before the battle recommenced. 'Do you have access to any of Otto's business things?'

Susannah Wragg shook her head. 'But I can give you the number of his assistant, Hugo. He should be able to help.'

–

'Bloody Nora, that was intense,' Hickman breathed when they were back in the safety of the pool car, driving away. 'I wouldn't like to be in that house any longer than I had to be.'

'Me neither.' In the rear-view mirror, Wheeler caught a glimpse of a stony-faced Sheila Kersey staring after them from the doorstep of the farmhouse before the bend in the track hid her from view. 'Odd about the threats. Why say he'd reported them if he hadn't?'

'With that lot?' Margi chuckled in the passenger seat. 'Easier to get them off your back than tell the truth. I don't imagine it's a bundle of fun having that mother-in-law on your case.'

Wheeler was inclined to agree. 'So, we need to talk to Otto's assistant regarding the threats. If he kept any of the letters, that would be great.'

'And the link with Lingham and Stapleforth was interesting. Might they have been threatened, too?'

'Who knows, Marg? It's a link, though. That's something.'

'What about this Mattie Kemp? Did Otto leave Susannah for her? Or did she threaten him to keep him from going back to his wife?'

'Both decent possibilities. Call it in, would you? The link with Lingham and Stapleforth, too. See if we can find an address for Ms Kemp. Makes sense to try and catch her while we're on the road.'

As Hickman placed the call, Wheeler stared at the road ahead. Why had Otto Wragg lied about reporting the threats? And had that decision cost him his life?

TWELVE

MINSHULL

The scent of fresh coffee welcomed Minshull back into the CID office, the weary smiles of Ellis, Anderson and Bennett making sense the moment he spotted the Tutti's branded bags and coffee cups on Bennett's desk.

'That bad a day, is it, Guv?' he grinned, dropping his jacket to the floor when Anderson held out a coffee cup for him.

'I prefer to think of it as a perfect day for a treat,' Anderson grinned. 'I take it you don't object to cream, sugar and calories with your coffee?'

'Wouldn't dream of saying no.' The paper bag Ellis passed him revealed a large, cream-filled *maritozzo* bun. If it was possible to catch a piece of heaven in a grease-spotted paper bag, Minshull was pretty sure it would look like this.

His colleagues returned to their own pieces of heaven as a satisfied silence settled over them all. It was a tiny, bright moment in a day fraught with horror and confusion, but every detective savoured it. That's how you got through each shift in this job: lurching from one glimpse of light to the next.

The coffee and bun wouldn't solve anything, but it gave Minshull a moment to regroup.

'Dave out?' he asked between delicious bites.

'Visiting Otto Wragg's family,' Anderson replied, screwing up the empty deli bag and aiming it at a wastepaper basket by Wheeler's desk. When it caught the edge of the bin and rolled in, Anderson lifted both arms in celebration.

Bennett and Ellis hid their smiles.

'Have we heard back yet?'

'Waiting for it. We're also waiting for Lingham's solicitor to stop yakking with him so we can continue.' It was clear from his grim expression what Anderson thought of both Lingham's legal representative and the unnecessary delay.

'Perhaps Mr Carmichael can persuade Lingham to co-operate,' Minshull countered.

Anderson huffed. 'If he does, I'll buy him his own bun.'

'Now that would be a treat, Guv,' Ellis said, a much-missed twinkle in his eyes.

'Carmichael getting free food?'

'No, Guv, us getting to see a Scot spend money.'

Ellis ducked just in time to avoid the empty takeaway coffee cup Anderson threw at him.

Minshull smiled and returned to his desk, picking up his notebook and flicking to the list he'd been steadily compiling since the investigation had begun. It appeared to be growing of its own accord, more names materialising on the page with each new piece of information they gathered.

He ran his finger down the regimented line of boxes he'd drawn next to each name, a daft habit he'd acquired at school and never quite lost the thrill of. A simple tick for each task complete was the best reward. In its small way it settled his mind, providing him with a way forward.

Right now, forward motion in the investigation was even more desirable to Minshull than the admittedly delicious Roman buns Anderson so loved.

They just needed one thing to join up, to start a chain they could follow.

As he was consulting the list, his phone rang.

'Sarge, we've just visited Otto Wragg's family, and some interesting stuff came up.'

'Go on, Dave.'

'Turns out Otto's a property developer. Small but growing operation. But get this: he had a silent partner investing in the business. Tim Stapleforth.'

Minshull raised his hand, catching Anderson's attention. 'You're sure about this?'

'Absolutely. His brother confirmed it. And there's more: the properties he's developed have subsequently been let out by Lingham-Quartermain lettings.'

'Mark Lingham's company.'

The bun lowered from Ellis' lips as he stared across the office at Minshull.

'The very same. So we can prove that three of our four suspected murder victims not only knew each other but were benefitting financially from doing business together.'

'That's a heck of a link. Excellent work, Dave – Margi, too. You on your way back?'

'Not yet, Sarge. Wragg's family also mentioned a young woman in the village – Mattie Kemp? Looks like she's Otto's new flame – or at least that's what his former mother-in-law believes. I've asked Control to check for last known addresses for her, but the family are certain Ms Kemp still lives in Evernam.'

'Mattie Kemp.' Minshull added the young woman's name to his list, tapping the page with his pen as he processed the new information. 'Okay. Talk to her today if you can, and let me know when you're returning.'

'Will do, Sarge. Oh, one more thing: Otto's brother and estranged wife reckon he'd had some trouble lately. Threats, delivered in letters. He told his brother he'd reported the threats to us, but there's no record of it.'

'Strange. Okay, thanks, Dave. Carry on and keep me updated.'

Ending the call, Minshull's eye was drawn to the last-but-one name on the list, recently mentioned by Lingham and now Wheeler. He looked at his team.

'Okay, everyone, here's the latest. We now have a definite link between Otto Wragg, Tim Stapleforth and Mark Lingham.

Otto's property development business was being invested in by Stapleforth, then the properties were let by the agency Mark Lingham co-owns. Someone needs to get in touch with Lingham's business partner, Gavin Quartermain. He might know more about the whole arrangement.'

'I could call him,' Ellis offered. When Minshull hesitated, he added, 'I don't know him, Sarge. He's been mates with Mark for years but he's not one of our lot. Doesn't play cricket, isn't interested in rugby or even drinking in the pub. Workaholic, I reckon.'

Minshull felt for the DC, who was likely to be prevented from so much of the groundwork for this investigation purely by dint of potentially knowing the men who'd died. It was a shame: his observational skills, better than anyone in CID, frequently picked up details the other detectives missed.

'You can call to make an appointment. But Dave will visit tomorrow morning, first thing.'

'Understood, Sarge. Thanks.' Ellis made for his desk, until Anderson blocked his path.

'Eat your bun first, for heaven's sake. I know you want to get involved, but allow yourself a bit of joy.'

With a rueful grin, Ellis returned to his treat.

–

An hour later, Minshull's desk phone rang, shaking him from his post-cream-bun afternoon slump.

'Custody suite here, Sarge. Mr Lingham's solicitor is requesting another interview. Apparently, his client's remembered something.'

'Great, thanks. We'll be down in ten.'

Anderson appeared to be in the same post-bun haze as Minshull had been, head half-bowed over his desk. Minshull's rap on his office door roused the DI from his almost-slumber with an ungraceful snort.

'Yes, Rob?'

Minshull suppressed a grin. 'Jasper Carmichael's requested an audience with us. Lingham's memory is returning.'

'Right.' Anderson scrambled to his feet, unhooking his jacket from the back of his chair and grabbing his notes as he followed Minshull out into the main office.

'We're going to interview Lingham again,' Minshull addressed Bennett and Ellis. 'Carry on with next of kin checks, Kate. And Drew, find out anything you can about previous owners of 62 Januarius Street. We need the fullest picture possible.'

'Sarge.'

'If Dave gets back before we do, ask him to do some background checks on Lingham, please.'

'No problem, Sarge.'

'Cheers.' He turned to his superior, who was waiting by the door to the corridor. 'Ready, Guv?'

'Oh, I'm ready,' Anderson growled, heading out.

THIRTEEN

ANDERSON

Mark Lingham sat passively beside his solicitor as Minshull started the recording.

Jasper Carmichael was grim-faced, pointedly avoiding eye contact with his client. It reminded Minshull of the expressions of mothers brought into Police HQ to collect troublesome teens – the firm square of the shoulders, the clench of the jaw, the sense of suppressed fury barely held at bay...

'You asked to talk to us again, Mark. Can you tell me why?'

'My memory is coming back,' Lingham said, his eyes fixed at a distance just beyond Minshull and Anderson's chairs. 'Some of it. I was confused before.'

'What have you remembered?'

'My errand in Evernam... It wasn't an errand. It was a meeting.'

'Who with?'

'A prospective client.'

'At the retail unit?'

'Yes. No – *near* the unit.'

Minshull caught the slip, storing it for later. 'A potential property client?'

Lingham nodded. 'A local landlord was interested in my company letting flats above a couple of the shops he owns in Januarius Street.'

Minshull made a show of noting this down. 'And his name?'

'It's not important. He didn't show.'

'All the same, it would be good to check.'

'He's out of the country.'

Convenient, Anderson thought. He said nothing, observing the exchange.

'But you'd agreed to meet him?'

'I did, but... I got my dates mixed up, so he wasn't there. And when I called his office, they told me he was in Spain.'

'O-kay...' Another pause while Minshull made a note. The words were immaterial, the time it took to write them merely a tool to keep Lingham on his toes. 'So, what time had you assumed you were meant to meet him?'

'Nine a.m.'

'And how long did you wait before you called his office?'

'I don't know, twenty minutes?'

'Didn't you try his mobile phone first?'

'No, just his office.'

'So, at approximately 9.20 a.m., you ascertained that the landlord was out of the country, and you'd made a mistake regarding the date of your meeting. What happened next?'

'I...' Lingham made to reply, his voice scratchy. 'Can I have some water, please?'

Minshull picked up a water bottle from beside the recording machine and filled Lingham's dented cup. In his first interview, Lingham had played the drink card several times to halt proceedings; this time Minshull was wise to his trick.

'So what happened next?'

'I walked down the street and noticed the door to the unit was open. There were builders in there last week, and they had the back door open then, so I thought I might be able to nip through to the parking area at the back to save time.'

'To your blue Transit van that was parked behind the row of shops?' Minshull asked, checking his earlier notes.

'Yes.'

'You thought you could go through a private building that you don't own instead of walking a little further down the street to the side alley that would take you directly there?'

Lingham blinked. Carmichael made irritated notes.

'It was pension day, I think. The post office is next door, and there was a queue of old people blocking the street. I was... anxious to get home. Feeling stupid after my mistake. Mixing up the meeting dates, I mean. I knew Isabel would be annoyed. It was my turn to take the kids this morning, but she had to do it because of my meeting. But if she found out I could've done the school run after all... well, you know how it is with women when they think they've been duped.'

'No.' Minshull's reply was flat and fast. Anderson folded his arms.

Lingham stared back, his mouth open.

Minshull held his stare for just a moment too long before returning his attention to his notes. It was an effective ploy: as Minshull took his time writing, Anderson could see Lingham's shoulders tensed against the enforced silence.

'Is that why you were anxious to get back? To avoid a confrontation with your wife?'

'Yes. I just told you.'

'I would have thought your wife would have been far more concerned with the suicide note you left for her.' Minshull looked up slowly.

The horror on Lingham's face was his reward.

'I...'

'You intended her to find it, no?'

'I didn't... I wasn't thinking clearly...'

'You left a suicide note for your wife to find when she returned from taking your kids to school,' Minshull stated. 'But you'd arranged to meet a prospective client in Evernam that morning. Which you went to do, but discovered you'd made a mistake. So then you were keen to get home... Do you see how confusing this is, Mark? Had you planned to take your life after you'd signed a new client? Or were you just trying to scare your wife?'

'I hadn't planned... We hadn't...'

'We?'

'I–I mean *me*. Obviously.' Lingham rubbed his hand over his forehead, his fingers coming away damp from sweat lining his brow. He grasped his plastic cup and drank more water, a dribble sloshing out of one corner of his mouth and running freely down his chin, seemingly unnoticed by him.

Minshull and Anderson waited, their breathing steady.

For once, the solicitor didn't seem to know what to do, bright eyes beneath lowered brows darting between his client and his notes.

'Why did you meet the others in that building?' Minshull asked. None of what Lingham had said had yet explained the presence of the other four men, and it was time he accounted for them. 'Tim Stapleforth, Otto Wragg, Krish Bhattachama and Jack Markham, known as Denzil?'

Lingham winced with each name given.

'I didn't know they would all be there...'

'How did you get access to the unit? We already know the rear door was bolted and the street side was locked.'

'I said it was open, but maybe...' Lingham was rocking a little now, his seat squeaking in time. 'Someone must have had a key.'

'Who? One of your friends? You?'

'No, not me, I... Krish, probably. He always knows someone.'

'He knows the owner of the property?'

'Maybe. I couldn't say.'

'Did the client you were supposed to meet send Krish instead?'

'What? No, no, I didn't say that...' Lingham's eyes were wild now, flitting between Minshull, Anderson and the recording machine.

'Let's go back a little. You're saying that one of you, possibly Krish Bhattachama, had a key for 62 Januarius Street, and they let you and the others in.'

'I – I guess.'

'So you didn't arrange to meet a potential client after all? You arranged to meet Krish Bhattachama, Otto Wragg, Jack Markham and Tim Stapleforth in the empty unit?'

Lingham's head bowed. 'Yes.'

Now Anderson was alert, the sudden shift in the interview's dynamics startling.

'Why?'

'We needed somewhere to talk.'

'About what?'

Lingham shrugged like a surly teen.

'You couldn't have talked in the pub, in one of your homes, out in the countryside?'

'No. It wasn't possible.'

'Why not?'

'We didn't want anyone to overhear us.'

'With respect, Mr Lingham, you haven't answered the question.' Anderson could hold his peace no longer. 'Why choose an empty unit none of you had any access to? Unless…'

'Krish had a key,' Lingham blurted, glaring at Anderson. 'His father-in-law owns the unit.'

Finally, they were getting somewhere. Anderson's shoulders protested as he kept his spine straight in his chair. His whole body ached from too much work and too little sleep. He knew Minshull was as shattered as he was, but both stared down Mark Lingham now, determined to kick his lies out of the way to get to the truth.

'Krish had a key.'

'Yes.'

'And you weren't meeting his father-in-law as a prospective client. You were meeting your friends.'

'Yes – I told you.'

'At Krish's invitation?'

Lingham hefted a sigh. 'I guess. Yes.'

Were they any closer to the truth? It felt like a break-through, but could they trust it? Pulse pounding behind his stony exterior, Anderson waited for Minshull to note this, then leaned a little towards Lingham and his solicitor.

'Why did the five of you agree to meet there?'

'It was part of the plan.'

'What plan?'

Lingham glanced at his solicitor, who waved him on with his pen. 'We were supposed to be getting out of the village, starting again.'

'Starting where?'

'Abroad. Far away from the village.' Lingham seemed to shrink in his chair as he rubbed his eyes. 'Otto had a devel-opment in Gran Canaria we were all going to run. We were meant to be leaving today.'

Anderson caught Minshull's look and nodded for him to step in. He needed the break to get his head around this sudden curveball in Lingham's story.

'Did you all leave suicide notes?' Minshull asked, incredulity only just hidden in his question.

'We were meant to.' Lingham failed to make eye contact. Was this yet another lie?

'But they didn't?'

'I'm guessing not.'

'Why the decision to leave? What were you running away from?'

'Families. Businesses. We got talking at the cricket club months ago and decided to get out of the country.'

'Why? Is your business in trouble, Mark?'

'No. Gavin practically runs the business anyway. He'll be better off without me. Issy and the kids, too. I don't add anything to anyone's lives, I'm bored and useless, and I can't do another forty years of this shit. I've just reached the age where if I don't make a break, I never will.'

Anderson watched Lingham as his head bowed lower with each new admission. Was it really a case of a mid-life crisis? Anderson had laughed off the possibility earlier, but had Minshull been onto something?

'Okay, why did you meet in the unit?'

'So we wouldn't be seen.'

'And you planned to go from there? To the airport?'

Lingham nodded into the collar of his sweatshirt, his chin dipping beneath the fabric. 'I had my bag packed, and the others had theirs in Krish's car parked out on the street. It felt dangerous, you know? Fun. We had a few hours before we needed to be at the airport, so we had a drink to celebrate...'

'A drink?' Anderson asked.

'Someone brought a bottle of champagne and we...'

'Who brought the champagne?'

Lingham's gaze clouded. 'One of us – I don't remember. I poured it out for everyone...'

'At just after nine a.m.? Bit early to be drinking, wasn't it?'

'We were celebrating.' Lingham stopped, his eyes growing wide. 'We had a drink...'

'So you said.'

'No... you don't understand... We had a *drink*...'

His arms folded across his body, the rocking recommencing as he hugged himself. Tears filled his eyes, his face contorted in sheer horror. Carmichael put a hand on Lingham's arm, but his client appeared not to notice, a long, low wail emitting from his mouth.

The change from lucid conversation to the babbling, incoherent mess Lingham had been in the beginning set Anderson's nerves on high alert. 'Mr Lingham? Mark?'

'It was in the drink,' Lingham moaned.

'What was?' Anderson urged.

'We had a drink and... And then I woke up and... and they were *dead*!'

FOURTEEN

BENNETT

Minshull and Anderson burst into the CID office like two men possessed.

Kate Bennett looked up from her screen, where she was constructing lists of wider contacts for the four suspected dead men.

'Call Dr Amara,' Anderson barked as he ran towards his office. 'Ask her if she can find any traces of sedative in the stomach contents of our deceased.'

'You think they were drugged, Guv?'

'According to our little lying friend in custody, they may have been.'

Minshull's expression was grave as he approached Bennett's desk. 'We need a medic at the custody suite to take a blood sample from Mr Lingham. As soon as possible, please. He claims he shared a celebratory drink of champagne with the four victims and then woke up in the crime scene with their bodies around him. I want bloods taken while there's still a chance it's in his system.'

'Do you believe him, Sarge?' Ellis asked, from the neighbouring desk to Bennett's.

Minshull rubbed the back of his neck. 'I'm not sure I believe anything he says. He just changed his story three times in our interview.'

'And his solicitor didn't stop him?'

'Nope. I think it took him by surprise as much as it did us.'

'Bloody hell. Does he realise how bad it makes Lingham look?'

'I imagine he does now, after the event.' Minshull pulled over a chair from DC Evans' empty desk, flopping down on it. 'The only conceivable way forward for Mr Carmichael is to allow Lingham to shoot his mouth off so he can claim mental trauma and diminished responsibility further down the road. But it's a dangerous line to take.'

'It would explain how the guys were overpowered, though.' Ellis tapped his chin with his pen. 'I mean, I know Mark Lingham. He's quick and he's lean, but he isn't strong. I've been trying to make sense of how he could have done it. Even with his speed, I don't think he could physically overpower any of them. They have at least a foot on him in height, and they could throw him across a room easily. But if they were rendered helpless by a sedative...'

He paled, and Bennett's heart went out to him. Analysing the suspected manner of your friends' deaths with any objectivity must be a terrible task.

'Exactly that.' Minshull sent Ellis a respectful smile. 'Which means Lingham could have drugged them all with the champagne they drank and slit their throats with little resistance. That would explain the amount of blood on him when he was found.'

'Why were they drinking champagne first thing in the morning in a derelict shop?' Bennett asked. This case made less sense the more they knew.

'They were planning to do a moonlight flit... No, a *daylight* flit,' Minshull corrected himself with an apologetic grin. 'If there is such a thing.'

Now Bennett had heard everything. She thought of Isabel Lingham in their picture-perfect home and the neatly stacked boxes of toys belonging to their children. What kind of man planned to leave all that by the cruellest means ever? 'Is that why Lingham left the note? To make his family believe he'd killed himself?'

'So he says.'

'*Bastard.*' The words were unleashed before Bennett could think better of it. She couldn't help but think of Ross, her soon-to-be ex-husband, and the ease with which he'd lied to her for years as he started a new family with another woman behind her back. Realising her slip, she reeled her anger back. 'I mean, be upfront: tell them you're leaving. Don't fake your death to traumatise them forever.'

Minshull observed her for a few seconds before he replied. Bennett wished for the ground beneath her chair to open up and take her down into the depths.

'No, you're right. It's a shitty way to leave,' he conceded. 'Kate, when you talked to Isabel Lingham, did you get any sense that things weren't good between her and Mark?'

How could anyone know what was happening in someone else's marriage unless they were specifically told? Bennett thought of all the people in her family who had assured her Ross was a great guy and regarded the act of abandoning her for a family he'd started while still married to her as just a blip. Even her own mother, who she'd always assumed would take her side, now made mention at every opportunity that 'Ross must have had good reason' to do what he did: a thinly concealed accusation that Bennett was at fault for her ex's behaviour. That she hadn't been enough.

She caught the glance Ellis sent her as she cobbled together a reply, thankful that he knew about her home situation. An ally at the desk next door was surprisingly welcome. 'The only thing Mrs Lingham said was that Mark had been through 'rough patches', but I took that to mean his own mental health rather than their marriage. She just seemed terrified for his safety.'

'And when you told her where he'd been found?'

'She was angry, but she quickly regrouped to support him. If they've had problems, she's hiding them well.'

Her last sentence could have been a description of herself. Bennett slumped a little as Minshull walked over to the white-board bearing the crime scene photos and notes on the case.

'You okay?' Ellis whispered, wheeling his chair a little closer to Bennett's desk.

She nodded and shooed him away. It was enough that he understood. Besides, he had his own demons to contend with.

'Where are we at with relatives and contacts?' Minshull asked, his back to the team as he surveyed the sketchy information they'd collected so far.

'We're trying to contact Krish Bhattachama's wife, but so far, no joy,' Bennett replied. 'Jack Markham's father was listed as his next of kin, but he died last year.'

'I called the company Denz works for,' Ellis said, checking his ever-present notepad. 'AgriLite Engineering over in Bury St Edmunds. He's a salesman for their farm machinery division. His manager mentioned a girlfriend – he's trying to track down a contact number for us. I should hear back from him soon.'

'Great, thanks. Has he mentioned a girlfriend to you before, Drew?'

Ellis grimaced. 'Never by name. Denz always seemed to have girls around him. Safer not to know.'

'I see. Well, when we can get formal IDs on the deceased, we can widen the net. Until then, let's just gather as many contacts as we can so we're ready to go.'

'Sarge.'

Minshull added new notes to the whiteboard. 'I know Dave isn't back yet – has anyone else been able to check Mark Lingham's social accounts? If he's been spending more time with the dead men lately while they were planning to run away together, we might see some evidence of it there?'

'He posts on Facebook mostly,' Ellis said. 'I follow him on there and Instagram.'

Bennett could hear the strain in Drew's reply. It must be horrible for him, not only battling the strong possibility that he'd lost four of his social circle in one fell swoop but also watching a fifth friend questioned on suspicion of their murder. While the bodies were yet to be officially identified, there seemed little doubt that they would be the people Lingham had named in his initial interview.

If – when – it was proved, what would that mean for Drew Ellis?

Evernam was such a tight-knit community, with the pub, rugby and cricket clubs being the hub of the village social life. Ellis had moved there from St Just, home to Bennett, Anderson and Wheeler, largely because the rugby team he played for had welcomed him into Evernam life and made him feel he could make it his home. He'd left St Just after the Hannah Perry case that had forever changed his feelings about that village. Would this case cause him to leave Evernam, too?

'Give the profile links to Kate, would you?' Minshull asked.

'I'll do them,' Ellis protested. 'I don't mind.'

'Mate. Let Kate handle this. You've enough going on.'

The gentleness of Minshull's reply had the desired effect. Ellis nodded and solemnly wrote them down. As he passed the paper to Bennett, she caught his fingers with her own, giving them a squeeze. When she looked at her colleague, she could see the struggle in his expression. Quickly, she let go, turning her attention back to her screen.

Over by the whiteboard, Minshull stared back.

FIFTEEN

WHEELER

Two hours on a wild goose chase. Addresses that Control had provided proving inaccurate, new addresses they were directed to being wrong. For someone who had lived in the village for years, Mattie Kemp had moved home a surprising amount. And worse than the never-ending parade of former abodes was the shocking willingness of everyone Wheeler and Hickman encountered to pass judgement on the young woman.

'Can't keep a home, that one. Not surprising she's trying to wreck someone else's.'

'Are you after her for unpaid rent? I heard she's got several landlords baying for money.'

'A wrong 'un, she is. Attracts trouble like a magnet in a scrapyard.'

The damning opinions followed Wheeler and Hickman like dragging dead weights, slowing their progress and hampering the search.

Wheeler was beginning to wish he'd never suggested they try to find Mattie Kemp straight after visiting Susannah Wragg and her battling family.

It was pointless.

The first two addresses they'd visited turned out to be dead ends: former residences she'd rented for six months or so before moving on. A third belonged to her rumoured uncle and his family, but a neighbour informed Wheeler and Hickman that they were away on holiday. She wasn't even certain they were related to Mattie Kemp.

There was no answer at a fourth address: the property looked in bad repair from the outside, and despite two hanging baskets that looked relatively healthy to Wheeler, it could well be unoccupied now.

Every member of the public who had helped with these accommodation suggestions wanted to discuss the Januarius Street bodies, which slowed each interaction down to a frustrating snail's pace. Wheeler had given the stock reply about the investigation being ongoing and their priority being to the families of the victims so many times he was pretty sure he'd be reciting the words in his sleep.

I'm afraid I can't comment on that... An official statement will be made soon... I'm not able to discuss that... Sorry... Sorry... Sorry...

Wheeler leaned against the CID pool car as PC Hickman headed into the newsagents in Evernam High Street, enjoying the break of afternoon sun that had momentarily parted the stubborn rainclouds. He was worn out already, and it was only the first day of the investigation. Quite what state he and his colleagues would be in by the end of it was anyone's guess.

He should admit defeat in the search for Mattie Kemp and go back to the office. But that could wait a moment. All he needed was five minutes to breathe...

'Excuse me, officer?'

Wheeler swallowed an inward groan and plastered a friendly smile where a scowl wanted to sit. 'Yes?'

The woman standing beside him offered a shy smile. 'I heard you were looking for Mattie Kemp.'

Bloody hell, news travelled fast in Evernam! Living in St Just, Wheeler was used to village grapevines, but Evernam's grapevine made his home village's internal communication network look like a slow-rolling boulder.

'Who told you that?' he asked, carefully. The last thing Wheeler wanted was to fuel local gossip any further than their fruitless search for the young woman would have done today.

'Aldo Wragg. He's my friend. Mattie is, too. And for what it's worth, she isn't guilty of all the crap Sheila Kersey's spouting.'

Wheeler observed the young woman as if he was seeing a mythical creature. He'd encountered so much negativity surrounding Mattie Kemp that this woman's positivity came as a shock. 'Do you know where I can get hold of her? It's very important.'

'I have her mobile number.' The young woman checked either side of her as if snipers might have her in their sights. Then she produced a crumpled till receipt from her pocket. 'Do you have a pen?'

'Er, yep, one mo...' Wheeler scrabbled in the back pocket of his suit trousers to find his trusty Biro. As he handed it over, he remembered the well-chewed base and split lid. But it was too late to offer an alternative: he saw the rise of the young woman's eyebrows before she removed the lid, her fingers curling over it in her palm as she wrote a number on the back of the receipt.

'There.' She handed the pen and paper back to him.

'Thanks so much – um?'

'Gaby Hall.'

'I'm DC Dave Wheeler.' He offered his hand, which the young woman accepted. 'I really appreciate this, Gaby. Can I ask, how well do you know Ms Kemp?'

'Really well. I was at school with her. We've stayed friends ever since.' She leaned forward, lowering her voice as if the street might betray her words. 'Mattie isn't the husband-snatcher Sheila Kersey wants everyone to think she is, DC Wheeler. My whole family love her, and my younger brother Lukas childminds for her sometimes. She's had a rough trot over the years and been treated badly by the village, so she's wary of people. But I think she'll want to talk to you.'

Wheeler pocketed the number. 'That's great. Thank you.'

'You're welcome.' Gaby smiled and started to leave, but turned back. 'Look after her, please? Plenty of people round here want her gone. They'd be only too happy to see it.'

'Of course. But why are people so against her?'

'Because she listens.' She gave her watch a nervous glance. 'I really have to go.'

'Right. Thank you...' Wheeler began, but she was already hurrying away.

Because she listens? What did that mean? And why would anyone have a problem with it? There weren't enough good listeners these days, in Wheeler's opinion. Folks too eager to exercise their mouths, not their ears.

'No Curly Wurlys,' Margi Hickman announced gruffly, walking out of the newsagents. 'So I got you a Twirl instead. Reckon getting a chocolate bar means the last two hours haven't been completely wasted, eh?'

'They haven't been, as it turns out,' Wheeler held up the receipt.

'What's that?'

'Only Mattie Kemp's mobile number.'

Hickman stared back, chocolate bars in hand. 'How on earth did you swing that?'

'Ways and means, Marg—' Wheeler grinned, tapping the side of his nose, '—ways and means. Let's get in the car, and I'll give her a call.'

Wheeler couldn't hide his smile as he swung into the driver's seat of the pool car and dialled the number. He'd convinced himself they weren't meant to find Mattie Kemp but the chance meeting with Mattie's friend and the jackpot of the mobile number renewed his hope. Now, phone pressed to his ear and the call slowly ringing out, he resigned himself to wait for her voicemail. It was still a result, he reasoned, so still a cause for congratulation.

Halfway through one finger of his chocolate bar, the call suddenly connected, causing Wheeler to sit up straight and brush chocolate flakes from his shirt.

'Hello?'

'Good afternoon, can I speak to Mattie Kemp, please?'

There was a long pause. Then, 'Who wants her?'

'I'm Detective Constable Dave Wheeler from South Suffolk Police. I need to talk to her urgently.'

'About what?'

Wheeler rubbed his aching temple, forgetting the melted chocolate on his fingers. He looked in the rear-view mirror, his reflection gawping in dismay when he saw the sticky mess on his face. Hickman stuffed her giggles behind the back of her hand.

'We really need to talk in person. We're in the area now, actually. Any chance we could pop over?'

'No. I'm not at home this afternoon.'

Wheeler accepted the point scored. 'So I'm talking to Ms Kemp now?'

A long sigh. 'Yes.'

'How about tomorrow, then? Morning, maybe? It really is important.'

'I'm out after ten. If you can get here for nine, I should be in.'

'Okay, that would be great,' Wheeler replied, punching the air and grinning at Hickman. 'We'll see you then.'

–

The mood in the CID office was muted when Wheeler returned. The news Minshull greeted him with made his head spin. Lingham's lies, the pact to leave the village, the possibility of drugged champagne – it was a ride Wheeler hadn't been prepared to take.

When he was fully appraised, Minshull offered him a smile that faded as soon as it appeared.

'How'd you get on, Dave?'

'We tried to find Ms Kemp and had no joy for a couple of hours. Turns out she'd moved countless times in recent years and now, thanks to village rumours, has pretty much gone into hiding.'

'Rumours about what?'

Wheeler flopped down on his desk chair. 'About her involvement with Otto Wragg – and others. About why she's

102

moved about so much. His mother-in-law didn't hold back on her opinion of Ms Kemp, and by the sounds of it, she's been pretty vocal in the village, too. Word's certainly spread: it turns out half of Evernam has her pegged as a homewrecker now.'

'So, she did she have an affair with Otto Wragg?' Bennett asked. Wheeler knew it would have hit a nerve with Bennett, her own marriage in tatters after her ex-husband went looking elsewhere.

'We don't know that for sure,' Minshull warned, but Wheeler was keen to answer Bennett's question.

'Well, no, maybe we don't, but here's the thing: the family thinks she did. Most of the village, too. It does seem like the most obvious conclusion. Susannah Wragg is heavily pregnant – around eight months, Margi Hickman reckons – with three young kiddies already to look after. It must have been something drastic to make her throw her husband out.'

'Could the threats Otto Wragg received have been linked to this alleged affair?' Minshull asked.

'It's possible,' Wheeler conceded. 'That might explain why he didn't report them to us when he'd told his brother he had.'

Minshull considered this as the team looked on. 'So, given the village were against him, and his friendship – or whatever – with Mattie Kemp was causing issues for him, it's easy to see why Otto might want to leave Evernam and get a fresh start with Lingham and the others.'

'That's true. But we did find one person in Evernam who believed Mattie. A young lady – Gaby Hall – who said she was Ms Kemp's friend. She blamed Otto's mother-in-law, Sheila Kersey, for spreading rumours about the affair. But then she said something odd: she reckons they've all turned against Ms Kemp because she *listens*.'

Ellis frowned. 'Listens? Is that a euphemism for something?' He ducked a swipe from Bennett, his grin unapologetic.

'You heard anything about this, Drew?' Wheeler asked. 'Being in the village and all?'

Ellis sagged at the question. 'Otto never said anything to me. But I don't pay much attention to gossip, to be honest. People go nuts about any scrap of scandal in the village. It's better to stay out of it.'

'Probably for the best, eh?' Wheeler offered him a friendly grin, then turned back to the team. 'That comment, though – *she listens* – it struck me as odd. Unfortunately, Ms Hall was in a hurry to leave, so I didn't get to ask her what she meant. *But*, long story short, I phoned Mattie Kemp on the number Ms Hall gave us. We can go to see her at nine a.m. tomorrow.'

Minshull brightened a little and Wheeler congratulated himself for delivering a bright spark for the investigation. 'Great work. I'll go with Kate tomorrow – if you don't mind, Dave? I need you to visit Gavin Quartermain, Lingham's business partner. Ellis has set up an appointment for 9.30 a.m.'

'Suits me.' Wheeler did his best to stretch the knots from his aching shoulders. 'I've had enough of a runaround trying to track Ms Kemp down today. An office visit to see someone who is expecting me to arrive will do nicely. Just – go easy on Ms Kemp, will you, Sarge? Sounds like she's had a pretty rough trot lately.'

'Of course. Thanks, Dave.'

While the team returned to their work, Wheeler switched his computer back on. It was a relief to return to a familiar task, allowing his battered mind to rest. The buzz of the office, admittedly subdued at present, was a soothing backdrop he could relax against. He needed that, after everything today.

The phone rang, and Ellis answered. After a short exchange he raised his hand – something he'd done since his first day in CID, an endearing gesture that made Wheeler chuckle. It now seemed completely at odds with the strapping bloke Ellis had become, after beginning his detective career as a lanky, shy kid three years ago.

'Sarge, I've just had a call from Pauline Wilks at the front desk. Krish Bhattachama's wife is here. She wants to see you.'

'Oh? Okay.' Minshull stood immediately, grabbing his suit jacket from the back of the chair, his expression grave. 'Tell Pauline I'm on my way.' He glanced at the team. 'And cross everything for me, yeah?'

Wheeler and his colleagues raised their crossed fingers in solidarity as Minshull left the office.

SIXTEEN

MINSHULL

Questions beset Minshull as he hurried down to Police HQ's reception. What did Krish Bhattachama's wife know? Had the Evernam gossip reached her yet? Had she been searching for her husband and put two and two together when she saw the police presence in the village? Or had someone told her to come to Ipswich and ask for the DS leading the investigation?

And what could he say to her that would do anything other than shatter her world?

It was a bittersweet pill to see pieces of the puzzle coming together, particularly when lives had been lost. But the extraordinary nature of this case magnified the experience. It made everything guilt-laden and fleeting, every step forward made in painful, pinching shoes.

It was part of the job, though. You accepted the knotted, barbed bits as much as the exciting, fulfilling ones.

Steeling himself, Minshull pushed open the double doors that led towards the front entrance. As he did so, a high, piercing sound broke through the muted air. Minshull slowed, inclining his head to work out where it was coming from. The direction may be unclear, but there was no mistaking the sound:

A baby crying.

It seemed out of place, instantly concerning here. Police HQ was not a place you ever wished to see a child, let alone a baby. The sound floating down the corridor set his nerves on edge. Everything about this case felt off, deliberately cruel – and the unmistakable sound of an innocent seemed to underline this.

Krish Bhattachama was a dad – a new dad at that. It meant the news Minshull carried could destroy not just one world but two, a new life that shouldn't have to learn how unfair life could be yet.

Desk sergeant Pauline Wilks, legendary for her gruffness and unflappability, was pink-cheeked and nervous when Minshull entered the front reception area. She nodded at the woman sitting alone on the row of blue plastic chairs, but she didn't need to: the loud wails of the baby in the sling the woman wore were enough to direct him.

'Mrs Bhattachama?' Minshull approached, his words almost lost amid the cries. 'Hello, I'm DS Rob Minshull.'

'You can call me Ani.' The young woman gave a fleeting smile and stood slowly, shaking her head at Minshull's proffered hand to help her to her feet. 'I'm fine, thanks. Just give me a minute.'

Minshull nodded, his hands returning to the safety of his jacket pockets. 'If you'd like to follow me?'

'Family room's free if you need it,' Wilks confided as Minshull passed her desk.

'Cheers.'

He swiped his card on the reader and held the door open for Ani Bhattachama and her still sobbing baby.

The family room was a grand name for the grey, uninspiring space just before the pass-locked entry doors that led to the custody suite. It was about the size of two of the interview rooms joined together and contained a sad, saggy sofa and an apologetic armchair that might once have been comfortable. A pathetic potted palm next to the sofa did little to appease the overwhelmingly depressing atmosphere, while a low coffee table bore two unappealing South Suffolk Constabulary coasters and a creased box of tissues.

The room seemed infused with sadness – no surprise, given its use. No good news was ever delivered here. No hope offered within its mournful grey walls. This was where alleged assault victims gave their testimony, where families of missing people had their worst fears confirmed. It was where young children, exposed to horrors no human being should ever witness, were asked to draw pictures of what happened, and where parents were told their children were never coming home.

Minshull hated this place. The baby in Ani Bhattachama's sling seemed to sense it, too, its cries intensifying.

'I'm sorry,' Ani Bhattachama apologised over the protestations of her child. 'He's hungry.' She sat on the sofa and dropped a large bag from her shoulder, rummaging inside it with one hand to produce a plastic bottle and a small carton of baby milk.

'Here – let me hold that,' Minshull said, springing forward to take the baby bottle. Ani offered a weary smile and opened the carton while Minshull unscrewed the bottle's teat.

It had been several years since he'd done this for his sister, Ellie, but the action returned surprisingly easily. He held the bottle out while the young mum poured the milk into it, replacing the teat and handing it back.

'Thanks,' she said, untying the sling to free her son, cradling him in the crook of one arm and accepting the bottle with the other.

It was only when the infant was quietly feeding that Minshull realised he'd been holding his breath.

'My husband is missing,' Ani stated, settling back a little, resting her forearm on the arm of the sofa for support. 'I didn't want to wait for you to come to me.'

'When did you last see him?' Minshull asked, the relief of his routine's return considerable. He loved his nephew and niece, but always felt like an awkwardly fitting spare part around other people's kids. Being able to do his job was infinitely easier.

'Yesterday. He was on his way out to the pub, as ever. Or that's where he said he was going. With Krish, you never know.'

The baby wriggled a little beneath the bottle. Ani modified her position to accommodate him.

'He didn't return home last night?'

'If he did, I never saw him. His car's not back. I don't know where it is.'

There was a hardness to her replies, an edge to everything. What was behind that?

And as for Krish Bhattachama's car, Minshull already knew its whereabouts. After Mark Lingham's recent revelation regarding the plan to leave the village, uniformed officers at the scene had confirmed the car parked a little further up the street had luggage visible on the back seat. It was being brought in for investigation.

A fact he would appraise Ani Bhattachama of soon, but not until he'd delivered the devastating news of her husband's death.

Steeling himself, he continued the questions he'd prepared. 'How did your husband seem yesterday, when you spoke to him?'

'Evasive.'

'You think he had something to hide?'

'I know he did.'

Minshull waited for more, but Ani Bhattachama was gazing intently at her baby. Changing tack, he tried again.

'Did your husband ever have any dealings with a man called Mark Lingham? Or his company, Lingham-Quartermain?'

His question was met by a blank stare. 'I have no idea.'

'Did he ever mention them?'

She shook her head. 'My husband had fingers in many pies, but he rarely included me. Especially once I was expecting our son.'

'So it's possible he could have had dealings with Lingham?'

'Why are you asking me this? Do you think Krish is with this man? I don't know where my husband is, Detective. That's the point.'

'Forgive me.' Minshull held up a hand in apology. 'Is that what made you come here?'

A sigh, then, although her expression gave no sign of resignation. 'It's all over the village: bodies found in that old shop. They said you were the one to ask for.'

Usually, Minshull was just 'a copper', 'a plod', or any one of a plethora of less-than-attractive names levelled at him. His dubious fame in Evernam sat strangely with him – he wasn't sure he liked being so identifiable. Anonymity was suddenly attractive…

'Do you think your husband could have been in the shop unit?'

Ani was still for a moment, observing her contentedly feeding son before raising her eyes to Minshull. 'I don't know. But the way things have been… it's possible.'

It was time. Minshull could delay the news no longer.

'I'm really sorry, but we believe he could be,' he said, as gently as he could.

Ani Bhattachama took the news with surprising calmness.

'We're contacting all the next of kin of the persons we believe were found in the shop,' Minshull continued. 'We'll need to have a formal identification to be able to confirm. Is there someone you'd like to call to be with you?'

'No. When will it be?'

'Tomorrow, we hope. As soon as possible if not. Once we have confirmation of identity, we can start looking for whoever did this.'

'Did he suffer?' The question was a stab from nowhere, so sudden that Minshull momentarily faltered.

'Until we get the pathologist's report, we…'

'*Did* he suffer?' She was staring at him now, fire in her question and her frame.

'Given the injuries, I'm afraid it's likely. Our pathologist will be able to tell us more…'

'Good.'

'Sorry?'

'I hope he suffered. Shit he's put me through this year, he needed to.'

The change in the young woman was startling – and Minshull was completely unprepared for it. 'What happened this year?' he managed.

'Affairs. Lies. Broken promises. All while I had this one to contend with and no help from anyone.' She shook her head at her now dozing baby, easing the teat of the empty bottle from his tiny lips. 'I found receipts for meals out, hotel stays and jewellery I never received. He's been taking money from the family business to do it – I only found out because our accountant decided to break his silence when he wasn't paid.'

'I'm sorry to hear that.'

'So, yeah, I hope the bastard suffered. Saves me having to divorce him.'

Wow... Minshull had heard some hard statements in his time and considered that he'd pretty much heard everything, but this was a new one.

'Did he know you'd found him out?'

'He did yesterday.'

'The last time you saw him?'

Ani nodded. 'He told me I was insane, of course. Claimed it was pregnancy hormones still messing with my head. But he couldn't explain the receipts or the accountant gunning for him. Or the texts I found on his phone.'

'How did you leave things?' Minshull almost winced as he asked.

Ani Bhattachama's eyes met Minshull with diamond-sharp clarity. 'I told him to drop dead. Seems he listened to me for once.'

SEVENTEEN

ANDERSON

'*I'm here in the small, usually sleepy Suffolk village of Evernam, where today details are emerging of a shocking multiple murder. Eyewitnesses report as many as six body bags being removed from this disused shop behind me today, taken away quickly by private ambulance. One person told me they saw a man covered in blood staggering from the building. It is unclear whether or not he survived.*

'*Large sections of the road have been cordoned off while police and forensics teams work inside the building, and diversions are in place preventing traffic from entering Januarius Street. Local people who arrived at the scene were turned away, and now uniformed officers are guarding the immediate area. While we've yet to receive an official statement from South Suffolk Police, who are conducting this investigation, we have been told that the deaths are being treated as suspicious.*

'*People here are scared. With a potential murderer still at large and police noticeably tight-lipped, nobody in Evernam village is going to rest easy. We'll keep you updated...*'

'Bastards!' Anderson spat, punching the off button on the TV remote. His team stared hollowly back from their seats, gathered together by the whiteboard for the last briefing of the day. He knew they would share his sentiments, even if most of them didn't possess the energy required to match his outburst. 'Could they not have given us a day before they got their grubby mitts on the story?'

'Punch bags of choice, aren't we?' Ellis said. 'Local yokel coppers tackling a major murder case.'

'Amazed they didn't bring in the "usually concerned with chasing sheep rustlers and stolen tractors" line,' Wheeler scoffed.

Anderson took little comfort in its omission. It was impossible to ignore the fact that they were chronically under-funded as a rural force and now staring wide-eyed down the barrel of a murder investigation that would test the mettle of even the largest forces in the UK. Added to this, his suspicion was growing that the reason for South Suffolk's woefully low budget was the high-ups sharing the view of the journalists. Would that the only cases that crossed their patch were as simple as a stolen Massey Ferguson or a herd of missing sheep...

'I heard they've already set up camp in the village,' Bennett said, instantly turning to Ellis. 'Sorry, Drew.'

Ellis shrugged off the concern, but his face told a different story. 'It was always going to happen.'

'Could have done without the *bloodied man in the street* mention,' Anderson growled.

'Hard to keep it quiet, Guv,' Bennett replied, 'considering half of Evernam saw him.'

Anderson conceded the point. Lingham staggering around like a blood-drenched madman would be catnip for the bastard hacks. Probably all their Christmases coming at once.

None of it was good. All of it would mean untold shit aimed at his department. With the wrath of DCI Sue Taylor no doubt fast on its heels...

'*Six* body bags?' Wheeler chuckled. 'I bloody hope there aren't two more bodies we missed.'

'Builds up the story,' Bennett replied. 'Makes us look like the Met.'

Ellis scowled. 'We don't want to look like them. I'd rather be a *bumbling local bumpkin*, thank you.'

'Press hauling us over the coals already?' Minshull asked, walking back into the office and dropping his interview folder on his desk. 'Didn't take them long.'

'Never does,' Anderson hissed, the sting of the news report still smarting. 'How did you get on with Mrs Bhattachama?'

'Um… *interesting*.' Minshull perched on the end of his desk. 'She was furious with her husband. Turns out he's had multiple affairs, financial irregularities, questionable business dealings, you name it. The last thing she told him was to *drop dead*.'

The team winced as one.

'Bloody hell,' Anderson said. 'Did she have any idea who might have wished him harm?'

'Besides herself? She didn't say, but we might be looking at several individuals, given his track record.'

'So you went in with tissues and ended up needing a fire-proof suit?' Wheeler joked.

'Something like that. What's worse, she had a two-month-old baby with her.'

Wheeler's grin vanished. 'A baby?'

Minshull nodded. 'She calmly told me she hoped her husband suffered and had wished him dead, while she was feeding her son.'

Shoulders stiffened across the team. Anderson sensed much not being said. Tension balled in his own body, too.

He chose his next question with utmost care. 'Should we be considering Mrs Bhattachama as a suspect?'

It seemed preposterous to even entertain the theory. But Anderson acknowledged that a woman wronged by her partner could have as much of a reason to wish him harm as anyone. More so, some may argue. And if the betrayal left her alone as a brand new mum…

'Let's wait until we have a formal ID,' Minshull replied – the weariness in his response suggesting he might have battled the same thoughts, too. 'But I think we need to talk to her again once we know for certain who our victims are.'

'Okay.' Anderson turned back to the team. 'What else do we have?'

'I spoke to Dr Amara. She says toxicology results should be back tomorrow,' Minshull said. 'And now we've talked to Mrs Bhattachama, we're just waiting for Jack Markham's girlfriend to get back to us. If she does before midday tomorrow, we'll arrange the formal ID for tomorrow afternoon. Dr Amara's on standby for that.'

'Good. Anything else?'

'I looked into Michael Stapleforth,' Bennett said, her glance at Ellis not lost on Anderson. 'Turns out he's been in and out of trouble going back years. Intimidation, affray, drunk and disorderly. Mostly cautions, but he did twelve months for burglary in 2004.'

'I don't expect his mother mentioned that,' Anderson remarked.

'Funnily enough…' Minshull's smile was as grim as everyone else's. 'But it explains why her first thought was Michael being in trouble.'

'I expect, as a councillor, she's keen to keep the criminal record of her son under wraps.'

'She's done a good job, then: it's the first I've heard of it,' Ellis replied.

'No gossip in the village?'

'Plenty, but not about him. I don't think he lives in the area now – I've never seen him in Evernam.'

'Good to know.'

Anderson hoped his thanks conveyed his sympathies. Ellis was only just learning how tough having a connection with a case could be. Tomorrow, if the formal identifications went ahead, he'd face the full extent of his loss. Not only would he have his own grief to contend with, but also a significant change in his professional involvement in the ongoing investigation.

He would be sidelined – deliberately and necessarily so: his connection with the deceased and, potentially, the suspects, barring him from having as active a role in proceedings as his colleagues. For a detective as dedicated and ambitious as Ellis, that could prove even harder to accept than the loss of his friends.

Forcing his thoughts away, Anderson returned to the task at hand – the only way he knew to keep going. 'So, plan of action for tomorrow morning. Rob?'

'I'm talking to Mattie Kemp at nine, with Kate, if that's okay?'

Bennett nodded. 'Fine by me, Sarge.'

Wheeler held up his hand. 'I'm talking to Lingham's business partner, Gavin Quartermain, at the company offices tomorrow, 9:30 a.m.'

Minshull noted this. 'Cheers, Dave. Drew, can you keep chasing Jack Markham's girlfriend, please, and field any calls that come in from the other families? We'll need to make sure Yvonne Stapleforth and her husband are ready to come in for formal identification, whether they believe Tim could be one of our victims or not. We have to be ready to go when we have everyone else.'

'Yes, Sarge.'

'Thanks.' Minshull turned to Anderson. 'Guv, we'll need access to phone records for the four deceased, and it would be good to check recent email exchanges, too. Can you sort those?'

'Consider it done.' Anderson checked the clock above the whiteboard. 'If that's everything, I say you all head off home. I'll hang back to brief Pete York for the night shift.'

Wheeler grinned. 'And nab some of his excellent coffee, no doubt.'

'Allow me some bloody perks, Dave,' he smiled back, knowing he'd been rumbled. The thought of the night detective's now legendary coffee, brewed to get him through long, lonely hours in CID, had been keeping Anderson going for the past hour. 'So, possible IDs tomorrow provided, we should be able to get all next of kin confirmed. And let's hope the bastards in the media cut us some slack so we can get on with our work.'

'Guv.'

'Cheers, Guv.'

He watched his team slowly disperse back to their desks, exhaustion evident in all of them. They needed a break – in more ways than one. Heading back to his office, Anderson prayed to the gods of providence for answers. Any glimpse of light in this stubbornly shadowy case would be a gift...

EIGHTEEN

CORA

By the time Cora returned home, all she wanted to do was get outside. She'd spent the entire afternoon cooped up in the cramped South Suffolk LEA Educational Psychology Unit and almost an hour and a half in her car in near-stationary traffic. She needed fresh air and space to think.

Changing into her running gear, she left her apartment and ran down the winding road to Felixstowe's North Beach, the rush of salt-scented sea breeze that met her an instant reward.

As she passed through the small park that stretched adjacent to the beach road, a wave of hidden voices rose up beside her from the wind-strewn litter blown to its peripheries.

So tired…

Just another five minutes…

My feet hurt…

Don't want to be here…

The emotional fingerprints of countless strangers found their voice in Cora's mind, a constant feature of her life since she was sixteen. But where the unseen voices once made navigating every day a battle, now she found comfort in her ability. Leaning into it had been the best decision she'd made, opening doors she would never have expected.

Not all the doors had been easy, but she was proud of what she'd achieved.

With practised ease, she gently muted each new voice that rose up to meet her, as if they were passers-by in the street and their conversations merely part of the soundscape of the seafront with the barking dogs, mewling gulls and waves breaking on the beach.

Her legs were stiff from her day, so she settled into a gentle pace. No personal bests required: just a steady, measured stretching of her muscles. It was a beautiful evening, with a pale yellow sun already dipping its toes in the silver horizon, painting an arc of tiny white altocumulus clouds pink and gold in the blue sky as it set. The breeze coming off the sea was blissfully cool after the storm-threatening closeness of the afternoon – a perfect companion for Cora's run.

Here she could think, away from the images, conversations and questions that had characterised her day. She pushed them aside and focused on her breath, the steady pounding of her feet and the wide sweep of the ocean beside her.

She had almost reached Felixstowe Pier when a buzz in her pocket summoned her attention. She stifled a groan. She'd almost left her phone at home but had pocketed it as a last-minute thought. Now she wished she hadn't. Slowing to a walking pace, she glanced at the screen, answering when she saw the identity of the caller.

'Evening, Rob.'

'Evening. I'm not interrupting you, am I?'

He was, but he didn't need to know it. 'I'm just out for a run.'

The sigh that met her words made Cora smile. 'Sounds like heaven. I bet it's gorgeous by you.'

'It is. Sun's setting, lovely cool sea breeze, hardly anyone around...'

'Okay, stop, or I'll be jumping in my car.'

'With the traffic in Ipswich, you'd be lucky to get here before nightfall.'

'Rub it in, why don't you, Dr Lael.'

'More than happy to, DS Minshull. Are you still at work?'

'No, Joel let us go after the last briefing, so I've just got home.'

'How's it going?'

Minshull's groan was the twin to Cora's earlier. 'Everyone's wrecked. I don't know how we're going to get through it, to be honest.'

'I saw the news reports.'

'Hmm. Flattering, weren't they?'

'Where did they get *six* bodies from?'

'Who knows? It's pretty telling when four brutally murdered corpses aren't newsworthy enough for them. Look, I don't want to keep you...'

'It's fine...'

'Thanks. I was just thinking, the objects we found around the bodies this morning are likely to be held up for a while with Forensics before we get them back. They've got a backlog of stuff to test – the knife we found, clothing from the bodies, swabs taken from the scene. It all has to be looked at before they'll get to the belongings.'

'It sounds like a huge job,' Cora replied, gazing out to sea.

'It is. But rather than wait for the team to get to the objects found around the bodies, I wondered if you'd be up for inspecting them at the lab? You've viewed items before they've been tested in the past – this would be no different.'

Cora jogged to a nearby bench on the promenade, watching the strengthening path of sunlight stretching from the sunset across the waves towards her as she sat down. 'When?'

'Soon. We have the prospect of formal identifications happening tomorrow, so I need to attend to that first. But maybe the day after? Could you get away from work?'

Cora smiled against the phone, remembering Tris Noakes' fulsome enthusiasm for her working on the new case. 'It won't be a problem. Tris says he'll cover my caseload when I'm needed. I realise you can't say exactly when, but as soon as it looks possible, let me know? I'd like to give Tris as much notice as I can.'

'Of course. Thanks, Cora.'

Cora stretched her legs out, pushing her lower back against the bench seat to ease out a knot at the base of her spine. 'No problem. Are you okay?'

There was a marked pause before Minshull replied. 'Let's just say I'm not stopping to think about it. Better to keep going, I reckon.'

Safer, maybe, Cora thought. Not necessarily better. But it was understandable given the pressure Minshull and the team must be under. Cora had found the prospect of being involved in the investigation daunting enough: she couldn't imagine what it must be like to be as deep into it as Minshull was. 'Try and rest if you can tonight,' she said, knowing he probably wouldn't. 'And if you need to talk...'

'Thanks, I appreciate that.' His reply was genuine, but designed to gloss over what Cora had just said. 'Anyway, I'll let you carry on. Do a lap for me, yeah?'

'You mean a slightly slower one than I'd do?'

'Harsh. Probably fair, though.'

Cora smiled as she stood. 'You just need more practice.'

'Well, when the Evernam serial killer decides to hand themselves in, I'll start coming back for Sunday runs with you.'

'I'd like that. Have a good evening. Get some rest.'

'Yes, *mum*...' He paused, the line falling silent against the waves and gulls around the promenade. 'I appreciate your help. Honestly. Have a good evening.'

Ending the call, Cora closed her eyes, filling her lungs with salt-sharp air. The prospect of what lay ahead both scared and thrilled her. But there would be time to consider it later. For now, her run was calling. Switching her phone off completely, she zipped it into her pocket and set off along the sun-gilded promenade once more.

NINETEEN

MINSHULL

Mattie Kemp's home was a sharp contrast to the other houses Minshull had visited during this investigation. A small semi-detached property linked to an identical one on its left. In the 1950s, when it was built, it would have been a desirable design, its sleek lines and wide, generous windows attractive from the road. So, too, the strip of lawn that ran from the roadside to the front door alongside a neat drive long enough to accommodate one car.

But the years had not been kind to 16 Knightsway Road. Paint flaked from the once-white frontage, revealing the original beige pebbledash beneath. The windows were the kind of double glazing that kept condensation between the glass panes and not much heat in, their plastic frames yellowed with time. The lawn hadn't been mowed for months, but rather than the burgeoning wildflower meadow so coveted by devotees of No Mow May, it was a mess of foot-high grass and sprawling brambles, peppered with broken children's toys and the detritus of the street that had blown into its clutches. A single hanging basket swinging aimlessly next to the front door was the only visible attempt to improve the frontage of the house.

Minshull glanced at Bennett beside him, noting how carefully she kept her reactions in check this morning. Both had been quiet on the drive here from Ipswich, and Minshull wondered if Bennett had slept any better than he had last night. Talking to Cora had helped; his idea of bypassing the wait for the Januarius Street objects to be released a significant plus at the end of a hard day. Lightness seemed in short supply: he'd take it where he could today. 'Nice hanging basket,' he offered, inviting Bennett's response.

'Looks homemade,' she replied firmly. 'I love those petunias.'

Fair enough, Minshull mused as they walked up the drive to the front door, his fun denied. Bennett was a better person than he was. Not that it would come as a surprise to anyone to learn that. He shouldn't judge, and he knew better, considering the years he'd witnessed his father boxing and labelling everyone and everything at will.

The thought of that chastised him.

Ringing the doorbell, he looked at Bennett. 'Takes skill to make something like that. Maybe I should have a go.'

'Nah, Sarge, you'd be a danger to anything green,' Bennett returned, the appearance of her wry smile both a relief and an admonishment.

The sound of a chain being slid into place called their attention back to the battered front door. It opened a crack, offering a glimpse of a young woman's pale face.

'Yes?'

Minshull held up his warrant card. 'Hi, Miss Kemp, I'm DS Rob Minshull from South Suffolk CID, and this is my colleague, DC Kate Bennett. My colleague DC Dave Wheeler spoke to you yesterday. Is it okay to have a quick chat?'

'What's this about?' Nervous fingers grasped the edge of the door. Minshull noticed the alternate pink and yellow varnish on Mattie Kemp's fingernails that was as chipped as the paint on her front door.

'It's regarding Otto Wragg,' Minshull stated, hoping it was enough. Would the news have reached her yet? If she'd been as involved with the dead man as Wragg's mother-in-law had alleged, she must have noticed his absence at least? Wheeler had reported that the older woman was adamant Mattie Kemp was to blame for the failure of her daughter's marriage. Was Mattie aware of the allegation?

The blue eyes widened in the gap between door and frame. Then the door slammed shut. Minshull groaned and was about to raise his hand back to the bell when the rattle of the chain sounded again, and the door opened fully.

'Come in, quick,' she rushed, ushering Minshull and Bennett into a narrow hall and closing the door behind them. 'Through here.'

Though the carpets had seen better days, the house inside smelled fresh and clean. Minshull kicked himself again for expecting damp and neglect. They passed a small kitchen and a stairwell leading to the first floor, emerging into a sitting room at the back of the house. There was just enough room to fit a two-seater sofa and a high-backed armchair that looked as if it might have been inherited with the house. A flatscreen TV had been fixed to the wall above the fireplace. Beneath it, the mantelpiece bore a simple wooden clock flanked by two unlit candles. The candles were the type favoured by Minshull's mum, scented so strongly that they were as useful as air fresheners as they were sources of light. The labels bore names that evoked images of an American country kitchen – Sugared Apple Crisp and Warming Peach Pie. Around the base of both candles were piles of hand-painted pebbles, the kind Minshull recalled seeing along the seafront during his Sunday morning runs with Cora.

As Minshull sat on one side of the sofa, his gaze traversed the space, taking in details that added to his own sense of shame for judging this home before he'd seen it. A white folded-leaf table with two chairs was placed next to a single patio door that led to a tiny square of garden. Beside the table stood a narrow, washed pine unit with three white-painted wicker baskets as drawers, the handles of each wrapped in yellow gingham ribbons. More painted pebbles were arranged across the top, each one bearing a different design.

They were beautiful. Had Mattie Kemp painted them?

A handmade four-pennant banner reading *HOME* was artfully draped across the mantelpiece, and a cluster of white heart-shaped frames of varying sizes had been arranged together on one wall. From where he was sitting, Minshull was too far away to make out all the images, but he recognised the young woman sitting opposite him and Bennett in three of the frames.

It felt *hopeful* – a surprisingly strong emotion for such a diminutive space – as if Mattie Kemp had surrounded herself with lovely things to keep her mind from the horrors of village condemnation and gossip that awaited her outside.

She sat with her hands wedged between her knees, her shoulders hunched as if protecting her ears from the news that was bound to be spoken.

'Thanks for seeing us,' Minshull began, feeling the need for an opening gambit that would put the anxious young woman at ease. 'We just have some questions regarding Otto.'

'Is it true?' she rushed, her stare passing between Minshull and Bennett. 'Is he dead?'

'I'm afraid we believe he might be. We're hoping his family can identify his body later today,' Minshull replied, as softly as he could. But how could news this devastating ever be gently delivered?

'What happened?'

'We're still piecing the details together, but we believe Otto's body is one of four discovered in an empty unit on Januarius Street yesterday morning. We believe he and three others were murdered.'

'Murdered?' The blue eyes grew wider. 'Are you sure?'

'Yes. Our pathologist has confirmed it. I'm so sorry.'

She nodded. Between her knees, her pale fingers laced tighter. 'How do you think he died?'

'Our investigation is ongoing, so I'm afraid we can't disclose that.'

Another nod.

Minshull braced for tears, or anger – he'd seen both many times when delivering such news. But instead, Mattie remained emotionless, staring at the detectives as if she was waiting for more.

'Can I ask, Miss Kemp…?'

'Mattie. My given name is Martha, but nobody calls me that anymore.'

'Mattie,' Minshull corrected, careful to keep his tone steady. 'When was the last time you saw Otto Wragg?'

'On Sunday.'

Bennett made notes beside Minshull, the scratch of her pen abnormally loud in the small, quiet room.

'And where was that?'

'Here. He came here.' She eyed Bennett's notepad. 'He *visited*. He didn't stay.'

'And how did he seem?'

Mattie shrugged. 'The same as he always was.'

'He didn't mention any problems – at work or at home?'

A frown creased Mattie's brow. 'What's that supposed to mean?'

'I'm just trying to establish…'

'You've heard the gossip, haven't you?'

'No, I—'

'Sheila Kersey shouting her mouth off again, I'll bet.'

'Ms Kemp – Mattie – I'm just trying to establish Otto's recent movements and his state of mind.'

'We aren't having an affair, if that's what she told you.' The hands had emerged from their knee prison now, fingers wringing with anger as Mattie Kemp faced the detectives. 'That's what she's told half the village, I know. I've stolen Otto from his loving wife and kids and broken up their perfect home. That's what she's told you, isn't it?'

'We're just trying to build a picture of where Otto went and how he seemed in the days and hours prior to his death,' Bennett cut in. 'We're not accusing you of anything.'

The young woman took a long, shuddering breath. 'It's all a lie to protect her precious, perfect family. Only they aren't perfect. If people knew the real story…'

'Which is?' Bennett was pushing her luck, Minshull thought, but he trusted her to go with it.

'Not for me to say.'

A dead end.

Minshull regrouped. 'Did Otto ever mention anything about threats?'

'What?'

'Letters that he received at work?'

'What kind of threats?'

'We're still investigating. His brother mentioned he'd received some threatening letters at work, and Otto said he'd reported them to us. We have no record of that, but I wondered if he'd said anything about it to you?'

'No.'

'Did he talk about anything that was concerning him?'

'Why would he?'

'Well, because...' Minshull broke off, flailing now.

Mattie's eyes narrowed. 'Because you think I'm shagging him? Go on – say it: it's what his bloody mother-in-law wants everyone to think.'

'How would you describe the nature of your relationship with Mr Wragg?' Bennett asked, cool-headed as ever. Minshull wished himself anywhere but here.

'Not friendly. Not cosy. Not anything *certain people* are telling anyone who'll listen. He left his wife for other reasons, although she and her mother have decided to ignore that fact. All because of me, apparently, which is a joke. He comes here when he wants to feel good about himself.'

'How do you mean?'

Mattie Kemp shifted in her seat. 'He comes here to talk. About how stifling his marriage is, about how great his business is going...'

'So you're friends?'

'No.'

What was that supposed to mean? 'Then why does he come here?'

Mattie sighed. 'I do bits of admin for him. Invoices, quotes, material estimates.'

'And how did you come to do that for him?'

'I got the work through a virtual assistant agency. Only the person who ran it decided to declare themselves bankrupt and do a runner, with months of money owed to me and the others on their books. Otto asked if he could come and see me to discuss working with me directly. We got talking about other stuff – things he said he couldn't talk about with anyone else. I listened because I thought he'd send more work my way if I did. And he just kept coming after that.'

'So the last time you saw him, it was to discuss work?'

The young woman's eyes dipped. 'Yes.'

Her reply didn't fit her body language. Minshull noted the fingernails with their chipped paint, picking at a thread in one of the rips in her jeans.

'And did he mention any of the other things? His wife? The rumours about you both?'

'No. Not the last time I saw him.'

'And nothing about any threats?'

Mattie glared at her own skin visible beneath the denim tear. 'I told you, no. I can't imagine Otto being threatened by anybody.'

—

'Did you think she was being evasive?' Bennett asked as they walked from the house back to the pool car.

Minshull thanked his stars that he'd had Bennett there with him. 'You thought that too?'

'When you asked about what they discussed? It was obvious. Total averted eye contact, nervous fingers, tapping feet.'

'Very odd.' They reached the car, and Minshull unlocked it, walking to the driver's side as Bennett got into the passenger seat. 'When she mentioned Wragg had visited once and then just carried on, did you think she sounded weary of it?'

'Can't be easy,' Bennett said, fastening her seatbelt. 'She has to see him because he's giving her work, but then he expects to talk about personal stuff – which is completely inappropriate.'

'And then she gets labelled a scarlet woman for it by the village,' Minshull added.

Bennett sniggered, causing Minshull to look at her as they reached a set of temporary traffic lights on red on the edge of the council estate.

'What?'

'*Scarlet woman*, Sarge? Did you fall asleep in the 1800s and wake up here?'

'Some bloody awful dream if I did,' Minshull laughed, appreciating the opportunity for a joke. 'So, what do you think?'

Bennett was quiet for a while, watching the green hedgerows and fields pass by the passenger side window as Minshull drove on.

'I think she knows a lot more than she told us,' she concluded at last. 'Secrets in Sheila Kersey's "perfect family", things Otto felt he could only discuss with her. And there was something off about the way she described their relationship.'

'I agree,' Minshull replied, even if the inconsistencies weren't enough yet to suggest what the truth might be. 'We bear this in mind, and we keep digging. There's more going on here than we know.'

TWENTY

WHEELER

The offices of Lingham–Quartermain were well-appointed and had the outward appearance of success. Stylish desks and light fittings, generous sofas, and walls painted in subtle shades of blue and grey in the calm and comfortable reception made the space feel coolly professional.

Wheeler felt like he was cluttering the aesthetic just by being there.

It was what his wife Sana would call 'all sleek clothes and empty pockets'. Wheeler smiled at the thought of that as he moved out of the way of another agent, who bustled stylishly past. What lay beyond the expensive fixtures and impressive front-of-house operation?

A receptionist who couldn't be more than about eighteen sent him a dazzling white smile from behind her green glass desk.

'Mr Quartermain will see you now, Detective Wheeler.'

Thanking her, Wheeler opened the turmeric yellow door beside the reception desk and walked inside.

In the equally sleek office he entered, Gavin Quartermain rose from his chair, hurrying over to shake Wheeler's hand.

'DC Wheeler, apologies for the wait. It's been crazy here.'

For us, too, Wheeler thought, accepting a seat at a low coffee table across the office from the letting agent's desk.

'Coffee?' he offered.

'Not for me, thanks.'

'Okay. Good. I might...' he nodded in the direction of reception, scurrying back to his desk to send his request to the receptionist, then returning to the matching turmeric yellow seat beside the one on which Wheeler sat. 'Right. Sorry, where were we?'

One thing was abundantly clear about Gavin Quartermain: he did not fit the surroundings of his company. He wore a creased suit that had seen better days and narrower waistlines and likely hadn't seen an iron or the inside of a dry cleaners' for quite some time. He possessed the air of a man forever halfway to doing something else. Even his sentences often failed to complete, his mind skipping off in another direction before returning reluctantly to the first.

'I need to ask you some questions, sir, regarding your business partner, Mark Lingham.'

Quartermain's flustered face immediately fell. 'Ah. I heard.'

'You heard? May I ask who from?'

'Well, Isabel called me first, of course. That's when I knew something wasn't right. Then friends from Evernam started saying Mark was out in the street – well, you know...' He swept a hand down his body as if indicating the blood. 'Honestly, it's a shock. Mark's the last person you'd expect to go off the rails.'

'Is that what you think happened?' Wheeler asked, surprised by Quartermain's bluntness.

'Well, he's not in his right mind, is he, if he's...' His words drifted away from him, replaced with a weary shrug. 'It's the worst time for him to do it. The workload here is insane. Not that Mark always noticed...'

'How do you mean?'

'Oh, you know, too many fingers in too many pies. Too many shiny things catching his attention that were more fun than working.'

The resentment was barely concealed. Wheeler noted it.

'How has Mr Lingham been recently?'

'His usual self, I'd say. Before *this*, at any rate. Flitting from one project to another, like nothing else mattered. The life and soul of the party, charming everyone within fifty paces… Easy, when you can do it. Me, on the other hand…' Quartermain broke off again.

'Stuck with the work, eh?' Wheeler risked. It sounded like nobody listened to Quartermain. Maybe he'd get more out of Lingham's weary, dishevelled business partner if he approached this interview like a friendly chat.

Quartermain observed Wheeler with surprise. 'Always. Fifteen years since we set this place up and it seems like every year I'm given more to carry while he does his own sweet thing.'

'Was Mr Lingham aware of what you really thought about his behaviour?'

'No,' Quartermain returned, a bitter laugh dancing through the word. 'Mark will ask once how you are, and by the time he's used your answer to draw breath, he's off to the next thing.'

'Frustrating, I imagine.'

'You have no idea.'

Wheeler checked the list of questions he'd written in his notebook in the car park. None of them felt appropriate now, in the light of Quartermain's not-so-glowing report of his business partner. Discarding them, Wheeler felt his way into the conversation.

'Were you expecting him in the office yesterday morning?'

'No. I had some investors in, and I didn't want Mark stuffing it up.'

'You think he might have done?'

'I know he would. He always does, particularly when he has other things on his mind. He's obsessed with a project he's been cooking up. Something he reckoned he couldn't share "until it was ready". I've heard that before, and it's a load of…' He gave a heavy sigh. 'I like Mark. I always have. But he's been about as much use as a chocolate teapot this year.'

The pact. The plan to abandon everything in Lingham's life, including his business partner. Quartermain wouldn't know what hit him when it all came to light. Wheeler stuffed the knowledge behind his simple question. 'Any idea what the project was?'

'Probably a woman,' Quartermain replied, sudden horror dawning on his face the moment he'd said it. 'You won't repeat any of this to him, will you?'

'We're just trying to build a picture of Mr Lingham's state of mind prior to the incident,' Wheeler answered, as kindly as he could. 'Anything you can tell me will really help.'

The huge sigh Quartermain hefted wasn't lost on Wheeler. What was the dynamic of their working relationship? Was Lingham the salesperson, the showman, to Quartermain's behind-the-scenes workhorse? Could the business survive without its absent partner?

'Whatever he was chasing, it excited him. He sparkled with it... Wrong choice of word, I know, but it's the only way I can explain how he was. It's what made him so impossible to ignore when he proposed we set up this agency. That energy. That drive. When he puts his mind to something, nobody can stop him.'

Wheeler tried to make out the contrary emotion in Gavin Quartermain's remarks. Was he in awe of Lingham's character, or bruised by it? Might Lingham suspect more than his partner realised, and was this the reason Lingham planned to abandon him?

'When was the last time you saw Mr Lingham?'

'In the office? Probably a week ago.'

'And outside of it?'

Quartermain's gaze drifted to the halogen spots in the ceiling of his office. 'A few days back. I went to his home to drop off some paperwork for a foreign property he had a private buyer for.'

'Foreign?'

'Gran Canaria. Nice if you can get it, eh? Better than mouldy old farm properties and run-down commercial premises like we deal with here. I'd love to have a hotel to develop in the sunshine.'

It matched Lingham's mention of Otto Wragg's development, supposedly the centre of his plan for a new life abroad. Did this confirm the rest of Lingham's story, too?

'And how did he seem?' Wheeler asked.

'Optimistic. Planning grand gestures for the business with all the money he reckoned he was going to make.'

'Was that connected to his secret project, do you think?'

'I don't think so. Unless... No, it wasn't connected.'

What was Quartermain about to say? Did he know more about Lingham's escape plan than Wheeler had first suspected? Or was it another example of Quartermain's chaotic mind?

'Unless...?' Wheeler encouraged.

'It couldn't have been connected,' Quartermain rushed. 'I mean, I'd seen the paperwork and everything. Hardly a secret project if he'd shown me the details, eh?'

Sensing a slammed door, Wheeler changed tack. 'Can you think of anyone who might wish Mark harm?'

'No. Not at all. Mark didn't have enemies. He was too busy impressing everyone to rub anyone up the wrong way. That was the problem.'

It was a firm answer. But was it the truth?

TWENTY-ONE

ANDERSON

At his desk, Anderson felt the old familiar pang of nerves as he waited for news. After yesterday's revelations, the prospect of what today might bring was unnerving.

Minshull and Bennett visiting Mattie Kemp.

Wheeler talking to Gavin Quartermain.

And calls were due any moment from Dr Jo Warwick – the duty medic who had taken blood from Lingham last night for testing – and Dr Rachael Amara regarding Anderson's requested post-mortem toxicology tests on the deceased.

When they all arrived, would they prove or disprove Mark Lingham's story?

And if he hadn't drugged the champagne himself, who had?

Anderson had many valuable skills and abilities, but waiting was not one of them. He'd already paced his office, jogged down to the Custody Suite to check that Jasper Carmichael had arrived to brief Lingham before the next round of interviews, and refilled the tea caddy from the large bag of Yorkshire Tea he'd covertly smuggled in for the CID kitchen at his own expense (and for the sake of his own sanity). DCI Taylor had yet to find it: neither would she find the woeful excuse for teabags her measly budget had provided for, now lying at the stinking bottom of the industrial wheelie bin in the car park of Police HQ.

Operating CID with one detective down and a major murder investigation to contend with was ignominy enough. Being asked to do it with sub-standard tea was unconscionable.

The sharp trill of his desk phone sent him into action. Snatching up the receiver, he barked, 'DI Anderson.'

'Joel, good morning. It's Rachael Amara.'

She sounded as exhausted as his team. 'Rachael, hello. How's it going?'

'Heavy work with four guests on my slab, but worth the effort. You were right: they were drugged. I found significant quantities in their stomachs.'

Anderson realised he was gripping the handset. 'Which substance?'

'Isopropyl alcohol. Used to make rubbing alcohol and cheap solvents for cosmetics and skincare products. Pretty easy to come by, relatively inexpensive, but if ingested in large enough amounts, it can leave people disoriented, dizzy, unable to control their balance or speech. Fast working, too.'

A hunch proven, Anderson thumped his desk in celebration. 'Excellent work. You found the substance in all of the deceased?'

'All four, yes. Together with considerable amounts of champagne.'

Anderson breathed a long sigh of relief, the mention of champagne the crowning detail. 'That's wonderful news.'

Dr Amara gave a wry chuckle. 'Look at us, eh, Joel? Who else would think of celebrating four men being drugged with champagne prior to their murder?'

'This bloody job,' Anderson returned. 'It makes monsters of us all.'

As he spoke, a notification appeared on the screen of his computer. Opening his email, he found a new message from Dr Jo Warwick that made his old cynical heart leap like a lamb.

'And that's the jackpot!'

'Are you rich beyond your wildest dreams now, Joel?' Dr Amara asked, a smile in her tone. 'Able to book that round-the-world trip for you and Ros?'

'Better. The duty medic who did blood tests on Lingham just sent over the results. Traces of isopropanol and acetone.'

'Only traces?'

'That's what we wanted to know,' Anderson explained. 'Lingham was in control of his body enough to leave the shop unit and alert passers-by. The victims were presumably overpowered easily, allowing the murders to take place.'

'Did Lingham give them the champagne?' Dr Amara asked.

'He told us he did. Poured it, at any rate. But he claims he didn't know the champagne was drugged until it *occurred* to him in interview.'

'If he was dizzy, disoriented, drunk-like in his movements when he left the scene, it would support the theory that he only took a sip from the drugged champagne.' Dr Amara mused. 'Which could explain why his memory was affected. It's possible he was still suffering some after-effects of the isopropyl alcohol.'

'Or that he was lying about his memory.'

He could picture the pathologist's smile down the line. 'That too. I guess it comes down to who you think is responsible for the murder. If Mark Lingham is a victim, as he claims, then you have a killer at large. If not, you may well have a killer in custody. I don't envy you the task of deciphering which it will be.'

'I don't, either.' Anderson chuckled as he reached for his mug of illicit tea. 'Now, about the bodies…'

'They're ready to be viewed for ID now.'

It was the news Anderson had hoped for, but it brought with it a wash of regret. For four sets of loved ones – and for DC Ellis – it signified the end of their hope.

'Thanks, Rachael. We'll contact the next of kin and arrange times with you for identification.'

'My pleasure, Joel. We'll be waiting.'

TWENTY-TWO

BENNETT

Kate Bennett had begun to think they would never find anyone to identify Jack 'Denzil' Markham.

No immediate family had been located for him, and when Ellis contacted Markham's employer, AgriLite Farm Machinery in Bury St Edmunds, his manager refused point-blank to identify Markham if no other family members or close friends could be found.

The initial contact for an ex-girlfriend Markham had dated while working at AgriLite turned out to be fruitless, too. Ellis frustratedly admitted he knew nothing of the woman when Bennett asked him, not even her name.

When Erica Edison's name and email address finally came to light, Bennett discovered Erica had emigrated to New Zealand five years ago and hadn't spoken to him since she left the UK. It struck Bennett as odd that people Markham had worked with for so long apparently cared so little about him.

'He just doesn't do small talk,' Ellis explained when Bennett asked why. 'Or other people's dramas. So they have nothing in common to bind them. The thing with Denz is that he's just out for an easy life. His job bored him to tears and was a pain to drive over to every day, but it was good money. Denz always said the farm machinery more or less sold itself.'

'How come you all became friends, then?'

'Because we talk crap and we buy him beer,' Ellis replied. 'And because he's the best batsman on the cricket team.'

As reasons for friendships went, it was simple but effective.

How, then, had Jack Markham – known by everyone in the village as Denzil or Denz – become embroiled in a dangerous drama that could have cost him his life?

Bennett worked steadily through social media links, messaging the few people Denz Markham had tagged in his photos. It seemed doomed to become another blind alley until she received an email to the police address she'd attached to her messages.

Denz is my partner. I haven't seen him since Friday, and I'm scared. Do you know what's going on?

It was signed *Jasmyn*. No surname, but a phone number. When Bennett called, the quiet young woman who answered confirmed her name as Jasmyn Searle.

'Can I come and talk to you?' Bennett asked, pointing at the phone when Minshull looked over from his desk, following the gesture with a thumbs-up sign. The smile she received in return encapsulated what this stage of the investigation was like in CID. Many dead ends instantly forgotten when one glimpse of light appeared.

'No. I don't think that's a good idea. Can't we just talk here, on the phone?'

'It's really important I talk with you in person, Miss Searle. Are you sure I can't visit you at home?'

'I'm not comfortable with that.'

Bennett changed tack. 'How about coming to South Suffolk Police Headquarters in Ipswich? We can talk in confidence here.'

'I don't know. I don't think I should leave the house.'

It was such a stark statement that Bennett momentarily struggled to find a reply. Jasmyn Searle had a voice like thin porcelain, the kind that may shatter at any moment.

'How about I pick you up? Or meet you somewhere?'

'It's really important?'

'Yes. I'm afraid so.'

'And I'm not in any trouble – with you?'

It was such a strange thing to ask, but real fear lurked around the shape of the question. Why would she think that?

'Not at all.'

The pause that followed tipped Bennett's nerves on edge. What if Jasmyn changed her mind and ended the call?

'Okay. If you promise that nobody else will be there.'

It took an effort for Bennett to keep the rush of adrenaline she felt from leaking into her reply. 'You have my word.'

An hour later, Bennett's mobile buzzed on her desk. Checking the message, she stood quickly.

'Sarge, she's here.'

'Okay.' Minshull nodded. 'Good luck.'

'I think I might need it,' Bennett replied, heading for the door.

–

At the rear gate of Police HQ's car park, where Bennett had arranged to meet her, a timid young woman was waiting. Despite the pleasantly warm September day, Jasmyn Searle was dressed in thick layers. Long sleeves were visible beneath a baggy jersey dress, worn over midnight-blue leggings and black boots. A hooded cardigan was tied around her waist like a belt, adding another layer to what must have felt like a prison of fabric enclosing her small frame.

A brief smile transformed her face as Bennett greeted her, vanishing the moment their tentative handshake was over.

'If you'd like to follow me, we'll go to the family room,' Bennett said gently. 'It's quieter and more private in there.'

She led Jasmyn into the building from the fire escape ramp that rose from the car park at the rear of the building. The young woman didn't speak, merely flashing occasional, fleeting smiles when they made eye contact.

It was the longest journey within Police HQ that Bennett had ever made.

By the time they reached the family room, Bennett was completely on edge.

Jasmyn appeared even more fragile and liable to break in person than she had sounded on the call. Bennett wished now that she had accepted Wheeler's offer of assistance so that the family room felt less like sides drawn in battle. It would have made the news she had to deliver a far less daunting prospect, too. Even as they sat facing each other, at either end of the soothing blue sofa, Bennett worried she might shatter Jasmyn into tiny shards, impossible to repair.

'Thanks so much for coming in,' she began. 'I understand how daunting this must be.'

'It's scary.' Jasmyn's gaze darted from wall to ceiling to floor, as if seeking escape routes. 'Denz is always home, even if it's late. But it's been days since he was there.'

Bennett steeled herself for the task ahead. 'I am so very sorry, Jasmyn, but we have reason to believe that Jack and three of his friends died in Evernam yesterday morning.'

She waited for the news to sink in. How was it possible to gauge the correct amount of time for this to occur? With a colleague beside her, she could have had a second opinion. But here, she felt exposed.

Jasmyn didn't move or speak. Had she heard Bennett?

With no other option, Bennett continued. 'We're treating the deaths as suspicious.'

Jasmyn blinked. 'He's dead?'

'We believe so. There has to be a formal identification to confirm it. We may ask you to consider doing this if we can't find his family.'

'I don't think he has any family. None that he wants to keep in touch with, anyway. He's been with me for eleven years, and I've never heard him even mention them.'

'Does he have any photos of family members? Or relatives he follows on Facebook?'

'I've never seen any. He says he likes it just being us, that I'm his 'found family', and that's all that matters.'

Bennett thought she saw a shudder pass across Jasmyn Searle's shoulders.

'We're just trying to work out what happened. And why he and his four friends went to the empty shop at 62 Januarius Street in the first place.' Bennett gave a small smile to coax words out of the young woman. 'Did he mention going there?'

'No.'

'Or that he was meeting his friends?'

'No.'

'Do you know his friends?'

'No. I'm not supposed to talk to anyone.'

'Why?' The question escaped instinctively: there was no way Bennett could stop it.

Jasmyn picked at the zip fastener of the hoodie, still tied around her waist. 'I'm not meant to talk to anyone. Especially not his friends. He's mentioned them a couple of times, but I've never met them. I'm not even sure they know about me.'

Ellis certainly didn't – not that it was much of a litmus test for what the others knew. Considering his stance on approaching personal conversations with his friends, it was unlikely he would have been having heart-to-hearts with Markham.

'Has he ever mentioned his friends by name?' When Jasmyn shook her head, Bennett pushed a little more. 'Can you recall any names he's mentioned?'

The young woman hugged her elbows to her body. 'Um, Mark, I think? And maybe a Tim?'

'That's great, thanks.' It was something, at least. Bennett gave her an encouraging smile as she wrote the names in her notebook. Two out of four...

'Do you want me to see the body?' Jasmyn asked suddenly, raising her eyes to Bennett.

'It may come to that. If you did, is there someone who could come with you?'

'My mum.'

'Okay, good.'

'So are you taking me there now? To the morgue?'

'If that's something you think you can do. We can call your mum to come here if you'd like.'

'I hope it is him.'

Her words cut the air in the cramped space.

'Sorry?'

Fists balled beneath the long hems of Jasmyn's sleeves. Tension danced along her jaw. 'Because he's made my life hell.'

Bennett could only stare back.

'I've never told anyone that because it's Denz's rule to keep quiet, to stay away from everyone else. Even my mum doesn't know.'

Bennett's training clicked into place as her own emotions threatened to betray her. 'Has he hurt you?'

'Every day.'

'Can you tell me how?'

'When he's angry, he uses his fists. When he wants to keep me in line, his silence.' Jasmyn's reply was flat, emotion beaten out of her over what could be years of sustained abuse. 'He's angry every day. And it's always my fault, even if I don't know what I've done. I've run out of excuses at A&E, about where the injuries come from.'

Stunned, Bennett let her professional guard drop, speaking to Jasmyn as one shattered woman to another. 'I am so sorry you've had that happen to you.'

The young woman acknowledged this with a slight bow of her head. 'I can't even cry about it anymore. I'm like a shell...' She gave a cough and pulled her sleeves further down over her hands. 'So, yes, I want to see Denz today. I want to make sure he's dead.'

TWENTY-THREE

WHEELER

Waiting was the worst part of this job. Wheeler caught himself watching the clock over the whiteboard again and forced his eyes away.

Jasmyn Searle's arrival at Police HQ – and the subsequent arrival of her mum to accompany her – had set wheels into motion. The other next of kin or nominated persons who had been on standby since Dr Amara's call first thing were all summoned to the pathology lab's viewing gallery.

Since the call had come in that next of kin for all four dead men had arrived at the pathology lab for identification, Wheeler had been on tenterhooks.

It didn't matter that everything pointed to the bodies being the men Lingham had named in his initial interview: until each was formally identified, the investigation was stuck.

Dr Amara had described her plan to keep the families separated from one another when she'd called following confirmation of all parties being ready for the identification.

'We'll instruct them to come to different doors at twenty-minute intervals,' she'd explained. 'We have the deceased arranged on gurneys in two viewing galleries, with a pull-around curtain separating them, so we'll display one half of each gallery at a time.'

It was clever but, by necessity, time-consuming. Which meant more waiting...

At the desk next to his, DC Drew Ellis was working with fierce concentration. Wheeler's heart went out to him. Bad enough waiting for news of one loved one: waiting to hear the fate of four friends would be hell. He must already fear the worst, but Wheeler knew only too well that a spark of hope always burned until confirmation came.

The other side of Ellis, Bennett kept her head down. She'd returned from her interview with Jack Markham's girlfriend two hours ago, ashen-faced and quiet. From her report of what Jasmyn Searle had disclosed, it was no wonder. How could anyone do that to someone they said they loved?

Now, Wheeler saw Bennett's carefully concealed glances at her colleague. At least she and Ellis were getting on, which could be good for both of them. He knew about Bennett's home situation and had done what he could to support her, but having someone closer her own age to talk to was important. Maybe if she was supporting Ellis, she wouldn't feel so self-conscious about him supporting her.

'Any news?' Anderson's whisper by Wheeler's ear brought him sharply back from his thoughts. How such a big bear of a bloke was able to move with such stealth around the office still foxed Wheeler after twenty-odd years of working with him. *The Silent Ninja* his team called him out of earshot. If Anderson knew about this unofficial nickname, he'd never said. Although Wheeler suspected Joel would be quite flattered by it...

'It's going to take a while, Guv. Four lots of IDs, shepherding them all around the building so they don't meet, making sure they leave at the right time – that won't be a quick job.'

'I know that. But *bloody hell...*'

'A word, Guv?' As if he'd heard Wheeler's prayers across the CID office, Minshull appeared, his own silent ninja skills clearly improving. As the DS steered Anderson away towards the DI's office, he shot Wheeler a rueful grin.

At least there was this: the team being united, despite all the crap. It was how they would get through it, despite the constant nagging doubt that they could. They were exhausted, but exhausted together. The pressure bearing down on them from all sides was equally shared. Wheeler knew how easily that strength could be lost, however, which was the reason for his unofficial patrolling of the CID team's space. So what if the others called him a Mother Hen? He knew his own strength lay in the protection of everyone else.

It didn't make the time pass any quicker, mind.

He forced his attention back to the catalogue list the Forensics team had sent across, detailing the objects that had surrounded each body at the crime scene. It read like an obscure puzzle in a quiz show: find the link and you'd win the jackpot. Except the prize for solving this conundrum was a macabre bounty: a potential reason for each victim's murder.

But what could that be?

For some of the items it was easy to imagine a use: a coil of rope, a roll of electrical tape. The others made no sense at all: an open padlock, a broken camera lens, a battered toy car, a bag of coins covered with soil, a list of first names, a Do Not Disturb sign...

With the formal identifications now underway, Minshull had made his planned call to Dr Cora Lael. He and Wheeler were due to meet Cora to inspect the items at the lab two streets away from Police HQ. Wheeler had seen Cora's ability in action several times, but the significance of her inspection of the Januarius Street objects seemed the greatest yet. What she heard could help them solve the puzzle of who had placed the objects there – maybe even why.

If an unknown killer had set the scene and drugged Lingham and his friends prior to their murders – as Lingham was insisting and both the suspect's blood test and the victims' toxicology reports appeared to support – Cora might confirm a new voice attached to the objects.

If she heard differently, it might steer the investigation in an entirely different direction.

Right now, any step forward would be a win.

But until Dr Lael arrived to inspect the objects, Wheeler opted for some old-school investigation of his own.

He pulled a pad of sticky notes from the top drawer of his desk and cleared a space in the area immediately in front of his computer monitor. He copied the list of belongings onto the bright yellow notes, one per body, plus one for the fifth empty space, and stuck them to his desk in the order in which he'd seen them at the scene.

Images of the blood-soaked unit flashed back into his mind, and he quickly pushed them aside. He'd been locked in a battle with them since yesterday morning when he'd seen it for real, the horribly vivid mental pictures not easily dismissed. He rubbed his eyes, then studied the layout.

Were they clues to the identities of the four men? A coded message only their loved ones could decipher? Or something else?

An accusation, perhaps?

The sudden ring of his desk phone made Wheeler jump, snatching up the receiver on the second ring.

'DC Wheeler?'

'Dave, hi. Rachael Amara. We have four positive IDs.'

It was simultaneously the best news they could have hoped for and a completely crushing blow. Once it was shared with the CID team, everything would change:

Four men savagely murdered.

Four motives to unpick.

A killer potentially still at large...

Ellis was staring at him, with Bennett at his shoulder. Minshull and Anderson hurried back into the office. Wheeler stared resolutely at the sticky notes, placing the pad at the centre of the five object lists and carefully noting down details as Dr Amara gave them. It mattered to get everything right, to deliver the awful news to Ellis in front of the team with absolute clarity.

It was the only kindness Wheeler could offer to counter the terrible truth.

'Okay, thanks, Doctor, I've got that.'

'No problem.' There was a distinct pause, the rapid clicks of a ballpoint pen sounding in the gap. 'Give Drew Ellis my best, okay? I know this is the worst news.'

'I will. Cheers.'

He slowly replaced the receiver.

'Well?'

Anderson was at his desk, Minshull beside him. Ellis stiffened to Wheeler's right, Bennett watching him carefully.

'Dr Amara saw all four family groups at twenty-minute intervals. The team did a brilliant job of keeping them apart. She's emailing a list of who was in each party, so we have a record.'

'And?' Anderson's impatience was tempered by care, his question as soft as he could make it.

'Four positive IDs. We can now confirm that the bodies found at 62 Januarius Street on the morning of Monday 9th September, are those of Otto Wragg, Tim Stapleforth, Krish Bhattachama and Jack 'Denzil' Markham...'

The chair beside him was kicked aside, its seat spinning empty as the CID office door slammed back against the filing cabinet behind it.

Ellis was gone, his startled colleagues staring in his wake.

'*Shit*,' swore Minshull, striding across the office.

'No, Sarge, let me.' Bennett was on her feet, already at the door.

'I should...' Minshull began, but Wheeler cut in.

'Let her go, Minsh. It's better if it's Kate.'

Minshull brought his hands to his head, adrift in the centre of the office. 'What a nightmare.'

'It's what we needed, though.' Anderson's tone was all apology. 'I appreciate this is devastating for Drew, but now we know who the victims are, we can proceed.'

'*Four* of his mates, though, Guv. Nobody should have to deal with that. Poor kid.'

Anderson, Wheeler and Minshull stared at the slowly closing door.

'We find who murdered them,' Anderson stated, grim resolve setting his jaw. 'We nail them to the bloody wall when we do. And we do it for Drew.'

TWENTY-FOUR

ELLIS

It was too much.

He knew the news was coming, had prepared himself for it as best he could. It was inevitable, given the man in custody was so close to the four men he'd named in his first interview. In such a small village as Evernam, it was unlikely to be anyone else.

Ellis had so often seen Lingham and the others sitting together at the village pub, The Shire Horse, heads bowed together over their pints, thick as thieves. The pub's landlord, Roli Chisholm, reckoned they were starting a boy band and had taken to calling them *Midlife*, cracking jokes about them catering for the musical needs of older ladies in the village. It had been a source of great hilarity among the regulars of The Shire Horse.

But hearing Wheeler's confirmation that the bodies were those of his friends soured the joke.

His own response shocked him, but he was on his feet and running from the CID office before his mind could override the impulse.

Even as he fled down the stairs and kicked open the fire door at the end of the corridor, Ellis knew he shouldn't have left like that. Everyone in CID was personally affected by this case: why should he expect special licence to be hurt? Minshull and Anderson would be well within their rights to discipline him for storming out.

He gripped the iron railing at the edge of the stone staircase leading to the car park, gulping lungfuls of air, the warm early autumn day swimming in his vision.

It was the finality of it that devastated him: the positive identification from those closest to the dead men, irrefutable and unavoidable. The death of the final shreds of hope Ellis didn't realise he'd been clutching until now.

He thought he'd prepared himself for the news. He'd thought of little else since Mark Lingham had named Tim, Otto, Krish and Denz. He hated his own response, his utter lack of control. After three years in CID, he should be able to deal with the worst news. He should be able to cope.

Why couldn't he hold it together?

'Hey.'

The gentle pressure of a hand at his back made him start, wiping his face hastily as he looked up to see Kate Bennett's concern.

'Go back inside, I'm okay.'

'You're not.' She pulled a folded tissue from her jacket pocket, offering it to him. 'And I'm not going back in without you.'

'You're bloody annoying, do you know that?'

'It's been said.'

Ellis observed her before taking the tissue, hating that she had seen his tears. So much of life in CID required you to keep your head up, to stuff down your true feelings to save face in front of your colleagues. It became as natural as breathing: editing every action to comply with the image you wanted everyone else to see. Being the youngest DC on the team brought its own pressures: Ellis had worked hard to shed the image of the gangly youth, wet-behind-the-ears and too earnest for his own good, that he'd been when he'd first joined CID. He wasn't the baby any longer. He'd more than proved himself.

Until now.

Storming out made him look like a petulant teen. Crying in front of Kate Bennett made him no better than a kid. He didn't want anyone to be reminded of the jokes that had plagued his first year in CID. Especially not Bennett, who had revelled in mocking him most. They'd become closer since she'd admitted what was happening to her at home, spending time together as friends outside of the office. He loved that, but it could only work if she considered him an equal. He wasn't ready for her to see this level of vulnerability.

But he was in pain and couldn't contain his emotion. For the sake of his own preservation, he lapsed into silence, staring back out at the lines of police cars and personal vehicles. Bennett said nothing, waiting beside him.

Finally, he let out a shaky sigh.

'I didn't want it to be true.'

'I know.'

'It was just hearing Dave say it…'

'It's horrific.'

'I should have been ready…'

'Ready for what? You couldn't prepare for a shock like that, Drew. Not losing your mates. Even if you already suspected it.'

Ellis swallowed the thick emotion that rose in his throat. 'But Minsh and the Guv…'

'They're fine. They're just worried about you.'

'I shouldn't have run.'

Bennett shrugged. 'Better than pretending it didn't matter. Or trying to hide from it. That's how people lose their shit, mate. Take it from one who knows, okay?'

When Ellis looked back, Bennett offered the smallest smile.

'Thanks. I think I just need a moment.'

'Of course. Get some air. Grab a drink. Do what you have to. We'll be fine up there for a while. Minsh, Dave and Dr Lael will be off to Forensics shortly, and the Guv and I can hold the fort. Nobody is expecting you to cope with this on your own, Drew. We're all here for you. *I'm* here.'

'Thank you.'

Ellis had already pulled Bennett into a hug before he'd realised what he'd done. He froze, flushed with embarrassment, not knowing what to do. He'd crossed a line he couldn't retreat from: he shouldn't stay there, but to push her away now would be wrong.

'Sorry...' he began, expecting his colleague to break free.

But Bennett didn't pull away. Instead, her arms wrapped around his back, holding him close to her. Ellis leaned into Bennett's embrace, the strength of it soothing, the warmth of it surprising.

In this moment, it was what he needed.

After what felt like an age, Bennett's hold loosened a little, and Ellis pulled back. She looked as flushed as he felt – which he didn't know what to make of. Embarrassed, they traded wry grins.

'I should get back,' Bennett said. 'Take some time, yeah?'

'Thanks, Kate.'

What else could he say? He hoped the two words he'd managed to speak expressed everything he felt. But how could that ever be possible?

Bennett patted his arm and headed back inside the building.

Still reeling, Ellis turned slowly back to the car park.

TWENTY-FIVE

CORA

The items had been placed around the table in the small lab, carefully arranged in the groups in which they had originally been placed around the bodies found at 62 Januarius Street. The evidence bags that encased each one glistened under the laboratory spotlights.

'Like a nightmare jumble sale, isn't it?' Dave Wheeler's joke was a moment of lightness, but even his perennial smile faded the moment he'd made it. 'You just take your time, Dr Lael. No rush on these ones.'

'Thanks, Dave.'

The door of the lab opened and Minshull hurried in. 'Sorry – sorry. Got held up. Cora, thanks for this. I hope Tris was okay about the short notice? We didn't know when we'd have the formal IDs of the bodies.'

Had she had a boss less interested in her ability, the sudden phone call summoning her to Police HQ today might have caused an issue. But Tris Noakes was a blessing Minshull should thank heaven for. 'He was fine. It's a paperwork week this week, so I was due to be in the office. If I'd been on a home visit, it would have been trickier to get here quickly.'

'Well, paperwork's loss is our gain,' Minshull grinned. 'Thank you.'

'No problem.' Cora surveyed the piles of belongings in their shiny plastic evidence bags. 'Where should we begin?'

'It's up to you. Dave's going to take notes. I'll observe – and I'm here if you need assistance.'

'Okay. Let's start at the side nearest the wall and go clockwise around the table.'

It was agreed, Cora and Minshull moving to the first pile of objects and donning plastic gloves and paper face masks while Wheeler settled in a chair at the head of the table, pen at the ready.

'So, Pile One – these items were found around Tim Stapleforth,' Minshull said, picking up each bag in turn and describing its contents for Wheeler's notes. 'An election rosette. A child's toy car, damaged on one side. An old cricket ball. A Do Not Disturb door hanger sign, potentially from a hotel. And… *this*…' He held up the last item, a bag with another bag inside it and piles of coins. 'A bag of old coins. Looks like someone's dug these up from the garden – the bag is half-filled with soil.'

Wheeler made notes while Cora carefully picked up each bag in turn, inspecting the contents from every angle.

'Tell me when you're ready to open them,' Minshull said, his respect for Cora and her ability encouraging.

'Ready,' she said, braced for the rush of object voices that would follow.

Minshull unzipped the first evidence bag.

Cora opened her eyes. There was no decipherable voice attached to the election rosette. The sound was muted, crushed, as if several audible elements had been smudged together. How was that possible? Cora was used to detecting distinct sounds and emotions from the objects she encountered. Everything spoke to her: from the litter blowing along Felixstowe's streets to discarded newspapers in coffee shops and stacks of leaflets on shop counters.

When she'd inspected items that had been handled by gloved hands, she only caught echoes of peripheral sound. But this was completely different: the voices were there but distorted and disrupted beyond all recognition.

Why was that? Had it been in too close contact with the other objects, or partially wiped before it was set in place around Tim Stapleforth's body?

'Cora?' Minshull and Wheeler were watching her with concern. She would normally have responded by now: they had worked together long enough for Cora's usual process to be familiar to them.

'The sound – it's there, but not distinct.'

'Try the next one,' Minshull frowned, unzipping the bag containing the damaged toy car.

Cora accepted the bag from him, frowning when the same indecipherable crush of sound emitted from the battered toy.

'I don't understand this.'

The cricket ball and bag of soil and coins were the same; Cora's heart sinking with each one when the muffled sludge of voices spilled from the evidence bags. When none of the first set of objects yielded anything distinctive, Cora stood back from the table.

'Hang on.'

'Do you need to take a break?' Minshull was watching her carefully.

'No. But I think I need to slow down. There's nothing beyond a muddle of sound with each of these. Everything's so distant, almost as if the object voices have been recorded in another room.'

'Could there have been too many people handling them?' Wheeler's question was a good one, and something Cora hadn't considered.

'It's possible, Dave.'

Minshull tapped his chin as he stood beside her. 'What about taking them as groups rather than individual items?'

'That would be no different,' Cora replied. 'The attached sound is the same.'

'Would it, though? Whoever put them in place obviously planned to do it beforehand. So, presumably, they brought all the objects together to the shop unit to prepare for the arrival of the men. Might the fragments of sound combine if the objects are brought together?'

Minshull's theory impressed Cora. Not so very long ago he had been too cautious around her ability to ever consider suggesting how she might utilise her skill.

It was worth a try.

She returned to the first group of objects and moved the evidence bags together. Then, she and Minshull carefully opened the top of each bag.

This time, the sound was stronger, amplified by the collective as Minshull had suggested. Cora pulled out a stool from under the lab bench and sat down, focusing her mind on the grouped items.

A wider soundscape met her – sketchier, with the sense of voices rather than anything distinct. With more space between the sounds, she had to stretch out her search area, but as she steadily built up a picture of the aural layers, some elements began to emerge.

'The space around them is confined,' she began, sharing what she sensed as she experienced it, a live interpretation in real time. 'Very confined, as if they've been squashed together. The air is constricted because of it. And I'm aware of heat, here...' She brought her hands to within millimetres of her face. 'The sound is very muted, but I can hear two voices, like rhythmic hums.'

'Can you make out what they're saying?' Minshull had moved beside her, and his question was softly delivered.

'No. But one voice is dominant: the other *staccato*.'

'How do you mean?'

Pressing into the rhythm of the voice sounds rather than searching for specific words, Cora became attuned to the tension between the two. 'It isn't an equal conversation. One voice is speaking the majority of the time. It's as if the speaker feels entitled to say as much as they want, while the other speaker's job is to punctuate it with occasional comments.'

'Bit like when Sana's talking to me,' Wheeler grinned over his notepad. 'She's the brains of the outfit; I'm the *yes, no, oh that's interesting* man.'

'Exactly like that,' Cora smiled.

'Okay.' Minshull stared at the bags, his mind clearly scrutinising the new information. 'We already suspect the job required more than one person to carry it out. So what you're hearing tallies. But are we looking for a mastermind and a sidekick? Or could the dynamic be reversed?'

'Minion doing all the talking, Bond villain replying occasionally?'

'Dave, you're on fire today,' Minshull returned.

'Had a drop of twenty-year-old, oak-casked Hebridean single malt last night,' Wheeler chuckled. 'Slept like a baby.'

'Maybe you should bring some in for the rest of us. I don't think I've had a decent night's sleep in months.'

'That's because you never rest, Sarge.'

Cora smiled as she switched from the voice sounds to the strange, warm, cramped air around them. She had a sudden sense of moisture, too, where the heat touched her face. Condensation? Damp?

'I think everything was thrown together and stored somewhere near where people met,' she said. 'A cardboard box in a kitchen, maybe, or a living room. I think the sound voices have imprinted from wherever they were kept. And, as I suspect whoever put them in place was wearing gloves, the sound imprint from their storage location has been left on them.'

Minshull frowned. 'So someone wearing gloves wouldn't imprint any new voices or sounds on the objects?'

'Precisely. The sounds from wherever the objects had been kept would remain, undisturbed.' She looked at him. 'Is any of this useful?'

'Yes – absolutely. It's building up a picture, and that's where we start.'

Wheeler surveyed the objects covering the table. 'Question is, what's all this stuff got to do with the bodies?'

'I don't know. But I don't think any of the objects belonged to the victims,' Cora replied. 'I would hear distinct voices from them if they did.'

'And you say they're all carrying the same sound?' Wheeler asked.

'Yes, so far.' Cora moved along the line of open bags until she came to the fifth. With the items grouped together, the change in sound structure of the final object group was more pronounced. 'No, wait… These four object sets carry the same sounds I've just described. But this one—' she waved her hand over the group of items found without a body at their centre, '—is different.'

'In what way?'

Cora focused in closer on the altered sound. The fifth set had none of the blurred soundscape of the other four. Instead, it was characterised by heavy, urgent breaths. 'It sounds like a single person breathing heavily. Like they were in a hurry.'

Minshull looked at the fifth set of items. 'Like they were panicking?'

'Yes, possibly. It's pronounced, driven. Urgent, even. And the sound is very present. I can sense it now that the objects of this group are together.'

'Lingham claimed he woke up to find himself surrounded by the objects,' Minshull said. 'So could he have panicked and laid out a fifth set of belongings that hadn't been packed with the others?'

Cora considered this. 'It's possible, yes. Also, look at these objects: the four sets found around the four victims don't make any kind of sense. They're unrelated, totally random. I think the only thing they have in common is the person they were laid around.'

'And the fifth?'

'There's a coherence to them: a jacket, Mark Lingham's driving licence, a leather bag, a phone, money… They could all have come from inside that bag.'

Minshull's frown lifted a little as he ran with the theory. 'So Lingham could have panicked, grabbed his bag and shaken the objects around himself to make it look like he was the fifth victim.'

'Who miraculously survived.' Wheeler shook his head. 'That's what I don't buy, Sarge. You saw those bodies: they were killed by identical cuts, made in haste. *Slash, slash, slash...* No time to fight, no chance of survival. If the killer struck with such force and speed, why leave Lingham alone, sleeping like a baby? Why not just dispatch him like the others and be done with it?'

'That's why I think it was staged.' Cora agreed. 'Looking at the photos of the objects in situ, even the placings weren't right. The other four sets of items had been arranged with considerable precision.'

'Like the method of murder.' Minshull agreed. 'So why the change, if Lingham was the killer? You don't go from being a precise operator, executing a strategic plan, to a shit-scared rookie, chucking items everywhere.'

'So maybe Lingham is a victim after all?' Wheeler suggested.

The disparity was difficult to dismiss – but Cora couldn't believe Mark Lingham was wholly innocent any more than she believed his explanation of how he'd survived the fate of his friends. 'I heard two voices from the other four sets of objects: one confident, one subordinate. I think Lingham was working with someone else.'

'And what, they left Lingham behind?'

'Maybe. What if they'd planned it as a team, but Lingham couldn't handle the reality of the attack?' Cora looked between Minshull and Wheeler. 'If his accomplice ran, abandoning Lingham at the scene, he could have rearranged the bodies to make space for a fifth, bloodied himself more and staggered out into the street to make it look like he was a survivor.'

It was a horrific thought. But no more shocking than the murder scene had been. Who knew what witnessing such brutal, merciless executions – four, in quick succession – could do to someone?

'I think Cora's right,' Minshull said. 'So, we work on the theory that Lingham didn't work alone. Which means that at least one other person was involved. What we need to do now is work out why Lingham added those objects – and find who he was working with.'

Cora began to relax her mind from the sounds, comforted that the sounds she had deciphered had at least given Minshull and Wheeler a workable line of enquiry. As she did so, another sound appeared across the first four groups of objects: an audible shadow at first, sufficiently different in shape to summon her attention.

'Wait,' she said, holding her hands up for quiet.

The detectives' conversation died at her signal.

'What do you hear?'

The shape of the shadow shifted and grew as Cora pushed aside the curtain of muted sound to reach it. The edges were spiky and shrill, where the previous object voices had been flattened together. It sounded like a…

No.

She was mistaken.

She had to be…

Confused, she pulled back, her brain jarring from her sudden retreat through the layers of sound. 'It can't be. It's not possible.'

'What is it?' Minshull and Wheeler were staring at her now as she moved along the lab bench, the sound the same with every object group, even the one where she'd first heard only insistent breaths.

Hardly believing her own assertion, Cora faced her colleagues.

'A baby. I can hear a baby crying.'

TWENTY-SIX

CORA

'A baby?' Minshull's consternation matched her own. 'Are you sure?'

Cora wanted more than anything to assign the soundscape to another source. But once she'd heard the well-hidden sound, it was impossible to deny its origin. 'It's a baby crying. I'm certain of it.'

'Why would a baby be at a crime scene?' Wheeler asked, visibly shocked.

'Hang on, wait.' Minshull held up his hand. 'It might not have been at the scene. Cora, you said the other sounds suggested the audible imprint of the location where the items were stored prior to being taken to Januarius Street? Maybe the objects were taken from a house with a crying baby.'

Cora faced him, conviction building in her gut. 'I don't think it's as simple as that. The more I focus on it, the more prominent it becomes. It feels newer, more immediate, like the breaths I can hear over the fifth set of objects.'

'It could be an anomaly. A fragment of sound from outside that somehow latched onto the items...' Minshull broke off, Cora's expression acting like a swift knife. 'What I mean is...'

'It's a sheen of sound,' she insisted. 'It covers all of them equally. Even the fifth set. Meaning the baby crying is from the location of the crime scene, not the gathering of the objects or a sound from the street.'

Minshull glanced at Wheeler, who stared helplessly back. 'How does this help us? There couldn't have been a baby in the unit. Unless you're suggesting our perpetrator is an infant?'

'It's as present as the breaths,' she insisted, irritated by his flippancy. '*In* the room, not imprinted somewhere else.'

'We found nothing at the scene to suggest a baby was there. We would have found it if it was.'

'Obviously you weren't looking closely enough.'

'Dr Lael – Sarge – come on now,' Wheeler interjected, nerves present in his plea.

They eyed one another with weary anger. Cora waited, holding back the torrent of argument she wanted to let flood. Then, another possibility edged around the impasse of their disagreement.

'Take me there.'

'Where?'

'The crime scene.'

Minshull dismissed this immediately. 'Out of the question.'

'Why?'

'You know why.'

'If you take me there, I can listen for peripheral sound. If the baby crying doesn't appear, we'll know your theory is correct, and it's sound from wherever the killer gathered the objects.'

'I really don't think...'

So strong was the idea that Cora dug her heels in. 'SOCOs have already removed the bodies and the objects. There won't be anything there now.'

'There may still be bloodstains.'

'I've seen those before,' she insisted. 'With the Abbot's Farm body.'

She saw her argument land at last, Minshull's hands dropping to his sides in defeat.

'I'll have to clear it with DI Anderson.'

'Of course.' She softened her tone, meeting his stare. 'Without seeing the crime scene, I can't be certain I'm presenting you with the fullest version of events. I won't need long to check it.'

The traitorous flash of a smile on Minshull's lips was her reward.

'Okay, stay here with Dave. I'll call to ask the Guv.'

—

Whatever Minshull said to his superior worked. Half an hour later, they were in a CID pool car driving towards Evernam. Minshull was noticeably quiet on the journey over, eyes fixed on the road ahead as Cora watched the rain-soaked greens and greys of the countryside passing in a blur from the passenger side window. She couldn't gauge his mood. Was he annoyed at having to return to the crime scene with the investigation in full swing? Or trepidatious of what Cora might sense in the Januarius Street unit? It was impossible to tell.

The SOCOs' van was parked beside the unit, the street still cordoned off, although the persistent rain had worked some of the police tape free. A despondent PC in a decidedly damp luminous jacket waved Minshull and Cora through with little more than a respectful nod.

Reaching the entrance to the unit, Cora braced herself. The sounds may well be muted now, but they would still be present, as they had been at previous crime scenes she had visited. She wordlessly donned the blue plastic shoe covers Minshull had handed her before they'd left the car.

'Are you okay to go in?' Minshull was studying her preparations.

'Yes,' Cora replied, steadying her breath as she stepped in.

The moment she crossed the threshold, intense fear balled at the centre of her chest. Constricting, gripping, pushing her senses to high alert. She had learned to accept the physical sensations that often accompanied emotional sound, but their intensity here was stronger than she'd encountered before.

Terror.

Pain.

Betrayal.

Cora moved further into the unit, careful not to read anything into the waves of her physical emotion, allowing them to register against her body as if she were wading against an insistent tide.

Around the room, SOCOs were making their final round of investigations, white-suited officers with hoods up and masks on, quietly and methodically cataloguing the remaining details. Brian Hinds raised a gloved hand to Cora and Minshull, returning immediately to his work. There was no need for conversation: everyone in the unit was there to do their job. For the first time, Cora included herself among them. Despite the sudden, visceral emotion she was experiencing, the reality of her acceptance within the group of officers gave her a strong sense of belonging.

Nobody questioned why she was there or what she was doing.

Nobody, that is, except Minshull.

He was watching her, hawk-sharp, as she moved to the heart of the space. He didn't pass comment, but his scrutiny remained an unnerving presence in the periphery of her vision.

Large areas of stained concrete floor indicated where the bodies of the four dead men had lain, almost identical shapes creating a horrific bloom, like the dark crimson petals of a flower. An area to the right of the others had less blood, but Cora knew from the graphic crime scene photos she'd been shown in the CID office that this was where the objects had been discovered without a body to surround.

Like the four sets of objects she had inspected back at Police HQ, the sound was muddied in the unit, the individual voices smeared together, impossible to pull apart. But here in the murder scene, other sounds joined them.

Screams.

Moans.

Terrified utterances, their words long since lost. Only the fear remained.

It hit Cora like a body blow, forcing breath from her lungs. She stopped still, closing her eyes, pushing her mind out towards the snapped edges of sound that were flapping like the loosened police cordon tape on the street outside. Unlike previous emotional echoes she had encountered before, muting each individual sound was impossible. The voices here were too twisted and melded together to separate.

Instead, she pulled the threads of emotional sound she could catch, dragging down their collective volume until other, quieter sounds could be sensed, deeper within the audible soundscape of the unit.

She moved as close to the bloodstains as she could, careful not to cross the markers laid out by the scene of crime officers. At the edge of the marked area, she crouched down, switching her attention to the layers of sound emitting from the darkly stained floor. Where the objects surrounding the four bodies had been placed, she sensed the same jumble of sound she'd experienced while inspecting them; a few inches above ground level held the cries of the victims, now muted in her mind. Slowly, she rose to her feet, searching vertical layers of sound, as if inspecting rising lines of sediment in a water jar, seeking out new, quieter sounds once masked by the immediate layer of terror and death.

At almost full height, it appeared: far, far back in the sound-scape, but growing in stature as Cora sent her mind to it.

Unmistakable.

Irrefutable.

And yet, rationally impossible.

'I hear it,' she said aloud, her voice thick with emotion. 'A baby crying.'

The blood drained from Minshull's face. 'You're sure?'

'Absolutely certain,' Cora replied, the sound around her undulating as if her head were underwater. 'Here: at this height.'

'Just where you're standing?'

'I don't know,' she said, starting to slowly move around the bloodstained circle, the shrill sound held firmly by her mind.

Minshull watched her progress, tension locking his shoulders.

She already suspected, but she had to be sure. This was her only opportunity to be here, her only chance to prove or disprove her theory. As she navigated the circle, the sound remained, almost as if an invisible figure carried the baby alongside her. The infant's shrill cries remained at the same height, at the same volume, not breaking the circle.

'It's all the way around this area,' she reported, her hand making a wide sweep of the bloodstained floor. 'At this height. Almost as if the sound is being carried at a consistent distance from the floor.'

Minshull crossed his arms, looking out across the floor. 'Definitely a baby's cry? Not an animal – like a cat?'

There was no mistaking the sound, but Cora understood the detective's caution. It *didn't* make sense. Why would a baby be present at the scene of four brutal murders?

'It's a baby,' she replied. 'But I don't know why it's audible here.'

'Okay,' Minshull replied, the argument settled. 'I'll ask Brian to check for any signs of a baby or an infant. And then we should go.'

Cora turned back to the bloodstained circle, the confirmation the crime scene provided presenting more questions than it answered. Why were individual sounds muddied? Why were the baby cries present?

As Minshull approached Brian Hinds, Cora muted the baby cries and moved to the site of the fifth group of belongings. Focusing her mind on the air immediately above the concrete, she searched for the other sound she'd heard from the belongings found there. It arrived, closer to the surface than the infant cries: frantic, short breaths, a strong shot of panic replacing the physical blow of fear that she'd sensed in every other area of the floor.

The cries of the dying men were here but distant, the volume of the frantic breaths far louder, assuming centre stage.

Whoever had placed the fifth set of objects around the empty space had done so in a hurry, acting on impulse. Where the muddied sounds attached to the other four object sets suggested a certain order and intent, the fifth set gave Cora a strong sense of afterthought, a deviation, maybe, from an original plan.

Had Mark Lingham panicked following the aftermath of his friends' murders and added a fifth arrangement of objects to suggest he was an intended victim, not a culprit?

TWENTY-SEVEN

MINSHULL

'A *baby*?'

Anderson's expression mirrored Minshull's own.

'She's certain that's what she heard.'

'Why would a baby be at the scene?'

'Your guess is as good as mine.'

'It couldn't be a hangover from a previous use of the building?'

'Not possible, Guv.' Minshull had considered this too, but information recently unearthed by Ellis about previous owners of 62 Januarius Street had confounded the theory. 'It was previously an off-licence, a dry cleaners' and, most recently, an ironmonger's shop that lasted less than six months.'

'So, unless our baby was supplying Evernam with tools, nuts and bolts, it's unlikely.' Anderson's grim humour was a thin veil for his frustration. 'How certain was Dr Lael of what she heard?'

'Absolutely convinced. Taking her to the crime scene only confirmed it.'

Anderson leaned back in his chair. 'I don't want to dismiss Cora's ability. We've learned to doubt it at our cost. But as far as the investigation is concerned, I think we park the baby thing for now. Note any individuals connected to the case who may have a baby or have access to one, but beyond that, leave it as a notable anomaly.'

'Krish Bhattachama's wife brought a baby with her when she came to see us,' Minshull mused. 'But she has an alibi that checked out.'

'Fine. Let's leave it there then. I'm sure Dr Lael will be working on other aspects of the case with us. Best to let her get on with it.'

It was as Minshull had expected and really the only sensible course of action, given the increasingly pressing demands of the investigation. More immediate concerns must take precedence.

Nevertheless, the suggestion of a distressed baby at a murder scene haunted his thoughts as the detectives gathered for a briefing. He wouldn't mention the crying baby to the wider team. Until he could make sense of it, he couldn't expect his colleagues to.

He watched the CID team stifling yawns and making surreptitious stretches, the physical toll of the investigation evident on all of them. Ellis was with them, supported by his colleagues. By rights they should take him off the investigation altogether, but his knowledge of Evernam and his insistence that to be involved would be better than being kept away had secured his position. That and the ongoing problem of a lack of manpower, which tended to override all other concerns.

Wheeler was watching Minshull carefully as he assumed his position beside the large whiteboard near his desk. There hadn't been time to brief Wheeler fully on what Cora had sensed at the unit, but he knew enough from the experience at the Forensics lab to be unnerved by it.

'Okay, everyone, let's get an idea of where we are.' Minshull pulled the lid off a whiteboard pen and added notes to the collection of photographs and names already displayed on the board. 'So, as of this morning, we now have confirmed identities of all four bodies found in Januarius Street. Krish Bhattachama, thirty-nine. Jack, known as Denzil, Markham, forty-two. Otto Wragg, forty-one. Tim Stapleforth, forty-three.'

The pen tapped each photograph of the murder victims in turn, the sound as final a tolling funeral bell. Minshull sent Ellis a nod of solidarity. Ellis looked on impassively.

'Each man was killed by a single, catastrophic knife slash to the throat. Identical wounds on all of them, made from the same direction, which suggests one person carried out the killings. However, we aren't ruling out more than one person being responsible. To move the bodies into their very specific positions and place the objects around each one would, I suggest, have been too great a task for one individual to execute in the time available. What we need to establish now is who else may have been involved.'

'Sarge, are we treating Mark Lingham as the potential killer?' Bennett asked.

'For now, yes. He was arrested at the scene on suspicion of murder because he was claiming it was his fault. We've yet to establish conclusive proof that he carried out the killings, but we have enough to charge him with conspiracy to cause bodily harm.' He turned to Anderson, who was watching, stony-faced, from the side of the room. 'Any news on how long we can keep him in custody, Guv?'

'I just talked to Lydia Macfarlane from the Crown Prosecution Service. We've been granted an extension of thirty-six hours. It isn't as much as I'd hoped for, but it is a way forward. It's vital now that we find proof to secure a charge. I want to push for a murder, not manslaughter or conspiracy. But we can't guarantee that without good, solid evidence...'

The thud of the CID office door cut Anderson's words short.

As one, the team turned.

'Don't let me stop you, DI Anderson,' DCI Sue Taylor barked. 'Please, carry on.'

'I didn't know you were joining us, Ma'am,' Anderson returned, his tone bearing no sign of the irritation Minshull knew would be blazing within him.

'Given the severity of the case – and the unprecedented nature of it for our force – it's my business to be informed. As you were, DI Anderson.'

Stung, Anderson gestured to Minshull to continue. The stiff-shouldered team looked on.

The DCI's sudden arrival was the last surprise Minshull needed.

'Ma'am. Guv. So, as I was saying, we have four positive IDs, and our current suspect, Mark Lingham, is gradually revealing more to us about the events leading up to the murders. What we know so far is that all five men, including Lingham, had ingested isopropyl alcohol via a bottle of champagne they shared. Lingham had only a trace in his system, which Dr Amara informs me would have been enough to disorientate him, slur his speech and affect his ability to move but wouldn't have incapacitated him as significantly as it did the other four men, who had ingested significantly greater amounts.'

'Dr Amara has confirmed this?' DCI Taylor interrupted.

'Yes, Ma'am. Toxicology reports have confirmed it beyond doubt.'

'Why were they drinking champagne so early in the day?'

'According to Lingham, the five men had planned to leave the country for a new start, abandoning their homes, families and businesses. They had arranged to meet in the Januarius Street unit before travelling to Stansted Airport for a flight to Gran Canaria. The champagne was to toast the successful execution of their plan.'

DCI Taylor accepted this without comment, waving her hand for Minshull to continue.

What had prompted DCI Taylor to take an active interest in the case now? Could it have been the herd of reporters currently doorstepping homes in Evernam? Or the press contingent camped on the entrance steps to Police HQ? How invested was she in the success of the investigation, compared with her constant quest for an attractive media image for South Suffolk Police?

Shelving his suspicions, Minshull returned his focus to his team. 'So, next steps: we need to gather as much supporting evidence as we can. We need times and dates that the group met to discuss their plans, possible reasons why moving abroad was desirable to each man, and details of anyone who may have wished them harm.'

'Did they have any enemies that you knew of, Drew?' Wheeler asked.

Ellis stiffened. 'They rubbed people up the wrong way sometimes. Denz, in particular. He'd throw his weight around when he got drunk, start petty fights. Otto could be a sly one – you never really knew if you could trust him. And Tim, well, he was the one who handled disputes. I don't know how he did it, but one minute there would be a problem, and the next it would be gone. I don't know if he was just a brilliant negotiator or if he had other ways of solving things.'

'Wait – you knew these men, DC Ellis?'

Ellis paled. 'Yes, Ma'am. We played rugby and cricket together. I knew them socially, too.'

The DCI scowled at Anderson. 'You knew this?'

'Ma'am.'

'Then he shouldn't be here! It's highly irregular. And if the media got hold of it…'

'That won't happen, Ma'am.'

Taylor's crow-like stare swung to Minshull. 'Won't it, DS Minshull? How can you be so certain? If DC Ellis fraternised with four murder victims and our chief suspect in plain sight of the village, how long before someone in Evernam informs the press?'

Stop it, Minshull growled inwardly. He could see the DCI's words landing as blows on his young DC, with scant regard for Drew Ellis' personal grief. It was abhorrent. Screw the press: what mattered to Minshull was the protection and wellbeing of his team.

'With respect, Ma'am, DC Ellis is the best placed of all of us to understand the dynamics of this group. If anyone wished these men harm, it's likely he knows of it. And we are a man down, facing a multiple murder investigation that would challenge far bigger forces than ours.'

Bennett, Wheeler and Anderson observed him with incredulous stares. But Minshull wasn't finished. DCI Taylor could

173

think what she liked: what mattered to him was bringing the murderer of the four men to justice.

'We need him, Ma'am,' he concluded, chin high.

The DCI reddened.

Anderson gave a cough, signalling his willingness to step in. Minshull maintained eye contact with their silently seething superior officer.

'It's *irregular*,' she hissed, making to leave. 'I hear one note of trouble, and he's off the investigation. Do I make myself clear?'

'Ma'am.'

Minshull stood his ground until the DCI had gone. The team sagged in her wake.

'Sarge – Guv – if it's a problem...' Ellis began.

'No need, Drew,' Anderson replied. 'I'll handle DCI Taylor's objections. Rob's right: we need your insight. I can't have you active in visits or face-to-face interviews, but that doesn't mean you have no place in this investigation. Understood?'

'Guv. Thanks, Guv.'

Anderson gave a grim smile. 'Well, now the floor show's over, let's get back to it. Continue, DS Minshull.'

TWENTY-EIGHT

LANEHAN

PC Steph Lanehan was on her way back to Police HQ for a well-earned cuppa and ten minutes' break when the call came in. The apologetic tone of Sergeant Tim Brinton made her heart plummet.

'We've had a report from a member of the public. They say they've found a body hanging in Evernam Woods. I wish I could send someone else, Steph, but we're stretched too far. And you're closest. Can you get over there, please?'

It was inevitable. She'd dared to hope for a comparatively quiet day after the recent horrors she'd witnessed. She should have known better. It was as if the universe had heard and decided to chuck a spanner at her.

What a bloody week this was turning out to be.

A whole load of crap and more work than anyone could realistically deal with, and that was before the grisly discovery she and Rilla Davis had been first on the scene for: four slashed-throat corpses, one blood-soaked suspect. Press everywhere now and already condemning South Suffolk Constabulary without bothering to see what she and her colleagues were all doing.

It had been all over the news this morning, even the local radio featuring a report on it as she'd driven into Ipswich to begin her shift. It was the same old guff, but it didn't make it any easier to hear. The *local bumpkins* line being bandied about again, like it wasn't a kick in the guts to every exhausted officer

175

working their arses off trying to deal with a multiple murder case on top of everything else.

Now it was four p.m., but to Lanehan's weary body and mind, it felt like midnight.

She'd hardly slept since the discovery of the crime scene – the worst of her long police career: the images of the horrifically injured men burned on her mind like a sudden sunburst on a retina. She could still see them lying there when she closed her eyes: a grotesque, immovable tableau.

And now a hanging?

Would this ever end?

Lanehan was the last person to long for retirement, but her body ached for it today. With twenty years of service under her belt, she was still years away, but the appeal of not having to deal with the worst of society was strengthening by the day.

It threatened to break the surface of her carefully curated narrative about her job – that everything was okay, that the shit was just part of the joy. Even Fred had noticed, and her husband was famous for his unquestioning acceptance of her version of events. He'd challenged her in the early hours of the morning when he'd found her pacing the small kitchen of their terraced home, hands shaking.

'I know you don't want to hear it, girl, but maybe it's time to think of leaving.'

'You're right,' she'd returned sharply. 'I don't want to hear it.'

It had been the end of it then, but how much longer could she dismiss his concerns?

She turned the squad car around in a dusty entrance to a field, heading back along the road she'd just driven, towards the location Brinton had given her. Evernam Woods was a little-known local beauty spot; Lanehan was only aware of it because she and Fred sometimes walked their two springer spaniels, Cagney and Lacey, there. Would today's grim discovery prevent her from returning again?

She reached the sandy strip of ground at the edge of the woodland used by locals for parking, finding it strangely empty. Had word spread to others to avoid the woods today? Parking by the stump of a recently felled sycamore tree, Lanehan left the patrol car and followed a narrow, winding path down into the woods. Pulling her radio to her lips, she called in her location.

'Where am I looking, Sarge?'

'Caller said south-west side, about 500 yards in from the parking strip. Look for a tall beech tree in a clearing, surrounded by larches.'

'Do we know who the caller was?' Lanehan asked, pushing through swathes of nettles and brambles that were choking the path now. She was aware of gnarled tree roots criss-crossing her route, catching her boots as she stepped over them.

'Anonymous, I'm afraid. It might be a hoax...'

'Still got to check it out, though.' Did she hope for a false alarm, or was hope pointless in this case?

'We do. Are you close?'

'I think so. Can't see anything yet.' Lanehan stopped and looked around her. The tall beeches, silver birches and larch trees that made up most of Evernam Woods shaded the path here, interrupting the already weak light from the overcast sky above. She was suddenly very aware of being alone, wishing she had Davis alongside her. Angrily, she dismissed the thought. She'd tackled enough jobs solo before; this should be no different.

'Keep looking. If it's there, you should be able to see it soon.'

Lanehan took a shaky breath, the sounds of the wood closing in around her. She glanced back towards the car and let her gaze travel from there in a wide, sweeping arc across the trees, shrubs and undergrowth.

And then, she saw it.

Her stomach twisted as she reached for her radio. 'Got it, Sarge. Approaching now.'

Every step felt leaden, every breath laboured with anticipation. You couldn't ever be ready to see this, though Lanehan had encountered several such poor souls over the course of her police career. More in recent years, sadly, as the pressures of life, the dwindling rural economy and the ravages of the pandemic took their toll on young lives.

Could this body be connected to the four murdered men in the village? Or was it a wholly separate tragedy? The way things were going at the moment, Lanehan wouldn't be surprised by either.

Picking her way across dense undergrowth, barbed lengths of bramble snagging on the hems of her uniform trousers, Lanehan approached the body. It was facing into the woods, away from her, but as she neared it, she could see a black hooded sweat-shirt and black jogging bottoms, with trainers hanging limply beneath.

What immediately struck her was the lack of smell or flies, two indicators that usually accompanied a body in this state. Also, the absence of anything that could have been used as a jumping-off point. Had the deceased been killed somewhere else and moved here to be displayed amid the trees?

As she rounded the body, Lanehan caught sight of the face – and stopped. A synthetic face, its eyes scratched out, a cross of silver gaffer tape stuck across its mouth.

'It's a mannequin, Sarge,' she reported, a flare of anger igniting within her gut.

Tim Brinton's loud expletive expressed everything she couldn't.

'Exactly.'

'Are you sure?'

'Positive, Sarge. Shop window dummy, dressed in black hoodie and jogging bottoms with trainers. Looks like the clothes have been padded inside to make it look real. The hood is up, so I couldn't tell till I got up close and the right side of it.'

'Bloody bastards!'

Lanehan looked closer. 'There's a note, pinned to its chest.'

'What does it say?'

'One minute, Sarge, I'll try and get closer...'

Cursing her eyesight, Lanehan pulled a pair of glasses from her back pocket, a recent concession, well hidden from any of her colleagues. The last thing she needed was fielding their jibes about that. Putting the glasses on, she leaned closer to read the message, written in thick, black marker.

MARK LINGHAM:
SAY NOTHING
OR THIS COULD BE <u>YOU</u>

'Lingham?' Brinton repeated. 'The guy we brought in?'

'The same, Sarge. But what use is it here when we've got him in the cells?'

'A warning? Knowing news of it would get back to us?'

'Seems odd hanging it here. Most of the time this place is deserted. Bit pointless to go to all this trouble if nobody had found it.' But someone had, hadn't they? Because of a call from a concerned member of the public. An anonymous report. Lanehan punched her hands onto her hips, glaring up at the elaborate hoax. 'I'm going to need help getting this bloody thing down.'

'Don't move anything, Steph. I'll call SOCOs. Whoever did this knows about those bodies in Evernam. There could be forensic evidence on it. Secure the area as best you can and stand by.'

TWENTY-NINE

CORA

Nothing.

No voices, no peripheral sound, not even a sense of where the mannequin might have been before it was hung in Evernam Woods.

'Nothing at all?' Minshull's crestfallen expression was a kick Cora didn't need.

'They must have worn gloves. My guess is they wanted police to find this, so they were extra careful that no other traces were present.'

Minshull slumped against the desk where the fake body lay in a real body bag, the only official receptacle large enough to accommodate it. Anderson stared at the wall of Interview Room 4, chuntering under his breath.

'I can't believe we had to drag the duty pathologist all the way out to Evernam Woods to inspect this,' Minshull said.

'Report of a hanging body. She had to be called. Unfortunately, by the time Steph Lanehan established it was fake, they were already en route. At least it was Rachael Amara.' Anderson gave a bitter laugh. 'She's about the only one of the county team to appreciate the irony of a fake body hanging from a tree.'

'She'll be dining out on that story for months.' Minshull agreed, shrugging at Cora. 'You're welcome to do the same, of course.'

'It'll be my star turn at dinner parties,' she smiled in solidarity. But her mind was a brewing storm of frustration. First, the muddled voices from the objects found at the crime scene, and now the silence from this. The scratched-out eyes of the mannequin unnerved her, the secure cross of silver duct tape sealing its lips a silent threat in every sense.

It was a prop to achieve a sole aim: to intimidate Mark Lingham, the suspect still in custody in the cells not far from the interview rooms. Or was it intended to look that way – to plant the possibility of Lingham being framed for the Januarius Street murders?

'Could Mark Lingham have planted this before the murders?' she asked, voicing her thoughts.

Anderson turned back from the wall. 'What, strung it up as a decoy?'

'I mean, if you wanted to look like someone was threatening you, it's a heck of a tool.'

Anderson blew out a long breath. 'Do we think him capable of that kind of planning, though?'

'Is he capable of slitting the throats of four tall and fit young men and dragging them into that weird formation?' Cora countered. 'Because, despite the unlikeliness of that accusation, that's why he's here.'

'True, although the drugged champagne might have helped him.' Anderson cast a brief grin at Cora. 'Thinking like a copper there, Dr Lael. It suits you.'

'Maybe I'm spending too much time with you lot,' she returned, enjoying the uniform grins she received from Anderson and Minshull.

'Too much of a good thing, eh?' Anderson rubbed the two-day stubble on his chin. 'But supposing he did, who made the call? Who made sure we found it while Lingham was in custody?'

'An accomplice,' Minshull answered. 'We already suspected he didn't act alone – overpowering his friends, murdering them, arranging their bodies and the objects around them. Too much for one person to achieve in the time available.'

'Or he's telling the truth, and the real perpetrators are still at large,' Anderson countered. 'So the hanging body becomes a genuine threat to Lingham.'

Cora turned her back on the battered mannequin, facing the two detectives. Both theories were plausible, but both required several coincidences occurring at once. 'The threat only works if you tell Lingham, though.'

Minshull frowned. 'How do you mean?'

'Well, working on the theory that someone tipped you off so you could discover this: they must have believed that you would tell Lingham about the message and the fake body. If you chose to keep that to yourselves, the threat would be useless.'

'Which means we play into their hands if we tell him.' Minshull was beside Cora now, his stare passing between her and Anderson.

'And if we don't?'

'Then it's an elaborate waste of time,' Cora finished. She watched the weight of her words rest on her police colleagues.

'Can we trace the tip-off?' Anderson asked.

'Control are working with Tech, but it's unlikely,' Minshull said, turning back to the opened body bag. 'I just don't know why anyone would do this with such a considerable margin for error.'

'Why would anyone lure four men to their deaths in an empty retail unit?' Minshull replied. 'Or display their bodies as they were? None of this makes any logical sense.'

'Which makes everything a possibility.'

'True, Dr Lael.' Anderson looked as weary as he sounded. 'Right, let's get this back to Forensics and hope they can find something useful on it. No offence, Cora.'

'None taken,' she assured him.

But on the drive home, Cora allowed the sting of the words to take effect. Why hadn't she heard anything from the mannequin? Why were all her usual markers off with this case? And what use could she possibly be to the CID team with her ability so hampered?

THIRTY

ANDERSON

'The question now is how to proceed.'

Anderson let his gaze travel along the row of seated detectives at the briefing. He was fiercely proud of their determination to be here, despite all of them looking on the verge of collapse. It was past the official end of their shifts, but everyone had opted to work late in the hope of making headway with the case.

'We should tell Lingham.'

'No way, Dave.'

Wheeler frowned at Ellis. 'Why not? He's been leading us up the garden path for hours with his ever-changing tales. Maybe this'll shock some truth out of him.'

'It's what whoever did this wants,' Ellis argued. 'He'll clam up, and then where will we be?'

Minshull nodded. 'We can't risk that.'

'Dave's got a point, Rob,' Anderson returned, siding with his long-time colleague and friend. 'Lingham's led us a merry dance so far, and little of it is admissable evidence for the CPS. He's been prepared for what he's told us so far. He won't be prepared for this.'

'Unless he hung the fake body before he did anything else.'

The team turned to Bennett. It was what Cora had suggested earlier when she'd seen the mannequin. Was it really a viable theory?

'You think he did, Kate?'

'I think it conveniently fits his *sole survivor* narrative.'

183

'Really?' Ellis stared at his colleague.

'Really. If he wanted to prove someone had a vendetta against him, it would be a great way to keep the story going after the murders.'

'As long as the mannequin wasn't discovered before he was arrested. Which would be a significant risk. And as long as he could manage to climb up there to hang it by himself, which is unlikely.'

'I'm not saying either of those things aren't true. Come on, Drew, you've got to see how advantageous it would be for him. If he very publicly claims to have survived a multiple murder, and then receives a shocking warning supposedly from the killer themselves…'

Ellis gave a bitter laugh, the toll of discussing someone he'd known well evident in his response. 'So, before he lured four people to that unit, he drove out to Evernam Woods and hung a fake body with a message to himself?'

'It's possible.'

'Anything's possible,' Anderson agreed, although Bennett's theory was stretching the realms of possibility considerably. 'If he's responsible for planting that body, he'll be prepared for us to disclose it. It's a risk.'

'Unless he's talked himself in circles so much that he's dizzy,' Wheeler suggested.

'Meaning what, Dave?'

'Even if he did hang that dummy in the woods, he's clearly messed up with everything he's seen. He's panicking, grasping at straws, and we have permission to keep him longer than the initial twenty-four hours. Telling him now gives him all night to fret about it. His solicitor, too.'

Anderson sat forward. He'd seen that grim set of Wheeler's jaw before. It was a sign that he was ready to put aside his natural caution to focus on the task, and that only happened in the most serious of cases. 'Are you suggesting we disclose and then pull back?'

Wheeler nodded. '*Bedtime story* it, Guv. Even if he is prepared, his head's probably a mess after all the crap he's spouted.'

It made sense, and it could work. After the frustration of today's interview, Anderson was willing to give anything a try. But he needed everyone supporting the move, not least his DS. 'Rob?'

Minshull stared back for a moment. Anderson could almost see his brain working. Disclosing late in the day so that Lingham's solicitor would demand a recess to brief his client was a well-known trick, leaving Lingham to stew about it overnight. But it carried its own risk: Lingham could emerge with a counter story prepared or, worse, resort to no-commenting. On the other hand, it would play into his current story that he was an intended victim, suggesting that whoever had intended him harm was now intimidating him into silence.

'Let's try it,' Minshull said at last.

'Sarge...'

'I'm sorry, Drew. We need movement on this, and we're running out of time to keep Lingham in custody.' He glanced at his watch then turned to Anderson. 'Shall we do it now, Guv?'

Anderson gave a grim smile. 'No time like the present.'

–

'It's very late. Can't this wait until the morning?' Jasper Carmichael eyeballed Minshull and Anderson in the corridor outside the interview rooms.

'Time isn't on our side,' Anderson replied. 'If we wait for the morning, we'll only have a few hours until we have to charge or release.'

'And considering you have precious little on my client, you'll be doing the latter.'

Arrogant little shite, Anderson growled internally, behind a relaxed smile. 'Of course. Better to be safe than sorry, eh?'

It gave him no small amount of pleasure to see Lingham's legal representative on the back foot. Red-faced and weary, Carmichael threw his hands up and entered the interview room to await his client. Anderson winked at Minshull as he headed down to Sergeant Brinton's office in the custody suite. As victories went, it was a minnow. But that didn't mean Anderson couldn't enjoy it.

'We're ready for Mr Lingham in Interview 3, Tim,' he grinned, ducking his head around the door. 'His solicitor's already in.'

'Charming piece of work, eh?' Brinton chuckled.

'Oh, he's a joy. I'm thinking of hiring him for all my legal needs.'

Brinton picked up the phone receiver on his desk. 'Hi Zan, can we get Mark Lingham to Interview 3, please? Thanks.'

He gave a thumbs up. 'Have fun.'

Five minutes later, Lingham was installed beside his disgruntled solicitor, Anderson and Minshull taking their time to settle in the seats opposite. Lingham looked tired, but calmer than before. Was he confident in his plan, as Bennett and Dr Lael had suggested? Did he expect to be told that the mannequin had been found?

Carmichael made a show of inspecting his watch, an over-blown sigh accompanying it for extra effect. Minshull and Anderson remained stony-faced, waiting for his unconvincing pantomime to end. Then Minshull started the recording, noting the time, date and names of everyone present.

'Okay, Mr Lingham, there's just a couple of things we want to go over before we finish for the night. You said you met with Krish Bhattachama, Jack Markham known as Denzil, Otto Wragg and Tim Stapleforth at the unit at 62 Januarius Street on the morning of Monday 9th September.'

'Yes.'

'What time was that?'

'Sometime after nine, like I told you.'

Minshull turned the pages in his folder of notes, more for effect than genuine enquiry. 'Can you be more specific?' He looked up, expressionless.

Lingham drew a hand to his brow. 'I don't remember. Everything's foggy, you know, after the champagne.'

'About that,' Minshull said, pulling a sheet of paper from his notes. 'It turns out your suspicions about the champagne you drank were correct. Your blood test revealed traces of isopropyl alcohol. Rubbing alcohol, it's more commonly known as. It's used as a cleaning and disinfecting agent, mostly. Readily available to buy.'

He slid the paper to Carmichael and Lingham, who both leaned forward to inspect it.

'So, my client was telling the truth.' Carmichael stated flatly.

'About ingesting alcohol that had been tampered with, yes,' Minshull replied. 'According to our pathologist, Mr Lingham's four friends were rather more liberal with their drink. The rubbing alcohol would have rendered them helpless, allowing their murderer to act swiftly.'

'They were knocking it back,' Lingham offered, his reply surprisingly fast considering his earlier reticence to answer questions. 'I told them to take it easy, but they just kept passing the bottle between them, swigging straight from it.'

'But you didn't?' Minshull asked.

'Like I told you, I just had a small amount. I thought, you know, if Krish was meant to be driving us but drunk too much, I should hang fire in case I needed to drive instead.'

Minshull made notes.

Carmichael gave a cough and picked up the sheet of paper. 'In the light of these blood test results – and with the greatest of respect, DS Minshull – why is my client still here? He is clearly a victim, as were his unfortunate friends...'

'We still need to confirm aspects of Mr Lingham's story.' Anderson fixed Jasper Carmichael with a stare that could freeze molten steel. 'Unless you have any objection?'

The solicitor flushed but said no more.

Minshull looked back at Lingham. 'When you arrived, Mark, were the others all there?'

'Krish was there with the key. Denz was later than me. But not by much.'

'How much later would you say?'

'Five minutes? Ten? Something like that.'

'And Tim and Otto?'

'They arrived just after Denz.'

'And was there someone else present?'

Lingham stared back, blankly.

Minshull continued, his tone deliberately light. 'Someone who might have appeared to be a friend, but who betrayed you, Mr Bhattachama, Mr Wragg, Mr Markham and Mr Stapleforth? Someone who, ultimately, wished all five of you harm?'

Anderson kept his eyes on Lingham, who had started to inspect his clean hands again, as he had when he'd first been interviewed.

'I... no – no, it was just us.'

'Remind me, who brought the bottle of champagne?'

'Sorry?' His fingers rubbed harder at his palms. A tell, if ever Anderson saw one.

'The champagne you had a little of, but the others were—' Minshull read from his notes, '—*knocking it back... passing the bottle between them, swigging straight from it*. The champagne which you believe – and tests now support – the perpetrator drugged to render you and your friends unconscious.' He looked up. 'Correct?'

'Yes, yes, it is. I – sorry – I got confused.' Lingham glanced at his solicitor, who lifted a hand to signal all was well.

Anderson thought of the bombshell he and Minshull were ready to drop and leaned back in his chair. It was late, and he was in need of a pint, his wife and his bed, but he would stay as long as necessary to see this through.

'So, who brought the champagne?'

The fingers worked harder. 'I don't remember.'

'Who opened the bottle?'

'Not me. Probably Tim – champagne was his kind of drink. I can't open those bottles. The others mock me for it all the time...' His voice drifted a little as he rubbed his eyes. '*Mocked* me. They mocked me for it. I can't get used to talking about them in the past tense. It's such a shock...'

Undeterred by the performance, Minshull pressed on. 'You told us you poured the champagne?'

Chastened, Lingham nodded.

'Poured it into what?' Minshull asked.

'Sorry?'

'What did you pour it into? Did whoever brought the bottle bring glasses, too?'

'Cups. There were cups.'

'Plastic cups? Paper cups?'

'Yes. No, mugs. Sorry. There were mugs in the unit. Must have been left by the builders I saw in there last week.' Lingham relaxed a little, a nod from Carmichael, his reward.

'Not sure I would want to drink out of mugs left at a building site, but okay.' Minshull's smile was a barb to Lingham's celebration.

If Anderson had allowed himself to entertain the notion, he could almost have felt a fatherly pride at Minshull's remark. They might be worlds apart in their attitudes to most aspects of police life – and life in general – but in this one dig, he felt kinship with his DS.

'And nobody else was there? Nobody who could have slipped the isopropyl alcohol into the champagne?'

'My client has already stated there was nobody else there,' Carmichael snapped, another laboured look at his watch to emphasise his impatience. 'He told you he doesn't remember who brought the champagne.'

'I know that's what he said.' Minshull tapped his notes with his pen. 'But Mr Lingham also told us he suspected the champagne was drugged, and that his friends drank considerably greater amounts than he did. I'm trying to establish who might have been responsible for bringing drugged champagne to the meeting nobody else supposedly knew was taking place.'

Lingham glared back, but his defiance showed signs of decay. 'I don't know who it was or why they drugged the drink. I just know that I drank the champagne with the others, and the next thing I remember is waking up surrounded by their bodies.'

'So you have no idea who might have wanted to render you unconscious? Or to murder your friends?'

'I told you: no!'

Minshull rested his elbows either side of the open notes folder, fixing his stare on Lingham. 'Do you believe someone wished you harm, Mark?'

'Yes. Obviously.'

'Why do you think you were spared the fate of your friends?'

Anderson winced, but it was a great question.

The palm-rubbing began again, further undermining Lingham's defiance. 'I don't know.'

'Do you think whoever it was still wishes you harm?'

'What?'

'If you woke up alive but your friends didn't, that must mean something, mustn't it? They spared you for a reason. Could it be because you're more useful to them alive?'

While Lingham was processing this, Minshull continued, rounding down on the point, circling the ground, drawing the net closer. Watching him in action was a masterclass in patience and skill. Anderson admired the steady threads his DS wove around Lingham, ready to tighten them without warning.

'Here's what I think,' Minshull said. 'I think you know who did this. I think you understand why your friends died. And the fact of your survival terrifies you because the killer is still out there.'

'No... That's not possible...'

'Why not?'

'Because...' Nails joined the onslaught on his palms, angry red scratches appearing across the skin as Lingham's fingers worked away. 'Even if I suspected, I have no evidence... I can't remember... I was drugged, how could I know who did it?'

'I think you do know. And you're scared. And, judging by a recent development in our investigation, I can understand why.'

Minshull pulled two photos of the hanging mannequin from beneath his open page of notes, one showing the fake body in the woods from a distance, one close-up showing the scratched-out eyes, taped mouth and threatening message pinned to the dummy's chest.

Anderson nodded, and Minshull passed them across the table.

'We had an anonymous tip-off today about this. It was discovered in Evernam Woods with this message attached.'

A whimper sounded from Lingham, whose scratched palm flew to his mouth. Carmichael's eyes grew wide for a moment before his face reddened.

'You can't drop this on us! It needs to be properly disclosed!'

He slapped his hands over the photos, flipping the horrific images over. But it didn't matter: Lingham had seen them. And his spreading horror confirmed one of the possible theories the CID team had discussed: that whoever had hung it in Evernam Woods intended it as a threat to Mark Lingham.

'I demand time to discuss this with my client,' Carmichael snarled. 'We will need at least an hour in the morning before we talk to you again.'

'Of course. Our apologies,' Anderson replied, loving every moment of the solicitor's fury.

As a uniformed custody officer accompanied Lingham back to the cells and Carmichael stormed out of the building, Minshull and Anderson headed back towards the stairs.

'Nicely done, DS Minshull.'

'Cheers, Guv.'

'We'll brief the team quickly and call it a night. I don't know about you, but my bed's calling.'

'Amen to that. Might order a takeaway, too.'

'You should. I'd follow your lead if Ros would let me. But until the delectable Bengali Pearl in St Just offers a cholesterol-free menu, that's unlikely to happen.'

They reached the first-floor landing, Anderson holding open one of the double doors for Minshull to pass through.

'So, tomorrow?' Minshull asked.

Anderson grimaced. 'Tomorrow, we start looking for an accomplice. Someone who's still at large and needs Lingham to keep schtum.'

The purposeful disclosure of the hanging mannequin had served its purpose. There was no mistaking Lingham's response: the most truthful thing he'd given in Interview Room 3 since his arrival at Police HQ.

Fear. Abject, all-encompassing terror.

And now it would be Mark Lingham's uneasy cellmate all night.

THIRTY-ONE

CORA

Cora's heart was heavy as she drove home to Felixstowe. Her carefully masked concerns in front of Minshull and Anderson broke free as soon as she was behind the wheel. Now, the heavy traffic hampering her journey gave her too much time to dwell on all that had happened.

She faced a quandary: if she admitted her own frustrations to Minshull, might he doubt her again? The issue of the distant crying baby also remained, which so far nobody had been able to prove or disprove. Cora had half-hoped to hear the infant's cries attached to the mannequin's clothes, needing something more to support what she'd heard from the object sets and at the murder scene.

Nothing made sense yet: Minshull had been right about that. And the longer the disparate threads of evidence refused to be joined, the greater the chance the investigation would be undermined by weariness and doubt.

The media had predictably seized upon the lack of progress, despite the relatively short time since the discovery. They were already blaming it on a rural force unable, in their opinion, to cope with a major murder investigation.

Pressure was building on all sides, both externally and internally. Cora heard frustration and anger fizzing from every pile of papers, every waste bin and every dirty mug in the CID office sink. She saw it spilling from the body language of every detective and uniformed officer involved in the investigation: defeat, weariness, irritation, doubt.

Reaching her apartment on the cliffs above Felixstowe's North Beach, she called the only person who would immediately understand her predicament.

Dr Tris Noakes arrived at her door twenty minutes later, two packets of fish and chips in hand. He was a welcome sight in every sense.

'Thought you could do with a treat,' he announced, bounding into the apartment in that Tigger-ish way of his, heading straight for Cora's kitchen and pulling plates from the cupboard.

'You thought right,' Cora smiled as she closed the door and followed him. 'They smell so good.'

Her colleague beamed as he collected cutlery from the drawer. 'I didn't think you would've eaten much today.'

'Thanks, *Mum*.'

'Your mum loves me, and now you know why,' he returned.

Cora grinned back, wondering if she should regret introducing her mother to the ever-sunny Director of Educational Psychology a few weeks ago. Sheila Lael had been delighted with Tris – leading to many uncomfortable mentions of him since.

'Such a lovely man,' she'd cooed down the phone last week. 'Handsome, positive, clearly a fan of yours. I tell you, love, if Rob Minshull doesn't get his act together, Dr Tris would be a great catch!'

The memory made her wince as Tris ushered her to the table. At least Sheila hadn't expressed her opinion to Tris – yet. And with her mum currently away on a coach trip to Cornwall with her St Just WI friends, Cora was safe for the time being.

'*Eat*, Dr Lael. Or your mum will never forgive me.'

'You're enjoying this far too much,' she replied, smiling despite everything else playing on her mind. She had made the right decision calling Tris. It was good to have him here.

'Possibly. Also, I was worried about you. You sounded so upset when you called.' Tris blew on a chip. 'So, what's happening?'

194

'Someone hung a mannequin in Evernam Woods. They tipped off police so it would be found. It had a threat pinned to it meant for the man they currently have in custody.'

Tris stared back. 'Wow.'

'I know.'

'Connected to the murders?'

'Could be. That's partly why they called me in, to see if I could hear anything from it.' Before the inevitable question, she added, 'I couldn't. That's why I called you.'

Tris put down his fork. 'Okay, what's going on?'

Where to even start? 'Nothing's working, Tris. I couldn't separate the voices from the objects found around the body or at the crime scene. I got nothing from the mannequin, despite someone going to great lengths to make it. And then there's the baby...'

His eyes widened, involuntarily dropping to her stomach. 'Baby?'

'Not my baby, Tris!' His mistake broke the mood, a tiny moment of light relief.

'Oh. *Oh*. Sorry. It was just... That was a really daft thing to assume, sorry. I mean, you're not even seeing anyone right now... Not that it's any of my business...' Tris Noakes had many attractive attributes, the ferocity with which he could blush being one of the best. 'What baby are we talking about?'

The lighter moment passed, Cora's heart sinking as she began to explain. 'At the murder scene in Januarius Street, the only clear sounds I heard were frantic breathing around where the fifth set of objects without a body at their centre had been, and a crying baby.'

'Were the baby cries attached to a particular object or area?'

'No, that was the strange thing. It was as if they were following me around the room. No matter where I stood, the distance between the crying baby and the bodies remained the same. But it makes no sense: why would I hear a baby there? And why would it be moving?'

'You said the shop was currently unoccupied. Could the noise have been a throwback to its previous use?'

'It had been empty for almost a year, and before that, it was an ironmongers' shop. I've never sensed aural voices going back that far.'

'Could it have been a sound *like* a crying baby? An animal, perhaps? I know when the cats in my neighbourhood are fighting at night, they can sound very similar.'

'Maybe,' Cora replied. 'But why would a cat be there any more than a baby? The unit was supposed to be padlocked front and back – there was no way an animal could have got inside. And even if it had, it wouldn't have survived long without food and water.'

'Hm, good point.' Tris considered this while he ate. 'Ghost cat? *Paw*-ltergeist?'

'Helpful.'

He grinned like a cheeky kid. 'Made you smile, though.'

'It did. Thanks.' Cora speared a wedge of fried fish with her fork, surprised by how hungry she was. 'The problem is that if my ability isn't functioning as normal, what use can I be to Rob and Joel and the team? Right now, I feel like I'm just confusing matters.'

'Or maybe you haven't had a decent opportunity to tune into the voices yet. Can you inspect the objects again? Spend more time with them?'

'But that's my point: usually I don't need to revisit objects to hear voices. It should have happened by now. It's always immediate, all of the time.'

'A closer inspection might reveal more,' Tris argued. 'Away from the pressure of Rob breathing down your neck, waiting for answers. What you sense can be really subtle. What if there are further layers of sound waiting to be investigated?'

His words brought some comfort, although Cora's concern remained.

'But what if I've found the extent of my ability? What if it ceases to function? I've never pushed it as far as I have since working with the police. What if stretching it too far breaks it?'

'Don't think like that. You can't assume anything with this case. You've never used your ability in that kind of environment before, so give yourself a chance to navigate it properly.'

'You're right.' Cora nodded, the questions still nipping at her like summer midges.

'Besides, you *did* hear something. The panicked breaths and the baby's cries. Even if you don't understand why you heard those voices yet, it proves your ability is still functioning.' He screwed up the sheet of kitchen roll he'd been using as a napkin and threw it at her.

See what I mean? – the paper ball said in his voice as it landed on her empty plate.

She sent him a rueful smile. 'That still amuses you, doesn't it?'

'Always,' he grinned. 'And it proves my point.'

'Clever, Dr Noakes.'

Tris leaned back in his chair. 'Admit it: it's why you like me.'

Cora couldn't argue with that.

THIRTY-TWO

MINSHULL

He was lying. Of that, Minshull was convinced.

A night in the cells and several meetings with his solicitor had transformed Mark Lingham from a penitent confessor to a determined victim. The early hour wouldn't be helping, either, with Anderson requesting the team to start work at six a.m. to keep Lingham on the hop.

The disclosure of the mannequin's discovery had clearly unnerved him, as they'd hoped. But the longer they spoke to him, the more Minshull was convinced that Lingham's understanding of the truth was tenuous, to say the least.

'I didn't say that. I said whoever did this to me – to my friends – wanted to frame me for it.'

'So, who did this to you, Mr Lingham?'

'I told you: I don't know.'

'I think my client has more than sufficiently answered your question, DS Minshull.'

That was another thing: Jasper Carmichael had apparently googled 'how to be an effective legal counsel' overnight; his interjections frequent and his attitude bullish this morning. Yesterday, he had seemed happy to let his client dig a hole: today, he'd realised holes weren't the most desirable outcome. It was good for Lingham but annoying for Minshull and, judging by his superior's fierce foot-tapping beneath the interview desk, a red rag to an incandescent Caledonian bull for Anderson.

'I'm just trying to understand what happened,' Minshull replied, careful that none of his frustration was evident in his voice. While Anderson fidgeted and glared beside him, Minshull remained the picture of calm. Maybe the double-act would be effective. Precious else appeared to be...

'My client has told you what happened.'

'With respect, Mr Lingham has told us *some* of what happened. There are still areas he hasn't addressed. The purpose of this interview is to get as clear a picture as possible of what happened in the unit at 62 Januarius Street. If we are to find *the person responsible*,' he let his emphasis lean heavy on those three words, 'it's important we know everything.'

'Someone wants me blamed for this,' Lingham interjected, a dent appearing in the plastic cup in his hands as he gripped it. 'They want me sent down, or they'll kill me.'

The bedtime story had worked, then. Minshull pressed on. 'Why do you think someone would have hung that mannequin in Evernam Woods?'

'I told you: it's a warning.'

'Do you have any connection to the woods?'

'No.'

'Any links we should know about?'

'No.'

'Then why do you think the mannequin was left there? It seems strange to me, considering it was such a remote location. How would anyone know to look there?'

'Well, someone did. They told you about it.'

'Any idea why?'

'DS Minshull, what is this line of questioning trying to achieve? The mannequin was hung while my client was in custody here. It had his name attached to it. If you're implying that Mr Lingham had anything to do with that...'

'I'm implying that whoever hung it in Evernam Woods and tipped off police had a link to the four murders in the Januarius Street retail unit. Which means they had a link to your client. Which means he must have an idea of who that might be.'

Jasper Carmichael sat back in his seat, eyes trained on Minshull. 'I don't think you have anything. No evidence, no link, nothing to place my client anywhere near the site of the hanging mannequin.'

'We have *your client* running from an abandoned retail unit where four of his friends had their throats slashed, covered in blood and claiming it was his fault,' Anderson exploded. 'That's pretty compelling evidence.'

'I'm being set up!' Lingham whimpered.

'Then help me, Mark,' Minshull replied, his own frustration beginning to show. 'Who else knew of the plan to leave the country? Who else knew that you, Otto, Tim, Krish and Denz would be meeting in Januarius Street on Monday morning?'

'No one.'

'Could any of your friends have told someone? Let the details slip?'

'No. I told you. We kept it between ourselves. We couldn't risk anyone from our circles finding out.'

Our circles. A callous and dismissive way of describing wives and girlfriends, children, work colleagues and employees. How many lives had the plan – and the four murders – irrevocably altered?

'Could someone in your *circles* have uncovered the plan? Someone who stood to lose everything if you succeeded?'

'What? No.'

'You sound very certain of that.'

Lingham screwed up his features, the deep purple shadows beneath his eyes sharp against his pale skin. How much sleep had he managed last night? Minshull himself was feeling the effects of a broken night's rest, which culminated in him pacing his home at four a.m., unable to sleep.

'I told you: nobody else knew.'

In the seat beside Minshull, Anderson placed his hand flat on his notes, his signal that he wished to step in. Minshull was glad of it: with Lingham's continued denials, they were just going around in circles.

'Help us here, Mark,' he said, the merest hint of threat edging his words. 'If you're being framed for the murder of your friends, we want to apprehend the person – or persons – responsible.'

Was that a flinch? Lingham quickly regrouped, but his reaction to Anderson's mention of *persons* had been noticeable.

'Who might wish you harm?' Anderson continued. 'Who could gain from you being blamed for the deaths of your friends?'

'Someone who had a grudge against us. Someone who wanted us to suffer. *Me* to suffer...'

'Who holds a grudge against you, Mark?'

Lingham's eyes grew wide as if realising he'd said too much. 'Nobody.'

Carmichael glared at Anderson. 'We're getting into speculation here. I think we've established that my client doesn't know who must be doing this.'

'I'm trying to understand why your client would assume someone had a sufficient grudge against him to do this,' Anderson returned, switching his attention back to Lingham. 'What I don't understand is why the five of you chose such a strange location for your pre-flight celebration.'

'I told you: Krish had the key to the place.'

'So, could Krish or someone he knew have been in on the details? Is there anyone who might wish Krish harm?'

'I don't know! I've already told you: I'm being framed for the murder of my friends, and whoever did it is still out there. They want me to keep quiet and accept responsibility, so they hung that horrible thing in the woods. I didn't do this. They know it!'

–

'Pointless,' Anderson spat as they left the custody suite, Minshull almost breaking into a run to keep up with him. 'Why insist he was being framed and then lead us a merry dance to bloody nowhere?'

'He's bluffing,' Minshull replied. 'It's the only explanation.'

Had they been wrong to disclose the details of the mannequin last night? Minshull wasn't sure. Lingham had been spooked, but beyond that, where were they? No nearer to securing evidence and perilously close to the deadline for holding Lingham.

At the door to the stairs, Anderson stopped. 'We're stuffed, Rob. CPS won't give us murder if we can't conclusively prove Lingham premeditated the deaths.'

He was right, of course. But the fact spoken aloud by his superior made it a depressingly bleak prognosis. What did they have beyond a bottle of drugged champagne, four dead bodies and a hoax in Evernam Woods?

Wheeler raised a hand as Minshull and Anderson entered the CID office.

'Word, Guv?'

'In my office,' Anderson barked, striding past Wheeler's desk. 'Come with us, Rob.'

Wheeler and Minshull exchanged glances as they hurried in Anderson's wake.

'Okay, what is it?' the DI demanded as he flopped down in the chair behind his desk.

Minshull closed the door as Wheeler gingerly approached Anderson.

'I just had a call from Kirsty Morris in Forensics,' Wheeler replied. 'Results from the knife found at the scene in Januarius Street.'

Anderson brightened a little. 'Good. What's the verdict?'

'Lingham's prints are on the handle. Ninety-nine per cent match.'

'At last! I was beginning to think we were jinxed.'

Wheeler didn't smile. Nerves balled in Minshull's gut. Dave Wheeler without his usual sunny countenance was the darkest harbinger.

'There's more, I'm afraid, Guv. Alongside Lingham's prints, they also found four more sets.'

'You have got to be kidding me...'

Wheeler nodded. 'Significant matches for Krish Bhattachama, Otto Wragg, Tim Stapleforth and Denz Markham.'

Anderson's expletive reverberated around the walls of his office.

THIRTY-THREE

CORA

Teams of police support officers were still combing the undergrowth around the site where the hanging mannequin had been found, moving in carefully slow, methodical lines.

Cora watched their progression for a while, leaning against her car parked at the side of the road. In many ways, she felt like them: combing through a mass of brambles, ferns and tree roots to find anything that could make sense of this case.

Minshull didn't know she was here, although she'd brought her police pass with her, knowing that Anderson had given all the investigating teams word that Cora should always be allowed on site. She still wasn't sure why she had come: only that in the early hours of the morning, she had awoken with the strongest sense that she should be there.

Maybe the recent discovery, playing on her mind since she'd been asked to inspect the grisly object, had summoned her thoughts to this place. Whoever had strung up the mannequin meant it as a warning to Mark Lingham. Which meant that someone who had knowledge of what really happened in the Januarius Street unit had been here. Could they have unwittingly left a trail of audible evidence behind?

It was a theory worth pursuing. Especially as the voices from the objects and the bodies had been so frustratingly unhelpful.

Cora wasn't fully convinced she would join the teams on the search site, which was why she had arrived dressed in her running gear under a long green hoodie. She had no intention of getting in the way of her police colleagues. Their bowed heads as they searched spoke of so much more than concentration. Everyone was exhausted, the relentless twists and turns of this case sapping energy from them all. Knowing their moves were being scrutinised by an increasingly impatient and dogged media presence did nothing to alleviate the pressure, either.

Maybe she would just start with a run...

Her mind made up, she shrugged off her hoodie and threw it on the passenger seat of her car, reaching in for her water bottle. Locking the car, she set off at a gentle jog.

She followed the sandy path into the woods, pushing her way through the overgrown bracken and nettles that almost obscured it from view. The woodland felt cool, still dew-damp from sunrise, sounds muted here as if playing beneath a verdant green blanket, save for an occasional flurry of wings in the canopy above. The freshness of the morning and the satisfying stretch of her muscles were a reward. Were it not for the presence of police officers sweeping the area, this could easily be a pleasant pre-work run.

As she travelled the woodland path, Cora tried to picture someone dragging the prepared mannequin to the site where they had hung it. Had they worked alone? The mannequin itself was considerably large – the size of a full-grown adult – and padded to resemble a real body. Could one person have conceivably transported the mannequin here, or would the job have required another to help steer it through the winding, bracken- and bramble-tangled paths?

The footpath ahead of her twisted at sharp angles where it skirted the skeletal raised roots of trees, at times barely wide enough for one person to pass. Sharp, spiky, bramble branches caught Cora's leggings as she ran, as if the woods were trying to trap her. Could one person have navigated its barbs?

Which direction would they have come from? The road was her best guess. She'd consulted a map of the woodland area on her phone before driving out to the location, in order to get an idea of just how isolated they were. The only property anywhere near Evernam Woods was a development of holiday lodges about a mile from here on the other side of the woodland. It didn't make sense for anyone to lug that mannequin all the way through the woods when the road was so close to the chosen site.

Minshull had left Cora a voicemail message last night, informing her that he and Anderson had disclosed details of the hanging mannequin to Lingham before leaving Police HQ for the evening. It had arrived unnoticed while Cora and Tris were eating; by the time she remembered to take her phone off silent mode, it was too late to call Minshull back.

The 'bedtime story', he'd called it.

Cora was vaguely familiar with the term as a psychological trick. She hadn't been aware of its use within police circles, perhaps because it wasn't usual procedure. The practice of disclosing new, potentially damaging information late in the day and subsequently ending the interview before it could be discussed was designed to leave the person in custody to obsess about it in the cells overnight. The hope was that the enforced thinking time this afforded the suspect would scare information out of them next day.

As a psychologist, Cora understood why it could be both devastatingly effective and highly dangerous. Mind games as a form of control always carried consequences, not least that the fear they evoked could skew a person's recollections of events, rendering their resulting testimony unreliable.

Cora continued to run, aware of every sound around her. She pushed her mind beyond the brush of undergrowth, the creak of the tall trees in the strengthening breeze and the distant bursts of conversation drifting across the wood from the police team. If the path had been wider and less studded with potential trip hazards, she would have closed her eyes, but it wasn't possible here. Instead, she summoned her search for sound to the forefront of her mind, the passing swathes of green, brown and grey dappled with the pink–gold rays of early morning sunshine becoming little more than a kaleidoscopic light show to accompany the soundscape.

She reached a fork in the path, one side meandering off into a dark thicket of glossy-leaved wild rhododendrons towered over by arches of moss- and ivy-covered trees, the other turning sharply left and heading back towards the police team.

Which way now?

Judging by the first path, Cora thought it unlikely anyone would have come from that direction. It was far too overgrown, especially if they were dragging a mannequin.

The path back towards the police team and the road beyond was the more sensible option. A thud of disappointment registered within her. She'd hoped to hear some aural evidence of voices by now: the nearer she ran to the police cordon, the harder it would be to mute the layers of actual sound around her in order to listen deeper. But following the other route would be futile: judging by the way the thick greenery swallowed up the path, it was rarely, if ever, used.

She turned left, skirting a series of raised tree roots that criss-crossed the path. As she passed the last one, the toe of her running shoe caught the top of it, causing Cora to trip sideways into the thick bracken at the path's edge.

She stumbled a few steps into the undergrowth to stop herself tumbling over, her shoe connecting with something hard.

Get rid of it! screamed a voice at Cora's feet.

Every muscle in her body tensed, the scream reverberating as the voice repeated.

Get rid of it! Get rid of it!

Shocked, Cora steadied her breathing, focusing her mind on the sound. There was something else, hidden well behind the initial voice. If she could just reach past the shout... She closed her eyes, edging her mind beyond the yelling voice.

There – shrouded beneath the initial layer of sound, the sense of something else: a deeper burr of a response undulating between the shouted words.

The woodland, the search team and her own thoughts melted away as Cora pulled the secret voice layers to the front of her consciousness. With some difficulty, she took hold of the words she'd first heard, forcing down their volume, summoning the deeper, quieter strand of sound to the fore.

I'm…

I'm…

A thick ache appeared at the centre of Cora's brow as she picked away at the uneven edges of sound. It was as if the rest of the phrase she was pursuing was caked in thick mud, obscuring the shape of the words. Sensing the ground beneath her feet, seemingly far in the distance now as she focused on the sound realm, she began to crouch down, hoping the hidden voice might become clearer the nearer to the ground she could be. The shouted phrase continued its repetitious rage above her head as if Cora were beneath water, with the initial sound storming across its surface.

I'm d…

I'm doing…

I'm doing my…

The pain was increasing, Cora's own heartbeat joining its attempt to distract her from the slowly emerging second voice. With one determined effort, Cora pushed past them both, grasping for the rest of the phrase.

I'm doing my best.

With the final words came a sudden twist of pain at Cora's core. She gasped and clamped a hand to her abdomen.

Holding onto the uncovered voice and the physical pain, Cora retreated back through the layers of sound until she could open her eyes. Blinking away tears, the leaves and undergrowth of the woodland swam back into focus.

Gripping the second voice as tightly as she could with her mind, her hands began to tear back the scratchy bracken stems.

Suddenly, she saw it.

Half-hidden in the decaying leaf matter at the base of the bracken was a roll of dark green fabric, covered in what looked like faded golden stars. With the last of the vegetation moved away from it, the second voice – and its accompanying stab of pain – became clear.

Get rid of it!

I'm doing my best…

The second voice sounded physically hurt, as if it had been kicked. It felt like injustice, a physical ache registering where Cora imagined real injustice would.

'Officers! Over here! I've found something!' she called, waving her arms until one of the support officers raised their head.

As she waited for them to reach her, Cora turned her attention back to the object hidden in the undergrowth.

With its current position and the covering of leaves, it was impossible to tell how long it was, but it appeared to be rectangular and quite flat, the material following its contours. Cora knew better than to touch it, although the temptation was great, the hidden voices attached to it compelling her.

Did it have anything to do with the hanging mannequin? It was some distance away from the site where the mannequin had been hung – too far, it could be argued. But in this pristine woodland so noticeably free of litter or any other detritus, it seemed strange that an object so carefully wrapped and hidden in the undergrowth should be here.

The voices bore no resemblance to any of those Cora had managed to decipher from the belongings found alongside the Januarius Street bodies. Neither did they sound like the muffled tones she'd picked up on the mannequin. Yet the urgency of the first voice, coupled with the hurt and injustice of the second, suggested the object in the green star-covered cloth had a dark story to tell.

The thud of running feet sounded to her left, hollow on the dusty woodland floor. Cora looked up to see the Operational

Support Group unit leader hurrying towards her, flanked by two support officers. One of them carried a large clear plastic evidence bag, the other a DSLR camera ready to record the object in its location.

She showed her police pass to the lead officer, who offered a brief smile in return.

'Dr Lael, hi,' he said, offering his hand to Cora. 'I'm Sergeant Stu Latimer, unit leader of the OSG; these are my colleagues, PC Georgie Rowan and PC Naz Mattu. What do you have?'

'This.' Cora stood and stepped back to allow the support officers to see the object.

'Okay, great job. Give us five minutes to photograph it, and then we'll lift it.'

The officers worked as Cora moved a respectful distance away. Leaning against the broad trunk of a sycamore tree, she held the two voices lightly in her mind, as if they were still attached by a narrow thread to the object being photographed and catalogued amid the bracken.

When the officers finished, Latimer beckoned her over.

'Right, Dr Lael, we're ready to lift it. Do you want to observe as we open it?'

'Please.'

Cora looked on as Rowan and Mattu knelt either side of the wrapped object and, on Latimer's mark, gradually eased it out of its leaf-matter bed, lifting it slowly to meet the open evidence bag Latimer held. Once safely inside, he brought the bag over to her.

'Ready?' he asked Cora.

Cora nodded.

Gently, Latimer began to unwind the green, star-printed fabric within the open evidence bag, the clear plastic catching fragments of leaf and soil from the object as they fell. As the layers of material were peeled back, the two competing object voices grew in volume. Cora braced herself as the final layer was removed, dark-stained metal catching the morning sunlight as the loud scream burst free of her control.

Get rid of it!

THIRTY-FOUR

MINSHULL

'A knife. Found one hundred yards from the site where the mannequin was discovered in Evernam Woods.'

Minshull observed the weary CID team, gathered for a mid-morning briefing. At the side of the row of chairs, Cora stood beside Sergeant Stu Latimer, who had come from the operation in Evernam Woods to report to the team about the knife, wrapped in a green scarf printed with gold stars, half-buried in the undergrowth. Minshull still couldn't get his head around why Cora had even been at the site, considering she wasn't supposed to officially be there. What had made her visit Evernam Woods?

There was time to discuss that later: what she'd uncovered there may well change the course of the investigation – if it was found to be linked to the mannequin, or whoever had hung it there. It was a breakthrough: how significant it could be, he couldn't yet say.

'Do we know if it's even connected to the mannequin?' Bennett asked, immediately lifting an apologetic hand towards Cora. 'No offence, Dr Lael.'

Cora waved away the comment.

'We don't,' Minshull replied. 'But its proximity to the fake body and the fact that the woodland contains no other indication of human activity makes it significant.'

Ellis tapped his notebook with his pen. 'Did whoever strung that mannequin up intend this to be found?'

'Honestly, I don't think so. If Lingham's response is genuine, we have to consider the mannequin was a warning meant for him, to keep him quiet or compliant with a plan. We'll be talking to him about this in detail after the briefing.'

Wheeler frowned. 'But he could still have planted the mannequin himself before killing the others.'

It remained a valid point, for which Minshull had little reply. With Lingham's rapidly changing version of events, it was entirely possible he was lying about the mannequin's discovery.

'We can't rule it out, Dave. Although, given the remote nature of the mannequin's location and the time it was found, that looks unlikely. Also, the margin for error was wide: what if the mannequin hadn't been discovered until after Lingham was charged? He would have had to arrange for someone to tip us off at the precise moment he was changing his story in interview. That requires a level of planning and accuracy I'm not sure Mr Lingham has the capacity for.'

'But the bodies arranged in the way they were – the objects around them, too,' Wheeler countered, 'I'd say that's proof of a lot of planning.'

'If he did it alone,' Anderson cut in. 'Which I highly doubt.'

'Then we still have nothing.' Ellis' statement kicked the air from the room as Minshull watched the detectives' faces fall. At such a critical point in the investigation, this spelled danger: any setback compounded the effect of all that had gone before it. With the team so demoralised, so exhausted, mistakes could be easily made. He had to steer them away from that path.

'No – no, hang on,' he argued. 'We now have a second knife, with a good deal of blood along the blade and handle. That presents us with possibilities we haven't had before. And if it isn't related to the mannequin or the Januarius Street bodies, then we need to find out where it came from.'

'If I can just interject here?' The team turned to look at Sergeant Latimer. 'I would suggest that whoever hid the knife in the woodland never expected it to be found. So whether it pertains to the current murder investigation or not, it represents a significant slip-up on the part of those responsible. The mannequin was moved with careful planning – gloves to prevent traces of identifiable DNA, an alert sent from an unlisted number to ensure it was found. But the knife Dr Lael discovered had been left uncleaned, hastily wrapped in what looks like a scarf, which suggests that fingerprints, hair strands or skin cells might still be present, with none of the other precautions taken. That's an advantage for us.'

Minshull was glad of the OSG leader's interruption. 'Good point, Stu. And yes, we now have evidence that could prove vital.'

'How long before we get the results back?' Anderson asked.

'I've requested a fast-track, but you know how overstretched Forensics are,' Latimer replied. 'All we can do is hope they get to it quickly.'

It wasn't ideal, but not much in modern policing was. Minshull caught Anderson tapping his watch. 'Okay, that's all for now. Thanks everybody, I know it's a slog.'

'Slog is being kind to it,' Wheeler joked, his smile failing to meet his tired eyes. Minshull appreciated the effort, even if the end result was unconvincing.

As the CID team wheeled their chairs back to their desks, Minshull headed over to Cora and Latimer.

'Thanks so much, both.'

'There's more,' Latimer said, lowering his voice below the weary hum of the CID office.

'I heard two distinct voices,' Cora said. '*Very* distinct.'

'Not peripheral like you heard with the object groups?'

Cora shook her head. 'No. A loud voice yelling, *Get rid of it!* And a quieter one replying, *I'm doing my best.*'

'Male or female?'

'The shout was female,' Cora answered, the speed and conviction of her statement all the encouragement Minshull needed.

'And the other voice?'

'It was lower in tone, but beyond that, I couldn't tell.'

'Any sense of age?'

'Both sounded adult, definitely older than children. I can't be more specific than that.'

Minshull nodded, his mind turning over the new information. 'That's okay. It gives us a head start. Hopefully, Forensics can flesh that out.' He observed Cora and Latimer. 'So how come you were there?'

'It's our luck Dr Lael chose Evernam Woods for her morning run,' Latimer joked, with a wink.

'Around the police cordon?'

'What, Sarge? You mean you don't automatically head to crime scenes on your morning run?'

'Funnily enough, Stu, it isn't my first choice.'

Cora flushed a little. 'I needed to see the place where the mannequin had been hung. I hoped I might understand why the peripheral sound was lacking on it.'

'I see. How's the ankle?' Minshull asked.

She smiled. 'I'll live.'

A thought occurred to Minshull, and he voiced it without hesitation. 'Did you hear anything from the scarf that was wrapped around the knife?'

Cora's smile faded. Minshull was sad to see it go. 'No. But, at the moment Sergeant Latimer unwrapped it, I was focused on the knife itself. If I'd had more time to inspect the scarf – or study it away from the knife – it's possible I might have picked something up. Or else the screamed words and the whispered phrase might be attached to both if they were placed together.'

'Right. Perhaps when we get it back from Forensics, you could take a look?'

Her smile returned. 'Happy to.'

A cough from behind him made Minshull turn to see Anderson waiting, a pile of notes under his arm.

'I need to get going. We're due back in with Lingham.'

215

'Will you mention the knife?'

'Until we know it's connected, there's no point,' Minshull replied. 'We have the mannequin and the note directed at Lingham: for now, that has to be our main line of investigation. If he talks, that is. He was spooked first thing, and now his legal representative is getting jumpy. Are you both okay to get back?'

'Cora's kindly offered to give me a lift back to Evernam Woods,' Latimer replied.

'It's the least I could do for interrupting your search,' Cora replied. It was clear that she and Latimer had struck up a friendship thanks to the gruesome discovery.

Funny, Minshull mused, the strange things that connected you in this job.

He escorted them to the door of the CID office. As Latimer began to walk down the corridor to leave, Minshull touched Cora's arm. 'Call you later?'

She smiled up at him – a genuine smile, which seemed to brighten the space around them. 'Please.'

Taking a breath as he watched them leave, Minshull headed back into the CID office to collect his notes. It was going to be a very long morning.

THIRTY-FIVE

ELLIS

As the team worked around him, Ellis was aware of being under surveillance. Glances from Bennett, frowns quickly switched to smiles from Wheeler, the shadow of Anderson falling across his desk at regular intervals. Only Minshull hid his concern well, although Ellis knew he'd be watching, too. It was meant kindly – and he accepted it as such – but it didn't help when getting through every hour of the investigation was battle enough.

He was lucky to still be on the case, he reminded himself, as he had constantly since yesterday's briefing. If DCI Taylor had her way, he would have been seconded elsewhere, which would be worse than anything. At least in this office he could feel like he was contributing to the search for his friends' killer.

But it was a battle he felt completely unprepared for. Losing four friends and knowing exactly how they died dominated his thinking. Trying to remain professional and detached from it all was nigh on impossible.

Last night he'd told his parents what was happening. He hadn't planned to: he just blurted it out after dinner, when his mum's gentle question about how he was opened the floodgates. It had to happen somewhere, and Ellis was glad it had been in the large kitchen of the family farmhouse, away from the scrutiny of his colleagues.

He'd sobbed like a baby, any hope of remaining in control abandoned the moment his parents gathered him into their arms. It had been coming since he'd heard confirmation of the bodies' identities and had almost happened when he'd spoken to Kate Bennett out on the fire escape. He could be thankful he'd avoided it then, at least. His impulsive hugging of her at the end of their conversation had bothered him ever since.

He was moving a bunch of his stuff back to his childhood bedroom tonight at his mother's invitation. She was right: being away from Evernam was probably for the best until the investigation ended. He'd more or less reached that conclusion already; the offer from his mum the final element that made up his mind. It wouldn't be forever. Just until they could nail the bastard who stole his friends' lives.

Shaking off the sudden flood of anger that surged within him, Ellis turned his attention back to the screen. Despite Minshull delegating the task of checking Mark Lingham's social accounts elsewhere, Ellis had decided to conduct his own covert searches. So, while his colleagues did their best to retain a respectful distance from him, he took the opportunity to search Lingham's Facebook account.

He scrolled through posts featuring the cricket club, Lingham posing in his club whites with various jokey captions about the prowess of the team and his own bowling record. He was the fastest bowler they had, a fact both celebrated and resented in equal measure by his teammates. The accolade made Lingham cocky, gave him a bit of a god complex that did nothing for his image. He was acknowledged as a vital team member to his face and a puffed-up, egotistical dick behind his back.

Lingham had been worse in recent months. Ellis, like most of his mates, had put this down to the big birthday looming on the horizon for him. By all accounts, Lingham had resisted the usual mid-life crisis crap at forty, but fifty appeared to be bringing it out in him. Ellis had heard rumours of another woman he had on the go – although, knowing Lingham, that could just be boastful bullshit. He'd been splashing cash, though, noticeably more in recent months. When anyone asked where his sudden flush of funds had come from, he'd offered a vague reply about 'deals being done, hustles being hustled' in that completely naff way of his. Maybe his business had hit a boom period. It was true that many of the farms in the area were being parcelled up and sold off as residential properties for well-heeled Londoners fleeing the city. Suffolk was the latest desirable bolthole destination, according to the papers, and Lingham was only too happy to cash in on wealthy escapees seeking a rural idyll.

Ellis didn't buy it, though. There was something irritatingly sneaky about Lingham's attitude that suggested darker events at play. It had jarred with Ellis the last time he'd seen Lingham and the four dead men: last week in The Shire Horse, the group taking their now regular table away from the other lads, their heads bowed together as if they were plotting to take over the world.

The plan. To leave everything and everyone in their lives to start again abroad. Lingham had a wife and three young kids Ellis had seen sitting in the stand at the cricket club, supporting him. How could he even consider abandoning them?

And what of Otto, Krish, Tim and Denz? Had Lingham duped them all into meeting in Januarius Street? Was the plan his cover for bringing them together, out of sight of the village? Had he planned to double-cross them all along?

Lingham had been mouthing off in the pub, bragging about the latest cricket game where he reckoned his bowling had helped them snatch victory from the jaws of defeat. It probably had, to be fair, but the way Lingham was showboating made a mockery of team spirit. He'd shouted the pub a round of drinks – to celebrate *him*, he'd loudly declared – and while most of those who rushed to the bar thought him a total knob, none of them were likely to turn down a free pint. Ellis and his best friend Joe Allingham had ordered double whiskies just to spite him, to the considerable amusement of Roli, the landlord.

'Reckon you lads have the best idea,' he'd chuckled as he'd turned to the optics. 'Might have a triple myself!'

What had Lingham really been celebrating?

Photos of his picture-perfect home, gatherings in the immaculately landscaped large garden and holiday photos with his wife scrolled past, Ellis not paying much attention to them. A photo of his youngest kid – a boy they'd named Seb – was accompanied by a birth announcement that somehow made Lingham look like he'd done all the work.

> Delivered safely at 3.28 a.m. Seb Cody Lingham, 6 lb 1 oz.
> He's got my eyes! Everyone is completely in love with him.
> Totally exhausted after two days of waiting and hard work,
> but we got there in the end!

No mention of his wife, or whether he was proud of her – even if he didn't mean it, that should have been there.

Bristling, Ellis clicked on the post, revealing four more photos attached. One with the couple's other two children – a boy and a girl – leaning over the hospital bed and beaming at their new brother, one with Lingham's parents proudly holding the tiny baby, a photo of Lingham gazing adoringly at his son and a group shot showing the family taking the baby home from hospital.

Ellis was about to click away from the post when something caught his eye.

He leaned closer to the screen, clicking on the photo to enlarge it. Then his hand shot up in the air, as it always did when he found something.

'Sarge.'

Minshull was over immediately, as if he'd been waiting for a cue to move. 'What've you got?'

'Look at this.' Ellis stabbed the screen with his finger.

'What am I looking at?'

'What Isabel Lingham's wearing.' Ellis zoomed in on the image until Isabel Lingham's head and shoulders filled the screen. It was unmistakable – and if it was a coincidence, it was a hell of a one.

Draped artfully around Isabel Lingham's neck was a green chiffon scarf, a pattern of stars embroidered in gold thread catching the light.

Minshull's jaw dropped momentarily. Then he regrouped. 'Kate, when you visited Isabel Lingham, did she mention they had a baby?'

Bennett moved to Ellis' desk. 'She said she'd dropped their youngest off at the childminder's after she'd taken the eldest two to school. I didn't think she meant a baby, though.'

Minshull looked back at the image filling the screen. 'When was this taken?'

Ellis checked the date. 'Five months ago.'

'So still a baby... That works...'

What was he mumbling about? Ellis cast Bennett a look and she mirrored it back.

'I mean, it could be a coincidence,' Ellis offered. 'It might be scarf a hundred other people own.'

'It might. Or it could be a huge advantage you've just found for us. Even though I said not to look...' Minshull observed Ellis with a rueful grin. 'Right. I need to get the Guv in here, and we need a meeting.'

'You reckon we take this to Lingham?' Wheeler asked, joining the detectives around Ellis.

'I reckon we ask the question,' Minshull replied, heading for Anderson's office. 'Good work, Drew.'

THIRTY-SIX

MINSHULL

The decision was unanimous. The scarf was requested from Forensics and delivered to his desk within two hours. Finally, it felt as if the case was moving.

Minshull maintained a cautious approach in front of the team, but inside he was buzzing. It might be a coincidence, but if Isabel Lingham's scarf was the bloodied item in the evidence bag he now carried down to the custody suite, it could change everything.

Had Lingham taken it to conceal the real murder weapon? If he'd hidden it in Evernam Woods, so conveniently close to where the mannequin had been discovered, did that suggest his involvement in its hanging after all?

Or was Isabel Lingham more involved than anyone had realised?

Then there was the revelation about the baby. Given how Cora's ability had found the knife that could well prove a link between Lingham and the murders, her insistence that she'd heard a baby's cry attached to both the objects around the bodies and the crime scene itself could no longer be easily dismissed. If Isabel Lingham was involved with the stashing of the knife – and had a small baby – could this be the evidence they so urgently needed?

Anderson said nothing as he strode beside him, but Minshull could feel adrenaline fizzing off his superior. He had that look of grim determination Minshull always saw when cracks began to appear in an investigation: the *Mountain Lion*, the team called it. Like Anderson had the taste for battle and was preparing to attack…

They had briefed Jasper Carmichael that they needed Lingham to inspect an item found near the mannequin. As they'd hoped, the solicitor had taken this to mean they were investigating the threat against his client. All well and good, Minshull reasoned. Better to let Lingham think they were believing his intimidation story than suspect they were about to throw an accusation his way.

It helped that a label had been discovered on the scarf, identifying a local textile artist. When Bennett had contacted the artist via her website, she had confirmed she'd had ten such scarves produced to her own design. They had proved too costly to take into full production, so she'd sold the samples at a series of craft fairs across South Suffolk, one of which had been in the neighbouring village of St Martin. It was therefore possible that Isabel Lingham could have bought it there – or that it had been bought for her by somebody who lived nearby.

A gift from her husband, perhaps?

As evidence, it was far from conclusive, but it significantly narrowed down the list of potential owners. That in itself was a major step forward.

Lingham sat quietly beside Carmichael while Minshull started the recording, stating the names of those present, the time and the date. There had been so many versions of the suspect in this interview room since the day of his arrest: Minshull wondered which Mark Lingham they would encounter this time. Despite the hours he and Anderson had spent interviewing Lingham in this room, Minshull felt no closer to knowing who he was. So many lies, so many twists of the tale, each one further obscuring the truth.

But Lingham was scared now.

That might be the difference they needed.

'Okay, Mr Lingham, as I know your solicitor has explained to you, we have an item found near the site of the mannequin in Evernam Woods that we'd like you to take a look at, please.'

Lingham nodded.

Anderson produced the evidence bag and slid it across the interview desk. Lingham kept his hands wedged between his knees as he leaned forward, Carmichael placing his notes on the interview desk to take a closer look.

Minshull watched Lingham's face. At first he betrayed no sign of any emotion, but as his brief turned over the bag and the line of blood-tarnished gold embroidery caught the light, he drew back, eyes filled with horror.

'Do you recognise it?' Minshull asked.

'I... no... no comment,' Lingham blustered.

It was exactly what Minshull had hoped for. He didn't have to look at Anderson to know he shared his response.

The question now was *why* he recognised it.

Was it damning evidence or an indictment on his wife?

'It's quite an unusual design,' Minshull continued, careful to keep his tone light. 'We contacted the small business that made it. The owner is local and said only ten of these scarves were ever made and sold. Which is good news for us because it means our search for whoever it belongs to becomes significantly smaller.'

Lingham was practically leaning as far away from the scarf as he could now.

'You seem distressed, Mark,' Anderson cut in. 'Is there a reason why?'

'No... I mean, it was in the woods. I don't want to think about the person who wanted to attack me.'

Minshull nodded, waiting for more. When none came, he pushed a little.

'And that worries you?'

'It *scares* me.'

'Why?'

'Because they want to frame me for this… this…' He swallowed hard, a light sheen of sweat visible on his brow.

'Do you recognise the scarf, Mark?'

Lingham stared at Minshull, his mouth dropping open.

'Because if you do, it could help us identify the person who threatened you.' Minshull took his time, his tone as gentle as he could make it. With a breakthrough so close, it would be too easy to let the rising adrenaline push everything forward too quickly, destroying their advantage. He'd made that mistake in interviews before. He didn't intend to repeat it today. 'It's our belief that this is linked to the hanging mannequin.'

'What makes you think that?' Carmichael asked, pausing from his note-taking and leaning in for a better view of the evidence bag.

Minshull caught Anderson's slight nod in the periphery of his vision. 'Because of what the scarf was wrapped around.'

Now Lingham visibly paled.

Anderson turned a page in his file, pulling a photograph from a plastic pocket. The bloodstained knife was stark against its regulation white background, ruled reference marks charting its length and width. As Anderson slid it across the interview desk, horror filled Lingham's stare.

'Do you recognise this knife?'

Lingham didn't reply.

'If you recognise the scarf, my guess is that this is familiar to you, also.'

Lingham remained silent, but everything about him screamed panic. The working jaw, the defined dip of his Adam's apple as he swallowed against a dry throat, the whitening knuckles where his hands folded together on the interview desk.

Minshull wondered what Cora would hear if she were here. She'd told him of the soundscapes she sensed around the emotional fingerprint voices – three-dimensional landscapes stretching away from the subconscious words, encompassing breaths, echoes and peripheral sounds. He didn't understand how it was possible, but he'd learned to trust what she told him. Questioning it had only revealed his own lack of trust.

What sounds might surround Lingham as he sat there, terrified?

'I think my client needs a break,' Carmichael said, breaking the silence. His concern was impossible to miss. Had the disclosure unnerved the solicitor, too?

A break was unfortunate; the respite it would afford Lingham a potential threat to the momentum they'd built. But it might solidify the evidence in his mind and force him to reveal the truth — or some of it, at least. Minshull would take either. They were close now. He could feel it prickling his skin.

'If you think it would be beneficial…'

'My *wife*!' Lingham rushed, the accusation cutting through the stale air of the interview room like the blade in the photograph.

For a moment, the only sound between them was the gentle hum of the recording machine.

Then Minshull spoke. 'Mr Lingham?'

'The scarf belongs to my wife.'

Anderson displayed none of the shock Minshull felt, his expression granite-hard, eyes laser-focused on Lingham. 'And the knife?'

'She wants me dead. I never wanted to be involved, but she…' He swallowed again, his voice cracking when he continued. 'She did this. She made the threat. It has to be Isabel. She's the reason I'm here.'

THIRTY-SEVEN

BENNETT

Minshull drove like a man possessed.

In the passenger seat, Bennett held on, trying to get her head around it all. She'd offered to drive, but Minshull hadn't listened. Now, as they sped towards Isabel Lingham's home, she wished she'd insisted.

He and Anderson had burst into the CID office like a fire was hot on their heels, Anderson barking to Bennett to accompany Minshull. *For continuity*, he'd insisted, although Bennett suspected it was more to do with having another woman present when Minshull delivered the devastating news.

She hadn't anticipated returning to the Lingham's worryingly perfect home so soon and never for the reason they were speeding towards it now. Added to this, things had hardly been friendly between her and Isabel Lingham when she'd left last time. She'd hoped PC Janey March might still be at the house, but Minshull said she'd been stood down as FLO once it was clear Mark Lingham was alive and in custody.

Bennett had a feeling Janey's legendary calmness would have been useful today.

'Do you think Mark Lingham is lying?' she dared to ask, as Minshull glared at the country road ahead.

'If he is, he's got a nerve,' Minshull growled back. 'Who accuses their wife of murder?'

'Maybe they're both involved.'

'At this point, I'd believe anything.' He slowed the pool car a little as they approached a crossroads. 'Did you get the sense that Isabel Lingham was hiding anything when you visited?'

'You mean apart from the fact that her youngest child was a baby?' Bennett sighed. 'No. She seemed like a woman terrified that her husband had killed himself.'

There had been the sudden change in her when she'd learned her husband had been arrested, though. It bothered Bennett: could that have been the truth breaking through the scared wife routine or a natural instinct to protect her partner?

Was Isabel Lingham an accomplice, an aggressor or an innocent accused?

'Maybe she's lying. Maybe they both are.'

Bennett's spine was pushed back into the passenger seat as Minshull hit the accelerator again.

'Sarge, calm down.'

'We need to get to her before Carmichael warns her.'

'That won't happen. The Guv's keeping him busy.'

'The Guv can't watch him indefinitely. Carmichael's the family solicitor: of course he's going to warn her the first chance he gets.'

'It's a conflict of interest, Sarge. He represented Mark Lingham first in this investigation, he has to honour that...' She gripped the seat as Minshull threw the car around a sharp left-hand bend. 'Slow down, *please*.'

'There's no time. We're almost out of our extra hours with Lingham, so we need concrete reasons to charge now. We have to get there, fast.'

'We don't need to get killed in the process, Sarge... *Minsh!* Slow down!'

Her use of his name seemed to pull Minshull back from the fog clouding his judgement. To Bennett's considerable relief, the car slowed.

'I just want...'

'I know. We'll get there.'

He glanced at her, then back at the road.

In the passenger seat, Bennett forced a breath. This wasn't going to be easy.

As they reached the drive of the Lingham's house, the red brake lights of the white Land Rover Evoque parked by the door fired into life, a white reversing light following.

Swearing loudly, Minshull swung the car across the back of the vehicle, skidding wheels sending up a sharp shower of gravel. The driver's door flew open, a furious Isabel Lingham jumping out. Minshull flung open his door and headed towards her, Bennett scrabbling to exit the car and reach his side in time.

'What *the hell* do you think you're doing?' Isabel yelled, the high wail of an infant from inside the Evoque rising in reply. 'Great, now he's awake. You could have hit my car. You could have injured my baby.'

'We need to talk to you,' Minshull replied, more forcefully than Bennett would have done. 'I'm DS Rob Minshull, and this is DC Kate Ben...'

'I know who she is,' Isabel snapped back. 'And you're the one holding my husband for a crime he didn't commit!'

'Which is why we need to talk to you, Mrs Lingham. We should go inside.'

'We'll do no such thing. I have to take my son out.'

'That will have to wait.'

'Excuse me?'

The wails from the back seat swelled in volume. Bennett caught the slightest wince from Minshull as he stood his ground. 'A serious allegation has been made against you, Mrs Lingham...'

'What the...? What allegation?'

'This really would be better if we talked inside,' Bennett urged.

'This is my home! You can't just come storming over here, making demands!'

Was it Bennett's imagination, or did Isabel Lingham's angry stare betray a flash of fear?

'I insist,' Minshull cut back. 'Fetch your son from the car and return to your house with us, please.'

Isabel remained where she was for a breathless moment, then wrestled the back door open, pulling a baby carrier from the seat. Incensed, the baby kicked his legs, tiny hands forming furious fists as his cries intensified. Slamming the car door shut, Isabel turned her back on Bennett and Minshull, storming along the lavender-lined path to the light oak front door, the detectives close on her heels.

'Do you have any idea how long it took me to get him to sleep?' she spat over her shoulder as she bustled down the hall to the main living area. 'I'll never get him down now. I hope you're ready for the shit that's going to rain down on the pair of you when my solicitor hears of this...'

'Your solicitor Jasper Carmichael, who is currently representing your husband in custody on suspicion of murder?' Minshull's reply was cold as steel.

'He represents me, too,' she shot back. 'As you'll both discover. Now say what you've come to say and then get the hell out of my home.'

'An accusation has been made against you, Mrs Lingham. By your husband.'

It was as if all oxygen was immediately sucked from the room, the pressure registering strongly in the centre of Bennett's chest. Isabel Lingham stared back, her baby clutched to her. When she spoke, her voice was a strained whisper.

'*What?*'

Bennett softened her tone as much as she could. 'Sit down, Mrs Lingham. Please.'

When Isabel didn't move, Bennett risked a step towards her, gently taking her elbow to steer her to one of the sofas. She sank slowly, her stare never leaving Minshull. Only when she was fully seated did Minshull move to sit on the armchair opposite. Bennett sat beside Isabel Lingham, the oppressive air in the room finally beginning to ease.

Bennett would wait for Minshull to speak, she decided, but the moment his frustration threatened to block the conversation, she would intervene. She couldn't trust him to be wholly objective in this state. Sometimes knowing your place with superiors was understanding where you could safely overstep the mark. It had been a long time since she'd seen Minshull so angry: this, combined with the exhaustion battering the whole team, could completely derail the progress of the investigation.

She may not agree with Minshull on everything – or his sudden promotion over her that still stung – but Bennett knew he would watch her back if the tables were turned. Part of having his back was preventing him making an emotionally-driven decision he would later regret.

Right now, they needed Isabel Lingham to talk.

No amount of personal anger was worth jeopardising that.

'An item of clothing was found close to the site of a hanging mannequin in Evernam Woods that carried a threat to your husband,' Minshull began – and Bennett was relieved to hear the coolness returned to his voice. 'We presented this piece of clothing to your husband in interview, and he identified it as yours.'

He pulled a photograph of the scarf from his pocket, handing it to her. Isabel juggled the still crying baby to her other shoulder, taking the photo from Minshull.

'Do you recognise this scarf?'

Isabel Lingham frowned at the image, a visible hardness setting in her expression. 'Yes.'

'Is it yours?'

'It could be.'

'Do you have your scarf here?'

'No.'

'Then could this be yours?'

'It could be. I can't say for sure.'

'Mrs Lingham, your husband told us this is your scarf. He's made allegations against you – serious allegations. We need to

231

talk with you in detail about them. Is there someone who can look after your son — and collect your other children from school?'

Shocked, Isabel turned to Bennett. 'Why can't we talk here?'

'It really would be best to do this at the station.'

'No.'

'Mrs Lingham...'

'No!' She faced Minshull. 'You can't just come here and demand this! What has Mark said? And why are you taking it seriously, given the state he's in? He's distraught, scared. Jasper said the doctor had been called out to him...'

'To test his blood, not because he required medical assistance,' Minshull replied, his voice thankfully kept low despite the wailing infant and his increasingly distressed mother. 'He's accused you of being involved. We have to take that seriously.'

'Involved in what?'

'We can discuss that at the station in Ipswich,' Bennett repeated. 'Now, who can we call to take care of your children?'

Fear filled Isabel Lingham's expression, her eyes glassy. 'My mother... I can call her... I... Why has he said that? Why would Mark say that?'

Minshull made to speak, but Bennett jumped in. 'We'll get to the bottom of this, okay? Let's call your mum and sort that first.' She locked eyes with the bewildered woman, a note of doubt sounding in her mind as Isabel nodded blankly along with her.

Did she know this was coming?

Was she hiding her guilt?

If so, where was the defiance Bennett had witnessed in her before? Where was her fury?

—

An hour later, Bennett and Minshull took their seats opposite Isabel Lingham and duty solicitor Abby Garstang in Interview Room 1. Jasper Carmichael had furiously insisted he should be allowed to represent Mrs Lingham, but Anderson had dismissed this in no uncertain terms:

'Your client is facing a murder charge. Focus on that.'

Bennett shared a brief smile with the duty solicitor. She was one of the best ones Bennett had met: fair, calm in the face of whatever she encountered, a steady presence appreciated by both the officers conducting the interview and those facing questions. Anderson had briefed Garstang on the accusations made against Lingham's wife as Bennett and Minshull were bringing Isabel Lingham into Police HQ. And he had been able to share a surprise notification from the Forensics team that set everyone's nerves on edge.

They were as ready as they could be.

'I need to show you the item in question,' Minshull began, passing the green scarf in its evidence bag to Isabel and the solicitor. 'Do you recognise this scarf?'

Isabel recoiled from the bloodstains as her husband had done before. 'I can't say if this one is mine.'

'But it matches the one you own?'

'Yes. But the *blood*...'

'We'll come to that in a moment. Can you think of any reason why your scarf would have been found in Evernam Woods, two days after four men you knew were found dead in a unit in Januarius Street, Evernam?'

'No! I don't know anything about it.' Isabel's stare narrowed. 'What does this have to do with the – *thing* – hanging in the woods?'

Bennett saw Minshull's eyes flick to her for a moment. He produced a second photograph from his file on the desk. Bennett braced, knowing what was coming.

'The scarf was wrapped around this and half-buried in the undergrowth, yards from the hanging dummy.'

Isabel's fingers trembled as they accepted the picture. 'No. That's not possible.'

Minshull glanced at Bennett, the time to reveal the bomb-shell from Forensics now upon them. Bennett steadied her breath, her toes bunched tight in her work boots as she held her composure.

'When we arrived, I received this message from our Forensics team.' He passed a sheet of paper to Abby Garstang, who shared it with her client. 'The knife has now been tested, and traces of blood from the four men discovered dead in Januarius Street on Monday have been found on it.'

'No...'

'The same blood was also found on the scarf. The bloodstains you can see here.' Minshull pointed to the blood patches with the end of his pen. 'From the amount and the placing of the bloodstains, we believe this scarf – your scarf, perhaps – was wrapped around the knife shortly after it had been used to fatally wound the four men.'

'No!' Isabel shook her head wildly. 'I said *no*.'

'In interview, we presented both the scarf and the photograph of the knife to your husband,' Minshull stated. 'And he said the scarf was yours.'

'It... can't be...'

Minshull remained calm, all traces of emotion stripped from his voice. Was he bracing himself as much as Bennett was?

'Mrs Lingham, your husband has accused you of wanting to end his life. Of hanging the mannequin in Evernam Woods and, by insinuation, of anonymously alerting us to its location. With what we now know about the blood on the knife, this is tantamount to him accusing you of murder...'

'No...'

'...Of killing Tim Stapleforth, Krish Bhattachama, Jack 'Denzil' Markham and Otto Wragg and coercing Mark into being part of the plan. He said it was your idea. He said you wanted him dead.'

'No. *No*, he's lying!'

The momentum seemed to shift in the small interview room, the necessity of what needed to follow sweeping all possibility of niceties away. Bennett gritted her teeth as Minshull launched the questions.

'Where were you on the morning of Monday 9th September, between the hours of 8:50 a.m. and 10:15 a.m?'

'What? I was taking my *children* to school. My *baby* to the childminder. People saw me. Everyone saw me...'

'But you called the police from your mobile at 9:10 a.m. to report your husband missing and a suicide note you found in your house. Which meant you had left the school and the childminder at that point and had sufficient time to return home, find the note and realise Mark was missing. *If* you were calling from your home...'

'I called from my mobile, standing in my kitchen. I'd found the note there, and I was panicking. My mobile was in my hand...'

'Or you could have called from the unit in Januarius Street.'

'No!'

'The suicide note could have been a decoy.'

'What are you suggesting? That I faked my husband's suicide note to cover for a murder?'

'Your house is on the edge of the village. By car, it would only take a few minutes to return here from Januarius Street.'

'And I left my husband there, did I? In the state you told me he'd been found? I can't believe I'm hearing this.' She leaned towards Minshull and Bennett, the fight suddenly returned. 'I was in total shock. I thought Mark was dead, or lying injured somewhere. I couldn't think of anything else. I called the police because I was terrified he'd taken his own life.'

Minshull didn't flinch, didn't even blink. 'Your husband has suggested you were involved in the murder of his friends and that you somehow coerced him into taking part. And then, after he had been arrested, he asserts that you hid the murder weapon in Evernam Woods and erected the hanging mannequin as a threat to stop him telling the truth about what happened.'

'He's lying!'

'A mannequin found yards away from *this* knife—' Minshull tapped the photograph of the weapon, '—found hidden in the undergrowth, wrapped in *this* scarf.'

'Mark had my scarf!' Isabel Lingham shouted, silencing Minshull and causing Bennett to start in her chair. 'He had it in his car! I haven't seen it for months since he...' She broke off, her incandescent glare trained on her hands on the desk.

'Since he what?'

Isabel gave a soulless laugh. 'Since he started having an affair.'

'An affair? Who with?'

'I should have known he'd lie... The absolute *bastard*...'

Minshull persisted. 'Mrs Lingham? Who was Mark having an affair with?'

'It was so bloody obvious. I suspected it for a while – things he told me that didn't feel right, his caginess whenever I asked where he'd been. So I followed them, late one night, while my mother was babysitting the children. Found them together at the edge of Evernam Woods, sitting in his car. She had my scarf around her neck, and he had his arm around her...'

'Mrs Lingham, who did you see with your husband?'

Slowly, Isabel Lingham raised her head. The hate that contorted her features when they came into view sent a shiver of ice coursing through Bennett.

'Mattie Kemp.'

THIRTY-EIGHT

CORA

'We're going to talk about happy and sad, okay, Mabel?'

Cora smiled at the little girl curled up against her mum on the faded yellow sofa in the small counselling room just down the corridor from the Educational Psychology Unit's offices. Usually, she saw the children she worked with in their own homes or in schools if there was a suitable room for the sessions. But where neither was possible, the counselling room offered a quiet alternative.

Five-year-old Mabel Yates had been referred to the unit by her school in Evernam after losing her father and grandfather within days. She had become withdrawn, unwilling to speak in lessons and could quickly become overwhelmed if her class-mates became too noisy or excited. She was a sweetheart: shy but imaginative, with a glossy bob of dark hair and big, soulful blue eyes. She clutched a purple toy bunny that had clearly been loved for many of her five years, watching Cora from the safety of her mum's side.

'Remember when you came last time, I asked you to bring me some things that mean happy and sad to you? Have you got them?'

Mabel nodded, and her mum handed her a child's tote bag printed with a cute tiger and toucan sharing a tea party. With some encouragement, Mabel left her mum and joined Cora by the small table in the centre of the counselling room, where a bright orange squashy beanbag served as a chair. Settling herself down with her bunny beside her, she held the bag on her lap.

'Okay, great. Can you find something in your bag that makes you feel happy?'

The little girl brightened and rummaged around in the bag, pulling out a tiny, crocheted teddy with a frayed green ribbon bow.

'Who's this?' Cora asked, her question gentle and softly spoken.

'Trevor,' Mabel replied.

It was unexpected surprises like this that made Cora love her job. It was good to be back today, returning to her regular routine after the upheaval and uncertainty of recent days. And while the thought of the murder investigation and her colleagues in CID was never far from her mind, Cora relished the opportunity to focus on her young charge – and the comically named bear. She shared a grin with Mabel's mum, Tina.

He listens to me – the girl's unspoken voice declared from the teddy.

Noting it, Cora moved on. 'Brilliant. Now, can you show me something that makes you feel sad?'

The blue eyes mooned up at Cora, mouth set in a firm line as Mabel returned to her bag. From within its jolly printed interior, she brought out a roll of fabric tied with a red ribbon. 'Grandad's tie,' she stated, her voice wavering.

I want him to come back – said her subconscious voice.

Cora's heart ached for her. 'Thank you for showing it to me. Pop it back safe in your bag now. How about another happy thing?'

Mabel nodded and reached into her bag again. She rummaged for a while, half-lifting items and dismissing them. Tina offered an apologetic smile.

'We had a whole pile of things Mabel wanted to bring. It took a while to narrow it down to this little lot.'

'That's okay. It's good she's engaged with the task.'

Cora waited for Mabel to make her decision. After much consideration, Mabel lifted a smooth, round, painted pebble, setting it carefully on the table.

My magic treasure – her voice said.

They all deserve what's coming – whispered another.

Cora's breath caught in her throat.

The second speaker wasn't Mabel's subconscious voice. It was older, its rhythm stilted, the vowels stretched as though strained through gritted teeth.

It shouldn't be there – not attached to an object that brought a five-year-old joy.

Keeping her smile in place, Cora pushed quickly through the initial layer of sound – Mabel's delighted voice – to the hissed whisper behind it. Had the pebble been discovered recently? The voice sounded fresh, its shape and insistence sharp and clear. Most original object voices faded over time, still discernible but less present.

They all deserve what's coming – the whisper insisted, over and over.

Aware of both child and mother watching her, Cora edged her mind around the accusing whisper, attempting to gauge the shape of the air around it. The three-dimensional soundscape was patchy due to the lack of time she could invest in exploring it, but there was something else, in the farthest reaches of the sound, something just out of reach...

When Cora had tried to explain this realm of sound to Tris, the best way she could describe the sensation was as a 'sound shadow' – shapeless at first, too far away to sufficiently discern its identity and origin, but strong enough to summon her attention, calling her deeper into the distant soundscape.

Knowing she was hurrying now, she pushed her mind further.

There.

A sound slowly began to take shape.

A baby's cry.

It was removed from the whispered voice, as if in an upstairs room away from the unseen speaker. But once Cora latched onto the sound, it was unmistakable. Finding what she'd come for, she retreated quickly through the layers of sound to return to the counselling room.

'It's really pretty,' she managed, forcing her dizzied attention back onto the painted pebble. It bore a beautiful painting of a pirate's treasure chest, with the spilling treasure inside picked out in sparkling gold paint. 'Did you paint it?'

The young girl's nose wrinkled. 'No, silly! I found it! It's my special magic treasure.'

'We found it in the village,' Tina explained. 'They're all over the place. Nobody knows who paints them, but it's become a regular thing to find them on the streets this year, in flower beds, on shop window ledges, everywhere. Mabel found that one about a week ago on the way home from school. I'd had to collect her early because...'

'...I was sad,' Mabel finished matter-of-factly. 'Mrs Jenkins said I had to stop crying, and I couldn't stop, so Mum came and got me.'

Mind racing, Cora turned to Tina. 'Can you remember where you found it?'

'Januarius Street, I think.' Tina's smile faded. 'Awful, when you think what's just happened there.'

'I heard,' Cora replied, the sudden mention of the case she was involved with a turn she hadn't expected. Could the pebble be related to what had happened in the empty shop unit? Or was it a complete coincidence?

There was something else, too: a frustrating sense of familiarity about the whisper. Its tone, the formation of the words, and the emphasis points that echoed another recent example she had encountered...

She couldn't think about that now: Mabel and Tina deserved her undivided attention. Setting her questions aside, Cora continued the session as planned.

But by the time she waved off the child and her mother at the door of the Educational Psychology unit, it was all she could think of.

She had heard that whispered voice before.

Of this, she was certain.

And suddenly, she knew where...

THIRTY-NINE

MINSHULL

'Mattie Kemp.'

Minshull pinned the photo of the young woman onto the whiteboard.

'So far, she's been mentioned by Otto Wragg's wife Susannah, his mother-in-law, Sheila Kersey and now Isabel Lingham.'

'Don't forget Gaby Hall,' Wheeler interjected. 'The young lady who gave us Mattie Kemp's number.'

'Of course – thanks, Dave.' Minshull wrote the new name on the list beside Mattie Kemp's photograph. 'Did Gaby mention the name of her brother?'

'Lukas.'

Minshull added that name, too. 'Strange that her name has come up so often. And the accusation from Mrs Lingham suggests Mattie might know more about what happened than she's told us. We need to ask Lingham about her. It's odd she hasn't made an appearance in his many versions of events, given what his wife's just told us.'

'Perhaps he's protecting her. Because of all the village gossip,' Ellis offered, frowning when Bennett scoffed beside him. 'Maybe he isn't having an affair. Just because everyone else thinks he is.'

'Chances are he is,' Bennett snapped back, her gaze instantly dropping to the notebook in her lap.

Minshull raised a hand to signal calm to Ellis, who had visibly slumped after realising his misjudged words. Of course Bennett couldn't be objective when infidelity played a role in the case. Neither could Ellis, come to that, given his deep connection to the murdered men. None of the team could claim complete objectivity: all had their own biases and misconceptions. The skill lay in bypassing those in favour of solid, irrefutable facts.

'We need to work out what the connections really are. Does Mattie Kemp know more about the Januarius Street murders than she's revealed to us thus far? Or is she merely the 'good listener' that Gaby Hall stated her to be?'

'Being good at listening doesn't make you a murderer,' Ellis replied. 'Or guilty of having an affair.'

'Neither does it excuse you interfering in other people's lives,' Wheeler added. 'Seems to me like Ms Kemp made it her business to be in the know. Maybe she thought listening to Lingham would give her bargaining power in the village when so many other people seemed to be against her.'

'She could be blackmailing him?' Minshull wondered aloud.

'If she is, could that be a motive for murder?' Bennett asked. 'Or framing Lingham for it?'

The CID office hushed as the team considered this.

Minshull stared at the new photo on the board, his gaze passing across the gathered images and notes collected there. It didn't fit anywhere obvious yet. If Mattie Kemp was involved, surely Lingham would have mentioned her before he implicated his wife? But the re-emergence of her name was a coincidence he couldn't ignore.

What was the link?

'We need to talk to her,' he said. 'Today.'

'Do we bring her in, Sarge?'

'I think so, Dave. I don't want to risk calling first and spooking her. I think we need to visit and insist she accompanies us back here for interview.'

'But has she done anything wrong?'

What was Ellis trying to prove? Minshull waited patiently for more, but it irritated him. Did Ellis want someone from the village to be innocent so much that he was projecting his fast-fading hopes onto Mattie Kemp?

When Ellis didn't elaborate, Minshull decided to push him.

'Do you know Mattie Kemp, Drew?'

'What? No – no, not really...' Evasive, for certain. Of all the team, Minshull could count on Drew for direct eye contact: now his stubborn gaze drifted somewhere over Minshull's left shoulder.

'Meaning yes, you do.'

'Sarge.'

'How well do you know her?'

Ellis knew he was beaten. His head dropping, he mumbled, 'She's in the pub most days I'm there.'

Minshull raised an eyebrow as the team turned to their colleague. 'How is that possible if she has a young kid?'

Ellis sank further in his seat. 'Lukas Hall looks after the little 'un in the evenings.'

'So you know Lukas Hall, too? Right, briefing over. Thanks, everyone. Drew – with me, please. *Now.*' Minshull held his irritation in check long enough to watch the others slope back to their desks before he led Ellis out of the CID office, striding down the corridor to the meeting room at the end.

Once Ellis was inside, Minshull shut the door with more force than was necessary.

'Sit,' he snapped.

Ellis complied, for a moment looking like the young kid he had been when he'd joined the team.

'I asked you before...'

'Sarge.'

'I asked if you knew Mattie Kemp. You've seen her name brought up. You knew Kate and I had visited her as part of the investigation. You had every opportunity...'

'I know, Sarge. I'm sorry.'

'You want to thank your lucky stars the Guv hasn't got wind of this.'

He was laying it on thick, he knew, and if Anderson could witness this conversation, he would be the first to pull Minshull back. But they were in the thick of the biggest murder case South Suffolk CID had dealt with in living memory, under the ever-critical eye of press, the local community and their superiors desperate to avoid another PR disaster. They couldn't afford for anyone in the team to be given an easy ride – no matter what they had personally lost.

Ellis stared at his feet.

'I know this is tough, Drew. No, actually, I don't know what you're going through. But I need you onside. The Guv and I have stuck our necks out for you to stay involved, directly contradicting DCI Taylor's wishes. I need you to be honest about what you know. You're our local eyes and ears in Evernam: it's why you're still on this case. If there are rumours, I want to know them, however unfounded you might consider them to be. If you've observed anything about anyone in the village, you have to share it.'

'Sarge. It's just...'

Minshull stared back. '*Just?*'

'I haven't done this before. Been personally connected. I don't know how to do it, what to say. And everyone tiptoeing around me isn't helping, either.' His voice cracked, but the Drew Ellis who raised his head and met Minshull's stare was defiant, angry. 'I didn't know Mattie was going to be so involved. I didn't know you wanted details about her or Lukas Hall.'

Weariness edged Minshull's irritation aside. The DC had a point. And Minshull's frustration was far from wholly caused by his colleague. Relenting, he sat down.

'I didn't know we'd need to know it either,' he admitted. 'We're flying blind with this. I hate it, but it's true. And mate, I don't want to make this shitty situation any shittier for you, but we need you and your observations. You leave the rest of us for dust with every investigation: you see things we all miss. I need

245

you to lead on local knowledge from here on in. Find us the advantage we're missing. Please.'

Ellis took a breath that shook his shoulders on the exhale. 'She came to the pub to brazen it out, I reckon. All those side-eyes and not-so-hidden whispers around her. Most people would have stayed away. Mattie never did.'

'Did you ever see her talk with anyone?'

Ellis shrugged. 'Roli chatted to her sometimes – he's the landlord. I heard she was doing some paperwork for him. Occasional stuff, not all the time. He had her back in there, and that kept everyone in line. You don't cross Roli if you want to keep drinking in his pub.'

'And Lukas Hall?'

The DC frowned. 'Seems a good kid. Shy, though. I see him cycling around the village most days. The kind of kid you could easily miss, you know? Not like most of the teenagers in the village who want you to know they're there.'

Minshull nodded, relieved Ellis was talking freely now. 'Did you hear anyone talking about Lukas babysitting for Mattie Kemp? What was the deal with that?'

'Mattie told Roli that Lukas wants to train to be a nursery nurse. There was some delay in him getting on a college course for it, so she offered him the opportunity to learn on the job.'

'How long has that been going on?'

Ellis shrugged. 'A few months, maybe? Her baby can't be more than seven months old. But I think she's spent time with Lukas for years, since he was little. His sister said that to Dave – I didn't know before, Sarge, I swear.'

'That's okay, thanks.' Minshull replied. 'What about Mattie? Do you know her personally?'

'A bit. I've chatted with her sometimes if the boys were late arriving. She's usually in the pub from seven p.m. till nine p.m. If I'm early, I sometimes buy her a half and have a natter.'

'The father of her kid not around?'

Ellis snorted. 'He didn't hang around after the night he got her up the duff, apparently.' He quickly corrected himself. 'I mean, after the night she conceived...'

'I get it, cheers,' Minshull said, waving away his explanation. 'Any word in the village regarding his identity?'

The eye roll this was met with told Minshull all he needed to know.

'Okay, let me rephrase: did anyone know the father?'

'I don't think so. Didn't stop the vultures speculating. All my mates were in the frame for it at some point or other, despite several of them being married. Otto, obviously – that's what led to all the crap with him and his missus. Denz, too, at one point.'

'And Lingham?'

Ellis stared back. 'I reckon he was the most likely.'

'Why?'

'Because he was seeing a lot of her. Like Isabel said. They weren't very careful about meeting up. Most people in the village had seen them together – you can imagine how Sheila Kersey and her mob loved that.'

'Did you ever ask Lingham outright about it?'

'No.' Ellis gave Minshull a look as if he'd just asked if little green men lived on the moon.

'Why not?'

'You don't ask stuff like that, Sarge. I mean, you might with your mates, but not with us.'

'And what about when Lingham and the others started meeting in their huddle?' Minshull asked, remembering the comment Ellis had made before when he'd been asked about Lingham and the four dead men. 'Did you think they might have been talking about Mattie then?'

Ellis considered the question. 'They didn't include her, I know that. Blanked her the moment they got together. I thought she'd fallen out with Lingham, and he was maybe bad-mouthing her like the rest of the village. They haven't openly talked for a good couple of months.'

'Could that be a smokescreen for an affair if too many people were noticing them together?'

'It would get the village rumour mill grinding over something else,' Ellis agreed.

It took them no further regarding the case, but Minshull felt they had established more about the affair rumours, at least. And Ellis had been given an opportunity to share what he knew. In hindsight, Minshull should have afforded him this opportunity at the start of the investigation, but it was easy to be wise after the event. Navigating his colleague's obvious grief was a skill Minshull was still acquiring.

'I'm glad we talked, Drew,' he said, checking his watch. 'But we should get back.'

The CID office was quieter than it had been for days when they returned. Anderson had come back from a meeting with DCI Taylor, the rest of the team ducking to avoid becoming targets for his resulting bad mood. Seeing Minshull march Ellis out wouldn't have helped, either.

As Ellis returned to his desk, Minshull's mobile rang. Ducking back out of the office he answered the call.

'Cora, hi.'

'I need to talk with you.'

Her urgency bristled his skin. 'Okay, shoot.'

'Not on the phone. I'm in the car park. Can you come down?'

'You're a member of the team now, you know.' He smiled against the phone, a stubborn note of concern refusing to leave. 'You have an access pass and everything.'

'I heard the voice again,' she rushed. 'The one I heard attached to the knife.'

Minshull's humour dissolved. 'Which voice?'

'The whispered one. And something else, distant from it. A baby's cry.'

Minshull was already racing for the stairs before Cora finished speaking.

FORTY

CORA

In amongst the parked cars, Cora paced, her eyes never leaving the fire escape and the ramp that rose to it. It was where Minshull would emerge, but after her breathless dash across Ipswich to get here, every second she waited felt heavy as lead.

It might be a mistake.

A coincidence.

But the memory of the sharp whisper, dripping with hate, enclosed around the brightly painted pebble in Mabel Yates' small hand was too insistent to ignore.

So, too, were the links between voice and circumstance.

The pebble had been found in Evernam, close to the location where four men were brutally murdered. It carried the same voice as the knife in the green scarf that had also borne the blood of the murder victims, but where that voice had been seeped in hurt and injustice, the words attached to the pebble were emboldened by indignation. It was as if the invisible whisperer was giving voice to everything they had wanted to say when the knife was hidden.

Cora couldn't ignore this.

She stared at the stubbornly closed fire door across the concrete of the car park, made glassy by the recent rain.

Come on!

Maybe she should have used her pass, as Minshull had instructed, going straight to CID instead of skulking here. She had every right to be in that office now. She was part of the team – everyone acknowledged it, so different from her first case with South Suffolk CID. What still held her back?

Old habits took time to die, it seemed. Years of hiding her ability away, of living on the peripheries of life and expecting suspicion, distrust and mockery from those who encountered her, had left scars that might never heal. Would she always default to those fears when she felt vulnerable?

She glared back at the fire escape.

Where was he?

Cora edged out from the side of her car, adrift. Now she was here, doubt chipped away at her resolve. What if she was mistaken? The last thing the investigation needed was another blind alley.

Tris had assured her going to Police HQ was the right course of action, when she'd hurried back to their office after Mabel and Tina Yates had departed.

'If you heard it, Rob needs to know. Go – I can hold the fort here.'

'But what if I'm wrong?'

Tris had sent her a withering look in reply. 'You know you're not: you're fizzing with it. I've seen when you're uncertain, and you don't look that way now. *Go.*'

The fire escape door slammed open, Minshull appearing at the top of the ramp, scanning the rows of parked cars for her. Cora raised her hand and headed for him, rainwater splashing over her shoes with her hurried steps. They met near the row of pool cars and liveried patrol cars, Minshull breathless when he reached her.

'Tell me,' he rushed.

'A child I'm working with brought a painted pebble to our counselling session,' Cora replied, the edges of her own words ragged from her race to Minshull's side. 'The whispered voice I heard from the knife and the scarf was attached to it, along with the little girl's own. She found the pebble in Evernam.'

'Where in Evernam?'

'Her mother said Januarius Street.'

Minshull stared back. 'And you think it's the same voice?'

'I know it is.' As she said it, Cora's resolve set firm. 'Whoever painted this also held the knife they buried in Evernam Woods.'

Minshull took a few paces away, his breath still uneven. Cora waited. It felt as if they were on a precipice, staring into a dark, fathomless void. If he didn't believe her now...

'I've seen painted pebbles.' The statement appeared to take him by surprise as much as it did Cora. 'In the house of someone who's just been accused of...' He turned back. 'It's very new. I have no way of knowing if it's true. But that accusation and what you've heard, taken together... How certain are you?'

Cora ignored her knee-jerk reaction that Minshull's question represented doubt. He had to check – especially if it aligned with a potential lead. 'As certain as I can be.'

Minshull nodded, looking up at the slate grey sky as if a way forward were written in the rain-heavy clouds. 'Could you tell if the voice was male or female?'

'No,' she replied, wishing now she'd been able to discern more from the hissed breath. 'But it was an adult rather than a child. I'm sure of it. The vocabulary, the structure of the phrase – it indicates someone older than a kid. And it had the same characteristics as the voice from the knife.'

'But you heard two voices then. How did this voice compare to the other?'

Cora cast her mind back to the memory of the paired voices hissing up from the bloodied knife. 'This one sounded subordinate to the other when it came from the knife.'

'Like the other was in charge?'

'Exactly.'

'Two people responsible, one taking charge. So if Lingham planned this with Mattie...' Seeing her frown, Minshull raised a hand as much to slow his speeding train of thought as to apologise to Cora. 'Sorry... Mark Lingham has implicated his wife in the murders, claiming she coerced him into killing his friends. Then his wife accused him of having an affair with a local woman, Mattie Kemp. Her name has also been mentioned by several people we've talked to, and it appears she has links with at least three of the murder victims. I'm going to talk to her now to ask about Lingham's wife's claims.'

'You think he and Mattie murdered his friends together?'

'At this point I have no idea.' Minshull rubbed the back of his neck, weariness evident in every movement. 'But there are too many coincidences now for none of them to be linked. You said you heard a baby crying, too? With this pebble?'

'Yes.' Cora hugged her arms around her body, a sudden chill raising goosebumps across her flesh. 'Far more distant than with the bodies in the unit. As if it was coming from a room above.'

'Like a bedroom above a living room?'

'Just like that.'

'Mattie has a baby, around seven months old.' Minshull gave an ironic laugh. 'Isabel Lingham has a five-month-old son. And one of the victims had a four-month-old, too – the last thing Kris Bhattachama's wife said to him was to *drop dead*. I've never had so many implicated infants to contend with.'

Cora watched him carefully. 'I don't know why a baby would be present in any of the object soundscapes, but I'm not mistaken.'

'I never said you were.'

'I know.'

They observed one another.

'Thanks for telling me,' Minshull said, moving closer, as if their conversation might be overheard by the rain-splattered cars around them. 'We're bringing Mattie in. Immediately. Listen, if I can take a pebble from her home when we visit her, could you listen to it for me?'

'Of course. Can you do that?'

Minshull's smile was a long-missed friend. 'Officially, no. If Joel found out...'

'It isn't admissible as evidence anyway,' Cora said, a sudden thought illuminating the tangle of contingencies in her mind. 'Don't bring it back here.'

Minshull's eyes narrowed. 'Why?'

'If you're found with it and you haven't used a warrant to seize Mattie's belongings, it could derail the case.' She was thinking on her feet now, her pulse kicking up a gear as a plan formed. 'So drop it for me.'

'Drop it? Where?'

'Outside Mattie's house. Is there a front garden, a driveway?'

'There's a patch of grass at the front that might pass as a garden.'

'I can work with that.' The idea firmed and solidified. 'Drop it as you leave, in the grass. I'll park my car nearby and wait until you've gone. Then I'll check the pebble. If I hear the same voice from it, I'll text you.'

He was watching her intently now, waiting for more.

'It doesn't help the investigation, Rob. I know that. But it could help *you*.'

Minshull's head shook, a slow smile spreading. 'Bloody hell, Cora, Joel was right: you're thinking like a copper now.'

It was a risk. A huge risk, if anyone worked out what they were doing. But if what Cora heard confirmed or disproved the suspicion against Mattie Kemp, it might afford Minshull the edge he so desperately desired.

'Let's do it,' Minshull agreed, determination setting his jaw. 'We're leaving imminently. I'll text you the address when I go back inside. Head there now and park somewhere out of sight. When you see us leave her house, that's your cue.'

'Okay.'

'Be careful.' His hand rested lightly on Cora's arm. 'Try not to be seen.'

Cora didn't flinch, the presence of Minshull's warmth on her skin feeling like a signal of faith she'd sometimes doubted he was capable of. 'I'll stay out of sight.'

'Thank you. Good luck.'

'You too. Go – I'll wait for your text.'

With a final fleeting smile, Minshull was gone, racing back across the car park to the ramp and the fire escape. When the door slammed behind him, Cora turned away, walking back to her car.

It had been a split-second assertion, bypassing her usual cautiousness.

But the memory of the voice – and the evidence Minshull had shared – compelled her. There was no time for caution now.

Seconds later, Minshull's message arrived.

Like an athlete at the sound of the starting pistol, Cora ran to her car.

FORTY-ONE

MINSHULL

The drive to Evernam was beset by obstacles. Temporary traffic lights that appeared to breed over every one of Ipswich's roads without warning, a delivery lorry reversing across their lane, and a broken-down bus partially blocking the main road out of the town compounded by unusually heavy traffic from rubber-necking drivers.

Bursts of the siren from the top of the pool car helped as they neared each obstruction. But the journey still took far more time than Minshull wanted. Asking Bennett to take the wheel this time – not trusting himself to drive with sufficient care and attention given the slamming of his heart in his chest – Minshull stewed in the passenger seat.

'Ten minutes,' Bennett said to the road ahead.

'Okay.' Minshull appreciated the gesture. In his head he was rehearsing the scene once they arrived at Mattie Kemp's house. Present the information as they had done with Isabel Lingham, insist she accompany them back to Ipswich, carefully slip one of the painted pebbles from the collection on the mantelpiece or the set of wicker drawers into his pocket while Bennett was accompanying Kemp out, shut the front door and discreetly drop the pebble into the overgrown grass at the front of the house.

It was simple enough to achieve – Mattie Kemp would no doubt protest being taken to Ipswich, thus keeping Bennett's attention on her and not on what Minshull was doing – but it still felt risky. Minshull decided he would scope out the living room the moment they entered, selecting the pebble closest to where he stood.

It was a hell of a lot of trouble to go to for the sake of a hunch. But if Cora heard the same voice from that pebble as she'd heard from the hidden knife and the painted stone belonging to the child, it would prove that Mattie was responsible for all of them. Prove it to Minshull, at any rate – the evidence would be inadmissible as far as the CPS was concerned.

But it would be enough for him.

He would know Mattie was lying if she claimed to have nothing to do with the murders. And it would change how he spoke to her in the interview. That might unlock something he'd otherwise miss.

Besides, Cora Lael was certain.

He'd seen it before, so knew he couldn't ignore it. If Cora heard the voice, she *heard* it. Minshull knew better now than to challenge it. She'd been right every time before. He had to believe she was right this time.

Isabel Lingham claimed to have seen Mattie and Lingham together, proof, she said, of her husband's affair. Mattie had to answer for that. Was she aware that Isabel Lingham had rumbled them? Was Lingham now pointing the finger at his wife as punishment for discovering his and Mattie's affair?

It was a twisted mess of accusation and insinuation, and truth had been lost between the strands. It was time to unravel it all.

'Do you think they did this together?' Bennett asked, voicing Minshull's thoughts. 'Lingham and Kemp?'

'I think she may have helped him,' he replied, hedging his bets. 'If he wanted to stitch up his friends he would have needed help to set it up. I can't see him being the mastermind behind it all. He's too flighty, too emotionally unsteady, to have planned it all alone.'

Bennett kept her eyes on the road. 'And there's the baby.'

Shocked by the mention, Minshull looked at his colleague. Did she know about what Cora had heard from the crime scene and the objects within it? 'What do you mean?'

'What if it's Lingham's kid after all? What if he planned to leave Evernam with Mattie and their baby after killing the others?'

Relieved by her explanation, Minshull pulled his focus back to the reason for their visit. 'But why kill them?'

Bennett shrugged. 'Money. He said they were supposed to be leaving the country together and investing in a property. Lingham's in property: what if the money the victims thought they were investing in the Gran Canaria development was going straight into Lingham's pocket instead?'

It was a good point.

If Lingham had been handling the purchase of the property in the Canary Islands, it was conceivable he could have acted as an agent for the other four men. If they'd paid him without question, the money could be moved anywhere from the point of collection. Lingham could have been building a considerable nest egg for his planned escape with Mattie Kemp.

But was that motive enough to murder four men?

If they were dead, they couldn't chase him, Minshull reasoned. And if what Lingham had stated in interview was true – a big *if*, judging by his past form – the four men had met in the unit under the illusion they were about to board a flight together to leave the country. It would have been necessary to contain them in some way to prevent them scuppering Lingham's plan.

It just seemed... *messy*. Unnecessary in its cruelty, in its brutality.

What kind of mind could conclude that a quadruple execution was the best course of action?

The edge of Mattie Kemp's estate loomed ahead, its tired houses and cracked roads resignedly allowing them in. As they turned into Knightsway Road, Minshull caught sight of the dark blue bonnet of Cora's car, obscured from view by a large Leylandii tree that shadowed the pavement, the straggling brown branches at its base arcing thickly over her hiding place.

She was ready.

The plan was in motion.

Forcing a breath, Minshull turned back to the view ahead. 'Are you clear on how we're doing this?' he asked Bennett, the question aimed as much at himself as at his colleague.

'I'll follow your lead,' she affirmed. 'Nod me in if you need me to take over.'

'Okay. We have to bring her in: that's the objective. No matter what, we will leave Knightsway Road with Mattie Kemp in this car. Clear?'

'Yes, Sarge.'

Kemp's house was unchanged from Minshull's first visit, the soil in the hanging basket a little drier, perhaps, but the first drops of rain hitting the pool car's windows and roof suggested that might soon be rectified. A BMX-style bike was resting against the pebble-dashed wall at the side of the house. Minshull couldn't recall it being there last time, but he hadn't been looking for it then.

Get in, get the pebble, bring Mattie Kemp out…

The plan ran on repeat in his head, an insistent, rhythmic mantra, as they left the pool car and made for the house. At the doorstep, he nodded at Bennett and knocked on the door.

Footsteps sounded, followed by a chain being drawn back. But the face that met them when the door opened wasn't Mattie Kemp's.

'Yes?' the young man asked, scrutinising Minshull and Bennett with pale grey eyes.

'Can we speak to Mattie Kemp, please?' Minshull asked.

'Why?'

'We visited a couple of days ago – she knows us. I'm Detective Sergeant Rob Minshull from South Suffolk Police. And this is my colleague, Detective Constable Kate Bennett. It really is important we speak to her.'

The young man frowned as his gaze passed between them. 'Okay. Come in.'

Minshull and Bennett followed him into the hall, past the kitchen, into the small sitting room they'd visited before. The moment they entered, Minshull scanned the room, spotting a pile of painted pebbles on an IKEA bookcase near the door. Now he was looking for them, he saw the pebbles everywhere. There seemed to be more than before, but was that because he was seeking them out?

'Mattie, these coppers want to talk to you,' the young man stated, observing Minshull and Bennett as if he expected them to make a sudden move he needed to block.

From the small sofa nearest the fireplace, Mattie Kemp looked up. A sleeping baby was cradled in her left arm, an empty feeding bottle tucked against the cushion beside her.

'It's okay, Lukas,' she soothed, her voice soft over the grizzles of her baby. 'I've met them before.'

Lukas Hall.

Minshull should have known.

Bennett didn't flinch beside him. Had she worked it out already?

'How can I help, DS Minshull?' Mattie asked. She indicated for him to sit, but Minshull remained standing.

'Information has come to light regarding your link to several persons of interest to us,' Minshull said, his words sounding horribly stilted despite following his training. 'We need to discuss these in detail with you.'

'Okay.'

'It has to happen at the station in Ipswich.'

Mattie stared back. 'Am I under arrest?'

'No.' Minshull kept his voice at the same volume as hers, conscious of the baby asleep between them. 'But we need to ask you questions that are recorded, for the benefit of us both.'

'She can't leave Amelie,' Lukas said, the volume of his voice causing Mattie to shush him. 'She can't,' he said, almost in a whisper. 'You'll have to do it here.'

'I really must insist…'

'She's done nothing wrong!'

'Lukas, *hush*. We can discuss this.'

The young man refused to be pacified. 'If she goes, I go too.'

'I'll be okay.'

'You'll be alone! You can't be alone!'

The baby stirred, a grumble causing all in the room to stop talking. When her breathing resumed a steady pattern, Mattie turned to Lukas.

'Could you get me a glass of water, Lukie?'

'But the coppers…'

'I need it now. Please?'

The young man scrutinised her smile for a moment, as if reading more from it than Minshull could. Then he harrumphed and shouldered past Bennett to leave the room.

Mattie gave a long, slow blink and looked back at Minshull. 'Sorry. He doesn't do well with people he doesn't know.'

'Is he your brother?' Minshull asked, knowing he wasn't.

'No — we're not related. But I've known the family since Lukas was tiny. He spends a lot of time here, which I don't mind. Especially since this one arrived.' She stroked her baby's head with the tips of her fingers.

'Is there someone you can call to look after your baby?' Bennett asked, as gently as she'd spoken to Isabel Lingham.

Mattie shook her head. 'There isn't anyone to call. I'm estranged from my family, have been for years.'

'I'm sorry to hear that.'

'It is what it is.' Mattie offered Bennett a brief smile. 'Lukas can look after her if it's just for a few hours. I'll tell him to call his sister if it's any longer. She'll come and help.'

'Okay, if you would. It's imperative we talk to you now.'

'Can I ask why?'

'It's related to Otto Wragg,' Minshull replied, deciding against mentioning Lingham. If they had been involved in an affair — and if Lingham could possibly be the father of her baby

260

– Minshull didn't want to give her any reason to refuse their questions before they could take her to Police HQ.

Was Mattie Kemp aware of Isabel Lingham's accusations against her?

Given what Ellis had said about Kemp braving the local pub most evenings, Minshull couldn't imagine her crumbling in the face of a fresh accusation of infidelity. But what if she'd been an accessory to murder? Would she provide Lingham with the alibi he needed?

There had been many theories in the CID office about Mattie Kemp, many possible lives for the young woman seated with her baby. Now he was in the room with her, Minshull couldn't make any of them fit. Could she have become tangled in a situation unwittingly? Might she be the innocent party after all?

Lukas returned with a glass of water, eyeballing Minshull and Bennett as he edged past. When he bent to deliver the glass to Mattie, summoning Bennett's attention to the motion, Minshull seized the opportunity to swipe a pebble. He'd already spotted the ideal candidate – large enough to offer a significant surface upon which emotional fingerprints might be laid, yet small enough to be concealed in the palm of his hand. Using a blue plastic glove laid flat on his palm, he picked up the pebble and pocketed it in one swift motion, tucking the glove around it where it lay.

By the time Bennett, Lukas and Mattie looked at him, the pebble was safely hidden.

'Lukie, I'm going to need you to take care of Amelie for me for a while,' Mattie said, pressing on when the young man began to protest. 'I *need* you to do this, okay? If I'm away for longer than two hours, call Gaby, and she'll come straight over.'

'I should be with you,' Lukas insisted again.

'I'll be fine.'

She stood slowly, gently placing the baby in his arms. He accepted, still shaking his head. 'But you need me.'

'*Here*,' Mattie insisted, stepping back as Lukas attempted to give her the baby. 'I need you here. Amelie needs you.' She nodded at Bennett and Minshull. 'I can call Lukas from the station when I'm coming home, right?'

'Of course,' Bennett replied.

'Then let's go.' The young woman picked up her phone, bag and jacket, making to leave quickly. Bennett followed, Minshull letting them pass before he made for the door.

'No!' Lukas called, the baby in his arms jumping awake.

Mattie appeared back at the doorway, her smile gone. 'I said not to wake her!'

'I can't let them take you! I should be there!'

'You should be *here*,' she returned, a sharpness in her reply that cut the air in the small room. 'This doesn't concern you.'

'But...'

'Do this for me, okay? I've made my decision.'

Lukas fell silent, mournfully watching them leave.

It was only when Minshull followed her and Bennett out of the house that it occurred to him how odd Kemp's parting words had been.

Checking that Bennett was fully occupied with helping the young woman into the back seat of the pool car, Minshull moved quickly to the location he'd selected for the pebble drop. He carefully lifted it from his pocket using the glove as a barrier, dropping it into the long grass beside a narrow strip of grey concrete that served as a path across the front of the house.

Then he hurried to the car.

As Bennett drove them out of Knightsway Road, Minshull resisted the temptation to look in the direction of Cora's hiding place. She would see him: that was all that mattered. Slipping his phone from his pocket, he typed a text, pressed SEND and leaned back in the passenger seat.

It was done.

FORTY-TWO

CORA

The pool car passed Cora's hiding place, Minshull staring resolutely forward as he disappeared from view.

Had he spotted her? Did he know she was there?

Cora waited, the interior of her car darkened by the shadow of the tall Leylandii tree beneath whose branches she had parked. Was the house unoccupied now? Would any neighbours be watching from behind their curtains? She suddenly realised she hadn't factored anyone else into her plan when she'd proposed it to Minshull.

What if someone saw her, or asked what she was doing?

The sudden light of her phone's screen coming to life stung her eyes in the gloom as Minshull's text arrived.

> Drop successful.
> In long grass at edge of path at the front of the house.
> One occupant still in house. Be careful. M

What?

Had Minshull expected there to be someone else in the house, or had it taken him by surprise?

Then Cora remembered the baby. Of course. Someone must be watching Mattie Kemp's child while Minshull and Bennett took her back to Police HQ.

But did they have sight of the front garden from inside the house? How would she reach the drop point without being seen?

Why had Minshull chosen to drop it there and not nearer pavement, where she could easily retrieve it? Only now that their plan was in progress did Cora realise her instructions to the DS should have been more specific.

There was no point in going over mistakes now: she needed to get to the pebble.

With a final check to ensure the street was empty, Cora left her car and walked up Knightsway Road, conscious of each window that overlooked her progress. All appeared empty and still. But Cora was attuned to every voice rising from the pavement around her from the smallest scraps of wind-blown rubbish, carrying the voices of those who had discarded them:

I'm so late...

Tired now.

Dickhead...

A child's whingeing complaint from a discarded sweet wrapper:

I don't want to!

A woman's voice, choked with tears, protesting injustice from the violent creases of a screwed-up letter:

He can't do this to me! I hate him!

Mentally muting each one in turn, Cora walked steadily towards Mattie Kemp's house. With the emotional echoes removed, it was a quiet road on a faded housing estate. All she had to do was walk to the front of the house, locate the pebble, and listen to the voices attached, then drop it back where she'd found it.

Unforeseen complications aside, it was a solid plan.

If it worked the way she'd envisaged on the drive to Evernam, it could all be done in a few minutes. She would return to her car, fire off a text to Minshull and leave. Rob would have what he needed, and she would have done what she came to do.

The houses on either side of the road were quiet, their windows dark against the yellow-grey light of the stormy sky above. A gentle patter of rain echoed around the street as the downpour the sky had threatened all morning finally arrived. It provided sound cover for Cora's footsteps on the pavement as she moved towards the house.

She opted to approach from the narrow drive side, edging up along the low, tarnished metal fence separating number 16 from its next-door neighbour, rather than run across the grass nearest the large front windows of the property. Cora kept as close to the divide as she could, her breath held as steady as she could make it.

She reached the point where the garden met the house and was beginning to cross the grass when the handle on the front door began to move...

FORTY-THREE

ANDERSON

Something had changed with Rob Minshull.

Anderson was sure of it.

He'd left the CID office at a lick of a pace, returning like an army general, barking orders to Bennett as he grabbed a bunch of pool car keys. They were bringing Mattie Kemp in – but what had ignited Minshull's fire between returning from Isabel Lingham's interview and the call that had summoned him outside?

Anderson watched his DS preparing notes with Bennett now, killing time while a duty solicitor was summoned to sit with Kemp. Not at her request, mind you: at Minshull's. Which was odd in itself.

Why did Minshull insist on a legal brief being present for a voluntary interview?

What did he expect to be disclosed there?

If time had been on their side, he would have pulled Minshull into his office to demand answers, but Ms Kemp had a baby at home and a temporary sitter who, according to Bennett's hushed remark when they returned, would be unlikely to manage alone for long.

A sharp ring of the CID phones caused Minshull and Bennett to look up from their notes as Ellis answered. Thanking the caller, he hung up.

'They're ready, Sarge.'

'Good, thanks, Drew.' Minshull stood, glancing over at Anderson as if surprised to find him there.

What was going on?

'Guv, I'm going to take Kate in with me on this. She's met Ms Kemp twice now, and it gives us continuity.'

Meaning Bennett was a fellow woman, Anderson interpreted. Neither he nor Minshull had the balls to say it out loud, but it was accepted as part of CID practice. Bennett being the only female detective on the team meant she was the first and only choice when it came to interviewing women. It was unfair to her but unavoidable – and, knowing Kate Bennett, she was likely wise already to their thinly veiled reason for selecting her.

'Fine. So, what's the plan?'

Minshull shifted a little, an action not missed by Anderson. 'We'll talk to Ms Kemp and ask what her involvement with Lingham and the others was. Provided she complies, we'll try to ascertain the part she played in it all, if any.'

'Or if the village gossips are just stitching her up because she's an easy target,' Ellis countered.

'That too,' Minshull replied, twisting to look at his colleague. 'And then we'll go back to Lingham with what we know. I'd like to do that with you, Guv. For *continuity*.'

The smirk this elicited from Bennett was impossible to miss.

'I'll go back in with Mrs Lingham, then,' Anderson said. 'Dave, would you come in with me for that, please?'

'What should I do, Guv?' Ellis' hand raised as it always did.

'Carry on with what you're doing.'

'But I've completed all the tasks you set for me.'

'Then find others.'

'Like what, Guv? I know I can't attend any face-to-face business, but with respect…'

The addendum did little to appease Anderson's flash of anger.

'*With respect*, DC Ellis, you are too closely involved with our persons of interest to be of any use to us in interview, as well you know.'

'But I'm sod all use in here.'

267

Bennett, Minshull and Wheeler fell silent. Anderson's words were ice-cold steel when they came, a tone that sent fear through every detective in the room.

'Watch yourself, Ellis. I understand the challenge this is for you personally, but you have to abide by best practice, as we all do. I will decide how we proceed. Not you. Clear?'

'Guv.' A little of Ellis' defiance faded, but his chin remained high.

'I should think so too. Dave, with me, please.'

'Yep, coming Guv...'

Keeping his eyes on his young DC, Anderson walked to the door, finally releasing Ellis from his stare when Wheeler reached his side, and they moved out into the corridor.

It was only when they were safely past the double doors at the end of the corridor and heading down the stairs to the lower floor that Anderson let the mask slip.

'What the *hell*, Dave?'

'Go easy on the lad, Joel. None of us know what he's going through.'

'Maybe not, but he's making bloody sure we're all aware he's going through it.' Anderson punched the doors open at the bottom of the stairs, Wheeler only just scurrying through in time before they swung shut.

'You have to see it from his point of view, Guv,' Wheeler countered, ever the voice of reason. 'All these revelations coming to light about his friends, people he knew, his home village – and he's not allowed to witness any of it, except what he learns second-hand when we all come back into the office.'

Anderson understood but wasn't yet willing to concede. 'We've always had one detective manning the office in every investigation. It's usually...'

'Les,' Wheeler finished with a kind smile.

Of course. Anderson hadn't realised the direction his diatribe was headed in, the dawning of it too late to stop, unlike Wheeler, who had obviously seen it coming.

DC Les Evans, their injured colleague, whose dubious presence was missed more than anyone in CID would admit aloud.

'Ah.'

'And Drew *isn't* Les Evans. Come on, Guv, you know as well as I do that most of the time we kept Les back in the office was to prevent some catastrophe, not to meet protocol.'

Anderson slowed, his boots suddenly concrete-heavy. 'I can't let Drew close to the people we're talking to.'

'I know that. But cut the lad some slack, yeah? Bad enough he's learning all this stuff about people he knows without him thinking we're penalising him for it as well.'

Bloody Dave Wheeler and his annoying fairness!

Anderson swallowed his irritation.

They reached the custody suite and were about to enter Interview Room 1 when a shout from further down the corridor summoned their attention.

Sergeant Lyn Vickery raised a hand as she jogged towards them. 'DI Anderson, DC Wheeler – a word, please!'

'Problem, Lyn?' Anderson called back, quickly reeling in his frustration. Lyn Vickery was the kind of Custody Sergeant you needed to stick around. Fierce when necessary, solid in the face of any level of crap the job chucked at her, she was an old-school style copper, the likes of which Anderson was certain he'd not see again. New kids coming in from training only saw the role of Custody Sergeant as a stepping stone these days, not a desirable destination. No way was he going to say or do anything that might make early retirement appealing to her.

'Big problem, Guv. Mark Lingham's solicitor just resigned.'

'*What?*'

'He cited a conflict of interest because Isabel Lingham is here.'

'I hope you impressed upon him exactly how irresponsible his *interest* is to abandon his client now?'

Vickery gave a weary laugh. 'Oh, I did. But it gets worse.'

'How?'

'He wants to represent Isabel Lingham instead.'

Anderson couldn't believe what he was hearing. 'Right, where is he?'

'In the briefing room.'

'Respect, Guv. *Calm…*' Wheeler muttered beside him in a hurried mantra as Anderson stormed towards the small room allotted to duty solicitors and employed lawyers to talk to their clients.

'I'll give him bloody respect, all right.' Anderson snapped back.

It was just possible the hinges on the briefing room door had never been utilised so forcefully since their installation.

Or that a single solicitor, seated on a scuffed grey plastic chair within the room, had jumped so high.

Jasper Carmichael almost dented the ceiling.

Anderson took no small amount of pleasure from that.

'DI Anderson, I must protest,' Carmichael began, scrambling to his feet.

'*Talk,*' Anderson barked.

'E-excuse me?'

Waiting until the door closed behind him, Anderson folded his arms across his chest and stared the solicitor down. 'Explain to me why you, a solicitor with clearly many years of practice behind you, would ever consider it appropriate to abandon your client at such a late stage in an investigation.'

Carmichael appeared to be on the cusp of exploding. 'That is between me and my client. You have no right…'

'I have every right, sir! Your client is potentially facing four murder charges. We have been granted more time by the CPS to secure a charge against him. As well you know. Time that is rapidly running out. This is the moment your client needs you most.'

Carmichael's eyes flicked to the side. 'There are things you don't know…'

'*Enlighten* me,' Anderson growled back.

'I'm unable to. Client confidentiality...'

No way, thought Anderson, *absolutely bloody not!* The solicitor couldn't hide behind that excuse.

'You resigned, didn't you? Client confidentiality no longer applies.' He rounded on the solicitor, the full extent of his height casting an imposing shadow over the man. 'What don't I know, Mr Carmichael?'

The weasel-featured solicitor nervously resumed his seat with a long sigh. 'I have been advising Isabel Lingham for longer than Mark knows.'

Wheeler was intently observing the exchange when Anderson glanced back.

'Why?'

Carmichael sniffed, taking a slug from a half-crumpled plastic bottle on the small table at which he sat. 'She's filing for divorce.'

Anderson had heard it all now. Although given how readily Isabel Lingham had thrown allegations at her husband, this latest development was perhaps not surprising.

'How long have you been advising her?'

'Unofficially, months. Officially, the last six weeks. She wants to ensure she maintains the family home and receives a generous settlement for the rest.'

'Has she cited a reason?'

'I can't go into details...'

'Then give me a *clue*,' Anderson shot back, his patience as thin as the hair barely covering the solicitor's reddened scalp.

'It won't be a no-fault divorce,' Carmichael stated. 'I'm sorry, that's the best I can do.'

'I'm guessing Mark is the one at fault?' The solicitor's slow blink confirmed what Anderson suspected. 'And you're following the money.'

'Excuse me?'

'Keeping Isabel Lingham sweet so you can benefit from the divorce settlement.'

'I won't dignify that with an answer.'

Infuriating, arrogant little shit with an overinflated opinion of himself, Anderson seethed inside. He'd happily punch the crap out of him if the investigation wasn't resting on Mark Lingham's interviews continuing without delay.

'What reason have you provided my colleagues with for resigning as Mark Lingham's brief?' he asked, his question a safer alternative to physical violence.

'A conflict of interest.'

'Because you're advising his wife on the best way to divorce him?'

'Yes, that. And also… My loyalties lie with Isabel. They always have.'

Anderson thought he'd seen every shade of brass neck in this job. It turned out his collection was missing an exhibit. 'Then why agree to represent him in the first place?'

'Because Isabel asked me.'

Now the dynamic was clear: for all Carmichael's bullishness during interview, his motive had always been serving Isabel Lingham, not her husband. Had Lingham's sudden accusation of his wife shocked Carmichael into resigning as his legal representative? Or, when faced with two of his clients potentially accused of murder, had Carmichael simply chosen the most lucrative side?

There was another possibility, of course. Anderson would lay odds on Wheeler subscribing to it, without asking him if his supposition were correct. Did Carmichael have information on Mark Lingham that could incriminate him? Had Lingham confessed to the murder of his friends – and was his solicitor jumping ship before his client went down?

FORTY-FOUR

CORA

The handle clicked as a key was turned inside. Then the door began to open.

Panicked, Cora dashed for the far edge of the garden, ducking beneath the large picture window to reach a thick, blue-flowered hydrangea bush that looked as old as the house itself. Its wide, glossy leaves provided a verdant sanctuary as she crouched down within its branches.

A figure emerged from the front door, a dark grey hoodie pulled low over khaki combat-style trousers with thick-soled black and white sneakers beneath. A black rucksack was secured across their back, its silver zips dancing in the light as the person pulled a red BMX-style bike from against the wall of the house and began to turn it around to face down the small drive.

The figure looked like a teenager, the oversized clothes and bike hinting at someone younger. Did Mattie Kemp have a younger brother, perhaps?

Cora remembered her own brother, Charlie, and his near-constant obsession with BMX bikes when he was sixteen, begging their parents for one of his own for Christmas. Cora's mum, Sheila, had been all for it; Cora's dad, Bill, initially refused, having heard too many horror stories of youths causing havoc on their bikes on the local housing estate. It had taken every ounce of her brother's natural charm to win Dad round. But, like most things in his life, Charlie had got what he wanted eventually.

He had spent so many summers riding that bike... Cora smiled amongst the hydrangea leaves at the memory. It had been all Sheila Lael could do to stop Charlie carrying his bike up to his bedroom at the end of each day.

Had this young person faced a similar battle to win their wheels?

The sound of a pedal being kicked and the squeak of saddle springs summoned Cora's attention to the departing figure. At least with them gone, she could reach for the pebble, listen to the voices attached and get out of there. She just needed to sit tight for a few moments more...

She followed the progress of the rider as they carefully steered the bike down the small strip of cracked concrete that served as a drive. Where the drive met the faded pavement, the rider twisted in their saddle to look past the hydrangea shrub to a point further up Knightsway Road.

And that was when Cora saw the baby, strapped in a sling carrier to the teenage boy's chest...

FORTY-FIVE

MINSHULL

In Anderson's wake, the CID office felt bruised from his outburst at Ellis.

Minshull watched the despondent DC staring hollowly at his computer screen, and his heart went out to him. He was there by necessity, of course. He knew this, as they all did, but his confession in the meeting room that morning about the overbearing concern he'd witnessed from everyone else on the team revealed a level of frustration Minshull hadn't anticipated.

'Sarge, we should go.' Bennett's statement was respectfully quiet, her eyes on Ellis, too.

'Okay,' Minshull replied, a thought stalling him. 'You go ahead: I'll meet you outside Interview 2.'

'Yes, Sarge.' Bennett hid her frustration about as well as Anderson hid his fury.

When she'd gone, Minshull approached Ellis. 'I know this seems unfair,' he said, giving the DC a sympathetic smile when Ellis looked up mournfully from his computer screen. 'It sucks, to be honest. But I have a job for you.'

He pulled his mobile phone from his pocket.

'I'm waiting for a text from Cora. It won't make sense when it arrives, but I need to know immediately. Can you look after my phone, please? And the moment Cora sends a message, come down to Interview 2 and interrupt us.'

Ellis accepted the mobile with a mixture of relief and confusion. 'No problem, Sarge.'

'Cheers, Drew. I'd use the opportunity of a Guv-free office to relax a little if I were you.' Minshull gave a knowing glance in the direction of the DI's office. 'Who knows when you might get that kind of luxury again?'

'Thanks,' Ellis replied, the word carrying so much more besides its own letters.

–

Bennett was waiting by the door to Interview Room 2 as instructed. She watched Minshull arrive, her folder of notes clutched to her like a shield.

'All good, Sarge?'

'Drew is fine. We just need to give him air. I think we've all been so keen to help him that we've ended up half-smothering the poor sod.'

'He's really going through it. He doesn't want anyone to know how much.'

'Which is why we're going to give him space from now on,' Minshull replied, knocking on the interview room door and pushing it open.

Bennett followed him, taking her usual seat by the recording machine.

Mattie Kemp was sitting next to a duty solicitor Minshull didn't recognise, a plastic cup of water encircled by her long fingers. With her hands on the interview table, Minshull could see the intricate patterns painted on her fingernails. It reminded him of the elaborate and simple designs on the pebbles in Mattie Kemp's small sitting room. Did she paint her nails like she painted the pebbles?

Minshull raised his hand to the duty solicitor. 'Hi, I'm DS Rob Minshull. I don't think we've met.'

'Mel Chatterjee – and no, we haven't.' She gave a brief smile. 'I've recently moved here from London.' She glanced at Mattie Kemp. 'I've explained to Ms Kemp that this is a voluntary interview and, as she isn't under arrest, she has the right to choose to talk to you or refuse questions. She's chosen the former.'

'Excellent, thank you. Shall we get started?'

Once the recording had begun, Minshull consulted the list of questions he and Bennett had agreed in the CID office earlier. It felt rushed, even though they couldn't have had any more time to prepare. At the start of the day, he hadn't imagined they would be speaking to Mattie Kemp at all.

And yet, here they were.

So, where to begin?

'Ms Kemp, we've asked you here because an accusation has been made against you that, linked to an item we found, may carry serious consequences. I need to ask you some questions that may appear intrusive, but they're necessary.'

Kemp nodded.

Minshull accepted that as his cue to continue. 'Okay. How well do you know Mark Lingham?'

'I work for him sometimes. Virtual office stuff.'

'And beyond that?'

'I see him down the pub sometimes. The Shire Horse in Evernam. Most of the village sees him there, though.'

Minshull nodded. 'And what about Jack Markham, known as Denzil?'

The slightest hint of a frown appeared. 'I see him around.'

'Obviously, we've already spoken with you about Otto Wragg.'

Kemp hefted a sigh. 'Yes. No prizes for guessing where the accusation has come from, then. What has Sheila Kersey said about me now?'

The solicitor lifted her hand a little way from the interview desk as if to halt Kemp before she went too far. Mattie Kemp bristled and said no more.

'The accusation didn't come from Mrs Kersey.'

'Then who?'

'I'll get to that in a moment. Can you tell me where you were on the morning of Monday 9 September, between the hours of nine a.m. and ten a.m?'

'Lukas and I were taking Amelie for a walk.' She looked at the duty solicitor. 'My baby. She wakes early and needs a nap around nine a.m.'

Mel Chatterjee smiled and made a note.

'Where did you walk?'

'Just down through the village and on to the woods. Lukas likes walking there.'

'Did anyone see you?'

'Plenty of people, I imagine. You can't sneeze in Evernam without curtains twitching.'

'Anyone specific?'

Kemp laughed, her eyes trained on Minshull. 'Take your pick.'

'Sorry, I'll rephrase: did you see anyone else on your walk? Anyone you stopped to talk to?'

'No.'

'Okay, thanks. What's your relationship with Lukas Hall?'

'Like I told you before: he's a good friend. I spent a lot of time with his family when I was a kid. His sister Gaby is my best friend, and when my parents were going through problems, her folks let me stay with them. Lukas was always around. I think he sees me as a big sister, which I don't mind.'

'And now he helps you with your daughter?'

Kemp nodded, biting her lip a little.

'I imagine he's a great help.'

'He is. One of the few guys I can trust.' The statement felt barbed despite her smile.

Minshull moved on to the next round of questions. He and Bennett had agreed to go in gently: to begin with her relationship to the people she'd been mentioned in conjunction with, then double down on the details. The aim was to keep

Mattie Kemp talking as freely and as voluntarily as possible, before hitting her with Isabel Lingham's accusation.

'If we can return to Mark Lingham now,' Minshull said, turning a page in his notes. 'You say you work for him as a virtual assistant?'

'Occasionally.'

'What does that work entail?'

'Correspondence with property owners and tenants, handling enquiries when his office is closed, checking day-to-day accounts. It varies from week to week. I've done less since Amelie arrived, but it's a useful source of income.'

'And when Mr Lingham sends you this work, does he do it in person or online?'

'Both. It depends on what he wants me to do.'

Minshull nodded, making a note. Would the work Kemp described include late-night meetings in his car on the fringes of Evernam Woods? 'How well would you say you know Mark Lingham?'

'Pretty well. I've known him for years and worked for him for the last five.'

'Do you ever see him socially?'

'In the pub. Like everyone else.' Her gaze narrowed. 'Has someone said something? About Mark and me?'

'Why would you think that?'

Kemp rolled her eyes. 'Speculation. Mostly about Amelie's father. They see me within spitting distance of a bloke and assume I'm sleeping with him. Is that what someone's said?'

'Would they have reason to assume that?'

'Not beyond their own filthy imaginations, no,' she bristled.

It felt as if they had reached an eddy in the conversation, swirling around the mention of the accusation. Looking at the remainder of the questions he and Bennett had written, Minshull made a snap decision he was certain his colleague would support.

279

'Ms Kemp, an accusation has been made against you. By Isabel Lingham.'

'Figures.' Kemp gave a snort, crossing her body with her arms. Defences armed, battle-ready. From the sudden change in her body language, Minshull wondered if she'd been anticipating this. If Isabel Lingham's suspicions were on point, Mattie Kemp must have known this was coming.

'She saw you in a car at the edge of Evernam Woods with her husband, late one night. She believes you're having an affair.'

'I bet she does.'

'Is she mistaken?'

'You have to ask?'

'Yes,' Minshull replied coolly. 'I'm afraid I do.'

Kemp observed Minshull and Bennett from beneath lowered brows. 'He's a friend. That's all.'

'So that night, in the car?'

'We were talking, okay? We'd gone there to be away from everyone's prying eyes. Some bloody chance of that.'

'Why worry about what people are saying if there's nothing going on?'

'You think it's as simple as that? Since I fell pregnant, it's all anyone in that damn village can gossip about. They think Mark's the father: that when I couldn't get him to leave Isabel, I latched onto Otto and wrecked his marriage instead. They have a whole sordid soap opera written in their thick heads about me, just because their own lives are so pathetically dull.' She leaned forward, fixing Minshull and Bennett with her stare. 'I've done nothing wrong. Apart from refusing to be driven away by their shit.'

She thumped back in her chair, the silence stinging in the wake of her words. Minshull returned calmly to his notes, processing what he'd heard. For someone so initially timid, Mattie Kemp's temper was a snakebite that struck from nowhere. What fuelled that? Righteous indignation or fear of the truth?

Beside him, Bennett made her own notes, a brief double-tap of her pen summoning Minshull's attention to a line she'd just written.

Ask about the scarf.

She was right – they had reached a point in the interview where this would have to be exposed. But Mattie Kemp was on the offensive now, which made mentioning the scarf – and the inherent accusation it carried – a risky endeavour.

Minshull selected the photograph of the scarf from his notes. Bennett had suggested using the photo rather than the actual item in its evidence bag as an initial plan to gauge Kemp's response. Having just witnessed her temper, Minshull was glad they'd chosen this course of action.

'Can you take a look at this picture, please? For the recording, I am handing Ms Kemp a photograph of exhibit EV126.' He slid the photo across the interview desk. 'Do you recognise this?'

The flash of recognition was fleeting, but Minshull caught it before Mattie Kemp could stuff it away.

'I don't know,' she managed, taking a long sip of water before returning to the image. 'I mean, it's hard to tell.'

'Look closely, please. There's some embroidery on the fabric that's quite distinctive.'

'Mmm, no, sorry.'

She was lying. Even if Minshull hadn't been aware of Isabel Lingham's testimony, he would have spotted it immediately.

He decided to continue on regardless, pushing his luck for as long as the duty solicitor would allow it.

'I ask because this scarf was found wrapped around a knife, concealed in undergrowth in Evernam Woods.'

'That explains the state of it,' Kemp joked. Nerves danced at the edges of her comment.

'The knife, we believe, was used to murder four men we know that you know well. Tim Stapleforth, Krish Bhattachama, Jack 'Denzil' Markham and Otto Wragg.'

'Why do you think that?'

'The blood of all four men was discovered on the blade. And on the scarf as well, where it had stained the fabric. There will be other things on the scarf, too. Fibres. Strands of hair.'

Kemp's hand flew to her ponytail subconsciously, quickly pulled back and tucked across her chest.

'Isabel Lingham told us she saw you in her husband's car, wearing this scarf.'

'What? No – no, she's made that up.'

'Why would she do that?'

'Because…' Kemp's gaze darted around the cramped interview room now. 'Okay, okay. I had that scarf. I remember now. It was raining, and we'd been for a walk in the woods, and Mark gave it to me to keep my hair dry when we ran back to the car.'

'Mr Lingham had the scarf with him on your walk?'

'He must have done. I think he'd found it in his car and put it in his pocket to take back to Isabel. Then he gave it to me. But I gave it back, the next time I saw him.'

'Which was?'

'Sunday afternoon. The eighth. He brought some files over for me to go through.'

Minshull wrote this down. 'You're certain you gave it back to him?'

'Yes,' Kemp replied, glancing at the solicitor. 'I'm sure I did.'

'Okay. Just out of interest, when was the last time you went to Evernam Woods?'

'I told you, Monday morning.'

'And not since?'

'No.'

'Not even a walk there with Lukas Hall? You said he likes walking there.'

'Not since Monday.'

A dead end.

Minshull regrouped. 'Ms Kemp, is there any reason why Isabel Lingham would think you were having an affair with Mark?'

'Because she's a spiteful, vile bitch.' The reply cracked like a whip. That flare of temper he'd seen back at her house directed at Lukas, and moments ago in this room. It seemed an anomaly in Mattie Kemp's personality, starkly at odds with her apparent openness and good humour.

It was the sign Minshull had hoped to see. He waited.

Sure enough...

'She's joined forces with Sheila Kersey now, spreading their poison all around the village. And people believe them because they're too thick to wonder why it's happening or see through the lies. This—' she waved her hand over the photo of the bloodied scarf, '—is just another way to get rid of me.'

'You think they'd do that? Accuse you of murder?'

'Why not? Sheila hates Mark because she thinks he turned Otto against the family. And Isabel had a huge row with Denz Markham in the middle of the pub last month. She accused him of trying to blag money from her husband that he'd never pay back. She hated Krish, too – did you know they dated before she got together with Mark?'

Winded from the sudden rush of information, Minshull listed each new revelation with increased annoyance. Just how many secrets were being kept in Evernam?

'What about Tim Stapleforth?'

His question was met by thin-lipped silence.

'Ms Kemp?'

'Tim Stapleforth deserved everything he got.'

'Why?'

Kemp ignored his question, turning to her legal representative. 'I've helped enough. I want to go home now.'

'Ms Kemp, there are still a few...'

'I *said* I want to *leave*,' Mattie Kemp bit back. 'Lukas can't look after Amelie much longer by himself. It isn't fair. And she's due a feed soon.'

'Just a couple more questions and you're free to go.'

Kemp appealed to her solicitor, who raised her hand. 'I think Ms Kemp has answered enough, DS Minshull. Unless you're planning to take things further, I think we're done.'

Loath though Minshull was to admit it, the solicitor was right: Mattie Kemp had more than complied with the requirements of a voluntary interview. Minshull couldn't hold her without a charge, but while his instinct insisted there was more to her involvement in the Januarius Street murders, he had nothing to prove it.

Bennett's expression was as helpless as his when he sought her assistance.

They had to keep Mattie Kemp there until they knew what Lingham was telling Anderson.

But how?

FORTY-SIX

CORA

'Rob, it's Cora. A teenager has just left Mattie Kemp's house on his bike. He has her baby strapped to him in a sling. I'm following in the car. He's heading towards the village. Call me as soon as you get this...'

Cora stabbed her finger on the end call button on her phone where it sat in its dashboard cradle. She hadn't waited to text Minshull as they'd agreed, too concerned with getting to her car and following the young man along the road from the estate to the country road beyond.

He could be taking the baby to a relative. Or going to visit a friend. But carrying a baby in a sling while riding a bike didn't look safe – for the baby or the rider. Worse, the baby had begun to cry, setting Cora's nerves on edge.

It sounded like the cries from Januarius Street.

The cries from the knife.

And the distant cries above the painted pebble.

But how could she know if it was the same child every time?

It didn't matter: Cora knew without a shred of doubt that she had to follow the young man and his precariously carried charge.

The radio cut out as her mobile registered a call.

ROB calling

Relief flooding her body, Cora answered the call.

'Rob – he's got the baby…'

'Hi, Cora, it's Drew Ellis. Minsh asked me to watch his phone for your message.'

'Where is he?'

Ellis sounded breathless, the thud of running feet audible behind his voice. 'Interviewing Mattie Kemp. I'm on my way down to get him. Hang tight.'

'Drew – I need people here now. A teenage boy just left Mattie Kemp's house, taking her baby with him. I think he's heading for the village.'

'What? Is it Lukas Hall?'

'I don't know, maybe? I have a bad feeling about this, Drew. I'm following him, but I need help.'

'Okay… I'm going to sort this, Cora. Keep your phone on and I'll call you back.'

The call ended as the rider ahead took a sharp right and disappeared behind a high tangle of shrubbery.

Cora stamped on the brake, stopping her car just in time to change her course.

There was only one place the road that Lukas Hall had taken led to.

Evernam Woods.

FORTY-SEVEN

ELLIS

Breathless, Ellis raced down the stairs and along the corridor towards the custody suite. He had almost reached the door of Interview 2 when Duty Sergeant Lyn Vickery blocked his path.

'In a hurry, DC Ellis?'

'Sergeant Vickery, I need to talk to DS Minshull. It's urgent.'

'You can't go in there. A voluntary is in progress.'

'No, Lyn – Sergeant – you don't understand. DS Minshull gave me his mobile phone and told me to bring it straight to him when a certain message arrived.' To prove his point, he wiggled the phone in the stony face of the duty sergeant.

'I just heard shouting in there, mate,' Vickery replied through gritted teeth. 'It's obviously kicking off, and if DS Minshull leaves now, his voluntary may well clam up.'

Ellis stared back. What was Lyn Vickery's problem? 'It's an *emergency*. I can't get DI Anderson or DC Wheeler because they're in with the suspect for the Januarius Street murder case. And there's nobody else in the office except me...'

Even as he said it, he knew what he was going to do.

'Okay, look, let me give you DS Minshull's phone and a message. You give it to him as soon as you can.' He pulled his notebook from his back pocket, copying down Cora's number first, then scribbling a note on a fresh sheet of paper, tearing it off and bundling the message and Minshull's phone into Vickery's hands.

'Well, I don't know... Where are you going?'

'I'm sorting it!' Ellis called over his shoulder as he ran back towards the stairs.

He was done with being sidelined in this case. Done with being chained to his desk, unable to get out with his colleagues while they investigated the senseless killings of his friends.

He'd tried to toe the line, to swallow his frustration and force his mind back on the job. But how was he supposed to do that?

The only solution Ellis knew when facing issues was to take action. Being a bystander didn't make sense to him. He'd joined the police to make a difference, and he couldn't do that stuck alone in an office, staring at a bloody screen.

Minshull had said he was the local knowledge in the investigation – well, nobody in the CID team knew the village and the surrounding area like Ellis did.

Anderson would lose his shit.

Minshull would have his neck.

But there was no time to consult them.

Dashing into the CID office, Ellis grabbed his phone and a set of pool car keys. Then he turned on his heels and ran down to the car park, punching Cora's number into his phone as he ran.

He'd call for back-up on the way.

FORTY-EIGHT

ANDERSON

Carmichael wasn't budging. But he knew more than he would ever tell.

In frustration, Anderson resorted to return to the organ grinder, leaving the idiotic monkey to stew in the meeting room where he'd commanded Carmichael to stay.

Beside his new legal representative – an associate of Carmichael's apparently, who looked barely old enough to have passed his Law GCSE – Mark Lingham stared sullenly back.

'I need you to be straight with me, Mr Lingham,' Anderson growled, his seething fury barely contained. The man he faced had brought it on himself. If he hadn't led them a merry dance, they might have found the persons responsible for the murders already.

Or maybe the person responsible was in the room right now.

'I *have* been...' One glare from Anderson cut short Mark Lingham's protest. 'I'm still in shock... I didn't know what I was saying.'

'Does that apply to everything you've told us?' Anderson asked imperiously, ignoring the warning looks Wheeler was sending him at the periphery of his vision. 'Like when you claimed you'd arranged to meet a prospective buyer who never existed, or when you implicated your wife in a quadruple murder?'

'What has Isabel said?'

'That's none of your concern. What should concern you is what you tell us, in this room, now.'

'I've told you everything I know!'

Not everything, apparently.

'Then tell me about Mattie Kemp.'

The name was a blow that registered at Lingham's core. 'Mattie?' he squeaked, hands clutching his stomach as if nursing a wound.

Anderson nodded. 'According to your wife, you two were having an affair.'

'What?'

'She followed you and Ms Kemp to Evernam Woods, a month ago. Saw you together in your car, with your arm around Ms Kemp and Mrs Lingham's scarf around her neck. The scarf that, according to you, your wife must have used to conceal the knife you used to murder your friends...'

'DI Anderson, be careful,' the twelve-year-old-in-a-suit opposite interjected.

Anderson grunted his assent. 'Apologies. Let me rephrase. Your wife has suggested that you were having an affair with Ms Kemp and that you gave her Mrs Lingham's scarf as a gift. She denies being involved in the murder of four men and has placed the blame squarely on you.'

'She's lying!'

'So tell me the truth. Because you said your wife coerced you into being involved in the murders of your friends. Do you wish to retract that?'

Lingham stared back and said nothing.

'I have four grieving families desperate for answers. Four dead men who deserve justice. And the only person who can help me provide both is you. So start talking to me, or you will be charged with the murders of Tim Stapleforth, Krish Bhattachama, Jack Markham and Otto Wragg. Four innocent men...'

'Innocent?' Lingham's laugh when it came was bitter, soaked in hate. 'Ask Mattie Kemp about their innocence. Ask her about *hers*.'

'What will she tell me?'

'Not for me to say.'

What the hell was Lingham playing at? Did he want a life sentence for four murders?

'Why are they not innocent?'

'Ask Mattie Kemp.'

'DI Anderson is asking *you*.' Wheeler's words were firm but fair – and far more professional than the volley Anderson would have launched. 'Because I reckon you know, Mark. And the more time we waste in here, the less chance you have to tell us your side of the story. Once this interview ends, we'll take what we have to the CPS, and you'll lose the opportunity to tell us what you know. In the light of this, do you wish to change your answer?'

Lingham hung his head, Wheeler's fatherly tone clearly cutting through the tangle of ego and lies he had surrounded himself with.

'We were only meant to scare them.' A sigh followed that syphoned the remaining fight from Lingham's frame. 'It was meant to be about the money.'

'What money?' Anderson's question bore none of his earlier anger.

'The money they would pay us when we scared the shit out of them.'

'They were your friends,' Anderson prompted. 'Why would you want to scare them?'

'They were no friends of mine,' Lingham scoffed. 'Not when I found out what they'd done.'

The young solicitor cleared his throat. 'Maybe we should break here.'

'No.' Lingham offered the solicitor a weak smile. 'I'm sick of this. I didn't kill them. But I got them there. And Mattie Kemp did the rest.'

FORTY-NINE

CORA

She almost didn't answer the call when an unfamiliar number flashed up on the screen.

'Cora, hi, it's Drew. Sorry, I'm calling from my phone.'

'Where's Rob?'

'They wouldn't let me see him, but he'll get my message soon.'

How could Minshull ignore this? And how could anyone stop him hearing about it?

Cora bit against her frustration, keeping her eyes set on Lukas Hall. She'd slowed to a crawl as the narrow lane had become more rutted and grass-strewn, trying to keep out of sight as the teenager picked his way over potholes and ridges in the road.

The wail of Mattie Kemp's baby remained constant. Cora had wound down the car's front windows to better listen, despite the sound twisting her nerves. If the baby was crying, it was alive.

'Where are you now?' Ellis asked, the line furring a little as Cora drove deeper into the countryside.

'I turned off the main road to the village, about a mile from Knightsway Road. The first one signposted to Evernam Woods. It narrows to a track quite quickly. He's just ahead of me and riding slower to navigate the terrain.'

'Okay, good. I know where it is. I'm about two miles outside Evernam.'

'Who's with you?'

There was a pause; the sound of a racing engine all Cora could hear on the line. 'I'm on my own.'

'What?'

'There wasn't time to put out a call. I'm coming to help you, and I'll radio for backup on the way.'

'I can't tell if he intends to hurt the baby, Drew.' Cora's fear found a voice.

'I'm on my way. Keep your eyes on him.'

'I will... Wait!'

Ahead, Lukas had stopped. He appeared to be searching for something in the low pockets of his combat trousers. Dropping something into the grass, he steered the BMX down a narrow gap in the thick vegetation at the edge of the woodland and disappeared down a gulley.

'He's left the road,' Cora rushed, pulling hard on the handbrake and grabbing her phone as she left the car.

'Where?'

'End of the track,' she replied, her heartbeat crashing hard as she locked her car and started to run. 'I'm going after him.'

'Keep your phone on. Keep talking to me...' As Cora neared the grass verge leading to the woodland path, Ellis' urgent request was suddenly drowned out by an urgent whisper, cacophonous where it should have been hushed:

They deserved what they got.

Every syllable doused in injustice.

In pain.

In caustic, unbridled *hate*...

Reaching down through the sound and tall grass, Cora found the source.

A painted pebble, like the one she'd seen in Mabel Yates' palm and the larger one Minshull had left for Cora in Mattie Kemp's garden, now residing in her jacket pocket.

Lukas Hall must have dropped it there for a reason.

293

And not just for her to find...

He had Mattie Kemp's baby and was carrying her deep into Evernam Woods. The whisper, loud as a scream, spoke of injustice done, of a voice ignored. It was a whisper that demanded to be heard.

And in that moment, Cora knew why Lukas had the baby.

'He's leaving a trail,' she breathed. 'Drew, tell Minshull that Lukas Hall has the pebbles. He'll understand. And please, call for help.'

'Stay where you are. I'll be there with you in one minute.'

'There's no time,' Cora countered, breaking into a sprint. 'I'm going after him.'

FIFTY

ANDERSON

'They thought they were going to run away from their problems. I had the plane tickets to prove it.'

Lingham scratched at the rim of his water cup. The plastic creaked and cracked beneath his fingers.

'Otto had found a hotel complex going cheap in Gran Canaria. The plan was to go out there, develop it into luxury apartments, flog them and move on to the next project with the profits. Only... it never existed. I pointed him in the direction of the listing, which I'd placed on a property website, then offered to handle the sale. Once he was on board, the others were easy to dupe.'

Anderson couldn't quite accept the newest version of Mark Lingham. But if it was an attempt to cover his back, he was going all out this time. 'Why?'

'Because of what Mattie knew.'

'What did she know?'

'Everyone has secrets. I mean, we all do. Just not like they did. I counted them as friends for years. Rugby and cricket, birthdays and weddings, lads' weekends and Christmas breaks – we've done the lot together. Good lads, everyone says. Salt of the earth. You imagine always hanging out like that, being old gits at the bar together one day. But that was before I knew...'

They were losing him again, his words meandering, his gaze drifting.

'What were their secrets?'

'Blackmail. Fraud. Affairs. Abuse...'

The words hung above the interview desk, four ragged spectres released, demanding notice.

For a moment, Anderson found himself at a loss to know how to proceed. Four serious allegations. Four brutal murders. But none of them planned? Was Lingham even aware of what he was saying?

'Are you suggesting they were killed because of those things?'

'They were there because of those things. I got them there because of those things. But not to kill them. To scare them into paying for what they'd done.'

'So what did the arrangement of the items around the bodies mean?'

'Clues,' Lingham replied. 'For them, not for you. They were meant to wake up, bound, arranged as they were, with clues to their crimes all around them. I had a knife. Mattie had one, too. We were going to confront them at knifepoint, get them shitting themselves thinking they were about to die. Then reprieve them when they were on their knees – for a price.'

Gone was the emotion of his former confessions. His matter-of-fact description chilled Anderson to his bones.

'And what did you plan to do with the money?'

'Give some back.'

'Some?'

'It had to be worth our while.'

Of course. Anderson should have guessed. Mark Lingham wasn't the charitable type – his preposterous attempts in this interview room to protect his own skin at all costs had said it all.

'So what changed?' Wheeler asked, mirroring Anderson's thoughts.

'The kid.' Lingham spat the word like poison from his tongue. 'She wasn't supposed to bring the kid.'

A sudden rap on the interview room door brought Anderson sharply back into the room.

'Come.'

Sergeant Vickery entered quickly, handing Anderson a slip of paper.

> *Lukas Hall on the run with Mattie Kemp's baby in Evernam Woods.*
>
> > *DC Ellis and Dr Cora Lael in pursuit. Support patrols deployed.*
> >
> > *Urgent assistance required.*

'We need to suspend the interview now,' Anderson barked. 'Has DS Minshull seen this?'

'I didn't want to disturb him, Guv. Sounded like things were getting heated in his interview...'

Anderson stared at the Custody Sergeant. '*Disturb* him, Lyn. He's the Senior Investigating Officer. Quickly!'

Vickery dashed out, making her hurried apologies as she left.

Anderson made to end the recording, but a thought pulled him back. He paused to look at Lingham. 'You said Ms Kemp wasn't supposed to bring *the kid*. Which kid?'

Lingham grimaced. 'Both of them.'

FIFTY-ONE

CORA

They deserved what they got…
    I tried my best…
    Nobody sees me…
    They'll see me now…

The whispers from the pebbles grew in volume and resolve, almost rising to a discernible tone in places. It was the whisper from the wrapped knife, becoming bolder the further it called Cora into Evernam Woods. There was no sense of the other voice she'd heard from that knife: it was as if the subordinate entity had shed the shackles imposed upon it by abandoning the other one.

Breaking free.

Going the way it wished.

Ahead of her, the increasingly insistent cries of Amelie Kemp drifted back through the thickening woodland, the baby laying its own audible trail for Cora to follow.

It wasn't the side of the woods where she had stumbled across the knife. This was the lesser-known northeast end of the woods, the oldest part, long since abandoned by those who maintained the peripheries. Here, the trees were twisted by time and neglect, their thicker trunks gnarled and converging, obscuring what few paths remained with their broken and ivy-choked branches.

The pebbles were becoming better hidden, but their voices betrayed their resting places. Cora had stopped collecting them after the first couple, relying on her ability alone to guide her steps. The recently imprinted thoughts from Lukas Hall's hands overlaid those left embedded in the paint, a double layer of sound rising from the ground as she passed.

The baby's cries were becoming more distant now. Cora picked up her pace as she held the phone to her ear, each step described to Ellis down a fluctuating line.

'I'm out of the car, and I'm following the path,' he puffed between the clicks and burrs.

'Look for the painted pebbles,' Cora rushed, climbing over a fallen tree and wading through waist-high bracken on the other side. 'Lukas is dropping them as he goes. I've left them for you to follow.'

'Genius, Dr Lael. The others are on their way.'

'And DS Minshull?' she hated herself for asking, the question revealing far more to Ellis than she wanted. But Minshull should be here. They were supposed to be working together...

'I've heard nothing yet. But he'll be here.'

Cora kicked aside a length of bramble barring her way, wincing when something sharp and hard bit her ankle. A front wheel was just visible, lying in the bracken and nettles, the undergrowth flattened by its weight; a handlebar twisted to the side, the metal object that had scratched her.

'He's abandoned his bike,' she reported.

'That should slow him down.'

Cora stared at the darkening tangle of trees lying ahead, the loudening whispers calling her on. There was no sign of Lukas Hall now, only the emotional echo of his grievances drawing her towards the deepest part of the woods, where layers of dark, forbidding green choked the daylight from view.

'Hurry,' she urged Ellis.

Because something far more concerning than the loss of visual contact with Lukas Hall had just occurred.

Amelie Kemp had stopped crying.

FIFTY-TWO

MINSHULL

Lukas Hall on the run with Mattie Kemp's baby in Evernam Woods.

DC Ellis and Dr Cora Lael in pursuit. Support patrols deployed.

Urgent assistance required.

It was a disaster.

'When?' Minshull demanded.

'Twenty minutes ago.' Lyn Vickery's expression was all apology in the narrow gap between the interview room door and the architrave where she'd slipped Minshull the note.

'Why wasn't I informed?'

'I heard your interviewee shouting. I assumed you wouldn't want to be disturbed.'

'You *assumed*...?' Minshull began, biting back his rage. 'Has DI Anderson seen this?'

'Yes, Sarge. He's on his way out now with DC Wheeler. There are two patrols already on their way.'

Why had Anderson left before him? What was the point of being SIO if your superior went on a shout without you?

And what the hell was Ellis doing, taking a car out alone?

Slamming the door, he returned to his seat, Bennett's concern immediate.

'DS Minshull has re-entered the room,' she said into the recorder, eyeing him.

'Will this take much longer?' Mattie Kemp asked, drumming her painted fingernails on the interview desk. 'I said I wanted to go home.'

'There's been a development,' Minshull replied.

Instantly, the fingers stilled.

'Lukas has Amelie.'

'I know. I asked him to.'

'He's taken her to Evernam Woods.'

The words punched the air from Mattie Kemp, her strangled cry filling the interview room.

'My colleagues are there,' he assured her, wishing they brought him the comfort he'd willed into them for the distraught mother. Ellis was out there, alone. Cora on the heels of a young man with a baby that wasn't his. 'They're on his tail. But you need to talk to me, Mattie. I need to know why he's taking her there.'

'Because we didn't listen,' she returned, her face flooded with tears. 'It's where he goes when he wants to make a point.'

'Where?'

'In the oldest part, where nobody else goes. He makes dens...' A sob escaped her lips. 'Stick dens, with the fallen branches he finds. He hides there until we beg him to come home. But he's never taken anyone else there... Not even me.'

'Does he want to be found?'

Kemp nodded numbly. 'He wants people to see him. There will be pebbles, left in a trail.'

Now, Minshull was listening, his senses on high alert. 'Pebbles?'

'He'll have taken the ones from my house. The painted ones. We paint them together when he comes over if Amelie's sleeping. He calls them the Find Me stones. Drops them all over the village to show he's been there.' She ran a hand through her hair. 'The last time he went missing, he took the pebbles and laid a trail. I only found him because I knew what to look for.'

'Why has he done this now? And why take your baby?'

'Because he thinks I dismissed him.'

'When?'

She ran a hand across her eyes, mascara seeping into the tears in a dark slick, like a mask. 'When I came with you. He thinks I'm here instead of him. That I'm trying to protect him… Please, you *have* to stop him. You don't know what he's capable of.'

Minshull wanted nothing more than to race from the room and follow his colleagues to Evernam Woods, but a swell of urgency in Kemp's words held him back.

'What is Lukas capable of?'

One word passed Mattie Kemp's lips before she crumpled into the arms of Mel Chatterjee.

'Murder.'

FIFTY-THREE

CORA

The light was almost impossible to see through the canopy now, the heavy raindrops splashing across leaves and branches, creating running gullies through the sandy ground at her feet.

The woods were awash with sound, both actual and hidden. It took all of Cora's concentration to raise the whispers from the pebbles over the sound of the rain, wind and shifting leaves.

And still no sound from the baby. Not even a sense of an echo.

'Cora, I'm by the bike now. Tell me what you can see.'

Phone pressed to her ear, Cora looked around for distinctive landmarks. But in the gloom, it was impossible to make out the individual details of the trees that converged, crossed and obstructed each other. 'It's dark here, the trees and undergrowth are so thick… There's a holly bush next to a fallen tree just ahead…'

In a sudden stab of memory, she recalled the painted pebbles in her pocket, the one from Mattie Kemp's garden and the first two pebbles she'd collected while following Lukas Hall before she'd started leaving them for Ellis. Pushing through the heavy swathes of nettles and brambles, she made her way to a shadowy protrusion that proved to be a moss-covered tree stump, the earth around it raised where the tangle of its roots had been dragged upwards by the force of the trunk snapping.

'Drew, I'm putting two of the painted pebbles on a tree stump between the holly bush and the fallen tree. Look for a red pebble and a yellow one side by side.'

'Okay. Can you see Lukas and the baby?'

'No. But I can hear him.'

Ellis' reply cracked and hissed through the rain-pelted woodland.

'I can't hear you. The line's bad. Keep talking to me.'

'...with you s... out and... way...'

Shielding her phone from the rain with her hand, Cora kept moving. Her clothes were soaked now, rainwater and mud seeping up the legs of her suit trousers, her toes swamped inside her shoes. Streams of water ran down her face, broaching the point where her mobile met her cheek, streaming beyond the cuffs of her jacket to her forearms, dampness converging at her elbows and across her back.

She willed Drew Ellis' voice to return as she sought each new iteration of Lukas Hall's furious whispers. Here in the unfamiliar, encroaching woodland, her aloneness was stark, terrifying.

The crackles continued from the failing call as, ahead, a shape began to form at a point that appeared lighter than the rest. The nearer Cora got, the better she was able to discern what lay ahead.

It looked like a structure of some kind, vaguely triangular in shape. Closer, Cora could see its walls weren't solid but rather formed from lengths of tree branches woven together.

A stick den.

Her brother Charlie had loved making them in the woods surrounding St Just, the village they'd grown up in. He'd been taken to an outward-bound centre on primary school trip, where his class had been shown how to construct shelters from sticks found in the woods, steadily building a hollow shape that they could sit inside when it was complete.

It had been years since Cora had last encountered one, but it was unmistakable.

This one was tall and wide – by Cora's reckoning, it could easily accommodate two adults inside. Its woven branch sides suggested they had been constructed and fortified significantly over time.

As Cora approached the clearing where it had been built, myriad whispers filled the air. Each stick, branch and twig of the den's construction was speaking, splintered copies of the teenager's voice twisting and weaving together, distorting at the points where they met.

Cora could only mute sections of the sound at a time, mentally grabbing handfuls and forcing down their volume as she searched for the most recent sound prints. Then she looked down, where a line of five painted pebbles had been laid, leading into the dark heart of the den.

'I've found a stick den,' she told Ellis, praying her words would arrive with him whole. 'I'm going in...'

Cora bent her head to enter – just as a baby's cry split the many-faceted echoes of Lukas Hall's thoughts.

'Lukas?' she spoke through the battle of sound surrounding her. 'I'm Cora. I'm a friend. I need to see you.'

'Not *you*,' Lukas Hall's voice growled, hot and close to her ear.

Cora turned – and found she wasn't alone.

Furious eyes bore into her as a sudden heavy blow knocked the phone from her hand...

FIFTY-FOUR

ELLIS

'Cora? You're breaking up... Keep talking, okay?'

Ellis looked up through the rain, trying to gauge where best to move to find a patch of reception. A pool of pale light just ahead seemed promising. Leaving the narrow path, Ellis waded through wet bracken to reach it.

'...ahead... den...'

Den? Was that part of a word lost to the crackles of the unreliable line or a word on its own? Was he looking for a den in this darkening, unnavigable part of the woods? Who would come all this way for a den?

Ellis had played in the woods on the north side of St Just village as a kid, as all the children in his school had. But there, the woodland was managed, the trees well-spaced and cared for, and the undergrowth kept at bay by regular clearing, allowing space for light and welcoming trails. It was a natural draw, with plenty of organic building materials for making dens left for eager young den-makers by the woodland managers.

Ellis couldn't imagine anyone being drawn to this dark and lonely place, let alone constructing a den here.

His radio buzzed into life in his other hand.

'DC Ellis, please give your location, over?'

Shaking the raindrops from his radio, Ellis held it close to his lips as he pushed through the ground cover.

'DC Ellis, received. I'm following Dr Cora Lael in pursuit of Lukas Hall, heading northeast in Evernam Woods. Over.'

'Received. Can you see them from your current position? Over.'

'Negative. I'm in contact with Dr Lael via mobile, but I'm losing the line...'

His boot suddenly connected with a wet tree root, sending him tumbling forward. His hand shot out to steady himself, finding the rough edge of a tree stump, slippery with moss beneath his fingers. Regaining his balance, Ellis looked to his left – and saw the pebbles. One yellow, one red, resting side by side at the centre of the exposed rings of the felled tree.

'I've found markers left by Dr Lael,' he reported. 'I must be close to her location now. What's the ETA of the patrols? Over.'

'Five minutes behind. Over.'

'DI Anderson to DC Ellis.' Anderson's bark cut through the damp air.

Ellis closed his eyes as he replied. 'DC Ellis receiving. Go ahead, Guv.'

'What the *bloody hell* do you think you're playing at? Do you have any idea how irresponsible your actions are? Putting yourself in danger, not to mention your colleagues who are coming to find you...'

As Anderson's fury raged on from the radio, Ellis kept moving, the darkest part of the woodland in his sights. He would deal with whatever his superiors wished to throw at him later. Right now, he needed to get to Cora.

He had spent too long sidelined in this case, robbed of the right to be fully involved, simply because he knew the victims and the man accused of murder. This was what he should have been doing all along – following his instinct, taking action.

Doing his bloody job.

Anderson and Minshull could think what they liked of him: when Cora had needed assistance, he had been the only officer on the ground. This was what he'd trained for, what he'd worked so hard to achieve. Sod the consequences...

A break in the gloom of the woodland's dark heart caught his eye, summoning him to approach.

Then he saw it.

A stick den, taller and far more complicated a construction than any he had built in his childhood. He would have lost his mind over it as a kid. The thickly woven walls and impressive height were the stuff of his boyhood dreams.

He began to move towards it, turning down the volume of the radio as he neared the clearing.

But what he saw next made him drop to the cover of the sodden bracken on the woodland floor.

Lukas Hall, a baby in a sling across his chest, one arm bent across the neck and shoulders of Dr Cora Lael, holding her fast.

And, just visible in the dim woodland light, a cold flash of steel from the knife he held to her throat...

FIFTY-FIVE

MINSHULL

'What's happening?' Minshull demanded, flooring the accelerator.

'Shh, I'm trying to listen,' Bennett returned, adjusting the volume on the police radio.

Minshull muttered something the rising volume of the radio drowned out, forcing his attention back to the road instead of the growing sense of dread building in his gut. Ellis and Cora, tracking a dangerous young man through the woods – and he and Bennett still too far away.

They didn't know Lukas Hall had murdered four men.

But Minshull and Bennett did.

The confession had come flooding out from Mattie Kemp, the terror of her daughter being alone with the teen she'd looked after for years dragging the truth from her.

When it came, Minshull had no choice but to stay and hear it.

'Mark picked up the keys to the unit last week and gave them to me on one of his visits to my house. He'd spun Krish a story about wanting to evaluate its current value as a gift to Krish's uncle for letting us meet there. I was supposed to slip in once they were all knocked out with the champagne, using a copy of the key Mark had made to let myself in.

'Lukas insisted on being there. He knew what we were planning, and he said he would help. It meant I had to bring Amelie with me – she was strapped to me in the sling – so Lukas helped Mark tie them up and drag them into position, while I arranged the stuff around them. It was annoying, but I didn't think it was a problem. Lukas is stronger than I am – stronger than Mark, too. He could be useful for once, and he liked that. But I wasn't ready for… I never thought…'

It had taken some time for Kemp to regain her composure sufficiently to continue, Minshull on edge as he waited.

'What happened?' he'd asked at last, desperate to leave.

'They woke up – saw all the shit – and we spelled out their crimes. It was working like we'd planned. They were crying, wailing, begging us not to kill them. Mark was swinging his knife around like an assassin, totally getting off on the power. It was disgusting. But we were following the plan, so I let it pass. I thought of the money we'd make – and the justice we were serving. And then Lukas grabbed my knife.'

'Did you try to stop him?'

'It happened so fast. I couldn't reach him. And I had Amelie on me – I couldn't think of anything else but protecting her.'

'What about Lingham?' Bennett had asked.

'He was too busy playing the part.' She'd hung her head then, the duty solicitor watching on as Kemp replayed the unfolding horrors.

'Lukas was so fast. He was yelling at Lingham, yelling at the others, about justice and someone needing to do something. And then he slashed Tim Stapleforth's throat…' She gagged at the memory. 'He just did it. A single stroke, like he knew where to hit. It was like a nightmare I couldn't stop. I screamed at him to drop the knife, but he ran over to Krish and slashed him, too, then attacked Denz next to him. Mark dashed over to Tim, trying to stop the blood, yelling and crying. He tried to get up and get to Lukas before he went to Otto, but there was blood on him, blood on the floor – he slipped and fell… I've never seen so much blood. And the sound… I can't get the sound out of my head…'

'Sarge, the Guv's calling.' Bennett put her phone on speaker, cranking up the volume over the hisses and clicks of the police radio.

Minshull nodded, and Bennett answered the call.

'Guv, it's Kate Bennett. The Sarge is driving. We're ten minutes away.'

'Ellis is there. He's almost with Cora.'

'And Lukas Hall?' Minshull asked.

'Still at large. With the baby.'

Minshull swallowed a ball of fear that threatened to choke him. 'Guv, Mattie Kemp made a disclosure to us before we left. Lukas Hall murdered the four men in Januarius Street. Kemp and Lingham set it up to terrify and blackmail the victims, not to kill them. Lukas Hall wasn't part of the plan, but he was brought in to help overpower the men. He grabbed a knife and took matters into his own hands.'

'Shit, Rob.'

'He may be armed.'

'I'll alert everyone. Are you sure she's telling the truth?'

Minshull had doubted it, but there was no mistaking Mattie Kemp's horror. 'I'm certain. She says they never intended to kill the men, just put the fear of God into them and use that as licence for extortion.'

'Why did she leave Lingham there?'

That was the strangest part of the confession. As Minshull turned onto the road leading to Evernam, he remembered Mattie Kemp's reply.

'He lost it. He was babbling, sliding on the floor between them, begging them not to die. Then he turned on me, said he was going to send me down for it. He said he was always going to pin it on me because I'd betrayed his friends. Lukas was crouched in a corner, watching them all choke, and he went for Mark. But I managed to grab him and drag him back. The only way I could get Lukas out of there was to say we were going to leave Mark there to take the blame. We ran out of the back door, locked it, and I tossed the keys in the wheelie bin for the next door shop.'

'So if we search there, we'll find them,' Anderson stated.

'Guv. I'm worried for Cora.'

He caught Bennett's look. It didn't matter what she thought – what anyone thought. He was the reason Cora was chasing a dangerous young man through Evernam Woods, unarmed, with no idea of the peril she was in.

'We'll find her. Ellis is there.'

'Tell him to be careful. And to get them out alive.'

'Road to the woods approaching, Sarge, ahead on the right,' Bennett urged.

Minshull slowed the pool car just enough to take the turn, then accelerated down the narrowing track. As he did, an urgent voice cut across the engine noise.

Ellis.

Scared.

Voice little more than a whisper, clear despite the surrounding sound.

'DC Ellis to control. Suspect is armed with a large knife and is holding Dr Lael. Urgent assistance required. I am on the ground and out of sight, but I'm going to try to get to him...'

'DC Ellis, stay where you are!' Anderson's voice now replied from the radio, like the omnipresent force his team suspected him to be. 'Assistance is on its way. Remain in position and await further orders. Do not approach Lukas Hall. I repeat, do *not* attempt to approach Lukas Hall...'

FIFTY-SIX

LUKAS

She said she was a friend.

But she was lying.

The woman with the red hair braced against his arm as he squeezed tighter. She'd been easier to knock over than the others, even without the dodgy champagne. He was stronger than she expected.

That felt good.

Amelie would need feeding soon. And the sling was suspiciously warm around her bottom, so she'd need a change, too. Had he brought all the changing stuff? He'd been so busy collecting the Find Me stones that he'd not paid attention to the things from the changing basket he'd stuffed into his rucksack.

Mattie would be cross.

He hated that.

He was a good babysitter for Amelie. The best. Better than Mattie sometimes, he thought, especially when she was tired, or when that bastard Tim had been around.

She didn't think he knew about that. Or the plan he'd heard her going over with Mark Lingham. He'd only been in the kitchen the last time Lingham had visited, but he might as well have been on Mars for all the attention they paid him.

They don't see me.

I'm a ghost.

Sometimes, he wondered if he really existed at all. Mum and Dad tutted around him, like he was a load of clutter in their way. Gaby was too busy with her school marking and her weekend gym visits and that rat-faced new boyfriend of hers to acknowledge his existence.

He'd thought Mattie had seen him.

But she'd lied, too.

She used to tell him he was capable of anything he put his mind to. She'd tell him it when they were painting the Find Me stones together.

'You're so much cleverer than anyone realises, Lukie,' she'd say. 'Don't let anyone make you think otherwise. You just need to find your power. Like Superman.'

'Is that why you're scaring Evil Tim?' he'd asked once.

Evil Tim. The nickname Tim Stapleforth had been given as they'd painted hopeful images in bright poster paints on pebbles Mattie found for Lukas. She'd made Evil Tim out to be a cartoon villain so Lukas wouldn't worry, but Lukas knew the truth. He'd heard those conversations, too. The threats. The fear in Mattie's voice.

She should have gone to the police when a tower of wooden pallets Tim Stapleforth had stacked too high fell on her at his packing warehouse where she worked before she moved to Evernam. The damage to her back was permanent, limiting the work she could do. She should have sued Stapleforth, but he'd scared her out of it. Arranged for accommodation in the village for her when her two previous landlords evicted her for non-payment of rent. Then, he came by whenever he wanted a power trip, reminding her of what she owed him. Throwing his weight around. Demanding payment in ways Mattie should never have to make.

Blackmail.

Fraud.

Affairs.

Abuse.

Being a victim made her listen to other people's stories, she said.

'Like you, Lukas. You listen. That's our power. People dismiss us, but we know so much more than they realise. That gives us the advantage.'

Mattie had listened to the girlfriend Denz Markham had terrorised for years when she did some office stuff for the farm machinery dealership. Heard how he'd beaten her so badly one night she'd thought she was going to die.

A boxing glove: his violence.

A blood-covered child's toy: the baby his girlfriend miscarried after a beating.

A list of girls' names: past victims.

A roll of electrical tape: his profession before he entered farm sales.

A battered copy of War and Peace: *he called himself 'The Count' – above reproach.*

She'd listened to Ani Bhattachama at her antenatal clinic, who'd told her of the women Krish was seeing, the emails she'd found from his sordid affairs, and the money he was wasting on his lovers while she struggled to make ends meet at home.

A bunch of receipts: money he wasted on affairs.

A brown document file: a threat of evidence.

An open padlock: secrets.

A broken camera lens: the profession of his latest mistress.

A coil of rope: his particular kink during sex.

And she'd listened to Joy Naismith, the shy nineteen-year-old who ran the mother and baby club at Evernam Library, when she'd burst into tears on the way home from the pub and confided in Mattie that Otto Wragg had tricked her into investing in a first-time buyers' scheme that had stolen her life savings.

A bunch of keys: his profession.

An estate agents' brochure, the property crossed out: fake properties.

A postcard from the Canary Islands: his plan to flee the UK.

A photo of a family, torn in half: victims of his property scams.

A hammer: the physical threats he made to his victims.

And the reason for Mattie's own hatred of Tim Staple-forth: the man who had blackmailed her to cover up her accident, adding demands for sex into the bargain. The man who threatened her when he assumed Amelie was his – even though Mark Lingham was the father.

A toy car, damaged: to represent Mattie's accident.

A Do Not Disturb door sign: intimidation and silence.

A cricket ball: his captaincy of the cricket team.

An election rosette: his mother's role as a councillor.

A bag of filthy coins: blackmail.

All of these stories of hate and injustice, Mattie had repeated over the Find Me stones as they painted them with hope and colour. Sometimes, Lukas wondered if she even realised he was there when she was doing it. Like he was another piece of furniture in the sitting room listening to her anger.

And he got angry, too.

It was why he'd insisted on going with her to the shop in Januarius Street. Mattie shouldn't get revenge by herself. Because he'd listened too: now he had the same power she did.

The red-haired woman made a sound like a cry and a cough together.

'Shush,' he said, frowning when Amelie stirred against his chest. 'Don't wake the baby.'

'She should be with her mum,' the woman spluttered. 'Mattie will be worried.'

'Mattie knows I take care of her,' he replied, not that the woman deserved an explanation. 'She knows I love Amelie more than anything.'

'Why don't we take her back to her mum together?'

'No.' He squeezed a little harder, the strained gurgle satisfying. 'We have to wait to be found. That's The Game.'

'The… game?'

How could she not know The Game?

Hide, leave a trail, get found.

316

What was the point of a stick den if you couldn't play The Game there?

Mattie knew it. She would follow the stones and come to find them. The red-haired woman knew nothing. She didn't know his power. To give her a clue, he rested the flat side of the knife blade a little closer to her skin.

It felt good in his hands.

Power.

Like it had in the shop.

I'm stronger than they realised. And so much cleverer.

They would find him soon. And then they'd see…

FIFTY-SEVEN

MINSHULL

The patrol cars were parked in an untidy line where the track surrendered to the woods, uniformed officers being briefed by Anderson, with Wheeler grave-faced beside him.

Minshull swung the car to the side of the track, killing the engine. He and Bennett hurried over to Anderson and Wheeler.

'What's everyone doing here?' Minshull demanded, paying no attention to the looks his colleagues sent him.

'Agreeing a plan of action, Sarge. We need to surround the area, approach from all sides.'

'Then why aren't you all out there now?'

'Rob...' Wheeler warned.

'No, Dave, Lukas Hall is armed and holding a baby and Dr Lael hostage. What more do you need to know?'

'We do this right or not at all,' Anderson stated.

'Guv, you're playing with lives!'

'DS Minshull, *stand down*,' Anderson commanded.

Minshull instinctively drew back, seething. It should be his shout, his job to lead. How dare Anderson muscle in now? It wasn't Minshull's fault that Lyn Vickery had decided to stop news of what was happening from getting to him.

Expression thunderous, Anderson addressed the gathered officers. 'Right, you know where to go. Be careful and monitor your radios. Do not approach unless expressly told to do so. Understood? Good. Go.'

Their colleagues thus dismissed, Anderson swung back to Minshull.

'Don't *ever* talk to me like that in front of others again.'

'With respect, Guv, this is supposed to be my gig. My call.'

'You weren't here. Someone had to step up.'

'But he has Cora.'

Anderson's fury faded. 'I know. You need to calm yourself, Rob. Your panic does nothing to help her.'

He was right, but Minshull couldn't think beyond the terror gripping him. 'I'm going in after them.'

Anderson gave a weary nod. 'I know you are. Just be careful. It isn't only Cora's life in danger. Kate, go with him. Make sure he doesn't get himself killed.'

Bennett barely had time to accept before she was running alongside Minshull.

'Which way?' she called as they leapt over exposed tree roots and slapped rain-soaked overhanging branches and stubborn brambles aside from the path.

'Straight in until we see it. Then we look for a route in, away from the front of the shelter.'

Across the woodland, the bowed heads of uniformed officers could just be seen in the encroaching gloom, a net being closed steadily, stealthily around the oldest part of the woods. It was both a comfort and a risk. Despite Mattie Kemp's insistence that Lukas wanted to be discovered, that he had no intention of harming the baby he adored, there were no guarantees of how he would respond to fifteen officers approaching the den.

The heavy rain clattering through the trees afforded them some sound cover at least, the fast footsteps of his colleagues masked well behind the loud, insistent drone. Minshull and Bennett pushed ahead, taking whatever route they could instead of following the narrow footpaths criss-crossing the dense undergrowth. Mud splashed over their trousers, rainwater finding its way into their shirts and down their backs. Still, they ran, the thought of Ellis and Cora and Mattie Kemp's baby fuelling their strides.

Where the wood darkened ahead, Minshull raised his hand and slowed, Bennett pulling level. A crack of a tree branch to their right caused them both to duck behind a rhododendron bush, water running down its glossy dark green leaves beside them. When no further sound followed, Minshull turned to Bennett.

'It's in there. The darkest part, Ellis said. He's gone to ground not far from here.'

'So where do we go?'

Minshull breathed hard against the burn at the centre of his chest. 'Head to the left. I'll take the right. Make as wide a sweep as you can, then move towards the middle. Beyond that dead tree.'

He indicated the tall promontory of leafless decaying wood, bleached and cracked by the elements, pointing like a withered finger to the crowded canopy above.

'Keep talking to me,' Bennett replied, phone in hand. 'I'll wait for your signal.'

'Agreed.'

Her hand rested for a moment on his forearm. 'Be careful, Minsh.' It was removed before he could reply, Bennett sprinting away from their hiding place, her head and shoulders bowed to stay beneath the line of undergrowth.

Minshull scanned the immediate area. His fellow officers were here, he knew, but the woods appeared still. They were hiding, waiting, steadily approaching the location Ellis had whispered into his radio.

Was Cora aware of them yet? Did she know he was there?

A fresh rush of fear flooded his body.

And Minshull began to run.

FIFTY-EIGHT

CORA

The blade was cold against her neck, the chokehold of Lukas Hall's arm constricting her airway, making every breath an effort.

But Cora was battling more than this.

The whispers she'd followed to the stick den were now screams from the knife, rage and intense injustice converging in a cacophony of noise. She tried to mute the multiple versions of Lukas' voice, but fear and the sheer force of his unspoken thoughts prevented her.

In the rare moments when they ebbed a little, she attempted to coax the young man to let go. Appealing to him on the baby's behalf did no good, Lukas insisting Amelie wanted to be part of The Game. Reminding him of Mattie's charge to look after Amelie only strengthened his argument.

At the next juncture, she tried again.

'The rain's getting worse,' she managed, her voice thin and strained against the pressure. 'It isn't good to be sitting here in wet clothes.'

'My den is a good shelter,' Lukas responded. 'I built it that way.'

'But Amelie needs dry clothes. And a change.'

Lukas paused, as if considering the strength of the unmistakable smell coming from the sling. 'Mattie will change her when she finds us.'

'What if she doesn't? What if…?' Cora began, the rest of the words squeezed unspoken from her. 'Lukas…' she managed to croak, '…*please*… You're *hurting me*…'

'Good.' His voice was sharp against her ear as the screamed thoughts rose behind it.

So, instead of speaking, Cora chose to listen.

They had it coming.

I just made it happen.

Mattie couldn't see it through. But I did.

I'm The Power now, not them.

They'll see me now.

See me now, bastards!

'They'll see you now,' Cora repeated slowly, pain threatening every word.

The screams ebbed for a breath.

'Because you're the power. Not them.'

Another ebb. The blade slackened a little at her throat.

Lukas didn't reply. But the sudden quickening of his breath registered a hit.

Cora waited a while before she spoke again.

Push and pull back – Tris Noakes' favourite phrase for approaching sensitive subjects with the children and young people under their care. 'Like a game. Advance and retreat, like a fencing volley.'

The memory of her colleague's decidedly public-school analogy gave Cora a glimpse of lightness amid the fear. Only Tris Noakes could think swordplay was a universally understood example to choose.

She wished he was here now, advising her, supporting her attempts to connect with Lukas. She wished *anyone* could be with her, in this dark, abandoned wilderness. All contact with Drew Ellis had been lost when Lukas had knocked her down, her mobile lying useless somewhere in the surrounding undergrowth. Even if Rob Minshull was on his way – or nearby – he couldn't contact her.

Ellis was somewhere out beyond the stick den, but since Cora had been held by Lukas, she'd seen no sign of him. She hoped he was safe: the courage he'd shown by racing out to Evernam Woods alone to find her was considerable. He'd done it for her: if she found a way out from this place, he would be the first person she would thank.

As for Minshull... she didn't know what to think.

Did he even know yet? Would he try to reach her?

Cora bit back tears as she resumed her study of the multitudinous assertions of her captor.

As she did so, Amelie Kemp awoke and started to cry.

FIFTY-NINE

MINSHULL

The cry was a beacon.

Minshull's head snapped round, his body following as he changed course and made for the sound.

He'd gone too wide, missing the shadowed heart of the woods by a considerable distance. Had it not been for Amelie Kemp's wail, he might have missed them entirely.

He honed in on the cries, the sound amplified by the echoes reverberating through the close-growing trees. It wrenched at his core, stoking his rising fear about the woman being held beside its source, but for once, Minshull willed the sound to continue.

Please let her be okay, he begged whichever deity may be listening in the rain-pummelled woodland, all too aware that his plea wasn't only for the baby strapped to Lukas Hall.

The cries grew louder, calling him through a dense patch of brambles that grappled with the fabric of his trousers as he tore himself free. Rounding a wide trunk of two trees that had grown together as one, he caught sight of something about ten yards ahead.

The flash of a raised hand, dropped quickly back into the undergrowth.

Instinctively, Minshull began to count. Three seconds later, the hand appeared again, held for three seconds, then disappearing.

Drew Ellis.

They'd discussed it once, months back. Ellis had been reading about non-radio communication used in surveillance situations and had been amused by the raised hand method. A hand raised for three seconds exactly then lowered for three. Repeated as needed to signal your location. The receptor would repeat the pattern, confirming both receipt and location.

'Like at school, where everyone had to raise their hands when the teacher wanted the class to be quiet,' he'd joked. 'A hand up for quiet, everyone's hands up in reply.'

It had made them laugh, then, in the warm, familiar confines of the CID office.

This place was far removed from there. But Ellis had remembered and was using the signal for real.

God bless that kid!

Minshull retreated behind the double-headed tree, raising his palm in the direction of Ellis.

Three seconds visible. Three seconds hidden. Three seconds visible again.

Peering around the rough bark, he saw the identical reply.

Then, across the glistening foliage as far from Ellis as Minshull was, another hand rose.

Three seconds visible.

Three seconds hidden.

Three seconds visible again.

Kate Bennett, now in position.

Bolstered by the presence of his colleagues and friends, Minshull began to move.

SIXTY

CORA

She saw the hand rise for only a moment, and then it was gone.

Lukas was whispering to the baby at his chest, begging Amelie Kemp to stop crying.

Hardly daring to breathe, Cora slowly lifted her cold fingers until her palm faced the patch of bracken where she'd seen the hand emerge, the back of her hand pressed flat against her torso, inches below the strong barrier of her captor's arm.

Sensing her movement, the hold on her neck increased.

Flashes of light like tiny stars began to appear at the peripheries of Cora's vision. The urge to close her eyes grew stronger, to give in to the beckoning blackness threatening to engulf her as she danced on the very edge of consciousness. Only the insistent hidden voices yelling from Lukas Hall kept her from falling.

Grasping them like an anchor, Cora forced her hand to stay open, praying that whoever had raised their hand would see.

Almost immediately, the hand appeared again, rotating to Cora's right before falling back beneath the heads of bracken.

A signal.

Assistance from that side. A net closing in.

Despite the pain and the cacophony of hidden voices, Cora's heart lifted.

She wasn't alone. Friends were watching…

SIXTY-ONE

MINSHULL

The wet leaves brushed his arms and face, painting rainwater streaks across his jacket sleeves, his cheeks and neck. He kept his body low, his progress slow but steady, pocketing his phone as he moved. He was too close to the stick den to use it now.

The baby's cries were more insistent, increasing in volume and temper the closer Minshull moved towards the sound.

He'd seen Ellis' signal and the subtle change in the direction and pattern.

Help from your right…

Minshull's cue.

Had Cora seen the signal, too? Had she been able to reply?

Ellis' hand rose from the bracken again, this time facing Minshull, the pattern returned to its original formation. A signal to him.

As the hand fell from view, Minshull saw the structure.

It was side-on, but unmistakable as a stick den. Minshull had never constructed one himself, but he'd seen plenty on his weekend runs that took him through the woodlands of a local nature reserve near Woodbridge, passing children delighted to have discovered the strange, otherworldly structures. They would be magical to find as a kid, conjuring thoughts of mythical creatures, fairies or dragons, building them for weary travellers to find.

In a sunlit patch of woodland, Lukas Hall's stick den might enchant onlookers, too.

But in the storm-grey light of Evernam Woods' ancient heart, it was an ominous sight.

Minshull judged the structure from as close as he dared to get, Amelie Kemp's furious objections masking the brush of bracken and bramble against his clothes as he took his position. It appeared to be solidly constructed, the layers of branch and twig erected in regimented rows to create a considerable barrier.

But it was just sticks woven together, resting on the sandy soil of the woodland floor.

If Minshull threw his body weight against the side of the den, would that be enough to fell it? And would Cora know that Ellis' subtle signal heralded Minshull's arrival?

Minshull had heard his colleague's urgent whispers over the police radio as he had neared the patrol cars, detailing the position Cora was being held in and the location of Amelie Kemp in relation to Lukas. But were they still in the same place? Being unable to check before he moved put him at a disadvantage. He could injure Cora, the baby or their captor if he judged it wrong.

He would only have one shot: it had to be right.

He raised his palm towards Ellis to signal he was in position. Ellis responded in kind.

The knife is at the side of her throat, in his right hand, his right arm across her collarbone, holding her in place. The baby is in the sling at the centre of his chest. He is leaning to his left with Dr Lael held to his right side, so the knife is away from the baby.

Picturing Ellis' report he'd received in a flurry of messages sent to his phone, Minshull settled his mark on the side of the stick den. He raised a closed fist to Ellis, signalling he was about to move.

Then, he began to run.

SIXTY-TWO

CORA

The right-leaning palm appeared again from the bracken.

As it did so, Lukas began to plead with the furiously sobbing Amelie, his attention drawn away from Cora, his emotional thought-voice revealing frustration and panic.

'Come on, Amelie, stop crying for me...'

Why aren't you asleep? Go back to sleep!

'I can't take you home yet. We've got to play The Game, haven't we? It's important...'

Why won't she play The Game?

'Shh... shhh, now...'

They have to see me. They have to understand...

Amid the screams of the baby beside her and the increasingly anguished thoughts of the man who held them both, Cora forced her breath to slow.

She'd gauged the direction in which the flat steel of the blade had slackened against her throat while Lukas tried in vain to calm Amelie, his attention distracted by the red-faced fury of Mattie Kemp's daughter. If she jerked forward, the side of her throat would slide along the flattened steel, the pressure on Lukas' forearm preventing him from turning the edge of the blade to cut her skin.

If she'd judged it correctly.

A sudden pounding of feet to her right spurred her into action.

Forcing all other thoughts and sounds from her mind, Cora threw herself forward. The jerk of the movement caught Lukas unaware. He yelped as Cora's shoulder pushed his wrist back, his hand flexing open. Released from his grip, the knife fell.

At that moment, the right side of the stick den imploded in a crash of splintering wood as Minshull's body tore through it. Cora rolled forward, pulling Lukas and the baby over her. The teenager's arm released her as he toppled overhead, a scream coming from the baby as they fell.

Gasping for air, Cora kicked the knife aside, lunging for Lukas Hall, who was writhing on his back. She made a grab for the baby's sling, but Lukas kicked out, his mud-covered trainer connecting with her stomach. The pain was intense as Cora doubled over, falling to her knees. A second kick connected with her jaw, wrenching her head back, the trees spinning in her vision as she fell.

A roar from behind her split the air, and Minshull was there, throwing his body over the young man's legs. A loud crack sounded as Lukas screamed in pain.

Suddenly, the entire woodland was alive with sound and the thunder of boots as police appeared from all directions, their sights set on Lukas Hall.

Cora tasted blood and raised her fingers to her stinging jaw, finding a diagonal slash across it where Hall's trainer had ripped her skin. Struggling upright, she saw seven uniformed officers with Bennett, Wheeler and Ellis, frozen in a stunned cordon around the prone body of Lukas Hall, Minshull staring up at the teenager from across his legs.

'Don't move,' Lukas snarled at them all, his hands digging into the sling on either side of the baby's head. 'Or Amelie dies.'

SIXTY-THREE

MINSHULL

There was nothing he could do.

Lying across Lukas Hall's legs, Minshull could only stare up in horror as the teen's fingers encircled the baby's neck.

A glance at his colleagues confirmed his worst fears. Nobody could move fast enough from their positions to stop Hall if he chose to carry out his threat. Even Minshull, in actual physical contact with Lukas, dared not move, despite the loud crack that had sounded beneath him, suggesting at least one leg broken. The smallest movement could be catastrophic.

Hall looked so young from Minshull's vantage point, barely able to grow stubble, let alone callously end the lives of four grown men. It would be almost easy to think him incapable of murder, if the memory of Mattie Kemp's frantic confession weren't playing on repeat in his mind.

'He was like an animal. He moved so fast – I couldn't even yell at him before he'd killed Tim. It was like he knew exactly what he was doing, where to hit them. Like he'd studied it. One slash – that was all he did. And I watched them fall. When he'd slashed Otto, he looked back at me... His whole face had changed, like – like a monster. He was laughing when he attacked them...'

Hall was capable of dispatching the men he considered evil. Was he prepared to take the life of an innocent?

Think! Minshull commanded himself. There had to be something he could do – but how could he move without Lukas responding?

'Lukas.'

From beyond where he lay, Minshull heard Cora's voice. Without moving his head, he shifted his gaze until he could see her at the edge of his vision.

She was crouched now where she'd fallen, somehow managing to right her body while Lukas was distracted. His stare swung to her, his elbows lifting as if reinforcing the threat.

'Don't move!'

'This isn't what you want.'

What the hell was she doing? Minshull glared to dissuade her, but Cora didn't notice, her attention trained on the young man on the ground.

'You don't know what I want!'

'You want to play The Game,' she continued, her voice steady, emotionless.

'They should know about The Game.'

'But they don't. So you'll have to show them.'

Deep lines creased at the point where his brows met. 'Will they play?'

'Can I move closer, please? I want to see Amelie.'

'No! Stay still!'

Cora raised both hands, edging forward imperceptibly. 'I'm here, okay? I just want to make sure Amelie's ready to see The Game when it ends.'

'She can see from here.'

'She can't see them seeing *you*,' Cora replied, as if that sentence made complete sense to her and everyone else present. 'That's the best part, isn't it? Do you want Amelie to miss it after you've worked so hard to make it happen?'

A flicker of doubt animated Hall's stare. 'No...'

'So take her out of the sling.'

'I can't do that.' Lukas looked down at the baby, who had fallen scarily silent.

Minshull saw Cora edge a little further forward. 'It won't work from down there. All she can see is you. How is she going to learn The Game if she can't see what the Finders look like?'

Hall's brows knotted, sending his eyes into deep shadow. 'If they move...'

'They won't.' Cora looked around the horrified police personnel. 'Statue-still, everyone, okay? All eyes on Lukas.' She returned her steady gaze to the young man on the floor. 'See? They want to play The Game, too.'

The shadowed eyes rounded the circle of police. 'Do they?'

Cora moved closer. 'Of course. Look how closely they're watching you.'

Lukas said nothing, but his hands pulled back a little.

Minshull's breath caught.

'Lift Amelie out, so she can watch, too.'

'Okay, but I'll hold her.'

'Of course.'

The young man's hands emerged from the edge of the sling, travelling over the fabric to the knot at the side. Cora remained motionless as the sling grew slack, Amelie resting flat on Lukas' chest.

'Careful, she's rolling,' Minshull called, seeing the baby's head loll to one side.

'Don't move!' Lukas yelled.

'He isn't,' Cora glared at Minshull. 'Only you are. Support her head – quickly now.'

To Minshull's relief, Lukas complied, sitting the baby up, one hand at the back of her head, the other supporting her back.

'Can she see now?' he asked, the note of uncertainty so at odds with his earlier threats.

'I think so. Now make sure she can see the Find Me stones.'

The young man's face fell. 'I don't have them! I dropped them all on the path to show the way. I can't finish The Game without them.' He looked over at the wreck of his stick den. 'I can't see any there.'

In reply to the rising panic of his voice, Amelie Kemp's face began to redden, the stirrings of distress sounding from her lungs.

'Let me fetch one.' Bennett's voice sounded shaky as she spoke up.

'No! Nobody move!' Hall's grip tightened on the baby's back.

Cora's eyes flicked to Minshull as she reached into her pocket. 'I have one.' She lifted up a palm-sized painted pebble bearing an image of a bright yellow sun. 'See?'

A shot of adrenaline coursed through Minshull. The pebble he'd taken from Mattie Kemp's house, dropped for Cora to find.

'Give it to Amelie.'

'Are you sure?' Cora asked. 'I'll have to move to do that.'

Lukas Hall's eyes flicked from the pebble Cora held to the baby sitting on his chest. Minshull saw resolve set his expression firm. 'Yes. Bring it to Amelie. Then we can finish The Game.'

SIXTY-FOUR

CORA

Breathless, Cora stood.

Her body screamed in protest, sharp needles stabbing her stomach where Lukas had kicked her, her jaw on fire. She pushed against the pain, consciously slowing every movement. Holding the sunshine pebble ahead of her where Lukas could see it, she began to move.

The eyes of the police officers were on her, heads nodding in encouragement as she shuffled forward. Kate Bennett, Drew Ellis beside her, Dave Wheeler's tight smile. Uniformed officers, some of whom she recognised. Steph Lanehan and Rilla Davis, their identical frowns willing her onwards.

Her police family.

It had taken three years and too many false starts, but she finally felt it. The closeness she heard Minshull and the others referring to, the feeling of a unified purpose, of having a team at your back.

She forced her face to relax into a smile as she headed for Lukas Hall. Despite her rising fear. Despite the still swirling growls of defiance coming from his thoughts, louder than anything he was saying as he lay on the woodland floor. The pebble was her shield, her ability the one advantage she had over him.

My power.

Reaching his side, she brightened her smile, holding the pebble down near the grizzling baby. 'See, Amelie? It's a Find

Me stone. That's what brings people to you when you want them to see you. That's right, isn't it, Lukas?'

The flash of recognition in the prone man's face gave her the chance she'd prayed for.

In a single movement, Cora threw the pebble down into Lukas Hall's eye and stamped hard on his bent elbow, whisking the baby from his hands as he screamed out in pain.

Amelie screamed in unison as Cora cradled her close, stumbling away into the sodden bracken as the police officers piled onto Lukas Hall.

His shouts and screams sent the woodland birds fleeing from the trees, the frantic beating of wings adding to the rush of sound that assaulted her from every side. But Cora held Amelie tightly, the warmth of the baby in her arms enough to counter it all.

And finally, after what had felt like a lifetime, she grasped the ugly snarls and terrified screams of Lukas Hall's thought-voices, firmly muting them to silence.

SIXTY-FIVE

ANDERSON

If he'd been reading the transcript of the interviews that followed the arrests of Lukas Hall, Mattie Kemp and Mark Lingham without being part of them, Anderson would have declared them a work of preposterous fiction.

A plot for revenge, enacted by Kemp and Lingham together as some kind of twisted justice league, and enough crossing and double-crossing to make James Bond dizzy. It shouldn't be real – except for the fact that four men were in a mortuary awaiting funerals as a result.

'It's bollocks, the lot of it,' he said, throwing the stack of interview notes onto his desk. 'Why go to all the trouble of the clues, the drugged drink and the ritualistic placement of the bodies when they could have just confronted each man and demanded money?'

Minshull looked as battered as Anderson felt, the added ignominy of a cracked rib probably edging the odds in his favour. 'Lingham wanted a spectacle. I imagine that drove it. Kemp went along for the ride, but I'm not convinced she didn't plan to frame Lingham for it all eventually. He'd refused to acknowledge Amelie as his baby, after all. That must have been the biggest betrayal, when he'd made her think she mattered to him. Kemp may have achieved some kind of justice for the crimes she'd discovered, but was that merely a means to an end? I still can't tell what her end game was. She just didn't bank on Lukas Hall taking it so personally.'

'That's one thing I'll never understand,' Anderson replied, the detail that had bothered him most from the interviews coming to the fore. 'Why, when Mattie Kemp knew Lukas Hall was capable of murder, did she choose to leave her baby with him?'

Minshull gave a shrug, a hand immediately moving to his injured rib as he winced. 'I honestly think she believed he loved Amelie too much to hurt her. He murdered the others because he'd learned to hate them, as Kemp did. Maybe she thought his love for her baby was enough to trust him.'

'Crazy.'

'Indeed. I think she intended to take the rap for him. I get the impression she felt responsible, for bringing Lukas to the unit and for the deaths that happened as a result. It seems her loyalty to him blinded her to the threat he'd pose to Amelie.'

Lukas Hall had been treated in hospital for a broken ankle and brought back to Police HQ for interview. His answers to Minshull and Bennett's questions about the plot and the murders had left them cold.

'They didn't expect it. That's why it worked,' he'd stated, matter-of-factly, a relaxed smile where Minshull had expected to see shock, anger, or hurt.

'How did it work?' Bennett had asked.

Hall had laughed in reply. 'They died.'

By contrast, Mattie Kemp was a wreck of a human. Facing the prospect of being separated from Amelie and the full weight of consequences now clear, she had spent the hours of interview that followed sobbing, shaking and rocking in her seat.

'I didn't think he'd heard me,' she'd insisted. 'All the time I was going over it, when we were painting those bastard pebbles, I was just talking out loud. Letting it out. It was catharsis for me. I never thought Lukas was listening.'

If justice had really been her motive, why had she hung the mannequin in Evernam Woods and hidden the knife close enough to be found?

338

'I didn't,' she'd replied, much to Anderson's disbelief. 'I just wrapped up the knife in the scarf and told Lukas to get rid of it. He was planning to keep it at home, like a trophy.'

Even now, it seemed incredible.

'She still maintains that Lukas hung the mannequin,' Anderson said to Minshull. 'But does she seriously expect us to believe he went home, made a life-sized dummy, cycled it out to Evernam Woods and hauled it into place?'

'He overpowered and murdered four men considerably larger than him,' Minshull returned. 'And moved their bodies when they were unconscious. What's the difference?'

'The story with the scarf got me.' Wheeler raised a hand from the door. 'Seeing as we're sharing.'

Anderson looked up as Wheeler entered. 'What did she say, Dave?'

Wheeler handed them each an apologetically pale coffee and took the seat next to Minshull. 'That she knew the scarf belonged to Isabel Lingham when she saw it on the back seat of Mark Lingham's car. The rain was an excuse to persuade him to lend it to her.'

It had been the only time during the almost ten hours of interview that Kemp had shown any fight.

'I kept it. I wanted a way to get back at her for the crap she was spreading about me with Sheila Kersey. The two of them, so high and mighty, telling everyone I was a homewrecker and not to be trusted. When Isabel's own husband had left me pregnant and fed me a pack of lies about caring for me. Like she even knew how rotten her own perfect marriage was. I took her precious scarf, and I kept it in my bag. I didn't know what Lukas was planning – I swear I didn't. But when we got out of the shop unit, and he still had the knife, I knew exactly what to wrap it in.'

'You would have implicated Isabel Lingham in the murders?'

Kemp's spirit had dimmed, but her grit remained. 'She was the reason Mark abandoned Amelie. She deserved it.'

'Has Mark Lingham said anything yet?' Anderson asked. The uniform grimaces from his colleagues spoke volumes.

'He's a firm no-commenter since he chatted with his new solicitor,' Wheeler replied. 'Turns out the power trip he'd planned doesn't extend to the interview room. But CPS reckons we'll have enough from Kemp and Hall's testimonies to fill the gaps.'

Minshull risked a sip of coffee, barely concealing his luke-warm reaction to it. 'He thinks he won't be charged now we've arrested Lukas. He's got a shock coming.'

'Shame, after he'd gone to so much trouble to stage it all,' Anderson mused, the merest hint of humour sneaking in. 'Like taking a fifer on the field and skulking off before tea.'

'Get you and your cricket analogies, Guv,' Minshull chuckled, surprised. 'You'll be singing "Jerusalem" and flying the Cross of St George before you know it.'

'And hell will become a freezer before that happens, *Sassenach*.'

'What's going to happen to Amelie?' Wheeler's question stole their smiles.

'Unclear at present. Ms Kemp has no family to speak of, not that she is in contact with, at any rate. We've had an offer from Lukas Hall's sister to take the baby in, but I doubt that's appropriate, given the charges her brother faces.'

'Gaby,' Wheeler corrected. 'Lovely young lady. And a good friend to Ms Kemp, it seems. I'll cross my fingers for a bit of hope on that score.'

If only a kind-hearted request to the universe could bring hope, Anderson thought. But he didn't say it. Sometimes, the stories you chose to believe were what made the world tolerable.

And, sometimes, the world might even surprise you.

SIXTY-SIX

CORA

The bruises across her stomach were blooming through an impressive palette of blues, purples and greens. The stitches in the wound on her jaw looked worse. They would fade in time, she'd been assured, like the scratch caused by Lukas Hall's knife on the left side of her throat had already done.

But Cora still felt it.

Shock hit her several days later, when the euphoria of rescuing Amelie Kemp and the adrenaline of the chase finally dissipated. It had been a week since then, and she was yet to have a full night of sleep.

It helped that she'd had Tris to talk it all through with. His fascination with how her ability had operated in such extreme circumstances was balance enough for reliving its horrors.

Minshull was helping, too. Although, right now, he was bordering on obsessive.

'Mind your step.'

'Stop fussing, or I'll push you into the sea.'

Surrendering, he held back, allowing Cora to ascend the stone steps from the beach alone. 'Better?'

She sent him a withering look from the promenade.

Jogging up to join her, Minshull fell into step as they walked on. 'I probably owe you an ice cream now.'

'I thought you'd never ask. Double-scoop of choc-cherry, please. And a coffee.'

'What?' He feigned shock, which convinced nobody. 'You're going to bankrupt me, Dr Lael.'

'The thing is…' Cora put a hand gently on her stomach with a theatrical wince.

'Yeah, right, I get it. Park yourself on that bench, and I'll be back.'

She watched him sprint off in the direction of the ice cream parlour further down the prom. He was trying – much harder than he needed to. But she appreciated the effort. It seemed they had regained an even keel after months of navigating choppy waters, and that was a reward she found she'd longed for.

It didn't make him any less annoying, though.

Ten minutes later, after ice cream, coffee and endless jokes that skimmed over the surface like the windsurfers bouncing across waves beyond Felixstowe Pier, Minshull sat forward on the bench. Cora watched his fingers working together as he leaned his elbows on his knees – a pose she'd seen often in the CID office when he was mulling over a problem, but rarely during his visits to her.

She waited, not sure what was coming.

'Can I say something?' he asked, at last.

'Of course.'

He kept his eyes fixed on the bright sails that danced across the horizon. 'I could have lost you.'

'I know.'

'I hate that.'

Breathing against the surprise, Cora watched him. 'You were there as soon as you could be.'

'I was SIO. I should have been first on the scene. I failed.'

'Rob, you didn't.'

He gave a grunt of dissension. 'I called it wrong. As SIO, I should have seen what was happening. This whole case… Maybe those bloody journalists were right. We weren't equipped as a rural force to deal with that level of crime. *I* wasn't equipped.'

'You can't think like that,' Cora countered, her heart going out to him. For a man so personally driven to seek justice, the challenges of the case had clearly taken their toll. 'You went after those responsible for the murders. And you found them.'

'And I almost lost you in the process.'

'It was my decision to follow Lukas. And Drew...'

'I should never have put him in that position, either. The whole case was a mess.'

'But Drew did what you needed him to do. And so did I.'

'You did more than anyone should have...' He looked at her, began to say something else, but instead turned back to the sea in frustrated silence.

Cora watched him for a while, waiting for more. But Minshull's shoulders remained hunched over his knees, the sense of unfinished words heavy around him.

'What are we really talking about?' she asked, when she'd dismissed every other possible route back to conversation. 'Rob?'

'I don't know...' His hand curled around the nape of his neck, rubbing the skin as if trying to remove the awkward question. 'I don't how to... Can we carry on walking, please?'

The moment was gone, snatched away like the ice lolly wrappers and fast food detritus lifted up from the promenade by the breeze.

I want chips now. Can we have chips?

No way I'm eating that.

I just want five minutes alone. Is that too much to ask?

Cora walked beside Minshull, muting each voice, the practice so familiar now it was automatic. Maybe this was what mattered – that they could return to this place, this way of being, regardless of what the job threw at them.

For the first time, Cora felt at peace with her unexpected police career. She'd proved herself, had been accepted and could finally count the CID detectives as colleagues in the truest sense of the word. It was a new way of thinking about her life, two

343

distinct strands, both calling on – and developing – her ability. It suited her.

After the horrors she'd witnessed in Evernam, maybe this was the best compensation.

They passed the Seafront Gardens on Underhill Road and reached the point where Bath Hill began its ascent towards Cora's apartment building.

'I'll be okay from here,' she smiled, her injuries urging her home to rest.

'You sure? I can walk you up.'

'I'm good. Besides, it's your day off. When was the last time South Suffolk gave you one of those?'

Minshull laughed. 'Good point well made. Call you tomorrow?'

'Please.' She offered a hug, and he accepted, the action unhurried, the emotion shared. 'Now get some rest.'

'Rest... *r-est?*' he replied, as if trying out a strange new sound. 'Nope. Never heard of it.'

'Idiot. Go home.' She started to climb the hill, her hands resolutely by her side, resisting the urge to support her aching core. She couldn't risk Minshull knowing exactly how much pain she was in. If she gave it away, he'd never leave...

'Cora.'

Surprised, she turned back. He had followed her a few paces up the road and now stood as if unsure of how to proceed. 'What?'

'I want more.'

'I don't understand...'

'More. Of us. Of *this*. I don't know how or when. Or if. But I want you to know.'

What could she say to that? What was he asking for?

'You don't have to say anything,' he rushed, eyes trained on her. 'I like how we are.'

'So do I.'

He was panicking now, scanning the area for an escape route. 'Bookmark it, then? To come back to?'

'Yes.'

'Okay, done. So… Bye.'

Smiling at Minshull's fast-retreating frame, Cora turned and headed home.

A letter from MJ White

Dear Reader

Welcome to the fourth case for Dr Cora Lael, DS Rob Minshull and the CID team from South Suffolk Police!

When I wrote the first book in the Cora Lael series, I couldn't have dared to dream I might write a fourth instalment, let alone one with a quadruple murder at its centre. This book is the darkest, bravest story I've written so far, and it was a learning curve in every sense of the word. Writing this book, I wanted to push myself further, much in the way that Cora is pushing the boundaries of her ability, daring to discover what she's capable of. In that sense, I feel even closer to Cora and her unique world, having gone on this journey alongside her.

In this story, I wanted to investigate the way that murder in a small, tight-knit community sends shockwaves out to every corner, affecting everyone who lives there and casting a harsh spotlight on local gossip and prejudice. I also wanted to look at the challenges faced by rural police forces, where resources are dwindling, law enforcement provision is stretched far too thin and public scrutiny of police conduct challenges every aspect of investigations. I hope the challenges faced by South Suffolk Police in this book cast some light on those challenges and pay tribute to hard-working officers who remain dedicated to serving rural communities.

Thank you for reading *The Deadly Echoes*. I would love to know what you think of it. You can find me on the links below.

Brightest wishes

MJ White

LINKS:
www.miranda-dickinson.com
Twitter: @wurdsmyth
Instagram: @wurdsmyth
Facebook: MirandaDickinsonAuthor
YouTube: youtube.com/mirandawurdy
Mastodon: @Wurdsmyth@mastodon.social
Threads: @wurdsmyth
Bluesky: @wurdsmyth.bsky.social

Acknowledgements

I'm thrilled that Cora's adventures are continuing, thanks in no small part to such amazing support from my fabulous readers. That's you! Thank you.

As with every book in this series, Cora's latest case wouldn't have made it out into the world without a brilliant team. Thanks to my editor, Keshini Naidoo, whose encouragement, insight and unwavering belief in this book inspired me to write the bravest version of what I wanted to say. Her unbridled glee at the prospect of Cora, Minshull and the team tackling a quadruple murder was something to behold, too! Thanks as always to my agent, Hannah Ferguson, for being a constant support and fierce advocate of my writing. Thank you to the fab team at Hera and Canelo – Thanhmai Bui-Van, Iain Millar, and Kate Shepherd – and to Lindsey Harrad for copyedits and Lynne Walker for proofreading.

My sincere thanks to PC Steve Franklin for his expert advice and insight into police life. Thanks also to former detective, author and police advisor Graham Bartlett for sharing his expertise regarding police interview techniques, which played a significant role in shaping the interview scenes in this book. Any mistakes in police procedure are mine alone.

Writing can often be a lonely business, so true friends are a gift. I want to offer special thanks to two fantastic author friends who have inspired me, muscled my writer doubts out of the door and listened to me witter on for hours about this book. Craig Hallam – giggler extraordinaire, my podcast co-host, supplier of the best memes at the perfect moments and a darn good friend. Thank you for being brilliant. And your books *rock*, so there! And AG Smith – co-conspirator over coffee, writer of the scariest stories that deserve the biggest audience (come on, publishers, snap him up!) and a total rock. Thank you for always believing in Cora, and in me. Great big love to Claire, Rosie and Flora, too.

Thanks to fab author chums for supporting me and my Cora Lael series – CL Taylor, Rob Parker, Neil Lancaster, Steve Cavanagh, Luca Veste, Chris Callaghan, Adam Simcox, Joanna Cannon, DV Bishop, Ian Wilfred and Mick Arnold.

Huge love to my followers on Instagram, Facebook, Twitter, Threads and Bluesky, and the gorgeous community of viewers who watch my weekly Facebook Live show, Fab Night In Chatty Thing, for rooting so much for Cora and the South Suffolk CID team. This book represents the next stage of Cora's adventure – and there's more to come!

Huge love to my Mum and lovely in-laws, Phil and Jo, for always believing in me and telling everyone who'll listen about Cora. Support like that really helps!

Big thanks to my gorgeous Flo for lending me her brightly painted pebbles to keep me company as I wrote, which found their way into the story. And all my love to my husband Bob, who has weathered every storm, shared every triumph and supplied me with enough tea to fill several oceans. I love you both to the moon and back and twice around the stars! xx

This is Cora's darkest, most complex and bravest case so far. Enjoy!

Miranda x

The Deadly Echoes playlist

For every novel I write, I compile a soundtrack playlist that captures the emotion and atmosphere of the story I want to create. Here are the songs and pieces of music that inspired *The Deadly Echoes*. Happy listening!

MAIN THEME of *The Deadly Echoes*: REBIRTH – Elephant Sessions – *For the Night*

BEYOND THE LIGHT – Second Light – *Beyond the Light – Single*

LUMINARY – Joel Sunny – *Luminary – Single*

JÖRMUNGRUND – Skáld – *Vikings Memories*

THROW ME A LINE – HAEVN – *Holy Ground – EP*

LIGHTS – Sohn – *Tremors*

RESCUE MY HEART – Liz Longley – *Weightless*

LUST – RURA – *Our Voices Echo – EP*

WAVES – Dean Lewis – *Same Kind of Different – EP*

I'LL BE WAITING (CHOIR VERSION) – Cian Ducrot – *Victory (With Choir And Strings)*

SHE'S DONE IT AGAIN – Stanleys – *She's Done It Again – Single*

NÍU – Skáld – *Vikings Chant (Alfar Fagrahvél Edition)*